# STRANGERS IN VENICE

## STELLA BLED BOOK TWO

## A.W. HARTOIN

Strangers in Venice

*A Stella Bled Thriller Book Two*

# ALSO BY A.W. HARTOIN

Nowhere Fast

Dry Spell

A Sin and a Shame

**Stella Bled Historical Thrillers**

The Paris Package (Stella Bled Book One)

Strangers in Venice (Stella Bled Book Two)

One Child in Berlin (Stella Bled Book Three)

Dark Victory (Stella Bled Book Four)

A Quiet Little Place on Rue de Lille (Stella Bled Book Five)

Her London Season (Stella Bled Book Six)

Double Duet (Stella Bled Book Seven)

**Paranormal**

It Started with a Whisper (Son of a Witch Book One)

Angels and Insects (Son of a Witch Book Two)

**Young Adult fantasy**

Flare-up (Away From Whipplethorn Short)

A Fairy's Guide To Disaster (Away From Whipplethorn Book One)

Fierce Creatures (Away From Whipplethorn Book Two)

A Monster's Paradise (Away From Whipplethorn Book Three)

A Wicked Chill (Away From Whipplethorn Book Four)

To the Eternal (Away From Whipplethorn Book Five)

*For Connor, my documentary-watching wingman and knower of obscure facts.*

# PROLOGUE

The men had talked at first, the irrepressible chatter of the terrified, but that had long since fallen off as the minutes turned into hours. Abel said little, not even his name. His name was more dangerous than being a Jew and that was what got him in the boxcar in the first place. That and some foolish choices.

But the choices weren't only his. A young man named Herschel Grynszpan murdered a German official in Paris, not realizing the Nazis would take revenge. In truth, they were only waiting for an excuse and Grynszpan gave them a good one, but Abel never imagined it would be this bad. He didn't think the SA would attack people in the street, drag them out of their beds and beat them, or arrest hundreds of men like himself and shove them into freezing cold boxcars, many without shoes or coats. No. He never imagined that.

The old man beside him patted his knee and said in soothing tones, "We will be there soon." He said that every few minutes, whether it was for Abel's benefit or his own Abel didn't know, but there was such kindness in his voice that Abel got a pang in his chest each time he said it.

"Yes," said Abel, but he didn't think it would be an improvement.

People came back from Dachau, but when they did, they weren't the same as when they went in.

He and the old man were huddled up with fifty other men wondering what would happen next. The only options seemed to be terrible or horrific. If only he hadn't come back to Vienna. If only he'd stayed in his flat. If only he had listened. If only he had believed. It could've been different. He could've gotten away.

Instead, he'd dropped off his clients, Stella and Nicky Lawrence, at their hotel, gone to his shop, and begun answering the correspondence that had piled up in the two months of his absence. Without any inkling of what was about to happen, he'd gone to bed in his little flat above the shop only to be woken up a short time later by his maid, Lettie, on the telephone.

"Oh, Mr. Herschmann, you are there. How I hoped you wouldn't be," she said in a rush, her strong Slavic accent muddling her words.

"What is it, Lettie?" It paid to be calm with Lettie. She got excited by a late milk delivery.

"They're coming. Now. Now. Now."

"Who is coming?"

"The brown shirts. You must go now. Hide."

Abel sat on the edge of his bed with the heavy black receiver in his hand, unable to think.

"Mr. Herschmann. Mr. Herschmann. Are you there?"

"Yes, Lettie."

"You must go. Hide."

"Why?" he asked sounding thick-headed and none too bright. "What are they doing?"

"They've set fire to your churches and they are arresting men. They are beating them. Come here. We keep you safe."

The thought of his little Bulgarian maid fending off the SA brought him to his senses.

"Lettie, it's all right. I'll be fine," Abel said, but he was already up and getting dressed. "It's Albert's shop. We changed the sign, the deed, everything."

"You think they are stupid?" she asked, her accent growing stronger.

"Not exactly."

"They came to the shop looking for you. Mr. Moore, he tells them that you are traveling, but they don't believe him."

"Who came? When?"

"The other ones. The ones in black."

*The SS.*

Abel slipped on his shoes. "When was that?"

"Last week. Mr. Herschmann, you must go. They were very angry. They know your name. You're not just another Jew."

Not just another Jew. Lettie was more right than she knew. "Don't worry. I'll figure something out."

"You come here."

"Thank you, Lettie. I appreciate it." He hung up and tied his shoes. Was Lettie right? Did he have to go? When the SS were told that he wasn't there, he really wasn't and not due to return for weeks. He hadn't contacted anyone about going home to Vienna instead of Greece, not even his business partner, Albert Moore, whose Aryan name was painted over the shop's door. But the Dutch historian, Dr. Van Wijk, had seen him on the train with Stella and Nicky, and Van Wijk was rumored to be working for the SS. He may have already informed them that Abel was back in Vienna.

He went to the window and peered out to find his street quiet. Some windows were lit up, but there were certainly no torches or pitchforks parading down the street and there wasn't much reason to target his area. Mainly gentiles lived and worked there with just a handful of Jewish shops and homes. Maybe it was fine.

But then he caught a glimpse of light far off to the right, a faint glow over a rooftop. Abel opened the window and leaned out. As soon as he did, he smelled a hint of smoke. The fire wasn't close. That was good. It probably wouldn't reach the shop.

He waited, listening for the sound of sirens. None came, but screams did. Across the street, his neighbor Mr. Nelböck leered out at him between lace curtains. The gruff old man was a bastard on the best of days. He'd welcomed the annexation of Austria and the loss of their independence with unrestrained joy, but he'd never said a word to Abel about it.

Mr. Nelböck wasn't content to stay silent for long. Lit by a dim streetlamp, he leaned out of his window, waving a hideous Nazi flag and pointing a plump finger at Abel, who he barely knew. "Now it's your turn, you fucking Jew chiseler!"

Abel went icy with shock. What turn was he supposed to be having? Mr. Nelböck imported fine French cheese and wine. As a historian and travel guide, Abel was hardly in competition with the man.

He reached up to close the window as Mr. Nelböck began screaming obscenities with his red-faced wife trying to drag him away. Abel slammed the window and locked it with a loud metallic snap as if that could keep hatred out. He had to go. No doubt now.

And that was when his foolishness took hold. He had three choices as he saw it. Lettie was too far away so that left Albert, Stella and Nicky, and Ho Feng Shan, the Chinese consul general. Ho was a lovely man, who looked upon the annexation with horror and the Nazis, in general, with growing trepidation. He would let Abel into the consul. The two men had become good friends after crossing paths at the Café Central. He was the first to suggest that Abel take steps to protect the business by transferring his half to Albert and putting his money in a Swiss bank account. But Ho was in the embassy district, nearly as far as Lettie.

Stella and Nicky were the closest. The young honeymooners were members of prominent families and Americans, as well. He could go to them. They were his friends and Stella, in particular, would certainly help him without a thought to her own safety.

Last was Albert, his business partner and closest friend. As the son of a British ambassador and a member of the nobility, Albert was untouchable, but he was farther from the shop than Stella and Nicky's hotel. The possibilities raced through his mind. Distance, time, safety. Arrest, prison. Escape, success. Failure, loss. Albert or Stella?

He thought he could make it to Albert. On balance, it was worth the risk, just in case Dr. Van Wijk did tell the SS about Stella and Nicky. He didn't know what would happen if he were found in their room. They could be arrested. If they touched Stella…no, it didn't bear thinking about. Albert would be fine, even if he was found there. The SS wouldn't dare harm him.

Abel threw on his coat and opened his dresser. In the false bottom of the third drawer he uncovered the diary written by his ancestor, Johannes Gutenberg, wrapped up tight in brown paper and string to disguise its worth. Besides the diary's intrinsic value it also contained the inventor's carefully guarded secret. The most famous German inventor had loved and married a Jew, Nissa, and she'd been instrumental to the invention of moveable type.

Abel's family had begun to suspect that the Nazi hierarchy was aware of the diary's existence and what it said. To Abel, Van Wijk's presence on the train confirmed it. The last thing the Nazis would want was Gutenberg's secret revealed. Gutenberg was a hero, proof of Germanic superiority. A Jew couldn't be part of the greatest invention of all time. That didn't fit the Nazi dogma and what didn't fit must be destroyed.

Abel slipped on his coat and hesitated. Nothing was guaranteed. He might have to give the book to Albert or his doorman or some stranger if he were desperate. He grabbed his fountain pen and unscrewed the top. Greece or France? Paris was closer. His cousins, the Sorkines, would know how to act. Abel quickly scribbled their address on the brown paper and tucked the book into the interior pocket of his coat. He left behind his mother's jewelry and his father's precious books, taking only a wad of Reichsmarks, his passport, his parents' wedding photo slipped out of its silver frame, his favorite picture of Stella, and the diary.

Dashing out the back into the night, he'd made his way towards Albert's flat using back alleys and neatly avoiding crowds of SA ruffians roaming the streets looking for hapless victims and randomly attacking shops and homes. The sound of breaking glass and screaming accompanied him everywhere. The smoke choked him and made his eyes burn. He couldn't escape it, only ignore it as best he could. At one point, he nearly ran into a group chanting, "Burn it down! Burn it down!" in front of a synagogue and found himself cut off. It would be easier to go to Stella and Nicky, but he stubbornly stuck to his plan, taking extra time to go around the mob.

What had he been thinking? So foolish not to adapt to circumstances. Abel tugged at his pant legs, trying in vain to cover his frozen ankles. He wrapped his arms around himself and wondered if he hadn't decided to stay on his chosen path would he be safe? And more importantly, would Stella be safe?

He almost couldn't bear to think about her. Stella Bled Lawrence. In the last two months they'd become deep friends. He'd never known anyone quite like her. Although predictably young and pretty, Stella was nothing like the other women Abel knew, a curious combination of naive and knowledgeable that he found both intriguing and endearing. She was the one who insisted they come to Vienna, claiming that she wanted to see everything on her grand tour honeymoon, but something in her eyes told Abel there was more to it. That was why he'd agreed to go, even with all his misgivings. He wondered if he would ever know what Stella was up to. She wasn't as flighty as she appeared and allowed others to believe. She was a Bled through and through, and Bleds were always up to something. He learned that from her Uncle Josiah.

Now, because he turned right when he could've turned around, he might never see her again. The thought pained him nearly as much as his head. Abel rubbed the side of his face where a jagged gash topped off a lump the size of a lemon. When he'd made his right turn, a ragtag group of young men had come out of the shadows and clubbed him with a brick. Stunned, he'd gone down on his knees, pressing the diary to his chest as they beat him, jeering gleefully at his pain. He managed to get the reichsmarks out of his pocket and toss them on the ground. His attackers fell on the money and Abel attempted to stagger away, but two of the younger men, boys really, noticed, throwing him to the ground and demanding his address and identification. He handed over his identity card and gave them the address of the Ministry of Justice.

So he'd avoided the SA, but ended up in the hands of a dimmed-witted mob who believed that he could possibly live on Museumstrasse and didn't think to search him. The precious diary was safe for the moment as they herded him down the street past a group of men ransacking a clothing shop and a grocery. Eventually, they lost interest in him and gave him to a group of SA who already had fifteen prisoners and Abel was absorbed into the group. The boys tried to make off with his identity card, but the SA leader saw it in the hand of one of them. Abel held his breath, sure his name would be read and recognized, but the SA only ordered the boy to give it back to him for "accounting purposes."

The would-be thief, a stocky boy of around seventeen with a broken front tooth and rancid breath hissed in his ear as he gave it back. "We're going to steal all your furs and gold. You'll have nothing. We'll have everything. Which way to Museumstrasse?"

Abel pointed in a random direction, dumbfounded that they actually thought he had furs and gold. Nothing about him said that. He wasn't even wearing a watch.

"Museumstrasse?" whispered a man next to him.

Abel shrugged.

"How stupid…"

"Shut up," said the guard and cracked the man in the head with his rifle butt.

That man was now sitting slumped over on Abel's right. It hadn't stopped with one hit or with ten or twenty. The man, Abel didn't know his name, had fought back, punching the guard in the throat. Rifles came out of nowhere and he went down in a flurry of kicks and butts to the head. It happened so fast, the way Abel imagined piranhas to attack in the rivers of South America. And he had stood there, watching, so shocked he stopped breathing. A guard pointed a rifle at him as a spray of blood went up, splattering the brown uniforms. "Do you have anything to say?"

Abel didn't, to his everlasting shame. All he could see was the long dark grey barrel and thought, *They are killing him. They will kill me.*

When it was over, the man lay a bloody pulp in the road and the guards yelled at Abel and the other prisoners to pick him up. They silently obeyed and to Abel's surprise the man wasn't dead. He breathed in rasping, tight bursts, and Abel felt a little piece of his heart break. He should've done something, knowing all the while that he'd have ended up in the same condition and the diary lost.

After walking for what seemed like hours, they ended up at the Westbahnhof with hundreds of other prisoners. Then dawn came and the trains started coming. As soon as he heard the dreaded word *Dachau*, he knew there was no hope. The concentration camp was nothing if not organized. He would be cataloged and the diary discovered. He would've failed where fifteen generations of his family succeeded.

The beaten man was the first one in the boxcar, tossed in like garbage by the guards, angry that he hadn't died. Abel tried to edge away from the line, looking for a place to run. A guard saw him looking and Abel readied himself for a terrible beating. But it didn't come. The guard merely shook his head and indicated that he had to get in line. He did, but he kept looking. He could just run and take his chances. Maybe if he ran to the platform they wouldn't shoot at him. The station was filled with people fleeing the violence, ordinary Austrians and foreigners. He had a few coins in his pockets. Maybe he could get someone to post the diary to Paris. He couldn't take it to Dachau. Hope didn't live there.

His eyes roamed over the crowd, readying himself and looking for the best place to run. He would die in the attempt, of that he was certain. But there or Dachau, it made no difference. He made his peace with the prospect and that's when his eyes found her. Stella, small and disheveled in her fur, standing on the platform next to Nicky, cool and aloof as always. There was someone else with them, but that person was hidden behind the broad-shouldered American. Nicky was talking to a conductor and pulled out his wallet. They were getting out of Vienna. They could take the diary. Abel tensed and Stella turned around. He froze. She saw him. He held his breath. Should he run? Now? Nicky stepped to the side and Abel saw their companion. Albert. Bloody. Wrecked. Barely able to stand. Stella was at the edge of the platform. He shook his head. No. He couldn't do it. They'd hurt her. The diary be damned.

She jumped, landing hard on the gravel and running pell-mell toward him. No amount of head shaking could've stopped her. Stella Bled Lawrence wasn't accustomed to the word *no*, but she was accustomed to love, loyalty, and getting her way. God help him. He gave her the book. If anyone could save it, it would be her.

It was done and couldn't be undone. Abel spent hours thinking of what he should've chosen. Lettie, not Albert. Left, not right. He tortured himself as much as the cold tortured him. The other men were the same. There was talk of emigrating, of opportunities not taken. Most thought this madness was temporary. It couldn't continue. How could it? The world would see what Hitler was doing and take a stand. Surely they would. Hope was still there. And if didn't die in that boxcar, it wasn't going to.

But not everyone felt the same way. One man panicked after the doors were bolted. He began screaming and ramming his head into the wall. They held him down, trying in vain to reassure him. When the train made the first of many stops, the man began screaming again, a high-pitched, wild shriek, and the guards pulled him out. Before they could plead for the bloody man who lay slumped next to Abel, the guards slammed the door shut. A shot rang out and the shrieking stopped. The men were silent as the train started again.

"Never ask for help," said a gentle voice somewhere in the dark. "Be nothing. No one. If you want to survive."

"How do you know?" asked another man. "Who are you?"

"I am nobody. Nothing. No one. But I will survive."

Abel didn't know how to be nothing. What was nothing? What did that look like?

Hours later, he still didn't know. He was a man. He couldn't let them think he was less than human, although it seemed they already believed that or they couldn't have done what they had done.

"Are we slowing down?" someone asked.

"I hope not," said someone else.

"How can you say that?"

One man cried softly, "We're going to die."

"Don't be ridiculous."

"They're going to kill us," said another.

"No, they're not. They'd have to explain what happened."

"Do they? Who do they have to explain it to?"

"We have families."

"As if they care," said Nobody.

"Do you smell something?" said someone close to Abel.

"I smell shit."

They all laughed, breaking the incredible tension.

"No, there's something else," said someone else after a minute. "What is that?"

No one answered, but Abel knew what it was. He'd gotten a whiff an hour before, not long after he'd heard a gulp and the man next to him shuddered for the last time. The body's bowels had released, but that smell had only joined the rest of the stench for men had been urinating and defecating in the corners of the box car since their journey began. Abel was the only one close enough to sense the sticky pool spreading out across the rough wooden floor. No one else had wanted to sit next to what amounted to a corpse, so Abel volunteered. It seemed a good punishment for his folly.

"I smell it," said another.

"Who farted?"

They all laughed again, but this time it was nervous laughter. The smell of death had begun to pervade the boxcar and they all knew it on instinct.

Quietly, the voice of Nobody asked, "Does anyone know his name?"

No one did. There were tears and prayers for the dead. Abel didn't pray. His prayer was already answered. In the pitch black, he felt over the dead man's chest and found in his pockets a couple of bills, a photo, and the all-important identity card.

*I'm sorry, my friend. But your name can save me. I will use it well.*

Abel put his own identity card, passport, and photos in the man's pocket, kissing the photos before he tucked them away.

"We are slowing down," said someone and they were. Up ahead the train's whistle blew and the car jerked.

"Maybe it's just another stop."

"We have to get there sometime," said Nobody.

"What will happen?"

"God knows."

The train ground to a halt and, a few minutes later, an armed guard slid the door open. He squinted into the boxcar and made a face. *"Mein Gott!"*

Several guards gathered and Abel shielded his face from the beams of light from their *Taschenlampen*. They discussed the body in irritated Bavarian accents and then started yelling for the men to come out.

The prisoners stumbled into the darkness with rifles pointed at them. Any thoughts of making a run for it vanished as Abel stood at the door, grasping the wood to support himself, legs weak and stiff. He felt like a man of eighty-seven, not twenty-seven.

A guard screamed at him and he climbed down and then turned to help the old man. He probably wasn't far off eighty-seven. Together they squinted at the small station with a sign that had "Dachau" painted in block letters on it.

"It really is Dachau," someone behind them whispered. A murmur went through the group, spreading as the cars emptied their sad cargo. Abel realized some had held out hope that they weren't really going to the infamous camp where Jakob Ehrlich died and where Alfred Haag the communist had been imprisoned for years. He, himself, had no such illusions. Dachau was where you went if you didn't fit the Reich's vision and, as Jews, they certainly didn't.

"Get going. We don't have all night," yelled a guard and they began walking along an eight-foot-high masonry wall topped by barbed wire. Abel walked, supporting the old man, feeling as if he wasn't really there. He wasn't going into a prison when only twenty-four hours ago he'd been sitting on tufted cushions in first class with Stella and Nicky. Where were they now? Had they gotten away? His last glimpse had been of Stella's agonized face as Nicky carried her off. The young American's level head would get them away and they'd take care of poor Albert. He must've had some sort of accident. The Nazis wouldn't dare attack him. That just wasn't possible.

The old man's legs buckled and Abel managed to keep him from going down, but a wave of dizziness came over him, blurring his vision. He hadn't eaten in well over twenty-four hours, but he wasn't really hungry. Fear sat in his stomach solid as a brick and taking up all the space.

"Thank you," said the old man, his hazel eyes soft and dreamy with fatigue.

"We're almost there."

"Yes, but where is there?"

"Dachau," said Abel. Perhaps he had lost his wits like the mad man on the train.

He squeezed Abel's arm, nodding and becoming taller and stronger. "It was meant to be."

The men stopped and clumped up as it was time to turn a corner. Being taller than everyone else, Abel could see that they were going around a curve, probably to a gate. The area wasn't very large and obviously not designed to handle such a large influx of prisoners. He dared to look at the guards and found them looking but not seeing the men in front of them. Many were bloody or hobbling on frozen feet. A few were weeping. The guards took no notice, simply doing their jobs as they had been ordered to do. A conscience was not issued with the boots and uniform.

"What do you see?" asked the old man.

They came around the curve and Abel's chest tightened. "A gate."

"What is it? Why do you sound like that?"

"*Arbeit macht frei*," said Abel, his voice growing hard with the words.

"What is this nonsense?"

"That's what it says on the gate."

The men around them read the sign and a collective shiver went through them.

"Work will set us free, eh?" asked one man. "I wonder when."

"Who says the Nazis don't have a sense of humor?"

"What kind of work? I'm a cobbler."

"I'm a banker."

"Painter."

"Baker."

"You'll hammer nails into boards and like it," said Nobody behind Abel.

"You are joking with us."

"Damned if I am."

"Why?" asked the banker.

"What's the point?" asked the baker.

"Misery," said Nobody.

None had an answer to that.

Abel squeezed through the narrow gate under the mocking words into a huge courtyard where men were lined up to go into a white-washed building to the right. On the left were rows of squat, narrow buildings.

"When do you think we can sit down?" asked the old man.

"A while yet. Don't worry. I'll help you. You won't fall," said Abel.

The old man leaned heavily on his arm and took Abel's hand between his gnarled ones. "Your hands are very soft and elegant for a bricklayer, Adam."

"What?" asked Abel.

The old man leaned farther into him. "Your name is Adam Stolow-icki and you are from Warsaw. You were visiting your sister, Helena, in Vienna. I am Jakob Zack, her neighbor."

Abel said nothing. He couldn't think, only touch his chest where the identity card was concealed.

"You understand me, Adam?"

"Yes, Jakob."

"Good. And do not forget you are a communist."

"That's not ideal."

"It could be worse," said Jakob.

"Really? How?"

"Let me think about that. First," Jakob scratched vigorously at the back of his neck, "touch my neck."

13

"I don't…"

"Do as you are told, Adam."

Abel slid his hand under Jakob's heavy collar and felt the warmth of fresh blood. "You're hurt."

"Blood can conceal many things, can it not?"

"I don't know."

"Fine soft hands of a teacher or doctor, for instance."

Their eyes met again and Abel understood. Jacob would help him with his very blood.

"Let me see," said Abel, looking at a broad gash and multiple cuts on the back of the old man's head, pretending to tend them with a handkerchief that Jakob gave him. He got crusted and fresh blood on his pale, patrician hands and had to swallow down the agony that it cost him to do it.

"What happened?" asked a man behind them. "That is nasty."

"I fell," said Jakob.

"Backward?"

"And through a window."

"I'd like to kill them," said the man through gritted teeth.

"Maybe you'll get your chance," said Abel.

"You and I together," he said, extending his hand. "Michael."

"Adam."

The men were separated from Michael into another line and Abel leaned over to Jakob. "It's a big chance you're taking. Why help me?"

"My son died here. I could do nothing for him. I can help you and you will live for him."

"What was his name?"

"Leopold."

"For Leopold then," said Abel.

*And Stella.*

# CHAPTER 1

The rain started the moment the train crossed into Italy as if the country expected them and wasn't thrilled about a repeat visit. Stella wasn't thrilled either, but there was a job that must be done and nothing could stop her from doing it.

"Where's everyone going?" she whispered, her breath steaming up the wide window of her compartment and obscuring her already dim view of the rain-soaked platform outside.

She squinted and the tip of her nose touched the cold glass. Vicenza? Padua? She couldn't make out the sign, but it definitely didn't say Venice. The station was too small and there wasn't supposed to be another stop after Verona anyway.

Nevertheless, people were scurrying through the torrents of rain with their luggage, disappearing into the darkness. Was this some sort of tourist destination that she was unaware of? No. It couldn't be. If there was something to see, Abel would've shown it to them.

Stella dug her fingernails into the edge of the window's shiny brass trim. Abel. Where was he? In Dachau? Had the Nazis discovered his identity? It hurt to think about him and what might have happened in the last two weeks or could be happening right at that moment. She did know that whatever they did to Abel, it would get them nowhere.

He couldn't give them what they wanted. He couldn't even say where Gutenberg's diary was, only that Stella had it, which they already knew or thought they did. The book was gone, packed up in a crate and headed to the States with the Boulards, Amelie and Paul. The trick was letting the Nazis know that it was gone without telling them where it was. Uncle Josiah was the one to ask about that and she hoped that she would see him soon, within a week or two.

Josiah was on his way to Munich to help Abel, but she wasn't fool enough to think that the Nazis would release him just because Josiah Bled asked them to. He would have to come up with a good incentive, something they couldn't resist. The Nazis had been trying for some time to get in contact with the Bled family in hopes of getting some sort of boost from the famous brewing family. Apparently, they thought their name valuable, and Uncle Josiah could use that. He could talk about a possible deal, tantalize, cajole and coax. He excelled at that. Talking was her beloved uncle's forte and talking was how they met Abel in the first place.

Uncle Josiah just happened to be in Rome when a group of importers were being sallied around the city in an effort to get them to sign with a Belgian brewing conglomerate. He *accidentally* ran into them and their tour guide, Abel, in a bar. By midnight, they'd signed an agreement with Bled brewing and by dawn, Uncle Josiah and Abel were drunk as skunks, bathing nude in the Trevi fountain, and being arrested by the carabinieri for public lewdness. A first for Abel, but not for Uncle Josiah, unfortunately.

Stella's mother, Francesqua, declared that they had to make it up to Abel because no one doubted for a moment that it was all Josiah's fault. He was a bad influence, the worst influence. People did things with him that they would never remotely consider otherwise. In the face of the family's recriminations about drinking, Uncle Josiah just grinned. Being drunk wasn't necessary for having fun, he said. It just sped things up.

Maybe he could work his magic in Munich. They had beer and schnapps. He had money and clout. That was a good combination for making a beneficial deal in the normal world. But who knew about the Nazis? Their motivations made no sense. Why attack their own population? There had to be a point, but it eluded her. Nicky said it was hatred. What kind of a person hated someone they'd never met and had no knowledge of? Stella couldn't understand it. She did understand that they had to get Abel out of Dachau. It was their fault he was there, hers and Uncle Josiah.

If he hadn't gotten Abel arrested, she and Nicky wouldn't have hired him as their guide for their honeymoon. They wouldn't have known his name. If Stella and Uncle Josiah hadn't wanted to help people smuggle their art out of Vienna before the Nazis got their greedy claws on it, he wouldn't have been in Vienna to be arrested. Their fault, so it must be their solution whatever the cost.

The train whistle blew even as more people exited the train. Then the O'Sullivans went by her window. She and Nicky had had dinner with them and they were definitely going to Venice. The old couple crept along the platform with no less than five porters and four carts piled high with luggage. They were Irish gentry and didn't go anywhere without a valet and a maid. Mr. Marchand and Mrs. Fawcett were holding enormous umbrellas over the couple's heads and they couldn't see Stella as she waved and tried to yank down the stiff window.

"Stupid thing." Stella hammered on the window, hoping Marchand would look up. He was French and had taught her a few essential phrases in his many languages. They had intended to continue lessons in Venice and she needed those lessons. "Nicky, help me. The window's stuck."

He didn't answer.

"Nicky, the O'Sullivans are leaving. Something's going on." Stella turned around and found, not to her surprise, Nicky was sleeping with his long legs stretched out and his new fedora perched over his face. Her husband had shown an amazing capacity to sleep. Once the train was out of Paris, he'd assumed the position and slept steadily for going on twelve hours, waking only to eat and ask if there were any new newspapers available. He hadn't even woken up when she'd left the train with Marchand in Milan to buy dictionaries or when she accidentally spilled tea on his legs when she awkwardly climbed over them.

"Oh, for crying out loud." She glanced back at the O'Sullivans' retreating umbrellas and then climbed over Nicky's legs, ramming open their door as loudly as possible. Nicky's emaciated body in his baggy suit didn't twitch. She slammed it closed and stalked down the corridor, glancing through windows at all the empty compartments. Their car had been nearly full of wealthy tourists, excited to see the sites they'd only read about. Now they were gone.

She exited the car and got hit with a blast of painful rain so powerful she didn't consider running after Marchand. Instead, she darted into the second-class car. The double rows of red-upholstered seats were empty. Not a single passenger remained. Stella didn't know if it had been full, but there should've been someone there.

The train whistled again and she saw porters and conductors rushing by. She looked back through the door and saw no one coming aboard so she marched through second-class and into the next car. Third-class and it was occupied. Barely. A family of five huddled at the back looked up and then quickly down, avoiding Stella's enquiring eyes. All except the youngest, a boy of four leaned into the aisle to get a good look only to be yanked out of sight.

"Pardon," she called out, coming down the aisle. "I'm sorry. Do you speak English?"

They didn't answer, sinking lower into their seats.

"I don't mean to bother you, but do you know why everyone is getting off the train?"

The parents, mute, shook their heads and Stella looked the family over. They were well dressed and not normally third-class passengers she wouldn't have thought and the luggage rack at the end of the carriage had only two small valises on it, hardly enough for a family.

"Oh," she said. "I..."

The door behind her opened and cold air flooded the carriage.

"Mrs. Lawrence, what are you doing here?" Monsieur Volcot, the first-class conductor, rushed down the aisle, red-faced and sweaty.

"Trying to find out what's going on," said Stella.

"What is going on? Nothing at all. This is the…Bisset family. They are traveling to visit their family in Bologna."

"I see," she said with an arched eyebrow. "I meant what is happening with everyone leaving the train."

Monsieur Volcot's cheeks got redder. "Yes, yes, of course. Venice, it is flooded." He gently turned her around and led her to the door.

"Venice is always flooded. It's practically a permanent condition of the place."

"Yes, but this is very bad. The rain has not stopped in three days." He opened the door and hustled her outside. In a flash, they were in the empty second-class carriage.

"So what? Venice is chock-full of boats. We were told it never shuts down for rain," said Stella.

Monsieur Volcot herded her down the aisle. "Yes. Normally, that is true. But this time it is."

"Shut down?"

"Yes."

"Why?"

"The rain will not stop for several days and San Marco is knee-deep in water. I only found out in Verona. They tried to tell me that the rain will stop tomorrow, but it won't, and I told our passengers that. No one could say when the basilica or the Doge's palace will reopen."

He reached for the door handle and Stella asked, "What will people do?"

"Make other plans. Perhaps go to Czechoslovakia until the waters have receded."

"I meant the Venetians," said Stella. "What will they do?"

Monsieur Volcot stopped and met her eyes. "They will do what people do when things happen beyond their control."

"Hunker down or escape, you mean."

"I believe so."

"So why didn't you tell *us* that Venice has closed up shop?" she asked.

A hint of a smile curved his thin lips. "Because Monsieur Lawrence told me that *you* will go to Venice come hell or high water. It was not a phrase that I was familiar with, but I understood the situation."

"He's right. Hell or high water."

"Yes, madam." He opened the door and a gust of wind nearly ripped it out of his hand. "Please return to your compartment, Madam Lawrence. We will be on our way shortly."

Stella stepped into the rain, but turned around. "Monsieur Volcot."

His face closed up, fear in his eyes. "Yes, madam?"

She leaned back toward him. "In the future say less about the *Bissets*. No one goes to Venice to get to Bologna."

He took a breath and whispered, "Yes, madam."

Stella darted across the passageway, leaving Monsieur Volcot frozen in the doorway.

Their compartment was empty. No long legs. No sleeping Nicky. Just his fedora sitting on the seat. The train lurched forward, whistle blaring. Stella ran to the window, but she couldn't see the platform through the great sheets of rain pelting the window. He might have gotten off. She never imagined he'd look for her. He slept through hot tea, for God's sake.

She grabbed her coat and ran out into the corridor, spinning around, unsure where to go.

"Stella, what are you doing?" Nicky came in the forward door carrying a coffee pot with a couple of cups dangling from his fingers.

"Oh, thank God." She leaned on the wall and clasped her coat to her chest. "I don't think I could've jumped off another train."

"Why would you?" Nicky walked down the corridor in that casual, unperturbed way of his, kissed her on the forehead, and ducked into their compartment.

"I thought you might've gotten off," she said.

"Why?"

"To look for me."

"I wasn't looking for you," said Nicky, balancing the coffee pot on the stack of newspapers and putting the cups on Stella's new favorite book, *The Hobbit*.

"No?"

"I knew you wouldn't get off the train." He looked around and rifled through the papers on the opposite seat. "Where's *The London Times*? Did you throw it away?"

"No."

"Where did all these dictionaries come from?" he asked, tossing aside her French and Italian dictionaries and a child's book, *Histoire de Babar le petit elephant,* that Monsieur Marchand had recommended.

"I bought them when I left the train," said Stella, coming in and plunking down on the seat just the way a lady shouldn't. It had been well-established in the last two weeks that Stella was no lady so she no longer bothered to pretend.

Nicky stopped searching. "You left the train. Why in the world would you do that?"

She held up the dictionaries he'd so casually tossed aside. "To buy these. If I'm going to learn, I need the tools to do it."

"Why didn't you wake me up?"

"You say that like I could," said Stella.

"You could and you should." He leaned over and slid the door shut. "If you think the SS has given up on getting Abel's book, you're wrong."

"Of course I don't think that. Peiper's like a bloodhound only starchy and with less moral fiber. And I *couldn't* wake you up," she said.

"You could."

"Look at your legs."

Nicky peered down at his formerly pristine pant legs. "What is that? It's crusty."

"Tea with sugar."

"You poured tea on me?" he asked astonished. "Why in the world would you do that?"

"I spilled it while climbing over your unconscious body," she said, rolling her eyes. "It was an accident."

He pulled up a pant leg and examined the reddish mark on his shin. "You burned me."

"And you still didn't wake up."

"Stella."

"Nicky."

They eyed each other until Nicky cracked. A smile broke through and they started laughing, almost upsetting the coffee pot.

"Good God, I was tired. I didn't know a person could get so tired," he said.

"Are you still tired?" asked Stella.

"I won't be after this coffee." He poured a cup and offered it to her, steaming hot and thick from an espresso maker. "How about you? Did you sleep at all?"

"No, I couldn't."

Nicky smoothed back his thick blond hair and straightened his tie. He looked every bit the man she married, but also not, at the same time. It wasn't the gaunt lines of his face or the bruises. He was different and she was different, too. But she didn't want to be different. She wanted to be Stella, the girl before it happened, and she wasn't. In Paris, she thought all she needed was clean clothes and a good meal. The Boulards had seen to all that. Her bruises were fading and would soon be invisible, but she wasn't Stella, not that Stella, not anymore.

"What is it?" he asked, sounding very much like he was afraid of the answer.

"I don't know."

"You do."

She told him the truth, but only the part she knew he would understand. She couldn't say that the moment that she finished reading *The Hobbit* a wave of homesickness had come over so strong that she'd nearly begun crying. She was tired. She was sore. Everything hurt from her swollen, frost-bitten feet to her battered nose. Stella Bled Lawrence was eighteen, married, arguably a murderer, and she wanted her mother.

"I keep thinking about Abel," she said.

"I do, too."

"When you're conscious."

He smiled and her homesickness got the tiniest bit better. "When I'm conscious."

"What do you think will happen?" she asked.

"To Abel? Nothing, I hope. Josiah will go, throw the Bled weight around, and get him out."

"You don't think they'll arrest him then?" asked Stella. That had been one of her nightmares. Josiah in Dachau with Abel.

"No, I don't think they can do that," said Nicky.

Stella took a couple of aspirin and washed them down with a sip of coffee. It wouldn't help her feet. They'd been getting worse. All the running in Paris had finally caught up to her.

"They would've arrested us if they'd gotten the chance," she said.

Nicky looked out the window at the long fingers of rain slithering across the window, his mask of indifference sliding into place. "Yes, that's true."

Once Stella would've thought him bored, cold, untouched by the danger, but she wasn't a newlywed any longer, despite the brief amount of time since the wedding. Peril had made them well and truly married and she knew him. Nicky Lawrence was seriously concerned so she didn't press.

"Actually, I'm more concerned about the Sorkines at the moment and what will happen in Venice," she said.

"Are you?"

She thought that might kick a crack in his composure, but it didn't. He sipped his coffee and chose a newspaper. *The New York Times* from four days ago.

"You realize that Venice is flooded and everyone left the train?"

"Yes."

"The Sorkines might've left Venice, too."

That did it. Nicky turned to her with a flicker of concern, no more. "That changes nothing."

"Yes, it does. We need to tell them about Abel and the book. If we don't find them, they might follow our trail to Vienna. They're not going to give up on the book any more than the Nazis, Peiper, in particular."

"You're not telling me anything I don't already know."

"We need a plan," she insisted.

"What would you like to do?" he asked, his blue eyes half-mast and completely bored.

She wanted to smack him, to shake something loose. "I want to know what's going to happen."

Nicky yawned. "I can't tell you that. I can't even tell you what has already happened." He tossed the old newspaper on the floor with a sigh. "This is maddening."

"Really?"

"Of course," he said.

"Good. I want you to be as frustrated as me," she said with a grin before coming to his seat and cuddling up.

"How is that helpful?" he asked, pouring her another cup of coffee.

"I don't know, but it is."

He rested his head on hers. "You are ridiculous."

"And sublime?"

"Without a doubt."

A quiet knock rattled the door and they looked up to find Monsieur Volcot standing in the corridor holding up a newspaper. Nicky waved him in, but the conductor hesitated, glancing at Stella. She smiled with what she hoped was reassurance and he came in.

"Monsieur Marchand sent these for you. He believed you would like to have the news," said Monsieur Volcot.

Nicky practically snatched the papers from him. "Thank you very much. What day are these? Yesterday. It's a miracle."

Monsieur Volcot smiled and nodded as he backed out of the compartment.

"Wait," said Stella and his face tensed. "Do you speak Italian?"

"Yes, madam. I do. A little."

Stella knew well enough that when a European said "a little" they meant a lot. "Are you busy?"

"Well…I…" He kept backing up and glanced around as if an excuse might emerge from the walls.

"There aren't any other passengers," said Stella with a well-placed wink behind Nicky's bowed head.

"Um…yes, madam. You are the only passengers at present," said Monsieur Volcot.

"Then would you mind helping me with some Italian phrases? Monsieur Marchand taught me a few, but it's not nearly enough." She held up her Italian dictionary. "I have this, but pronunciation is the sticking point."

"Well, I should be—"

"Give it up, man," said Nicky, waving him to the opposite seat. "She'll chase you down the corridor and who has time for that?"

"Very well," said Monsieur Volcot, sitting stiffly on the seat. "What would you like to know?"

"I know how to say hello and all that, but I need to ask for a hotel, a small, out of the way place, not so popular with Americans."

"I thought you'd been to Venice before."

"We have, but our…circumstances have changed," said Stella.

"I see." He flicked a glance up at the luggage rack above their heads. It held only Stella's battered handbag, a hatbox, and her new makeup case. "There are a few options I can recommend."

Nicky looked up. "We'd appreciate that."

"Close to the ghetto would be best," said Stella and Monsieur Volcot got stiffer. She hadn't thought it possible. The poor man looked as though he might pop a vessel.

"No need to look as though you're facing the firing squad," said Nicky, suddenly radiating charm, but it didn't change the petrified conductor's demeanor one bit. "She's on your side."

"Sir, I assure you, I don't have a side."

"We've been in Europe for over two months," said Nicky. "Let *me* assure *you* that there are definitely sides and unless you are a National Socialist, we're on yours."

Monsieur Volcot blew out a breath and relaxed into the seat back.

"I would recommend the Hotel al Ponte Vittoria. They are friendly and reasonably priced."

"Close to the ghetto?" asked Stella.

His eyes roamed over her face. It only took a second, but she'd come to understand that he was looking for a hint to her origins, as if being Jewish would be written on her forehead or in the slant of her pale blue eyes. Such a ridiculous notion. But since he was obviously protecting the family in third class, she decided not to take offense. Monsieur Volcot didn't want to hurt her. He wanted to know her. That was a dangerous thing. Stella had come to think of herself as a kind of disaster magnet. The Dutch historian, Dr. Van Wijk, her father's friend, Hans, Albert Moore, and Roger Morris the artist dead or very nearly so.

"Yes," he said. "Walking distance, but it floods very easily. It will not be passable."

"We'll find a way."

He smiled and said, "I believe you will."

Stella looked at that nice man, not young, not old, probably a husband and father, at the very least a good and loyal friend and a fresh wave of homesickness came over her. How she wanted to go home, to walk off that train, be safe, and cause no one any trouble anymore.

"You know our names," she said.

He tensed again. Monsieur Volcot had seen their passports. They could've been fake, but they weren't. "Yes, madam."

"It's a good idea if you forget them," said Nicky.

"Yes, sir. I forget many things. I am very unreliable that way."

"That's not usually an admirable quality." Then Stella added with a smile, "But in such cases as these, a good memory is unpardonable. This is the last time I shall ever remember it myself."

Neither man got her Jane Austen reference and her eyes fell on *The Hobbit*. Cyril Welk had given it to her and he certainly would've known the quote. She missed him, in spite of herself. The little spy had saved and then betrayed her, trying his best to keep her from

Napoleon's tomb and Nicky, but why? That she didn't know and feared she never would.

"My memory is terrible and I will never improve it," said Monsieur Volcot.

"Glad to hear it," said Nicky. "Now what's the name of that hotel again?"

"The Hotel al Ponte Vittoria. Very good people. Understanding and forgetful."

Stella shook off her sadness and picked up her dictionary. "Now how do I ask for it?"

They began their lesson, working through simple phrases and questions. The rain poured and Nicky read. In the short amount of time left before they arrived in Venice, Stella got everything she needed, except a plan.

# CHAPTER 2

*N*icky stayed perched on the bottom step of the train car and Stella ducked, trying to see around him in the narrow area. "Go. What are you waiting for?" It had taken them ten minutes to get through the mad rush of boarding passengers.

"It's worse than I thought," he yelled over his shoulder.

"What is?"

"The water."

Stella squeezed between him and the railing and was shocked to find what amounted to a waterfall in front of her. The platform had a roof that ended about five feet from the train and the rain was pouring off it in a solid sheet. She could make out the platform and it wasn't under water, which was the only positive.

Nicky's giant golfing umbrella was lost in Vienna and they hadn't known to buy a new one in Paris. Stella never owned galoshes in her life, but she wasn't even sure galoshes would do it. They needed something like the rubber overalls the men at the brewery wore to clean the vats.

"I guess we'll get wet," said Stella.

"Just when I'd gotten used to being dry and warm."

"Good things never last."

"Don't say that. You'll jinx us," he said.

"You don't believe in luck, but you believe in jinxes?" asked Stella, looking for a break in the water. There wasn't one.

"I'm beginning to. Let me—"

Stella jumped through the water and landed with an inelegant splat on the platform, sending rockets of pain through her damaged feet and up her legs. She stumbled forward and someone caught her. She gasped in pain, clinging to his black coat. It could be anyone. It could be an SS officer.

"*Signora?*" he asked in a lovely resonate tenor voice and Stella looked up into a pale face with gentle, brown eyes and a priest's collar under the dimpled chin.

"Oh, thank God," Stella burst out. "Sorry, Father."

He looked rather startled, but quickly asked, "*Non see la Signora Goldenberg?*"

Stella wasn't sure what he was asking, but she didn't know anyone named Goldenberg, so she shook her head no.

Down the line of train cars, the silent family dashed onto the platform and huddled together, looking around for someone.

"*Scusi, signora.*" The priest hurried over and hustled them away with a glance back at Stella. He couldn't get away fast enough.

Nicky came through the waterfall, lugging her hat box and makeup case. "Who was that?"

"I don't know," she said. "Not the Bissets though."

"Huh?"

"I'll explain later."

Nicky looked around at the platform with passengers rushing past them to board, but no staff in evidence. "Well, I was hoping there'd be someone to help."

Stella took her makeup case from him and found its weight surprising. She'd forgotten that she'd stowed Gabriele Griese's pistol in the bottom. The unwelcome reminder made the image of Gabriele's body slipping into the Seine bloom in her mind. Stella felt no guilt. It had to be done, but it was less than pleasant all the same, and she forced it away. "Come on. There has to be someone around."

They trudged off the platform and into the station, braving two more waterfalls and a puddle the size of Lake Como only to find the station practically deserted.

"It's like Vienna," said Nicky.

"Don't say that," said Stella, but he wasn't entirely wrong. When they'd left Venice, a person could barely move in Santa Lucia. There were buskers, hawkers of exotic food, and travelers, so many travelers, rushing to get wherever it was that they were going. Now they could hear their footsteps on the floor. "At least there aren't any of those hateful flags."

"You're right. No swastikas to ruin our day. I wonder how long that will last."

"Oh, come on. Germany can't take over everyone."

"Wanna bet?"

Stella ignored him and walked off toward a newspaper man who was shuttering his little stand. She didn't want to hear any more miserable predictions. Monsieur Volcot's new papers had only succeeded in making Nicky gloomy. It seemed the world did not care about what happened on the Kristallnacht, unless you counted a few stern words of disapproval. Everyone wanted to avoid another war and if the Jews had to be sacrificed, so be it, or at least that's what Nicky told her as she was practicing her vocabulary. He was on about the annexation of the Sudetenland and the future of Czechoslovakia. He might be right about them and some others. Austria, obviously, maybe Poland, but Italy, no. They were just so Italian. Rules were just considered suggestions. How many times had she heard *"Domani,"* when she asked when something would get done. Tomorrow meant tomorrow or the next day or more likely never. Italians wouldn't comply the way the Austrians had. Regulations didn't run in their veins. Wine did.

The station was a good example. Sure, it was empty and cold, but it didn't have a jot of the fear that wafted around the Vienna station. The travelers there had been terribly afraid, for good reason as it turned out, but the travelers in Santa Lucia were just soggy and irritated.

"*Scusi, signore.*" Stella asked if he had a water bus schedule. He stared at her bewildered so she tried again. He shrugged and shooed her away. She started to insist, but Nicky dragged her away. "Forget it."

"I know my pronunciation was perfect. You heard me. *Vaporetto.* That's what the buses are called. Wasn't it perfect?"

"Apparently, it wasn't. Let's just go out to the stop. I think they have schedules posted."

They pushed through a crush of sopping wet tourists hurrying into the station and came out onto the steps overlooking the Grand Canal, except the Grand Canal was more like a lake. The water was up over the steps that led to the vaporetto dock. People were wading through the water, holding luggage up over their heads and cursing in multiple languages.

"How deep do you think that is?" asked Stella.

"I don't think it matters."

"Easy for you to say. You're on stilts."

He laughed and tried to pick her up. "I'll carry you."

She pushed him away and took off her shoes, tucking them in her pockets.

"What are you doing?" he asked.

"I only have one pair."

"It's dirty and you might cut your feet."

Stella hoisted up her skirt and coat. "And there might be sharks. Come on. There's the vaporetto."

They walked down into the water and Stella regretted it almost instantly. The water was beyond dirty and ice cold. Her teeth were chattering before they made it half way. There had to be a hotel close by. She started to turn around, but Nicky shouted. "It's leaving. I'll catch it." He surged off through the grey water, waving his arms and shouting the only word he knew, "*Basta! Basta!*"

The water bus did not *basta*. It left, belching black smoke and creating waves that brought the water up to Stella's thighs. Being hammered into a beer barrel was starting to seem like an elegant way to travel.

"Swell," said Nicky. "Let's go back. There has to be someone who can help."

"There is," said Stella, pointing at a small and non-too-seaworthy looking water taxi on the other side of the canal. There was a captain in it, smoking a cigarette and smiling laconically at them.

"He'll charge an arm and a leg."

"And we'll pay it." Stella waved and shouted. The captain nodded, lit a second cigarette, and fired up his engine. The dingy craft bounced over the waves to collide with the dock and bobble around like a cork until the captain gunned the engine in a kind of coughing way and persuaded it to calm down enough so that they could climb aboard.

Stella slipped around on the waterlogged space between the canvas-covered helm and the glassed-in passenger area.

"*Buongiorna, signora*," said the captain, continuing to smoke the two cigarettes at once.

"*Buongiorno, signore*," said Stella while holding onto the back of the captain's seat for dear life.

Nicky stepped into the boat and lost his footing in the narrow stair. He fell on his rump, long legs and arms flailing. Stella grabbed the makeup case, but the hatbox went flying overboard. The captain gave him a hand up and asked something incomprehensible.

Nicky looked at Stella and every Italian word she'd learned flew out of her head.

"*Quoi?*" she shouted over the rattling engine, the rain, and the cargo boat that chose that moment to chug by.

The captain said something.

"*Quoi?*" she repeated.

"Isn't that French?" yelled Nicky.

"Maybe he knows it!"

The look on the weathered seaman's face said he didn't and that he was rapidly losing patience.

"Hotel!" yelled Stella.

"*Sì!*"

"We want the Hotel al Ponte Vittoria!"

He nodded vigorously and put his hand up to shield his eyes from a fresh onslaught of stinging rain. "*Sì* hotel."

Stella tried again, but her teeth were chattering so badly she couldn't get it out in anything that sounded like actual words.

"Show him the paper!" yelled Nicky.

"What?"

"You wrote it down, didn't you?"

She'd totally forgotten that she'd taken the precaution of writing down key phrases and the hotel. She'd forgotten so well that she'd shoved her wet shoe in her pocket on top of the list. It came out soaked and had to be peeled apart with her fingernails. The hotel name was mostly intact and when she showed it to the captain, he nodded. "Ah! *Sì! Sì! Sì!* Vittoria!"

"Yes! Yes! Vittoria!" yelled Stella and he pointed at the passenger door.

Nicky flung open the door and they squeezed into the small area that smelled like mold and wet dog. The bench seats had springs sticking out of them and had some stains that Stella chose to believe were either dirt or chocolate.

"Don't say it," she said, picking up a crusty wool blanket and wrapping it around her legs.

"Say what?" asked Nicky as he wedged himself between two wickedly sharp springs.

"Beggars can't be choosers."

"That phrase has never been more accurate."

"It's fine. We'll go to the hotel, defrost in the bath, and figure out what to do." Stella sounded cheerful, but homesickness was settling in for a long stay.

A faster boat blew past them and a huge amount of spray hit the windows, coming through the cracks and broken panes to soak Nicky from the back.

"The worst honeymoon in history just got even worse," said Nicky, his teeth beginning to chatter, too.

"It's not that bad," said Stella.

"We could be dead, I suppose." He stared at her from under his sagging fedora with water dripping off the tip.

"We could be Calvin."

"Calvin?"

"My friend, Emily's husband. They went to England for their honeymoon."

"Wise decision." Nicky took off his fedora and shook it, spraying the floor and Stella.

She wrinkled her nose at him and said, "He found out about a game they play called rugby."

"If you're trying to say that a rugby injury is worse than being chased by Hitler's thugs across half of Europe, getting frost bite, and nearly killed, not to mention this colossal disaster, I'm going to have to say no."

"He was hospitalized for a week and lost his vision in the left eye," said Stella.

"I'd take that over this honeymoon," said Nicky. "It's not over. We don't know where the Sorkines are and, if I had to lay bets, Peiper is going to turn up, sooner rather than later."

"Maybe he won't."

"He will."

"Then we better hurry up."

The boat turned onto a smaller canal and slowed down. Stella didn't want to think about Peiper. Not just then. Her teeth had stopped chattering and she leaned back to look out the window. Venice was lovely, even in a deluge. The ancient buildings loomed overhead with their faded colors and crumbling stucco, speaking of a more elegant age. Tiny little balconies in wrought iron sat in front of tall, narrow doors shuttered against the rain, but occasionally she'd catch a glimpse of a multicolored chandelier with snaking tubes of delicate glass and encrusted with flowers and leaves. Stella couldn't remember why she wanted to leave so badly. She'd been safe, but then again she hadn't been aware that safety wasn't guaranteed.

She wanted to go home and feel that safety again, but when she turned back to Nicky and saw his eyes trained on her, she remembered. Where was home? They hadn't discussed it. Home to her was St. Louis. It couldn't be otherwise. Nicky was a New Yorker and he worked at his family's company, United Shipping and Steel. He would think that they'd live there. Never mind the brewery.

Nicky started to say something, but the engine cut out and the captain banged on the glass. Stella threw off her crusty blanket and picked up her makeup bag.

"I hope you didn't have anything important in that hat box," said Nicky.

She laughed and nudged him with her shoulder. "I only have one hat." She flicked the formerly fabulous feather that now lay on her shoulder, limp like a black rat's tail.

"I'm going to fix that. Eventually."

"I'll settle for a hot bath."

The taxi glided up to a small dock under an elegant canopy and Nicky frowned. "We should've specified not too expensive."

The dock did have a pricey look about it, similar to the five-star hotel they'd stayed in before. The polished steps up from the boat had a non-slip covering and a brass handrail with a lion's head perched on the end.

"Too late now," said Nicky.

"Much too late."

The captain asked for their fare and Stella was forced to get out her dictionary that was nearly as bad off as her Italian notes, but she gathered that they could buy a boat for what he wanted. Nicky started haggling and Stella climbed out, wincing at the pain in her feet. They were under the canopy so at least she wasn't getting more wet, which was probably possible although she was sure that she didn't look it.

Nicky came up the stairs and said, "Well, that was a rip-off, but we're here." He tried the door, but it was locked. "This cannot be happening."

Stella pointed to the bell. "I think we have to ring to come in."

"Ring then."

She rang and they waited an exceedingly painful five minutes for a man to walk leisurely down the teak-paneled halls with a clipboard and a look that was both eager and haughty at the same time.

When he got to the door, he looked them over slowly and checked his clipboard, his liver-colored lips pursed in dismay. Then he looked around their feet and his frown deepened.

"What's he looking for?" Nicky knocked.

The man shook his head and made a shooing gesture at them like they were a couple of vermin that washed up on shore.

Nicky knocked again and the glass door rattled on its fancy brass hinges. "We can pay. We're Americans."

The man sneered at them and pointed at a black telephone on a little mahogany table.

"I think he's going to call the police," said Stella.

Nicky pounded on the door. "I'm wet. I'm tired. I'm rich. Let me the hell in."

The hotelier picked up the phone and began dialing. Stella grabbed Nicky's arm and wedged herself between him and the door. "Stop it. The last thing we need is the police."

"Maybe we do need the authorities. Maybe he needs to be taught a lesson."

"Aren't Italy and Germany allies? Do we want to be arrested by a Nazi ally?"

Nicky abruptly stopped, took off his fedora, and smoothed his hair. "No. Obviously not."

She pulled him away from the door as the hotelier began speaking into the receiver. "Hurry up. We need to be gone."

"Where are we going? Into the canal?"

She pointed at a second set of stairs that led to an arched bridge over the canal. They ran up the steps past a couple of drowned rats and a broken wine bottle to find a choice.

"Left or right?" asked Stella.

Down the narrow passageway, a man stuck his head out a door and raised a fist. "*Vittene, sporchi ebrei!*"

"Not that way." Nicky spun her around and they ran up the stairs of the bridge. Stella had forgotten how exhausting Venice was. Stairs everywhere.

Another narrow passageway waited on the other side. It was lower and flooded. Two men stood in the pouring rain, using what looked like an oversized bicycle pump attached to a hose. Water was trickling out a window through a wide tube. It was a mystery why they'd be pumping out the building when they were standing in four inches of water, but she saw why when they splashed down into the passageway. The door had sandbags stacked up in it and the interior appeared mostly dry.

"Once more into the breech," said Nicky, dragging her behind him and the man from the hotel came over the bridge and yelled at them as they splashed away.

The two men at the pump yelled back, making a rude hand gesture at the hotelier that Abel had called "the horns." People did it a lot in traffic. Stella averted her eyes. "The horns" were sometimes followed by crotch scratching and her day had been bad enough.

The hotelier stopped yelling, beaten back by the ferocity of the workers, but Stella and Nicky kept trudging away.

"*Sei ebreo?*" yelled one of the workers after them.

They ignored him and sped up.

"*Sind sie Juden?*" he yelled.

Nicky kept going, but Stella stopped and nearly got pulled off her feet.

"Come on, Stella!"

"I think he asked if we're Jewish," she said.

"So?" Nicky looked up at the faces that were popping out of the windows above them and was rewarded with rain in the face.

"I'd like to know why." She wrenched her hand out of his and turned back to yell, "*Nein! Kein Juden!*"

"Hello, Stella," said Nicky. "We're being chased."

"Not anymore. Thanks to them."

The men waved at her and they splashed over. The younger worker said something in German that Stella couldn't make out. "Do you speak English at all?"

"Ah, English," he said with a broad smile. "You are Americans, yes?"

"Yes," said Stella. "Why was he chasing us? We wanted a room for the night."

"Fabrizio hates Jews," said the man. "My sister she marry Lorenzo. He is a Jew." He shook a fist in the direction that Fabrizio had disappeared in.

"We're not Jews," said Nicky.

"You look like Jews."

"Because we're wet? Everyone is wet," said Stella.

"Because you have nothing with you. The Jews, they come from the North and they have nothing."

"Well, thank you for explaining," said Nicky. "We've got to find another hotel."

"There are many hotels, but some will not like no luggage," he said, holding out his rough hand. "I am Luca and this is my father Antonio."

"You're very good at languages."

"I studied in Rome before I come home to help my father," said Luca. "You want cheap hotel, yes?"

"Cheap is good," said Stella, "and near the ghetto. We are trying to find some friends and we think they might be there."

He nodded and spoke to his father. The older man nodded, considered, and gave a name that was very familiar.

"My father says that you want to go to the Hotel al Ponte Vittoria. They will take you."

Nicky pointed at the bridge. "Isn't that the Hotel al Ponte Vittoria with Fabrizio the Jew hater?"

Luca laughed. "No, no. That is Hotel Palazzo Vittoria."

"Well, that explains it," said Nicky. "How far is the other one, the good one?"

Between Luca and his father they got directions to the right hotel that happily wasn't too far. Ten minutes, Luca claimed, but it might as well have been an hour. Stella's teeth were chattering and her feet numb. It was a toss-up when she'd felt worse, just then or after she'd crashed Peiper's plane.

"Be careful," called out Luca after them. "It's different after the *Leggi Razziali*."

"The what?" asked Nicky.

"The new laws for the Jews. Life will be harder for your friends."

Nicky nodded and Stella whispered, "Here, too?"

"It started in September, but I didn't think it was that serious. No one said anything to Abel when we were here."

"Something new then?"

"Must be," said Nicky. "I told you Italy is next."

"They don't seem like the type."

"It looks like every country is the type."

Stella stood in front of the door of the Hotel al Ponte Vittoria with her finger hovering over the bell.

"What on Earth are you waiting for?" asked Nicky.

She looked left and right for an escape route, but there were no good options. They were in the narrowest passage she'd ever seen. She and Nicky had walked single file and he kept bumping the sides. Even the door was small. Stella sized. Nicky would have to stoop. But reassuringly, the name Hotel al Ponte Vittoria was painted above the arched door in graceful script and the passage wasn't flooded.

"Stella, please."

"I'm figuring out where to run if this doesn't work out."

"It's going to work out."

"That's what we always think."

"I see your point, but your lips are turning blue and icicles are forming on my elbows." He pressed her hand and she pushed the small button.

"Here goes nothing," she said.

"Right now, it's everything."

A few fretful minutes later, a woman opened the door. She wore a thick white apron and a welcoming smile until she saw the state of them. Stella's heart sunk and she got ready to run.

"We lost our luggage." She almost said that they weren't Jewish, but her heart wouldn't let her. It shouldn't matter.

"Do you speak English?" asked Nicky.

The woman stepped back and welcomed them in. "*Buonasera.* Yes, of course, I speak English. Let me apologize. I was startled by your appearance. You have had a difficult day, yes?"

"I can't even begin to tell you." Stella squeezed past her into a surprisingly large and pleasing hall with a fat umbrella stand on octagonal tiles dotted with Turkish rugs. The walls were a warm yellow and lit by small, tasteful chandeliers, Murano glass but a quieter style, only frosted glass and leaves. And it was warm, so warm and inviting Stella's eyes welled up.

"Excuse me," said Nicky and there was a thump.

"Oh, sir. Your head," said the woman. "Are you all right?"

"If you have whiskey, I will be."

She laughed. "We do."

Stella turned and saw Nicky standing in a growing puddle rubbing the top of his head.

"Oh, no," she said. "Your floor."

But the woman wasn't looking at the puddle under Nicky. She was looking at Stella's feet. "Antonio! Antonio!" Then came a burst of rapid Italian and a little old man came running down the hall, stooped, frowning, and carrying a pile of towels. He exclaimed and spread out a towel for each of them to step on.

"I'm so sorry about the mess," said Stella.

"It is nothing. I am Sofia, your host. We must get you out of those wet clothes."

"Do you have a room?" asked Nicky as the old man slipped off his sodden coat and held it up at arm's length, making a new puddle.

"Of course. It is the off-season and this rain." Sofia made a tsking sound that seemed to be universal among older ladies and eyed Stella's feet again before she helped her off with her coat and hat. "You will need a doctor. I will call our friend. He will know how to help you."

"Oh, no. I think it's all right," said Stella.

"Call the doctor," said Nicky. "The sooner the better."

"You have the currency to pay him?" asked Sofia.

"We have money, just no luggage."

Sofia's smile widened and Stella sensed a bit of relief. She accepted a towel and began drying off as best she could. "As for the doctor, I don't—"

"Stella, for once, can you not argue?" asked Nicky. "Look at your feet."

She didn't look, having learned that looking only made things worse. "It's fine. I need a bath and a bed. That's all."

They all looked at her silently and then Sofia popped into action, yelling for someone named Matteo. A young man about Stella's age peeked out from the large desk at the end of the hall and Sofia waved to him to come down. Matteo stopped next to Stella, doing his level best not to stare, nodded, and attempted to grab her.

"Hey." Stella slapped his hands and he jumped back.

"Matteo will carry you to your room," said Sofia hastily. "You cannot walk on those feet."

"I've been walking on them just fine."

Sofia set her jaw and Nicky said, "I agree, but I'll carry her."

"Nobody is carrying me. I'm not a child," said Stella, taking a step and flinching from the burning pain in her foot.

"Look at your feet and say that," said Nicky.

"I don't need—"

"Do it."

She sucked in a breath and looked down, preparing for the worst and getting more than that. Her feet looked like boiled pork sausages that had rotted. The skin was peeling and had split and somewhere along the line she'd lost several toenails. "Oh my God."

"All right then," said Nicky. "I'll carry you."

Sofia pointed at Matteo. "He is very strong and you are tired."

"I can do it," said Nicky and Sofia gave him a look that Stella recognized. Her imperious grandmother looked at Uncle Josiah that way when he said things like, "I think I'll have another double," or "What kind of fool do you think I am?"

Nicky shrank back and conceded the way that Uncle Josiah never did and Sofia waved at Matteo, who blushed to the roots of his wavy black hair. But he obeyed and swept Stella off her hideous feet.

Led by Sofia, he carried her down a warren of halls to a door with an ornate H on it. She opened the door and Matteo carried her to a canopy bed draped in green damask. Sofia bustled over to put down a double layer of towels and Matteo gently laid her down.

"May I help you with your stockings?" asked Sofia and Stella looked down in surprise. She'd forgotten she'd had stockings and indeed she now didn't. The silk had shredded and hung around her calves in limp, wet tendrils.

"It's okay. I can do it," she said sadly, but the stockings were the least of her worries. Her new red suit was a wreck, the skirt drenched, but, at least, the jacket and creamy silk blouse that Amelie had so lovingly selected had been protected by her fur.

"Don't worry," said Sofia, sensing her dismay. "There are shops nearby. They will accommodate you."

Stella nodded, wondering how she could possibly get there on those feet and in those clothes.

"Here." Sofia handed her a toweling robe. "I will have your clothes and coat cleaned."

Antonio knocked and came in, saying something about a *medico* and Sofia nodded. "Dr. Davide will be here in an hour. May I draw you a bath, sir?"

"Thank you." Nicky pulled out his wallet. "How much for a week?"

Sofia demurred, but Nicky insisted on paying ahead and she finally accepting a wad of lira.

"Another thing. Would it be possible to arrange a transatlantic call?" asked Nicky.

"You want to call your family?" interrupted Stella.

"No." He seemed puzzled at the suggestion. "Yours. To tell them we've arrived and...find out their news."

Stella folded her hands over her stomach. "I should've known."

"Excuse me, sir," said Sofia. "Our telephone doesn't not work. The rain has broken the lines. I could arrange for a call at one of the larger hotels, but it will take some time to arrange."

"When will it be fixed?" asked Stella.

Sofia asked Antonio and the old man shrugged, *"Domani."*

Stella and Nicky exchanged knowing glances.

"Never mind," said Nicky. "We'll telegram."

She nodded. "As you wish."

After Sofia and the others had left, Nicky stripped. Stella popped opened her makeup case and dug out the pistol. Nicky raised an eyebrow but said nothing as she shoved it under the mattress. Out of sight wasn't quite out of mind, but it would have to do.

"She didn't ask us to register, but I suppose we'll have to, at some point," said Stella as she unsnapped the remains of her stockings from her garter belt. "Do we tell them we're the Bled Lawrences?"

"I don't know why we would." He stood glaring at her in his sagging briefs with his formerly pristine body looking like he'd been to war, which in a way Stella supposed he had. She wouldn't really know because every time she asked about what happened when they were apart, Nicky promptly went to sleep.

"Because that's who we are."

"That may be who you are, but I'm still Nicky Lawrence."

Stella flung her stockings on the tile with a wet slap. "Okay."

"Don't say it like that."

"Like what?"

"Like it's not true."

"Okay."

"Stella," he growled.

She unbuttoned her jacket and examined her blouse before glancing slyly at her husband. "What happened to Hans after I left the two of you at the brewery?"

He picked up his robe and turned away from her.

"All right. How did you get to Paris?" she asked.

"Sofia probably has my bath ready." He stalked over to the door, whipped it open, and left without looking back.

Stella took off her jacket and unbuttoned her blouse. "That's what I thought."

Stella managed to get all her clothes off without standing up. She wrapped herself in her fluffy robe, propping her feet up on a wad of semi-wet towels with her blouse draped over them. It wasn't good for the silk, but a little stained silk was better than looking at those feet, in her estimation, and silk was the only thing that didn't chafe. Now they weren't burning as much as hurting, which under any other circumstances would've been horrid, but just then, it was actually an improvement.

Such an improvement that she laid back on the feather pillows and closed her eyes. The room smelled faintly of lemon verbena and cigarette smoke. It was almost like having her mother and grand-mother there with her but without the exasperation and worrying. The bed was comfortable and she was almost able to drift off when a quiet knock came to ruin it. She called for the person to come in. They didn't, not immediately, so she expected Matteo, but it was Sofia, wringing her hands and avoiding Stella's direct gaze.

"I have bad news. Dr. Davide, he is not here."

"Okay. It's fine."

"There is a baby coming. It's fast and he can't come."

"I understand." Stella was rather relieved. If a doctor didn't come, he couldn't tell her that her toes were going to fall off and he couldn't do anything about it. If her toes were going to fall off, she rather they just did it without an unhelpful warning.

"He has sent his associate," she said. "Would you like to see him?"

Nicky strode into the room, freshly washed with his blond hair combed back to show off the bruise on his forehead. "Yes, she would."

Stella sighed. "I guess so."

Sofia didn't move.

"Well?"

"There may be a...complication."

"Isn't there always?" Nicky picked up his clothes that had been drying on the radiator, his indifference masked frustration although to Stella it was quite visible. "He wants an outrageous fee? Is that it?"

"No, no. He is quite reasonable," said Sofia.

"Then get him in here. Those feet aren't going to heal up on their own."

"They might," interjected Stella.

Sofia kept wringing her hands. "She must be seen. I explained the feet to Dr. Davide."

"Then what's the hold up?" asked Nicky.

"Hold up?" asked Sofia.

"What are we waiting for?"

She nodded. "I see. There may be a complication."

"You said that already."

Sofia leaned back to look at their door, which was open. She went over and quickly closed it. "Salvatore is a Jew."

"And a doctor?" asked Nicky.

"Yes."

"A good one?"

"Yes, I trust him…with several of our guests," said Sofia.

Nicky's indifference fell away and the congenial Nicky took over. "Bring him in. My wife needs help."

Sofia relaxed but still had her hands clasped together. "You understand it's against our law."

"What is?" asked Stella, her throat suddenly tight and hot. "Being a Jew?"

"Not yet, but I do not think that is far from us," said Sofia. "Dr. Salvatore cannot treat gentiles." She paused and then asked, "You are gentiles?"

"Yes, and we don't care about that stupid law. Do we, Nicky?"

Nicky stood up, casual and loose, and Sofia stopped clenching. "We won't tell if he won't."

She smiled and went into the hall. Nicky got dressed and, a minute later, she returned with a middle-aged man with salt and pepper hair and wearing a well-cut pin-striped suit and a dark overcoat. He could've been anyone, practically anywhere with any religion. He could've been her father or Uncle Nicolai. Not Uncle Josiah. He'd never been that respectable in his life. The whole thing was beyond ridiculous. A doctor needed patients and vice versa.

"Dr. Salvatore," Nicky held out his hand, "thank you for coming."

"You are very welcome." The doctor paused. "I don't believe I know your name."

"Because I haven't given one."

Dr. Salvatore bowed his head slightly. "I understand and apologize."

"Think nothing of it. What do you know about frost bite?" Nicky lifted the blouse and Stella was certain she saw the good doctor wince ever so slightly.

"It is not my field of expertise, but I believe I can help." He opened his big black medical bag and asked for a basin of hot water. Nicky and Sofia got Stella situated in a chair and the doctor mixed several tinctures into the water and swirled it with a wooden tongue depressor.

He squatted in front of the basin and gingerly picked up her foot. "You have been walking?"

"Yes. I had to, but it wasn't this bad before. It just happened," said Stella.

"Have you been taking anything?"

"Just aspirin."

"That's very effective for swelling and pain. You should continue taking it." Then he surprised her by sniffing her foot. "You have been walking in the canal water."

"Yes. There wasn't much of a choice."

"It is very bad for the skin and yours was already damaged." He lowered her foot to the water. "This will hurt you."

"Swell," said Stella, gripping the sides of the chair.

He stopped and asked, "Would you like to continue?"

"Yes," said Nicky, but Dr. Salvatore didn't look at him as Stella suspected a doctor in the States would have. He only looked at her, only she mattered.

"Yes," she said. "I have to get up and walking soon."

He lowered her foot into the water and she gasped at the stinging heat, but then it was sort of tingly.

"Too hot?" he asked.

"I think it's okay."

He put the second foot in and then pulled out a syringe. Stella stiffened and then reminded herself, if she could give a shot she ought to be able to take one. "Is that for Prontosil?"

He pulled a small vial out of his bag and snapped it open. "You have medical knowledge?"

"Only about that," said Stella. "And Eukadol."

He drew the liquid into the syringe and Nicky asked, "What's that for?"

"To kill the infection."

"The water gave her an infection?"

"I believe it was already there and she reacted to the...soiled water," said Dr. Salvatore as he gave her the shot. It wasn't more painful than her feet which was all she could say for it.

"What's in your treatment?" she asked, grasping for a distraction.

"Copper salts, vitamins A and D, lavender, and pomegranate. I have used them to good effect on burns." He lifted her right foot and examined her toes. "This hurts?"

"A whole lot."

"Then I think you will recover well, but you must soak your feet twice a day and not walk."

Stella glanced up at Nicky. "That is not an option."

He checked the other foot and then stood up. "Your feet are in poor condition. Rest is essential for healing."

"I understand, but we need to find someone so I have to walk."

"I'll do it," said Nicky.

"We'll do it together."

"Who are you looking for?" asked Sofia.

"Our friend's family," said Nicky. "The Sorkines, Raymond-Raoul and Suzanne. They might have their daughter with them. Do you know them?"

Dr. Salvatore and Sofia shook their heads.

"What do they look like?" asked Sofia and Stella was stumped. She had no idea. They were related to Abel, but that didn't mean anything. She didn't resemble Uncle Josiah, except for the eyes.

"You don't know?" asked Dr. Salvatore.

"Not really." Stella pointed at her handbag. She'd managed to keep it dry inside her coat and the only clue she possessed was hidden in it. Nicky gave it to her and she pulled out the pictures Nicky had rescued from the rubble of Abel's flat. She showed them the young woman with braids and the German officer. "They could look like them."

"Or not," said Nicky. "Honestly, we don't know."

"It is important that you find them?" asked Dr. Salvatore.

Nicky nodded. "Yes, and they may be looking for us, too."

"I will ask those that I know. Perhaps they have been seen."

"They're Jewish," said Stella and then she paused. "I guess we don't know that for sure."

"I think we do," said Nicky.

"You know very little," said Dr. Salvatore.

"We know we have to find them," said Stella.

Dr. Salvatore opened a little box and got out another vial. A pair of deep grooves had appeared between his eyes. "You can't ask the carabinieri for help?"

"It's better if we don't," said Nicky. "But they aren't criminals, you understand."

"Just Jews."

Stella didn't hesitate. "Probably. We have some information for them. It's essential for their safety. We wouldn't want them going where they aren't wanted."

The doctor met her gaze and within those dark, concerned eyes was understanding. "I will do what I can."

"Thank you."

"Would you like something for the pain to help you sleep?"

"I thought you'd never ask."

# CHAPTER 3

*T*he first thing Stella saw when she opened her eyes was the same dismal grayness outside the hotel window. Rain continued to pound against the glass, making the view wavy and muted.

She knew she was alone before she sat up and looked. Nicky had that kind of presence. Maybe it was their connection or perhaps just his size, but she felt his absence like an empty stomach. There were no clues about where he'd gone and she didn't remember being put in bed or what had been done to her feet after the soak, but something had been done. They were propped up high and, judging by their size under the blanket, they were huge. On the upside, they only ached. The burning was gone.

She wiggled her toes to make certain they were still there and a mild pain assured her that they were. She tossed off the covers and found her feet wrapped up in cotton strips like a mummy and didn't resemble feet in size or shape. It was more like she had pumpkins at the ends of her legs, so she started unwrapping them with a tight knot of fear in her chest and prepared herself for blackened, dead skin. Instead, the swelling had gone down dramatically. Her feet, while still sausage-like, were half the size and the color was in the neighborhood of normal. Two more toenails had fallen off, leaving her with five, but she had working toes so she wasn't about to complain. Besides, nails grew back. Her older brother, Lucien, had banged his thumb with a hammer when he was learning how to make beer barrels. His whole hand swelled up to the size of a catcher's mitt and the nail popped off during a family dinner, landing in his pot roast. Her mother had fainted so it was a good thing she couldn't see her daughter's feet. Francesqua Bled didn't have a strong stomach for that kind of thing. Sausage feet might put her in a coma.

Stella touched her left foot and discovered that it was covered in a sticky substance that when sniffed made her terribly hungry. It was honey and something else that she didn't recognize. Dr. Salvatore was full of tricks. Why would honey be good for frostbite or anything other than toast?

Since it was clearly working, she rewrapped her feet lightly and swung them over the side of the bed. Her wet clothes were gone, but someone had thoughtfully, or perhaps distractedly, left slippers and a robe for the person who wasn't supposed to walk. She managed to stuff her feet into the slippers, took a deep breath, and stood up. No sharp pain, just a more intense ache that was completely livable.

"We're back in business." Stella peeked into the large wardrobe that took up half of one wall, but it was empty. She needed Nicky and food so there was nothing to be done but to go out in public, wearing her robe and slippers. One more thing to put her poor mother in a light coma.

That wasn't a cheerful thought, but Stella smiled as she hobbled to the door. Her mother was one thing. Uncle Josiah was another. She couldn't wait to tell him. He'd laugh and raise a glass. They'd raise many glasses when it was all done. And it would be all done. She was better. They made it to Venice intact, minus a few useless toenails, and they'd find the Sorkines.

She left the room unlocked, tied her robe tighter, and went toward the heavenly scent of fresh coffee and baking bread. She didn't see a clock or anyone else in the halls, but she'd be surprised if Nicky wasn't wherever that bread was. Since they'd left Paris, he'd been eating like he'd just discovered the existence of food. She fully expected to find him eating an entire loaf and throwing back Sofia's whiskey at an Uncle Josiah rate.

Stella kept hobbling and hobbling. She wasn't sure how much farther it was to the desk, it hadn't seemed such a long way when Nicky had been carrying her, but she definitely wasn't alone in the hotel. Men's voices echoed down the halls, coming from nowhere and everywhere all at once. None of the voices was Nicky's though. They spoke Italian, but she couldn't make out the exact words. Someone was demanding something and someone didn't like it. That much she understood and it made her nervous.

She crept down the last hall before the desk and saw room A's door crack open. An elderly woman peeked out, listening intently. Stella was about to ask if she spoke English when the woman saw her and abruptly closed the door.

Stella paused and thought she could hear German being spoken. She bit her lip and focused on those angry men again. They were definitely speaking Italian, but could they be the SS, fluent in the language? After a few more minutes, Stella's finely-tuned ear said no. The accents were Italian with no hints of the Germanic cadence that she'd come to know and fear. Unless they were myna birds like her, they were Italian. She took a breath and continued down the hall until she heard a word she did understand. *Medico.* The men went back and forth and she realized that one voice was Antonio, the old man. The others she didn't recognize. Then one of those voices said, "*Doktoro* Salvatore," and her heart shot up into her throat. She turned around and saw A's door open again, just an inch and a blue eye gazed at her curiously. Stella ignored it and started hoofing her way back to her room. Her feet began to hurt more and it was slow-going.

A's door opened a little wider and the lady asked something in Italian. Stella shook her head and automatically asked, "*Sprechen Sie Englisch?*"

The blue eye widened. "*Ja. Ja.* Are you Am—"

A loud bang echoed down the hall. It sounded like someone had kicked the desk and the old lady reached out to grab Stella's wrist. "Come in here. You must hide."

Stella wasn't sure if that was the right thing, but it was the only thing, so she went in. The old lady carefully closed the door behind her and it was Stella's turn to have wide eyes. The room, identical to her own, didn't only contain furniture. It had books, wall-to-wall books, stacked up on the floor waist high and covering the small side tables on either side of the canopy bed and the foot of the bed, too, where another elderly lady sat, swathed in a flower-patterned silk shawl and holding a steaming cup of what smelled like medicinal tea.

The first lady held out her hand. "Welcome, young lady. I am Karolina and this is my sister, Rosa. Please sit down."

Stella shook her hand and obediently sat on the one chair they had next to a small cabinet filled with liquor bottles. "Thank you for letting me in. I needed to sit down."

"Yes, of course," said Karolina as she bustled around the room straightening books and tucking in Rosa.

If they were sisters, Stella would drink canal water. The ladies looked nothing alike. Rosa was tiny and delicate with snow-white hair and a narrow face. Stella's grandmother would've called her bird-boned. If Rosa was standing, Stella guessed she would be well under five feet. Karolina, on the other hand, stood at a good six feet, maybe more. She had broad shoulders, heavy features, dyed red hair, and a restless vitality that was nothing like her "sister's" serene manner.

"Do you know what they were saying? The men that are yelling, I mean," Stella asked.

"They are the carabinieri and they were asking about you," said Rosa softly.

"Me?"

Karolina sat on the bed next to a pile of books by Rudyard Kipling. "Dr. Salvatore came to see you last night, didn't he?"

Stella wasn't sure what to say. The cops knew about her already? How was it possible? They hadn't even used their names one single time.

Karolina reached over and patted her leg. "Try not to be frightened. This happens now. The *leggi razziali* changed how the Jews live and work. Dr. Salvatore is a Jew. They are very interested in his patients."

Stella blew out a tensely-held breath, thought about it for a second, and decided she wasn't frightened. She was tired and irritated. "How do you know that I'm his patient?"

Karolina gestured to her feet. "I saw you last night. You couldn't walk and this morning the carabinieri are here. It was not difficult."

"Who would've told them about me? Why would anyone care?"

Rosa shrugged. "Who can say why? Money? Protection? There are informers everywhere."

"What happened to your feet?" asked Karolina.

"I had an accident."

"Only to your feet?"

"To all of me." Stella smiled and pointed at the faded bruises on her face. "How long before the carabinieri go away? I really need some coffee."

The ladies shrugged.

"Antonio will argue and they will go," said Rosa, "as long as they don't see you, it will be fine."

As if a signal had gone out, the men's voices got louder.

Stella started to speak, but Rosa held a finger to her lips. Doors were opened and slammed. Karolina's ruddy skin paled and she jolted up, looking at the window frantically and then at Rosa, who sadly shook her head.

"Lock the door," she whispered, but it was too late. The door flew open and a large man in a crusty, rumpled uniform marched in and pointed at Stella. He yelled something in Italian and she stared at him, unable to think what to do.

Antonio rushed in after the officer and got between the two of them. The carabinieri batted him out of the way and shouted again.

"I don't know what you're talking about," said Stella, giving him the steely-eyed gaze she'd learned from her grandmother.

"You are American?" he asked, deflated.

"Canadian, actually," she lied on instinct.

He eyed her feet and said slyly, "What treatment did Dr. Salvatore give you?"

"Who's Dr. Salvatore?"

He sputtered. "Your doctor. He came to you last night."

"My doctor is Dr. Davide and he's very good. My feet are much better."

"Dr. Davide was at a birth last night," he said in triumph.

Stella channeled her husband and yawned, leaning back in her chair and becoming almost limp with disinterest. "I know."

"What do you know?" he asked.

"That Dr. Davide went to a birth. He was very sorry, but he didn't have time to do more than give me a shot. Sofia mixed up the treatment after he left."

Another carabinieri came in and whispered in the big one's ear. A smile lit up his face. "You are a Jew. Dr. Davide cannot treat a dirty Jew."

Stella bolted to her feet, ignoring the pain, and stuck her finger into his chest. "I am most certainly not a Jew. But you, sir, are dirty. You should wash your uniform more often instead of running around accusing normal people of being Jews." She stuck out a hip and tossed back her curls with a haughty glare.

The other carabinieri sneered at her. "You tried to get into the Hotel Palazzo Vittoria."

"What of it?"

"You had no bags."

"That's hardly our fault."

"Where are your bags?"

"You'd have to ask our Wagons Lit conductor," said Stella.

"What happened to your feet?"

"I got them in your disgusting canal water. It's terrible for the skin."

He balled up his fists. "What is your name? Show me your identification."

"I am Mrs. Douglas Myna and my husband has my identification."

"Where is he?"

"Out."

"Where?"

"I'm sure I have no idea. Canadian men do not ask permission from their wives to leave their hotel," said Stella.

The big carabinieri reddened and he turned on Karolina and Rosa. "Show me your identification."

Antonio began shouting at the carabinieri and pointing at the ladies. Rosa's hands trembled slightly and she put them under the covers, almost upsetting her tea cup and saucer. Karolina watched the men with no sign of fear. She got their passports out of a drawer and handed them over as Sofia rushed in. "What is this? *Capitano* Bartali! How dare you enter the room of our esteemed guests?"

"I have a witness that saw Dr. Salvatore enter your hotel last night with his bag. If you have only gentiles, who was he seeing?"

"I told you," said Stella. "Dr. Davide saw me. Now get out and go have a bath."

"These women—"

"Have been seen by Dr. Davide," said Sofia, smacking him with her dish towel. "You know that. You questioned them last week. Signora von Bodmann is very ill. She must rest." She shooed the carabinieri out and then followed him, yelling what had to be Italian insults to his questionable character.

Antonio nodded. "*Ci vediamo.*" Then he closed the door as more shouting erupted in the hall but then it quickly faded away.

Stella fell into the chair so hard it hurt her tailbone. "Have you been seeing Dr. Davide?"

"Yes." Rosa began to weep, soft sobs that she was almost too weak to make.

"I'm sorry I brought them in here," said Stella, all her strength draining out of her.

"Bartali comes once a week to question us and he always forgets who we are," said Karolina. "I think he does it on purpose to terrify us."

"Where did you get your passports?" asked Stella.

"In Heidelberg at the rathaus."

Stella plucked their passports off the bed where Bartali had tossed them in a rage and examined them. They were very well done, like the one Kaspar had given her after the plane crash. "So you're Rosa and Karolina von Bodmann?"

"Yes," said Karolina crossing her arms.

"Really?"

"Yes. Why would you think otherwise?"

"Because you're not sisters. That's for sure," said Stella, yawning a real yawn that time.

"We are."

"You aren't. Bartali is an idiot. Look at you two. You couldn't be more different."

Rosa wiped her eyes. "We have the same father. Different mothers."

"My mother," said Karolina, "died young and father remarried Rosa's mother."

"It's a good story," said Stella. "He obviously bought it."

"It's the truth."

"No."

Karolina swallowed hard. "You aren't Mrs. Douglas Myna."

"No and I'm going to need a passport immediately," said Stella. "Will you help me?"

Karolina and Rosa looked at each other, but no help was forthcoming.

"I know you're not sisters because your accents are different."

Karolina puffed up. "They are not. We are good German citizens and loyal to our führer."

"Spare me," said Stella, pointing at Karolina. "You *are* German, maybe even from Heidelberg. I don't know. But you, Rosa, are Austrian."

"It's not true," said Rosa, weakly. "Look at our identification."

"I don't care what those passports say. I have a good ear and I know what I know," said Stella. "I'm not going to turn you in. I wouldn't do that. I just need passports."

"We have done nothing wrong," said Karolina.

"Neither have I. Please give me a name. Just a name."

The ladies looked at each other and Rosa nodded.

"Father Maximilian Girotti."

"Thank you," said Stella although looking for a priest in Italy was a bit like a needle in a haystack. Italy was lousy with priests.

"I'm sorry we can't tell you more," said Rosa. "He met us at the station. It was arranged by a friend in Heidelberg. We don't know his church, but he does live here in Venice."

Stella put her hand to her chest where Abel's precious book had once been. "That's all right. We'll find him."

The ladies nodded and Stella could see the fear in their eyes. She would never betray them, but they didn't know that.

"May I?" She pointed at the stack of Kiplings.

Karolina took a breath and said, "Of course. You are an admirer of Kipling?"

"Not particularly. I love *Rikki-Tikki-Tavi* though. My uncle used to read it to me." She picked up what looked like a first edition of *The Jungle Book*, royal blue with gilt lettering and elephants on the cover.

"Would you like to borrow it?" asked Rosa.

"You wouldn't mind?" asked Stella. "You're obviously collectors."

Karolina's lips went thinner and Stella had to do it. She opened the cover and it was as she feared. There on the inside was a bookplate, a beautiful one in an art nouveau design with a sensuous woman wrapped in a riot of leaves. Printed at the top was "Ex Libris" and at the bottom "Max Ladner." She picked up *The Second Jungle Book* and it had the same book plate.

"Which one of you is Mrs. Ladner?" Stella asked.

The ladies said nothing, but Rosa began to weep again.

"You're going to have to tear the ex libris out."

"No. Absolutely not," said Karolina.

"Your identification says Karolina von Bodmann."

"That is my name."

Stella went around the room picking up books and finding the same book plate in every one. "These books say that you aren't who you say you are. Bartali is just too stupid to know that people with

57

libraries mark their books. My father has his own ex libris. So do my uncles."

"We bought them," said Rosa trembling, "at a house sale."

"A huge collection of first editions? I don't think so. You have to strip the name out," said Stella. "It's not safe for you."

Karolina shook her head and traced her fingers lovingly over the cover of a book of poetry. "We will not do that, but I thank you for your concern."

"I understand." That's what Stella said, but she didn't understand. It was a slip of paper pasted in a book. They took the trouble to get fake passports, but that wasn't enough, not nearly. "In case someone asks me, what are you doing here?"

"We're moving to Tuscany for Rosa's health. She needs warm weather," said Karolina.

"Then why are you still here? It's cold and the city is practically empty."

Rosa held out a frail hand and Karolina took it. "My sister won't leave me."

That Stella did understand.

The lure of coffee was too strong to hide away and wait for Nicky to show up, so Stella hobbled down the hall towards the front desk in hopes of finding something to eat and the much-needed coffee. She'd even take that evil Turkish blend they tried in Rome.

When she reached the desk, she found it unmanned with a dirty boot print on the wood. Worse, there was no coffee.

"Hello? *Buongiorno?*" she called out and Matteo darted out a door behind the desk with his finger to his lips.

She clamped her mouth shut and raised her palms to say, "What?".

He pointed behind her and she turned around. Outside, beyond a set of arched double doors that she hadn't noticed before was Nicky and a man she assumed was Bartali. She could only see his hat through the small windows at the top of the doors. It amazed her that she could tell he was angry from only a hat, but the way it jerked and bobbed, the carabinieri had to be furious. Nicky, on the other hand, was calm and bland, barely blinking in response, which probably infuriated Bartali all the more.

Stella started for the door. If Nicky hadn't said his name yet, all wasn't lost. She could steer the conversation.

"No," hissed Matteo. "*Signora, por favore.*"

Stella glanced back and he shook his head wildly, pointing back at the door and saying something that was barely audible. All she caught was "Sofia" and "Antonio." But that was enough to make her hesitate. Sofia knew her "name" now. Hopefully, she would think to use it. But what if she couldn't make Nicky understand?

She went for the door again and Matteo darted around the desk and, without asking, bear-hugged her to carry her out of sight.

The door opened and Sofia's voice echoed down the hall, much louder than necessary. "I apologize, Mr. Myna. You won't be inconvenienced again."

The door slammed shut and Nicky said, "What in the world was that about?"

"Your wife met Capitano Bartali and—"

"She met him? How did that happen?" He was practically shouting.

Nicky, Sofia, and Antonio arrived at the desk and simultaneously turned to see Stella and Matteo standing off to the right. Matteo let go of her and jumped back, looking tremendously guilty.

"Where have you been?" Stella thrust her chin out. Her guilty? Not a chance.

"Me?" Nicky whipped off his fedora and ran his fingers through his hair. He was probably counting to ten or some such nonsense in order not to tell her off. He needn't have bothered. She was ready.

"Where'd you get the suit?" she asked.

He looked down at the grey suit he wore as if he didn't know how he happened to be wearing it or the galoshes that his pant legs were tucked into. "Sofia...never mind that. What happened? Why are you out of bed?"

"I woke up. You were gone and I was starving. I came looking for food."

That shut him up and he looked nearly as guilty as Matteo.

"You shouldn't have come out." He came over and swept her up in his arms before turning to Sofia and Antonio. "Thank you once again. Can you please bring us something to eat and coffee, if you have it?"

"Of course," said Sofia. Her voice was strong, but she was bracing herself on the desk. That's when Stella felt guilty. They came to that hotel and no doubt they'd brought a wave of misfortune with them.

"Thank you and I'm sorry," Stella called out from around Nicky's shoulder and Sofia gave her a weak smile in response.

"What were you thinking?" asked Nicky.

"That I was hungry, obviously," she said. "Where were you?"

"Out." He set her down to dig in his pocket for the room key.

"It's open."

He clenched his teeth and a muscle twitched on his jaw. "You left it open? Stella. God help me."

Stella put her little nose in the air and hobbled in. "I don't have a key and I'm not really worried about someone coming in to steal my rouge, are you?"

He closed the door. It was the quietest slam she'd ever heard in her life and her mother was the master of the quiet slam. "Someone could've searched our room."

"So what?" She threw her arms wide. "We've got a makeup case, a dead woman's pistol, my handbag with no money or identification in it, and a copy of *The Hobbit*. If they robbed us blind, we'd barely notice."

"That's not the point."

"What is the point then? And where were you? Don't say out."

"The ghetto."

"You went without me?" It was Stella's turn to clinch her jaw.

"You were asleep and time is of the essence," he said.

"Why didn't you wake me up?"

He hung his wet fedora on the radiator knob and slipped off his jacket. "Dr. Salvatore said you need as much rest as possible."

"I'm fine. My feet are better. A lot better, in fact."

"Not that much better."

"We can go now. Where are my clothes?" she asked.

"They're being cleaned, but it's too late anyway." He closed the wardrobe and sat down in the chair, stretching out his legs and kicking off the galoshes. "Everything's closed and the water's rising."

"Had anyone seen them?"

"No, not that I was able to ask many people."

"Well, it's the evening. That's to be expected."

"I searched all day," he said.

"All day?"

"All day."

Stella's brain couldn't comprehend what he was saying. "What time is it?"

"Nearly six." Nicky rubbed his eyes. "We need to soak your feet again."

"Is it…tomorrow?"

He chuckled. "It is. You slept for over twenty-four hours."

"How could I sleep that long? How could anyone sleep that long?"

"Darling, you were well past exhausted. You hadn't really slept since we left here two weeks ago."

"Still—"

A knock resounded on the door and Nicky went over to answer it. Sofia came in with a tray loaded with rolls, butter, and jam. A squat coffee pot and two cups sat in the center and Stella had to restrain herself from diving for it when she set it on the bed.

Nicky poured two cups and a generous amount of cream in hers. "Thank you, Sofia."

She turned to go, but he quickly asked, "Would you please explain why you keep calling me Mr. Myna?"

Sofia stopped at the door and looked at Stella.

"I did it," she said.

"What did you do?"

"The carabinieri wanted to know who we were. I had to say something," she said.

"You could've said our names, our real names." Nicky's jaw was back to twitching.

"Oh, yeah? You want our names in a report? Reports are read. When the SS come looking for us, and they will, they're going to go to the local authorities first."

"Sofia," Nicky nodded at their hostess, "headed him off, but he's going to come back looking for our passports, that are Canadian, apparently."

"We can pass for Canadians," said Stella before tearing into a roll slathered in a ludicrous amount of butter.

Sofia grabbed the bedpost and steadied herself. "I must ask, why does the SS want you?"

"We kept them from getting someone else's property and they aren't happy about it," said Nicky.

"I'm familiar with the Nazi's love of other people's property. What was it?"

"It's better if you don't know."

She glanced around, paling slightly. "Do you still have it?"

"No," said Stella. "But they probably think we do."

Nicky stood up and reached behind the chair. He pulled out the basin and asked Sofia to fill it with hot water. After she left, he began pacing. "We have to go. I don't know if we can wait until tomorrow."

Stella pried her swollen feet out of the slippers. "We're not leaving."

"We don't have Canadian passports."

"I'm not running away. We'll get passports and stay right here."

"Where are we going to get passports?"

"Father Girotti."

He gaped at her.

"He's here in Venice and he's done it before," she said.

"Why would some priest help us get fake passports?" he asked. "How do you know his name in the first place?"

Stella unwound the bandages from her feet, ignoring Nicky's wincing at the sight of them, and told him about Karolina and Rosa. He immediately went to her makeup case and pulled out *The Hobbit*.

He opened the cover and heaved a sigh of relief. "It's okay. No ex libris."

"Even if there was one, it wouldn't be Cyril's real name or a name that could be traced."

"You're right. That old codger is too smart for that."

Stella knew that to be true better than Nicky ever would. Cyril Welk helped them escape Gabriele Griese and the SS in the Vienna Westbahnhof. Stella met up with him again after she crashed Peiper's plane near a safe house. It was clear that Cyril was some sort of spy, but what side he was on was less clear.

Sofia came back in with the water and Antonio, who carried a little box filled with bottles that Dr. Salvatore sent. He couldn't take the chance of coming back so Dr. Davide would be by the next day. Stella was sad to hear it, but the worse news was that he wanted her to have another shot of Prontosil. Nicky and Antonio put Stella in the chair and Sofia mixed in the tinctures. The stinging seemed worse that time, but it also felt good in an odd way.

"So who wants to give me a shot?" asked Stella.

Nicky picked up the syringe. "I'll do it."

Sofia said she had to be going. The sight of the needle made her look like she needed to grab onto the bedpost again and Antonio rushed her out.

"How do I do this?" he asked, brandishing the needle and the little glass vial.

Stella told him and he gave her the shot like it didn't bother him a bit. "How many rolls do you want?"

"All of them. I'm starving." Stella licked her lips and reached for another roll.

Nicky read the directions that came with the syringe and cleaned it with a little bottle of spirits before he packed up the medications. "I hope I don't have to do that again."

"Well, there's still the Eukadol for later," said Stella, pointing at another vial.

Nicky grimaced.

"I can do it myself."

His blank face went back on and he said, "I'll do it."

She gazed at him, looking for something that gave a feeling away and found nothing but detached calmness. It was unsettling.

"What?" he asked.

"It didn't bother you to stick that needle in me. I hated doing that to Oliver."

Just the mere thought of Oliver brought back the smell and shock of the explosions at Hans Gruber's brewery and that dear man's death. Stella looked down at her hands and was surprised they were clean, not covered with sticky blood with its metallic tang so strong that she could still smell it weeks later.

"You did it well," said Nicky.

"Not as well as you. I can still see the blood and the meat of his arm when I think about it."

Nicky squatted in front of her basin with his hands on her knees. "It bothered me tremendously, but I didn't think it would help you if I showed it."

"It wouldn't."

"Now I have something to ask you," he said.

Stella bit her lip. She'd eaten and she was tired again. Fighting about the passports would just make him angry and change nothing.

"Why Douglas Myna?"

She brightened and sloshed her feet in the water. "Miss Myna."

"Huh?"

"I'm Miss Myna. Remember? It's my nickname." She imitated Sofia's accent perfectly.

He chuckled. "Right. I forgot. What about Douglas? I hate Douglas."

"Aunt Eulalie says you look like Douglas Fairbanks Jr.."

Nicky screwed up his mouth in the ultimate vision of displeasure. "Do you think that?"

"Maybe a little around the eyes." She grinned and slapped his hand. "You think you're better looking than Douglas Fairbanks Jr.."

He stood up and crossed his arms.

"All right. You are. But you're still Douglas. We can't change it now."

"And what is your name? Myrna?"

"As in Myrna Myna? I don't think so."

"As in Myrna Loy."

Stella made her own displeased face. "Myrna Myna sounds stupid. And how old do I look to you?"

"Myrna Loy isn't old."

"She could be my mother," said Stella.

"If she had you when she was fourteen."

She glared at him.

"Eulalie then. That way we won't forget." He leaned over and cupped her face in his hands. "You're prettier than Myrna Loy." He kissed her and she forgot about her feet and the pain where the needle went in.

"And don't you forget it."

"No chance of that."

# CHAPTER 4

*S*tella woke early; warm, cozy, and thoroughly confused. The darkness disoriented her, but she was more puzzled by the warmth and how very comfortable she felt. That wasn't a normal occurrence anymore and made her heart beat faster like when she first set eyes on Nicky Lawrence.

With the thought of her husband, Stella realized where the warmth was coming from. She slid her hand over and found Nicky's ribcage, still bony and defined but rising and falling in a lovely comforting rhythm. It was fine. They were in Venice and safe. She wiggled her toes to see how safe she really was. They hurt but less than before. She could run now, if running was required.

"Nicky?" she whispered.

He rustled around slightly and took a deep breath, so Stella threw back the covers and took a deep breath of her own before putting her damaged feet on the cold floor. To her surprise, there was only a little stinging and although she could feel the splits in the skin, they were different, itchy and healing.

She felt around in the pitch black, bumping into the bedpost, wardrobe, wall, and chair until she touched the heavy damask curtains. Drawing one to the side, she saw a hint of color through the rain above the ancient buildings facing the other side of the canal. Morning or, at least, the beginnings of it. They really needed watches, first thing, right after she got clothes and galoshes.

"Nicky," Stella said without whispering, but he didn't even move. A sliver of pale grey light ran over his face, highlighting the eye sockets that were still a bit sunken, jutting cheekbones, and pale bruises. She suspected he would've slept through a flashlight or flood lamp. You'd have thought he'd taken a shot of Eukadol instead of her. Nicky had given her the second shot right after she'd eaten a huge pile of linguine with clam sauce covered in a cloud of finely-grated parmesan, but she didn't really need it. She could barely keep her eyes open and only dimly remembered Nicky putting her in bed before the injection.

Sofia had thoughtfully brought her a sponge bag with their dinner so she picked that up after slipping on her robe and headed out with only the smallest worry about Nicky waking up to find her gone. He was forever thinking the opposite of what made sense to her so there was no point in trying to anticipate him.

The bathroom door hung open at the end of the hall and the closet-sized room was empty. Stella put her sponge bag on a hook, selected a towel, and proceeded to fill the bathtub that was really more like an oval washtub, tin with a wooden rim. Nicky called the bathroom rustic. Her mother would've called it medieval. The beautiful Francesqua couldn't have imagined her daughter, a spoiled Bled, sharing a tiny bathroom with ten other people and using a towel that had the texture of unsanded wood and was just as stiff.

But to Stella it was the height of luxury. The water came out piping hot and filled the room with a minerally steam. She breathed deep and thanked God for helping her to be there and then asked that he please help her to find the Sorkines before they got it in their heads to go into the Reich to search for Abel.

She asked for a sign, but one wasn't forthcoming so she washed and soaked until the water grew cold. On her way back to the room, she ran into Antonio, who made it clear that she wasn't to be up and about on her own. She waved that silly notion away, although it would be the same one Nicky would have, and tapped her wrist. After a short back and forth, he showed her his watch. Six-thirty. Not bad. She remembered the word for breakfast, and he pointed to seven on his watch.

"*Perfecto, Antonio,*" she said. "*Grazie mille.*"

He insisted on walking her to the room, got her a basin of hot water for her feet, and generally fretted like her old nanny, Mrs. O'Connell, a lady who liked worrying more than a nice draught of whiskey, which was saying something since it was the only thing that eased her rheumatism.

Stella shooed the nervous Antonio out of the room and mixed up her own foot bath. She soaked for ten minutes, got dressed in her red suit and blouse that Sofia had returned, vigorously towel-dried her hair next to Nicky's snoozing face, and, when that didn't work, she switched on the lights. Nicky finally stirred enough to reach for her and discover she was missing.

"No!" He sat up, his eyes darting around the room, then slumped back, exhaling a ragged breath. "Don't do that."

"Do what?" she asked while fiddling with the stockings Sofia brought. She had to wear stockings. It was practically indecent not to, but she didn't think they'd fit over the bandages she wrapped her feet in.

"I thought you'd…that someone."

"Got me?" She tossed the stockings aside. Indecent it was. "As if I'd go without a fight. Don't you know me at all?"

Nicky sat up again and pondered his wife. His expression said it all. He didn't and he wasn't crazy about that fact. "Why are you dressed?"

"Did you imagine I'd stay in my robe while searching for the Sorkines?"

"I imagined you'd stay here while I searched."

"You're bananas if you really thought that." She eyed her shoes, also freshly cleaned, and knew there wasn't a chance she could stuff her fat feet into them. "Hey, where did you get your galoshes?"

"Sofia has a store room full of them." He slid out of bed and pulled on his pants. "Don't get any ideas."

Stella put on her slippers and went for the door. "Too late."

"Where are you going?"

"Breakfast starts at seven."

"I'll bring you a tray."

"No, thanks." With that she went out wearing a smile and no stockings. Indecent.

Stella expected the breakfast room to be empty that early in the morning in a flooded city, but it was nearly full. To be fair, the breakfast room wasn't much larger than their hotel room and had only five tables and a long counter laden with piles of fruit, rolls, and drinks.

"Mrs. Myna," said Sofia when she turned around. "What are you doing up?"

Everyone turned to look and Stella immediately rethought her plan. She was recognizable, if not for being a Bled and her wedding that had been featured on society pages coast to coast, then for her beer. Her father had lovingly named a beer after her on her sixteenth birthday, Stella's Honey Lager. She hated it, both the beer—too sweet —and her face sketched on the label. But the beer sold like hot cakes and there was no chance her father would retire a winner.

Stella smiled and sauntered in. "I'm absolutely fine."

"And Mr. Myna. He is well?"

"Well and on his way."

Sofia's shoulders relaxed and she led Stella past another couple to the only empty spots, a small cafe table that would've been more at home outside. "Let me bring you coffee."

"I can do it," said Stella, reddening under the scrutiny.

"No, no. You must rest." Sofia bustled over to the coffee urn and Stella decided that a strong opening was essential to success. People believed what they were told or so her Uncle Josiah claimed. Say a man is wicked long enough and people will believe he's wicked. He would know since Uncle Josiah was generally considered to be wicked. If he was right, saying her name over and over would make people believe it was her name.

"Hello," she said with a little wave. "Do you speak English? I'm Eulalie Myna."

The couple nearest had the look of Americans. He wore a dull black suit, unimaginatively cut, and she wore a day dress in a loud combination of polka dots and stripes. Their faces had been clouded, but they lightened at her greeting.

"Hello, there," he said. "I'm Randolph Hutchins and this is my wife, Dolores. Have I met you before? You seem awfully familiar."

Stella stood up and held out her hand. "I don't think so. I'm pleased to meet you, Randolph. Please call me Eulalie."

Dolores frowned, but shook her hand. "You do seem familiar. Are you from Des Moines?"

Stella had to come up with something fast. "No. I'm afraid not. We're Canadian, born and bred. But perhaps you've heard of us?"

"I don't think so. Are you famous?"

There was a light in Dolores's eyes and Stella put it out. "Only for our honey. We're Myna Bird honey, but we're only on the East coast in the States."

"That must be it. We were in New York for two weeks waiting for our passage," said Randolph. "We must've had your honey."

"Very possible." Stella smiled warmly. "We're in the best hotels."

The couple smiled and glowed with pleasure at "the best hotels". They would stay in the best New York hotels or, at least, they were happy to have her think that.

Stella went around introducing herself to the group. Karolina was alone in a corner and she stood up, playing her part perfectly. "Mrs. Myna, it is so good to see you here."

Dolores noticed her feet and rather impolitely stared at her stockingless legs and bandages.

"Your reaction is better," said Karolina, pointedly looking down.

Stella held out her right foot. "Much better. I'm going out walking today."

"What happened, if you don't mind me asking?" asked Randolph.

"I had to wade through canal water when we arrived," said Stella. "I had a reaction. Dr. Davide fixed me right up though. He's very good. If you need anything, I recommend calling him at once."

The room came alive with discussions of toxic canal water, the never-ending rain, and the apparent difficulty of getting a train out. It seemed everyone wanted to leave but hadn't found seats yet. Karolina played along, saying that she would like to go home to Germany, but that Rosa was ill.

Stella sipped her delicious coffee and buttered a roll, while nodding and never forgetting to answer to her new name.

"Mr. Myna," said Sofia more loudly than necessary in such a small room. "I was wondering if you were lost."

Nicky stiffened at the sound of "Mr. Myna" and Stella could see him running it through his mind. "I was lost. If there was a wrong turn, I took it, but I can see my lovely Eulalie didn't have that trouble." He came over, gave her a kiss, and went to get coffee.

After twenty minutes, the guests left to start their days, which mainly consisted of trying to get on a train, any train. Stella and Nicky stayed with her downing her fourth roll and him drinking black coffee and glaring.

"What is it, Douglas?" she asked sweetly.

"You know what it is."

"I do know." She turned in her seat. "Sofia, do you have some galoshes I can borrow? We don't want to waste another day in your fabulous city."

Nicky gritted his teeth so hard she could hear it. "You stay in, darling. I'll go out and see how flooded St. Mark's Square really is."

"I won't hear of it," said Stella. "Sofia?"

Their hostess looked back and forth between the two set faces and then called to Matteo, unleashing a stream of Italian that Stella was pleased to understand a small amount of. He was to get her several pairs of galoshes. Matteo came back straight away and helped her try on three pairs. The one that fit was sadly two sizes larger than her normal size and she looked positively ridiculous with her man-sized feet.

"These will work fine," she said.

"Wait another day. Your feet will be better," said Sofia.

"Venice awaits," said Stella. "I can't wait to see it."

Nicky scowled but helped her up. "Maybe you could take a nap."

"At seven-thirty in the morning?"

"You have to rest."

"We have to—"

Antonio ran into the breakfast room and hissed at Sofia. Stella's chest got tight. Unless she was very much mistaken, Matteo had said that the carabinieri was there and he mentioned her name.

"*Sì. Sì,*" said Sofia calmly.

"What is it?" asked Nicky.

"Bartali is here. He would like to question you again about Dr. Salvatore."

Antonio gestured wildly and there was a shout behind him.

Nicky jumped and pointed at a narrow door Sofia had been using. "Where's that go?"

"The kitchen."

He grabbed Stella and almost pulled her off her feet. "Come on."

"Let him question me," said Stella, "the nasty worm."

"Passports."

"Oh, right." Stella yanked open the door and rushed into the kitchen, startling an elderly lady kneading bread. "*Scusami. Scusami.*"

Nicky closed the door and a voice burst out behind it, haranguing Sofia about Signora Myna. They spun around. So many doors.

The old lady pointed at one with a dough-encrusted hand.

"*Grazie. Grazie,*" said Stella and Nicky kissed her weathered cheek, making her flush.

The door led into an office, which led into another office, which led into the hall. Stella peeked out and she could hear Bartali. He was getting closer. Nicky ran across the hall to what looked like an exterior door. He yanked it open and beyond it was a dingy alley filled with water and empty wooden crates. "Come on."

"Do you have the passports?" whispered Stella.

"No, that's why we're getting out of here."

"Our passports."

He waved at her to get out. "No, but we don't need them."

The voices got louder.

"They might search the room," hissed Stella.

Nicky paled. "That must be illegal."

"I bet it's not, if he says we're Jews."

"Dammit." He tossed Stella over his shoulder and ran down the hall. She beat on his back. "Put me down. I'm not a sack of hops."

"I agree," Nicky said, breathing hard.

"Hey."

"Hey, yourself." He jiggled a doorknob. "Damn, I locked it."

He kept Stella on his shoulder, unlocked the door and ran in, banging her head on the door frame.

"Ow, that hurt," said Stella as he tossed her on the bed and went rooting around the wardrobe.

"Did you take them?" he asked.

"No." She went to the window and looked. No escape. Just a sheer drop into the canal. "Didn't you put them in the makeup case last night?"

"Yes. I forgot." Nicky got the passports and closed her case. Then he threw open the window. "You first."

"I'm not jumping into the canal." Stella backed away. Trains were one thing. Roofs another. A full dunking in a dirty bacteria-infested canal simply wasn't happening.

"I agree." He grabbed her waist and practically stuffed her out the window. "Stop smacking me. There's a boat."

Stella leaned over the sill. There was a boat ten feet below them and half submerged. "No. We'll never make it."

"We can do it."

"Maybe you can. I can't jump ten feet into a skinny boat on these feet." Stella pried herself out of his grasp and dashed as best she could to the door. She looked through the peephole and saw Sofia arguing with Bartali. He was trying to get a key ring out of her hands. Sofia glanced at the door and she must've seen Stella's eye because she handed over the key ring and pointed at the door across the hall.

"*Donna sciocca.*" Bartali fumbled with the keys and rammed each of them in the other door's lock until he finally found the right one. He went in and Sofia waved to her to get out. Stella opened the door and saw Bartali buried in the wardrobe, rustling around and cursing. Sofia shooed them away and Nicky picked up Stella, running down the hall.

They went through the warren of halls and ran smack into Rudolph and Dolores.

"What in the world?" asked Rudolph, jumping aside to make way.

"Why are you running?" asked Dolores. She was not interested in getting out of the way.

"I'm sick," said Stella.

"Call the doctor, man," said Rudolph.

"There's no time," said Nicky.

"She was fine a minute ago," said Dolores, frown lines appearing between her eyes. "Unless…"

"Yes," said Stella. "Unless, I'm in the family way and we have to go."

"Don't get so excited," said Randolph, primly. "Women are quite capable of handling this business on their own."

"Are they?" asked Dolores. "Are they really? Is that why you didn't call Dr. Alexander when I asked you to?"

"It was just a little cold."

"It was the flu. People die of the flu. They lose their babies," she said, backing her husband up into the wall.

"You didn't die."

"No thanks to you."

Nicky turned sideways. "Excuse us. In a hurry. Please tell Sofia where we've gone."

"She's with that carabinieri," Dolores called out after them. "He's looking for Jews."

Nicky ran to the desk and turned right to go out the proper front door.

"No," said Stella.

He stopped short and nearly lost his grip on her. "What?"

"Look."

There were men in official hats outside.

"The bastard brought reinforcements," said Nicky.

Antonio hooted at them and Nicky ran for him. The old man opened the little arched door they'd first come in and held a finger to his lips. As Nicky passed, mumbling his thanks, Antonio put an umbrella in Stella's lap.

Nicky ran out the door so fast he ran into the wall opposite, squashing Stella up against it.

"For goodness sake, put me down," said Stella.

And he did, bending over to catch his breath.

"No time for that." She grabbed his sleeve and pulled him away. "We have to hurry."

They dashed down the narrow alley to the bridge that led to the Hotel Palazzo Vittoria.

"Where exactly are we going?" asked Nicky.

"To find Father Maximilian Girotti."

"Did you ask Sofia about him?"

Stella groaned and said, "No. I didn't think of it."

"Then where do we start?" asked Nicky.

"In church, of course."

# CHAPTER 5

*L*ike most things in life, it was easier said than done. The first church they tried was locked. Locked. On a Sunday morning.

The next stop was a small high baroque church with a single nave and no side chapels. The double doors were open but the pews were empty. No mass times were posted. They hunted around for an office, but found all the doors locked.

"This is insane," said Nicky. "Anybody could come in here and steal the altarpieces. Look at that gold candelabra. It has to be worth a mint."

"Who would steal from a church?" ask Stella.

He raised an eyebrow at her.

"Not even the Nazis would do that," she whispered as if speaking their very name was sacrilege.

"I read it in the *London Times*."

"Where did that happen?"

"Germany. Mainz."

"But why?"

"Why did they burn the synagogues?" asked Nicky. "Enemies of the state, I assume."

"I wonder if the Vatican knows."

"If the *Times* knows, the Vatican knows. Why is no one here? Where's the priest?"

"They must not have a big enough congregation to have mass," said Stella. "We need a church that's actually up and running."

"I'd take a priest, any priest over going out in the rain again," said Nicky.

"It can't be helped."

"Maybe it can. Someone might be upstairs." Nicky looked up at the pipe organ that covered the entire front of the church above the doors and cupped his hands around his mouth, shouting, "Hello! Is anyone here?"

"Have you lost your mind?" Stella smacked him repeatedly. "We're in church."

"My job is to take care of you. I'm getting the job done," he said. "Hello?"

"Stop that!"

A loud, grinding click echoed through the nave, bouncing off the marble and sounding fierce in all that empty space. Then a head popped out from a door to the left of the altar. A dark-haired woman in a baggy blouse and skirt eyed them from behind the safety of the door.

Nicky raised his hand. "Hello. Do you speak English?"

She stared.

"Come on." He took Stella's hand and half-dragged her down the aisle.

"Slow down." Stella had plastered a smile on her face, but she couldn't keep up with Nicky's long strides. "Or just go."

He let go and went rapidly toward the woman. For a moment, she seemed transfixed by the stranger and Stella started to feel good about it. Nicky had a way with women. It didn't matter the age or whether they were married. It was a pleasure to look at him and talking to him increased their pleasure.

Not so with this Italian woman.

"Excuse me," he said. "I just—"

The woman pulled her head back and slammed the door. Another grinding click resounded through the church. Nicky kept on and knocked on the door. "I didn't mean to scare you. I just need some information. We're looking for Father Maximilian Girotti."

Stella came up behind him and said, "She doesn't understand you."

"You say it then."

Stella patted her pockets. "I didn't bring my dictionary."

"Swell." He banged on the door, rattling it on its hinges.

"That's not going to help."

"Tell me what *will* help then?" Nicky was angrier than she'd ever seen him. He usually went blank when riled, but, just then, he was fiery with two spots of color on his cheeks and he looked about to gnash his teeth.

"Don't get mad at me," she said, crossing her arms.

He grabbed her and hugged her tight to his chest. "I'm not mad at you. I just don't know what I was thinking."

"About?"

"Coming here. Doing this."

"We had to," she said.

"Did we?"

She looked up at him and it gave her a crick in her neck. "We owe it to Abel to at least try to find them."

He kissed the top of her head. "You forgot your hat."

"We better not go to a garden party then." She grinned up at him.

"Garden parties aren't on the agenda. How are your feet?"

"Fine." That's what she said, but the stinging had started again. "Let's go to that big church next to the Grand Canal."

"Which one? There's about a hundred and twenty."

"We passed it in the water taxi. Big, white columns."

"Are you joking?" he asked. "They all have big white columns."

"You know, we saw it last time we were here. You said it looked like someone used a shoehorn to fit it in."

He thought for a moment and then said, "At the San Stae vaporetto stop?"

"I have no idea."

"I guess we'll try that one." He banged on the door one last time. "God is not happy with you right now."

They hurried down the nave and out into the rain. Nicky put up the too-small umbrella and Stella said, "I think that was blasphemy."

"Aren't you supposed to offer succor to strangers in need?"

"Not crazy strangers."

"They're the ones that need it the most."

Stella shrugged. He had a point, but she said a little prayer, just in case.

Nicky, with an unfailing sense of direction, took them through narrow alleys, over bridges, and under the occasional archway. He carried her when the water got too deep and got his pants soaked in the process. Stella's teeth wanted to chatter so she knew he was freezing, but he didn't show it. The mask was on.

"There it is," he said as they emerged from a small alley.

Stella peered out at a huge baroque church covered in statues, columns, and bas reliefs. "That's not the one I meant."

"Well, we're going in anyway."

"It's pretty flooded," said Stella, doubting that they'd be having mass in such conditions.

The water from the canal was coming in waves to lap at the small steps in front of the twenty-foot outer doors that happened to be open. Another couple of inches and it would be over and seeping into the church itself.

Nicky didn't respond. He waded into the small square in front of the church and dragged Stella along. The water only came up to her ankles, but the waves from passing boats brought it up another six inches. Her feet were safe, for the moment.

They tromped up the steps and into the small atrium. Nicky tugged on the iron ring attached to smaller set of doors leading into the sanctuary. To Stella's surprise, they opened and she rushed inside as a blast of rain hit them from behind. The umbrella offered some protection, but they got wet from the waist down.

Nicky closed the door and stood there for a moment, looking wet dog dejected and holding an umbrella that was now saturated. "If they don't help, we'll have to go to another hotel."

"They have to help. I left Great Grandmother's hatpin in the room. I will not lose that on top of everything else," said Stella, marching to one of the four-foot high fonts on either side of the aisle. She dipped her hand in and crossed herself in an act of penitence, if nothing else.

The church was as empty as the last one, but huge in comparison. The walls were white with columns and statues like the façade. It reminded Stella of a Roman temple, beautiful, but too austere for her tastes. She liked her faith a little scruffy with color and feeling. That church gave off no feeling for her, unless you counted the floor. It had more soul. Her galoshes slapped on the marble that was beautifully done in diamonds of orange and gray. She looked up and overhead was lovely Romanesque vaulting. The church was a whole lot older than the overdone exterior let on. Someone had seen fit to redo it. Stella hated that. Leave things as they were meant to be.

"I don't see anyone," said Nicky.

"The door to the left of the altar is open. I think I see a light." Stella walked down the center aisle, heading for the door but stopped at a cordoned off area.

"I hope this isn't a sign."

Nicky came up behind her. "I thought we decided against signs."

"*You* decided against luck. I didn't."

"I feel the same way about signs."

"Look down."

A red velvet rope kept people from walking on a large rectangle in the aisle. There was more color than even Stella had a taste for. A motley marble border enclosed a tomb that was unusual to say the least. Directly in front of her was a skull and crossbones, white marble set in a black field. Around the rest of the tomb were more crossed bones and full-sized skeletons with raised scythes, looking like they were in the act of stabbing whoever had the misfortune to be buried there.

"That's unusual," said Nicky, "but it's not a sign."

"A jinx?"

"Definitely not."

"You don't know," she said.

A voice echoed through the church, assaulting them from all sides, and then an ancient priest hobbled with surprising speed down the aisle, waving a stout cane.

"That's more like it," said Nicky, totally unperturbed.

Stella backed away, her hands over her mouth. An enraged priest was a bad sign, a terrible sign. What had they done? At home, she'd seen Father Joseph angry when he had to counsel Uncle Josiah after his many misdeeds, but this was nothing like that. Father Joseph was practically a teddy bear in comparison, vein popping and all.

"Excuse me, Father," said Nicky.

The priest continued his stream of Italian, not stopping to breathe. He pointed his cane at the tomb and came around looking as if whacking them wasn't out of the question. Nicky eased Stella behind him and raised the umbrella. "Father, please listen."

The priest kept coming, his jowls flapping and his collar askew. Nicky stepped back and bumped into Stella. She slipped in their puddle and had to catch herself on one of the posts around the tomb.

"It's the water," she said. "Look."

They'd dripped a lot and it was spreading onto the ornate marble. The priest pointed at the tomb and behind them. Sure enough, they'd left a trail from the door.

"*Scusi. Scusi,*" said Stella with her hands clasped together, pleading for forgiveness, but he was not having it.

The priest kept yelling and they backed away, but he chased them, arms waving.

"We need Father Maximilian Girotti," said Nicky.

The name made no difference. He kept on yelling. Then a woman came out of the other door, raised her hands in horror and started yelling, too. But instead of a cane, she got a mop and came for them.

"They're crazy," said Nicky.

"It *is* very clean in here," said Stella. "Father, we need Girotti. Father Girotti."

The woman got to the tomb, brandished the mop at them, and started cleaning.

"How do you say it in Italian?" asked Nicky.

"What?"

"Father."

"Oh, Abel said *padre*, I think." She peeked around Nicky's shoulder and said, "Padre Girotti? Padre Girotti?"

"No Girotti!" yelled the priest. *"Basta con gli ebrei!"*

"Where is Padre Girotti?" Stella stepped to the side and put her palms together. *"Por favore*, Padre Girotti?"

He didn't care. He waved the cane in Nicky's face and chased them past the fonts so that they bumped into the door.

*"Por favore. Padre Girotti. Por favore."*

He poked at the door, but beyond him, the woman had stopped mopping. She yelled something about Padre Girotti and then went back to mopping. The priest yanked open the door, yelled, and they were outside in the continuing downpour having the door slammed in their faces. Nicky got the umbrella up, but the rest of them was half-soaked before he did.

"I don't like Italy much more than Germany at this moment," said Nicky, staring down at the water that was creeping over the step and was about ten feet from the door. "I wonder if he realizes that he's got bigger problems than our puddles."

"Hold on," said Stella. "Did you hear what she said?"

"What?"

"The woman with the mop. What did she say?"

"How would I know?" he asked.

"Did you hear *ebrei?*" asked Stella, yelling over the drumming of the rain on the taut umbrella.

"Maybe. I think the priest might've said it. What's *ebrei?*"

She grinned up at him. "Jews."

"Where are we going?" asked Nicky.

Stella didn't answer. She just kept dragging him through the rising water to the edge of the canal. "There's a taxi. Wave. Wave."

He whipped her around. "Where are we going?"

"To the ghetto."

"Because she thought we were Jewish?"

"I don't think she thought that," said Stella.

"I do. Everyone does. I guess we look like refugees."

Stella turned back around, frantically waving at the approaching taxi that happily wasn't a floating rust bucket but in good repair and shiny with fresh lacquer on the wood. "Wave. Wave."

Nicky gave up and waved. "This is going to cost us."

"We can find a bank and have money wired."

"To us? Using our names? I don't think so."

The boat slowed and, despite being buffeted by the waves, turned in the canal to head toward them.

"He saw us. He's coming."

"We don't have much money left, Stella."

"I'll think of something."

The taxi bumped the dock and Stella went for it. The captain emerged from the helm and looped a thick rope over the pylon. *"Buongiorna, Signora."*

*"Buongiorno. Inglese?"*

*"No, Signora."* He pointed to his left. *"San Marco piazza?"* Then, pointing to his right, he said, *"Santa Lucia?"*

*"Ghetto Ebraico,"* said Stella. "I think that's right."

*"Ghetto Ebraico?"* The captain eyed them and then said something rapidly that Stella couldn't make out.

"Fantastic," said Nicky.

"You understood that?"

"I understand money and he said he wants more, either because he thinks we're Jews or we're going to the ghetto."

Stella splashed in-between the men without any care for getting water in her boots and stuck her finger in his face. "You low-down communist piece of filth."

Nicky picked her up from behind and stepped into the boat, giving the captain a thumbs up. He got a sly grin in return and the man opened the passenger cabin for them. Stella sat down in a huff and tugged off a boot. Her bandages were pretty damp but only around the ankle. "We could've found another taxi or walked."

Nicky shook off his fedora and tossed it on the opposite seat. "Not in your condition."

"My condition is just fine. That man is a—"

"Capitalist, not a communist. He saw a chance to make an extra buck and he took it."

"It's disgusting."

"It's a fact," said Nicky. "You wanted to go to the ghetto. This is what it takes."

Stella forced herself to refocus. "You were there, in the ghetto, all day yesterday?"

He shrugged off his coat and shook it, spraying the cabin liberally. "Yes. What of it? I didn't find out anything."

"How many churches did you see?" Stella asked.

"In the *Jewish* ghetto?"

"Not *in* it. Around. Nearby."

He helped Stella off with her coat and shook out the fur. "Not many. I can tell you that."

"Any?" she asked.

"I wasn't looking for churches, but I think passed one," he said.

"Do you remember the name?"

Nicky leaned back on the seat and looked up at the ceiling. "No, darling, I don't remember the name of one church in a city jammed with them."

"Don't get snotty with me. A name would help." Stella used Nicky's handkerchief to dry her hair.

"How?"

"She said Father Girotti and *ebrei*, right?"

"So? We already know he helped your friends with their passports and you think they're Jewish."

"If he's a friend to the Jews then it makes sense that he'd know the community. He'd be nearby," said Stella.

84

Nicky shrugged. "Maybe."

"There is one more thing."

Nicky sighed. "How did I know that was coming?"

"I really couldn't say." Stella glared and then told him about the family on the train and how she ran into the young priest, who thought she was Frau Goldenberg. "I bet that's Father Girotti."

Nicky's eyes grew steely. "Why didn't you tell me?"

"I'm telling you now."

"Before. Why didn't you tell me before?"

"There wasn't much to tell. I didn't think it mattered."

"I'll be the one to decide that. I'm your husband," he said with a patriarchal tone.

Stella crossed her arms. "Congratulations."

"You know what I mean. As your husband, I'm entitled to know everything that happens to my wife."

"Then, as your wife, I'm entitled to know everything about you, right?"

"It's not the same," Nicky said, looking uncomfortable and Stella enjoyed it.

The captain banged on the roof as they slowed and approached a dock. Stella put on her boots and coat. "Are you coming?"

"How are you mad? You obviously should have told me."

"Lots of things are obvious." With that, she grabbed the umbrella, flung open the door, and marched out.

Stella was off the boat and scanning the buildings before Nicky managed to get his coat on. The captain was highly amused, which only served to make Nicky's frown deepen into furrows on his forehead. He haggled with the man and then paid him what Stella assumed was an obscene amount before clambering out of the boat.

"Hey!" yelled Stella and the captain popped his head out to squint at her through the rain pelting his face.

"Father Girotti?"

He shielded his face with his hand. "Eh?"

"Father Girotti. We want Padre Girotti."

The captain said something about Jews and Stella had an urge to punch him. Then he pointed at them. *"Ebrei?"*

"No," said Nicky, turning to Stella. "How do you say Catholic?"

"I don't know, but it can't be that different."

Nicky pointed to the two of them. "Catholic."

The captain smiled and patted his chest. *"Cattolico."* Then he came out and gave Nicky back some of the lira. Nicky accepted it but with gritted teeth.

"Father Girotti?" Stella asked, hopefully.

He shook his head.

"Um…church?"

He shrugged and shook his head again.

Stella crossed herself and put her hands together in prayer.

*"Ah, sì. Chiesa."* He waved for them to get back in. *"Chiesa di San Girolamo."*

Stella got back on the boat without looking at Nicky for approval. He followed saying nothing and the captain drove them farther up the canal. It was probably less than a fourth a mile, but it was kind all the same and Stella decided to appreciate it. The man had some goodness in him, even if it was selective.

*"Grazie. Grazie."* Stella got off and looked through the rain at a stuccoed wall with brick showing through the dilapidated parts. Above was a church as plain as plain could be without a statue in sight and only flat brick columns and simple pediments. Still, people were hurrying down the flooded walkway to an arched entrance in the wall where a wrought-iron gate hung open.

Nicky joined her as the taxi sped away and she said, "I think mass is starting. Let's hurry."

"Stella?"

"What?" she asked, tugging on his sleeve.

"I want you to understand what happened back there." He said it like she was a child or worse a simpleton.

"Oh, I understand well enough."

"I don't think you do."

She pulled him through the gate to a small paved courtyard with absolutely nothing to recommend it and the church wasn't any more attractive in full view either. But it was real, not new and improved for better flavor. That church was as the builder intended and Stella was disposed to like it, on principal.

She went toward the low steps, but Nicky held her back. "We have to settle this."

"What? That you think you're in charge? Fine. Go right ahead and think that. I'm getting out of this awful rain."

"I don't *think* I'm in charge, Stella. I'm your husband."

"So what? You don't own me, and I'm good at plenty of things that you aren't. Flying planes, for instance."

That stumped him for a second and then his eyes got shifty. Stella braced herself for a trump card.

"I'm older," he said.

"Barely."

"Six years isn't barely," he said with a smile. "And I've graduated from Yale."

"I don't need to graduate from Yale to know that age doesn't mean a thing." She walked away up the stairs into the plain church, lovely in its simplicity. All things should be so simple.

Nicky charged in after her, closing the umbrella and squeezing his large form past tiny Italian ladies, who viewed him with both admiration and irritation. "Age does matter. Your father is the CEO of Bled Beer because he's the oldest."

"No, he isn't." Stella darted to the right to try to get to an open pew but was beat out by a family of six.

Nicky caught up and asked, "He's not the CEO?"

"The oldest."

Stella found a pew in the back, knelt, crossed herself, and squeezed in next to a young man who was very happy that she did. Nicky barely managed to get his rear on the seat it was so full. "What do you mean he's not the oldest?"

"I mean, my father is not the oldest. Uncle Nicolai is the oldest. Nicolai, Aleksej, Josiah."

"But...but your father is the CEO."

"I know."

"Why isn't Nicolai in charge?" Nicky's frown was back and then some.

Stella sighed. How could a Yale graduate be so terribly dim? "Because when my grandfather retired, he picked his most capable son to take his place. My father. Age doesn't make a person better, just older."

"What did Nicolai say?"

"Nothing. We all knew who it would be. We *always* knew. Father started at the brewery at ten, years before my uncles. He loves it the most. He works the hardest."

"I thought he was the oldest because you're so old," said Nicky, flinching when Stella gave him a look that should've frozen the damp on his skin. "I didn't mean you're old. It's just your cousins are little girls. Millicent can't even walk yet."

"She can," said Stella. "She's just lazy."

"Well, I'm still your husband," said Nicky.

"I said it before and I'll say it again. Congratulations."

"Stella, someone has to be in charge."

"Why?"

"I don't know. Because that's how it's done."

She waved his protests away and leaned forward as a hush fell over the church. Three priests came in robed in heavy vestments and Stella recognized one of them as the priest from the train station. She elbowed Nicky and grinned. Success. But he looked at her with a curious expression, not his usual mask, more numb.

She turned back to the altar and breathed deep as the oldest priest began. He spoke in Latin, of course, but Latin was the same everywhere and the comfort, too. Soon, her mother and Aunt Florence would be taking Millicent and Myrtle to the cathedral, sitting in their pew and wearing their hats. Father and Uncle Nicolai would be late because they were at the brewery checking wort or deliveries or one of a million things that had to be checked on a Sunday morning and mother would be angry. Florence would smile into her gloved hand and then Grandmother would give Millicent and Myrtle little treats out of her handbag so they wouldn't fuss. Grandfather would help

Grandmother to kneel and she would kiss his hand. The old church they were sitting in was so different than the cathedral with its fresh paint and new mosaics, but the stories playing out around them, love, irritation, whining children, and the rest of it were the same everywhere.

They came to the Eucharist and the young priest led the prayer in a calm, tenor voice that settled on everyone like a much-needed blanket. People all around them were smiling. He was well-liked in this small parish and Stella had the feeling that many came to that humble church for the sole reason of hearing the word from him. It sounded sweeter, felt kinder.

But, as he was speaking, the church doors opened and icy air flowed into the nave, causing a collective shiver. The father finished the prayer and the doors slammed shut. The other priest took over and said The Lord's Prayer, but as the end of the service went on a whispering started and people were glancing back toward the doors. Stella turned to see what they were worried about, but she was too short to see.

She squeezed Nicky's hand. "Who is it?"

That shook him out of his revelry and he bent over to her. "What?"

"Who is it? Who came in?"

Nicky looked back and sunk down in his pew. "Bartali."

"Are you kidding?"

"It's him. We have to get out of here now," he said, beginning to stand, but Stella pushed him down.

"Wait," she said.

"He's here for a reason."

"It doesn't have to be us," she said.

"Remember how you believe in luck? Isn't this luck? Bad luck?"

Everyone started to stand for communion and Stella did, too. "I believe more in good luck and we're having it right now."

"We're not taking communion. That's crazy."

"It's perfect. We can't go straight for a door and if we stay here we're sure to be noticed. Look around. Everyone's taking communion. It's a mad rush."

And it was. No peaceful, calm procession for the Italians. They were out to get in line first like the priests were going to run out of wine or something.

"This is ridiculous," whispered Nicky.

"And perfect." Stella sidled down the pew, curbing her urge to look back and wishing Nicky could put on his hat. That blond was like a beacon among all the dark heads and black clothes.

When they got to the aisle, she bit back her politeness urges and cut off a lady to get Nicky ahead of another tall man in hopes that he would be shielded.

The Italians didn't mess around and the line moved forward quickly. When it was her turn, she knelt before the older priest and received her wine-dipped wafer with the younger priest she'd spoken to at the station holding the basin under her chin. She rose and broke tradition in what might be an unforgivable way. Stella turned to stand directly in front of the young priest, and said, "Hello, Father."

His eyes went wide as he recognized her and the older priest harrumphed and glared. Stella shuffled to the side, watching the priest from the corner of her eye. He was inattentive as Nicky took communion. He watched her instead, which got him a stern look.

They joined the crowd heading back to their seats, but when no one was looking they slipped out the door to the far right of the altar and closed themselves in darkness. After a few minutes when no one came after them, Nicky said, "Well, that's not going to make you popular."

"I wanted him to know I was here. He saw where we went. He was watching."

"This could be a huge mistake."

"He helped Karolina and Rosa."

"You don't know that."

"I do. I feel it."

He took her arm to lead her away when the door clicked and opened. Slipping inside was the young priest, highlighted with the light from the nave. He turned a knob and a single lightbulb overhead came to life, shedding a dim, yellowish glow around the chamber.

The priest closed the door and said, "*Buongiorno.*"

"Father Girotti?" asked Stella.

"No." He asked several questions that were far beyond Stella's comprehension.

"Do you know Karolina von Bodmann?"

The priest seemed puzzled and he asked several questions. Stella caught *Americani.*

She patted her chest. "*Sì, Americani.*"

He said something about Karolina and Germany, but since they couldn't understand, it was no use. Nicky squeezed Stella's arm. He wanted to go, but she wasn't about to give up. She liked him, this priest that wasn't Father Girotti. He helped the Goldenbergs. Only a good person would do that. Since he was a priest, it couldn't be for money.

"Frau Goldenberg?" she asked.

"*Sì.*" He nodded emphatically.

What was the word for help? She couldn't think.

"Passport?" She patted her chest again. "We need passports."

"Ah! *Passaporti. Sì.*" He glanced back at the door and then pointed at another door at the end of the chamber before rushing out.

"I guess we should go wait in there," said Stella.

"Or he wants us to go in there while he gets Bartali to turn us in," said Nicky.

"He wouldn't do that. He's a priest."

"Priests have to follow the law."

"We haven't broken any laws," she said.

"You just asked for fake passports."

"I didn't say fake." Stella marched through the long, narrow chamber that appeared to be a kind of dressing room for the altar boys and choir. Rows of hooks with dripping coats and umbrellas lined both sides with galoshes underneath and a couple of rickety wardrobes framed the door at the far end, probably where the robes were kept. The door itself was plain with heavy hinges and a unique lever door handle in the shape of an angel and her wing. She reached for the wing and Nicky grabbed her hand. "We need to get out of here."

"We will." She pulled the door open to reveal a small office with two desks in the middle pushed back to back, a simple coat rack with the obligatory wet coats and umbrellas, and bookcases covering the walls up to the ceiling.

Nicky crossed the room and opened another door. "It's another office and it's got a door. We might get out through it."

"I think we should wait," said Stella, wishing she could take off her wet coat, but wearing a red suit to mass was too rebellious, even for her.

"We're not waiting. He's not Girotti. We don't know who he is."

"I know he was at the station to pick up that Jewish family. They were terrified and desperate. He came for them. He did. That priest. I'm staying right here."

"No," said Nicky, taking a breath. "You're not."

Stella walked over to one of the office chairs and sat down. "You're not my father and I never obeyed him much anyway."

"Obey." Nicky puffed up and a slow smile came over his face. "You promised to obey at our wedding. Now get up, we're going."

Stella stretched and leaned back. The chair was quite comfortable, despite being wooden and cushionless. She could stay there all day, if required. "No, I didn't."

"Yes, you did. I was there, Stella."

"I guess you weren't paying attention then, which doesn't say much for your vows."

"Obey is part of the vows. You said it," said Nicky, but his confidence was faltering. She could see it and felt a small thrill of triumph. Obey, indeed. She'd show him obey.

"It's not required and we didn't have it in there."

"I heard you say it."

"Then you were hallucinating," said Stella. "Do you really think a Bled would promise to obey? Really?"

He began to pace and smack his fedora against his leg with wet slaps. "But it's in the vows."

"We took it out."

"When? How?"

"It was discussed," said Stella, getting bored of the conversation. She couldn't imagine why he cared so much about one little word, a word that wasn't really taken seriously. Did wives obey because they vowed to at their wedding? Hardly. "Are you hungry? I'm getting hungry."

"No, I'm not hungry. When was it discussed?"

Stella sat up, putting her elbows on the desk, and her clasped hands under her pointed little chin. "At mother's garden party, the one you were too drunk to attend."

"I wasn't drunk," he protested, looking around. "Where is that priest? We haven't got all day."

"Florence said you vomited in her favorite ficus and fell asleep in Millicent's trundle bed in the nursery."

"I...didn't know she told you that," said Nicky, blushing like Stella didn't know he could.

"She didn't. Millicent did."

"Oh, come on. The kid that can't walk."

"I told you she *can* walk and she can talk, too. You got drool on her dollies and she wasn't happy about it."

Nicky covered his eyes. "This is a nightmare. Who else knows?"

"Everyone, I imagine."

He looked up. "Your mother?"

"Why do you think she didn't mind me not *obeying* you? Mother was your only hope, in that regard."

"Why didn't you tell me?" he asked.

"Would you have called off the wedding?" Stella batted her eyelashes at him and smiled.

"You know I wouldn't have."

"Then what's all the fuss about? We were going to be married in any case."

"You exhaust me."

Stella grinned wider. "You'll get used to it. Mother did."

"What if—"

Stella shushed him. "Listen."

Men's voices came through the cracks around the door. The young priest, another man, and a voice that was unmistakable, the gruff carabinieri, Bartali.

The men were going back and forth about something, not exactly angry, more tense and a touch weary like this conversation had happened before and was fully expected to happen again.

Stella got up and went to Nicky, hugging him tight and watching the door.

"I want to leave," he said. "We still have a chance to get out of here."

"He's not here about us," said Stella. "I heard Goldenberg. He wants the Goldenbergs. That poor family."

"It's not illegal to emigrate," said Nicky, frowning.

"Maybe their papers were fake, too."

"Did you hear that? Von whatever. Karolina's name."

The voices went to two. Bartali was either silent or gone. Then the room filled with young, cheerful voices, boys and the choir were coming in to shed their robes and go home. Stella and Nicky watched the door and then at long last the angel wing moved. A man was talking, giving orders it seemed, and the boys called out in jest and joy. There was laughter and any nervousness that Stella had vanished. It would be fine. She knew it, like she knew it was right to come after the Sorkines, like she knew Uncle Josiah would find Abel and get him out of Dachau.

The door opened and a man slipped inside. Stella very nearly gasped. It wasn't the young priest but the old one.

"*Buongiorno.*" He didn't seem surprised to see them standing there, huddled and wet. "Hello. Good morning."

Stella was so surprised she couldn't say anything.

"You wanted to see me? I am Father Girotti."

Her knees went weak. Perhaps she was afraid. She just hadn't known it.

"Father Girotti," said Nicky in a rush. "Boy, are we glad to see you."

He chuckled. "I hear this often. Come. Let us go to my office where we will not be disturbed."

He crossed the room and ushered them into an office that was nearly identical to the first one, only it had a single desk and two comfortable chairs in front of it for them.

"Please take off your coats." The priest turned around and switched on a rusty little hot plate and set a kettle on top of it. "Would you like some tea?"

"I would," said Stella, "very much."

"Your coat," he said as she went to sit.

"Well, Father, you see, I didn't think we'd be going to mass today and—"

He held up his hand, rather stumpy and well-calloused. "God does not care if you are dressed in rags."

"What about red?"

He smiled. "Take off your coat."

They did as they were told and sat down as the priest took off his vestments and hung them on a hanger that he hooked onto a bookshelf. Then he found three tea cups in his desk and a small teapot. As he readied the tea, he asked, "Father Giuseppe said that you mentioned passports."

"Yes, Father," said Stella. "Karolina von Bodmann said that you helped her and her sister, Rosa."

He sat down heavily and his chair creaked in protest. "You're Americans?"

They hesitated, but Nicky said, "Yes."

"Why not contact your embassy?" He raised a dark eyebrow that set off his piercing green eyes.

"We need different passports," said Stella.

"False identities."

"Yes, Father."

The kettle spewed steam and he poured the boiling water into the teapot, careful not to spill a drop. "I must ask why. Have you done something illegal?"

The picture of Gabriele Griese's body sliding under the water flashed in Stella's mind, but she said, "No, Father. Nothing like that."

His eyebrow went up again.

Stella and Nicky looked at each other. They were there and he could help them if he chose to. They had to explain.

"We had some problems with the Nazis," said Nicky.

"And they wish to arrest you?"

"Probably."

Stella leaned forward and put her fingertips on the edge of the desk. "We're here in Venice to help someone. They're innocent, I swear to you, but the SS would arrest them if they had half a chance."

"These people are Jews?" asked Father Girotti.

"We think so. They're family to our dear friend and he is."

The Father swirled the teapot. "What happened to your friend?"

Stella's eyes filled with tears, unexpected and unwelcome.

"He was arrested in Vienna," said Nicky. "We think he was sent to Dachau."

"The Night of Broken Glass?"

"Yes, Father," choked out Stella. She could see Abel in the boxcar. She couldn't push the image away.

"Father Giuseppe tells me that you saw him at the station and that you saw the Goldenberg family, as well?"

"Yes, Father."

He considered that and her for a moment. "What are the names of your friend's family?"

"Raymond-Raoul and Suzanne Charlotte Sorkine," said Nicky. "You see, our friend had this package that the SS—"

Father Girotti raised his hand. "I don't want to know."

"Have you seen or heard of the Sorkines?" asked Stella.

"I haven't, but I will make inquiries."

"Can you get us the passports?"

"I can, but it's costly. I don't do this myself. I know certain craftsmen who have the ability and they must make a living like everyone else."

"We understand," said Nicky. "We're very grateful and my family, our families, will be grateful. I come from—"

"No, sir. I don't want your real names, only the ones you want to use."

"Douglas and Eulalie Myna," said Stella.

"Good names." He poured them tea and went to the door calling out, "Giuseppe!" The rest of what he said was lost and then he returned to the desk.

Since it seemed like a safe topic, Stella asked, "You speak English beautifully. Where did you learn it?"

"In your state of Wisconsin," he said with a wistful smile. "A lovely place. I was sent there when I was newly ordained to learn English and to understand Americans."

"Do you understand us, Father?" asked Nicky.

He sipped his tea and smiled. "No. Your country is a great one, but it is confusing to me. Such generosity, anger, greed, and love live there. Your country will not help the Jews, I fear."

"I think you're right," said Nicky, "and I'm ashamed to say it."

"You saw this Night of Broken Glass yourself?" He looked back and forth between them.

"Yes," said Stella. "It was horrible. They burnt the synagogues. People were thrown out of windows."

"I wouldn't have believed it, if I hadn't seen it for myself," said Nicky.

"Yes," said Father Girotti, getting thoughtful. "Seeing is believing."

There was a soft knock on the door and a boy's soprano voice called out, "Father Girotti?"

The priest rushed to the door and Stella noticed he was careful to only open the door far enough to let the boy slip in. Father Girotti returned to his chair and the boy stood awkwardly by the door, wearing his galoshes and a heavy raincoat made of thick canvas. He was plump and big-eyed with long lashes. Stella suspected he was quite a happy boy but being called into the Father's office was cause for alarm.

"This is Pietro Russo," said Father Girotti. "Pietro, these guests of mine" —he emphasized *guests*— "would like to meet your friend, Jacopo. Could you take a message to him for me?"

Pietro nodded.

"You can say hello."

A smile crept over Pietro's face in response to Stella's smile. Dimples popped out on his cheeks and Stella never saw a happier boy.

"Hello. Good morning. Good day," he said.

"Very good," said Father Girotti. "We are learning English. Pietro is a fast learner."

The Father wrote a quick note and gave it to Pietro, who nodded at Stella and dashed out another door.

"This will take a few minutes. You do not mind?"

"Not at all."

"I do have another question," said Stella. "Do you know Dr. Davide?"

"Everyone knows Dr. Davide. Do you need a doctor?"

Stella first explained her feet and their reaction to the canal water and then quietly said that there might be a need to see Dr. Davide before he came to the hotel.

The priest watched her for a moment and then steepled his fingers. "I think there is more to this story."

Stella said nothing, mostly because she couldn't think of anything to say.

"Is Dr. Davide a member of your parish?" asked Nicky after a moment.

The priest chuckled. "Davide? No, no. His faith is gone as is much of his soul."

"What do you mean by that?" Stella took a big drink of the tea and burned her tongue.

"You haven't met him, have you?" asked Father Girotti.

"Not exactly," said Nicky.

"Who has treated your feet? Dr. Salvatore?"

They stayed silent.

"Of course, he did. An excellent doctor and a good man. I send him as much business as I can, but it is difficult."

"Because of the new laws?" asked Nicky. "What's happened?"

Father Girotti explained the *Leggi Razziali* that went into effect on November tenth. They excluded Jews from owning any businesses or participating in any profession save a few. They couldn't teach at universities or schools that had gentile students. They couldn't marry gentiles anymore or leave the country with more than 120 lira. The list went on and on.

"I hope you were able to pay Dr. Salvatore," he said. "He has a family."

"We did," said Nicky.

"How are they supposed to live?" asked Stella. "What are they expected to do?

"I can't explain this madness," said the priest. "I don't know what they will do, but the community is not unsympathetic."

"Is that why you send patients to Dr. Salvatore?" asked Stella.

"I do as my conscience and the Holy Father commands."

Nicky sat up. "The Pope said to help the Jews. When?"

Father Girotti waved for him to settle down and got a paper out of his desk. "He did not, but I know many people and they tell me things." He explained that a friend of his told him that Pope Pius XI told a group of pilgrims, "It is not possible for Christians to take part in antisemitism."

"I hate to break it to you, Father," said Nicky. "It's possible."

He nodded sadly. "Indeed that is true. The people should listen to the Holy Father. He is leading albeit quietly."

Stella bit back a retort. There was such a thing as being quiet because you feared being heard and fear never helped anyone. Abel didn't need quiet words, neither did the Sorkines. They needed shouting, stamping of feet, and loud protests from His Holiness. Father Girotti saw her expression and smiled serenely. "I don't believe the Holy Father will be subdued for long."

"Why not? The Kristallnacht was weeks ago. People died."

"Because he also said, 'Spiritually we are all Semites.' That is all I needed to hear." But then he winked. "But I didn't require permission to be kind. It is a sacred duty."

"Not everyone feels that way. We've been chased away from a hotel and out of a church because they thought we were Jews," said Stella.

"I'm not surprised."

"I guess they didn't get the Pope's message," said Nicky.

The father slid the paper over to Nicky. "They got this message."

The paper was in Italian, but Stella could see that it was a Vatican paper by the emblems and script at the top.

"What does it say?" asked Nicky.

"That the Jews are controlling Italy and hurting our faith," he said.

Nicky made his hands into tight fists. "What happened to 'We are all Semites'?"

"The Pope didn't say these things himself, but it came out of the Vatican from the lower ranks. Our government is asserting its influence. Mussolini said the Jews are polluting our culture."

"Then it's no different than the Reich," said Nicky.

The priest jolted to his feet and sputtered, "We do not throw people out of windows."

"Sorry, Father," said Stella, hastily. "We know that. It's different."

"That carabinieri isn't different," said Nicky.

"Carabinieri?" asked the priest, his face flushed and Stella feared he wouldn't help them after all.

"It's fine," she said. "Nothing to bother you about."

"Which carabinieri?" he asked.

"Bartali," said Nicky. "He was at us about Dr. Salvatore and Stella says he's been sniffing around the von Bodmann ladies."

Father Girotti sat down, making his chair complain again. "Yes. Bartali was just here about the von Bodmann ladies. He is against the Jews. He listens to lies and hears the truth."

"He's the reason I lied about my name. If he put it on a report…"

"I understand. Stay far from Bartali."

"What about the other carabinieri?" asked Nicky.

He shrugged. "Who can say?"

A knock on the door brought the Father back to his feet and he went to the door, asking a quick question before opening it. A middle-aged man in a floppy hat and work clothes rushed in with a boy about

Pietro's age. That was where the comparisons ended. This boy wasn't round and jolly. He was the exact opposite and Stella's heart hurt to see his furtive eyes darting around the room, looking for danger. His father whipped off his hat and greeted the priest warmly while still seeming nervous and wary. He was out of breath to the point of panting. He must've run the whole way.

"Come. Come," said Father Girotti. "Have tea and let us discuss."

The man and his son accepted tea in two more cups that the Father found in his desk. Then he produced a tin of cookies and offered them first to the boy, whose sallow cheeks said he could've used the whole box.

"These are my friends, Douglas and Eulalie Myna. They require your expertise," he said, offering Stella a cookie, which she gratefully accepted. "Douglas, Eulalie, this is my friend, Alberto Gattegno and his son, Jacopo."

They said hello and Stella could see he was guessing at who they were and whether they were Jewish, but he couldn't come to a decision on either question. It seemed everyone was judging and guessing and she couldn't help thinking it would get much worse before it got better.

"Father Girotti's note said that you need a literary opinion," said Alberto. "You are Americans?"

"Yes, but we need Canadian passports," said Nicky. "What is your profession, Alberto?"

"I owned a bookshop and provided translations for those who required them, books, letters, documents."

Owned. Past tense. It hadn't been that long since the tenth, but long enough for desperation to creep in. Stella watched as they discussed the passports, how to do them, and when they'd be done. She couldn't work up any interest. Yes, they would have to use the photos in their American passports. Yes, that was a problem for going home. But for Stella, it was a problem for later. The Sorkines were not. Nicky'd scoured the ghetto. Where else would they go? Not to the tourist spots surely.

"Stella?" asked Nicky.

She looked up. "Yes."

"We're done."

They stood up and shook hands with Alberto and Jacopo, for good measure. Then Nicky handed over a stack of bills and Stella couldn't help noticing that they had little left. They would have to telegram the family and have money wired. No way around it. Then she brightened. She could use Miss Myna. Her father would understand it was her and it wouldn't tip off anyone who happened to be watching.

Alberto walked to the door and she asked, "Do you have any of your books left?"

"A few," he said and she regretted asking. The loss pushed him down into the folds of his coat, diminishing a proud man. "Why do you ask?"

Nicky frowned at her and Father Girotti wasn't pleased, but she went ahead. Sometimes you just have to. "Are any for sale?"

"They are in Italian and not in good condition. I only have them because Roatta—he took my shop—didn't want them. He said they were trash. They are trash."

"Are they any good for learning Italian?"

"I...I think so," said Alberto. "I have a children's songbook."

"I'll take it." Stella looked at Nicky. It wasn't much, but it was something that didn't look like charity.

Nicky understood and gave Alberto a bill.

"No, no. It is too much. This songbook, it is trash." Flustered, Alberto's accent got stronger and Stella took his hand that had fresh, broken blisters on the palm and said, "I want to learn Italian. It's worth it."

The man herded his thin son out of the room and couldn't meet anyone's eyes again. But it wasn't a mistake to help. It couldn't be.

"Now that's that," said Stella. "When will they be ready?"

"Weren't you listening at all?" asked Nicky.

"I didn't need to. You were. So when?"

"A few hours and we'll be legal, in a manner of speaking."

"Perfect," she said. "Can you give us directions to Dr. Davide?"

Father Girotti pursed his lips and stroked the rough wooden cross around his neck. "I think I had better send for him instead. He may be…indisposed."

Stella took her coat off its hook and said, "If he's indisposed, we better go to him."

"Mrs. Myna, perhaps Mr. Myna can go and you can stay here."

In response, she buttoned her coat.

"Stella," said Nicky. "Let's do as the Father suggests."

"Have you forgotten that we've people to look for?"

"We don't have that much time."

"It's time enough to go to Dr. Davide and start asking people," she said.

"Who? Who are we going to ask?" he asked.

She pondered that and came up with nothing, except simply knocking on doors.

"They don't know that anyone would be looking for them?" asked Father Girotti.

"No," said Nicky. "They have no idea. They're looking for our friend."

"Here in Venice?"

"Yes."

Father Girotti nodded and stroked his cross. "Why here?"

"Because he last contacted them here," said Nicky.

"What did he tell them?"

"I have no idea."

"Perhaps he told them your hotel," he said.

Stella dashed over, ignoring her swelling feet, and kissed him on the cheek. "Father, you're a genius. Of course, they'd go there first." She grabbed Nicky's coat and tossed it at him. "Directions. Do we have directions for Dr. Davide?"

"I guess *we're* going, Father," said Nicky.

"I never doubted it."

They got directions and the Father led them through the back hallways and out onto the canal walkway. "Good luck." He didn't say you're going to need it, but it was implied and Stella didn't mind.

They had a direction. They had a plan. All she needed was a plan.

# CHAPTER 6

"We could've taken a taxi," said Stella as they made their fifth turn and nearly walked into an over-flowing canal.

"No, we couldn't," said Nicky. "I'm not sure we have enough to pay the doctor."

"We can telegram my father to wire money." She'd been working it out in her head. A couple thousand dollars ought to be more than enough. Stella hadn't paid any attention to money before Vienna. She'd been spoiled, pampered, and praised all her life and thought little of it. Now that she'd seen the world and, in particular, little Jacopo's eyes. Children shouldn't look like that. He should look like Millicent and Myrtle, plump and full of mischief. She wanted to make him look that way. Maybe she could buy more books or make a loan. Alberto might take a loan.

"And give away our location?" asked Nicky. "Father Girotti made it pretty clear that Italy's going the way of Germany. We can't use the name Bled. It's like a beacon."

"We'll use Myna," said Stella. "Father will know who it is."

"You'd be sending the telegram to a Bled, Stella. Two and two still adds up to four."

"Oh, right. Let me think."

They splashed into a passage that looked minimally flooded but nearly went over their boots.

"I'm really getting sick of this rain," said Nicky. "For all we know, the Sorkines have sense and took themselves home."

"They can't go home. It's not like Peiper's going to forget their address and I think they knew he was coming," said Stella. "I know what we'll do. We'll send the telegram to Mavis's brother, Patrick."

Nicky stopped at a door and looked doubtfully at its peeling paint and rusty knocker. "This is it."

Stella peeked up at the building from beneath the edge of the umbrella. "A doctor lives here? It looks like a tenement."

"How do you know what a tenement looks like?" His mouth was twisted into a wry smile and Stella said haughtily, "Mavis showed me pictures of Dublin."

"Who is Mavis?"

"My friend. She was at the wedding, Nicky. Were you paying attention to anything at all?"

"I was paying attention to my bride."

Stella rolled her eyes. "Mavis is very pretty. Black hair. Freckles."

He was still blank.

"Irish."

"Her? Isn't she the laundress?"

Stella smacked his arm and said, "And my friend. We can telegram Mavis's brother for money."

"The laundress's brother has money?"

"No, but he's Mavis's brother and he knows me. He knows I'm Miss Myna. He'll go to Mavis directly and give it to her."

Nicky shook his head as if he had to expel that idea from his ears. "First of all, that's insane, and second, I'm not asking your family for money. I'm a Lawrence, for God's sake."

"We're asking for *my* money." Stella lifted the knocker and dropped it with a clunk.

"I'm not dipping into any trust fund or whatever your father gave you. I'm your husband and I'll provide for us."

"Don't start with that husband stuff again. It is my money."

"That your father gave you, so it's his money."

"I earned it." She banged the knocker again.

"By what? Being born."

"By working."

"Hey!" came a bellow from above. "Shut up down there. You're disturbing my beauty sleep."

They looked up and got instantly pelted with rain in the face. Two floors up, a man with a grey fringe of hair sticking out at all angles and wearing a grubby undershirt glared at them.

"Dr. Davide?" yelled Nicky.

"Yeah. What of it?"

Stella waved at him. "I'm your patient!"

"I doubt that! I'd remember you," he said.

"Eulalie Myna!"

"Oh, for Christ's sake! I'll see you this afternoon. I'm busy. Go away."

Nicky banged on the door again. "She needs to see you now!"

"You got money?" he asked, eyeing them critically.

"Some!" yelled Nicky.

"How much is some?"

Stella banged on the door herself. She was tired, rain was dripping off her chin, and her feet had swollen so much she might have to cut her boots off. "Now! Right now! It's an emergency!"

"You're disturbing my neighbors!" Dr. Davide yelled down.

"Open up!" Nicky kicked the door and it cracked open. It would've flown open and banged against the wall, but the entire first floor was flooded and it could only slosh.

"Never mind!" yelled Stella.

"Son of a bitch!"

They walked into Dr. Davide's house, if it could fairly be called that. Mavis's pictures of the slums in Dublin looked spiffy in comparison and Stella felt beaten down by the crumpling walls and fetid stench of stagnant water.

"Do you now agree that Father Girotti was right?" asked Nicky as he guided her around some debris floating in the water and bumped into a rotted box.

"I do not." Stella climbed onto the stairs and questioned the wisdom of it. They were wooden and none too new. "This won't take long."

"He can't be a real doctor."

"Father Girotti would've told us if he wasn't."

Nicky climbed on the stairs and they groaned and creaked.

"You better wait," said Stella. "I'll go up first."

"You're not going—"

She was already gone, climbing as fast as she could on the narrow stairs with her oversized and clumsy boots. She wanted to get up to what she hoped was a solid floor as much as she wanted to get away from Nicky. She hadn't meant to tell him about working or the wedding vows. She was never going to tell him about the wedding. Florence advised her not to. Men set a great store by such things and since he didn't notice, he couldn't care. It was sound advice. No secrets was still her motto, but Stella didn't really consider it a secret. He was there when it happened. She couldn't help it if he wasn't observant.

As for the job, it wasn't a secret if her drunk uncle already told her drunk fiancé that she was on her way to being a brewmaster. Like her father, she started at the brewery when she was nine. First, it was sweeping floors, an excellent way of getting out of lessons, if Uncle Josiah wasn't around to charm Miss Bloom, and Father never said no to her interest in brewing. She swept, shoveled hops, learned how to fix compressor valves, working her way up to mixing and bottling. It wasn't work like what Mavis did, morning until night. She did it when she could escape her tutors and her mother, who didn't think a proper place for a girl was in a brewery with those hard men and their high expectations, but she loved it.

And she earned, just a few cents at first, but now it was a tidy sum, earning good interest and waiting to be used. She didn't have a trust fund. The family didn't believe in them. Grandmother said money like that made people soft. She had no patience for soft people being rock hard herself.

The last stair groaned and Stella hurried onto the floor, which groaned just as much.

"Are you okay?" yelled Nicky.

"I'm fine! Come on up!"

"Yes, by all means come on up," said Dr. Davide, standing by the window with a glass full of a yellow liquid. "This isn't my home that you've invaded."

Stella straightened her coat and smoothed her hair that was slick with rain, doing her best not to breathe deeply. The untidy room smelled like unwashed hair and moldy bread.

"I'm sorry," she said.

"No, you're not." He downed the liquid and poured a generous glug from the unlabeled bottle on the sill. "What is so important that you interrupt my holy day?"

Stella walked across the room, dodging trash and a plate. She held out her hand and said, "Eulalie Myna."

He snorted and ignored her hand. "Sure you are."

"I am I assure you."

Nicky came up, looked around, and put his mask on. "She is and I'm Douglas Myna, her husband."

"Whatever you say. I want cash. No traveler's checks."

"Don't you want to know what the problem is?" asked Nicky.

He swirled his glass and leaned in closer to Stella. He smelled like Uncle Josiah after the binge when he'd gotten lost and fell asleep in the stable. "All right. I'll play. How're the feet?"

"Swollen," said Stella.

"That'll be 1000 lira."

"We're not here about Eulalie's feet," said Nicky.

Dr. Davide pointed a shaky hand at him. "I know that, boy. I've been in this festering city for a long time. People like you don't come to a doctor like me if they can help it. You're a Jew, right?"

"No."

Dr. Davide waved a finger at Stella. "What's with the face? Who punched you?"

"I fell."

"Yeah, there's a lot of falling going on in Germany these days. What do you want? I've got to finish that bottle. It's my civic duty."

"I told people at the Hotel al Ponte Vittoria that I'm expecting and something happened," said Stella. "I want you to tell them I'm fine."

"Make that 2000 lira."

"We don't have that," said Nicky.

"What baby? Eulalie isn't expecting," said the doctor before swilling right out of the bottle.

Stella clicked through a list of their possessions and they had nothing that was remotely worth that much. "We can get it."

"When?"

"It depends," said Nicky.

Dr. Davide pointed at the stairs. "Beat it."

"Is there an open telegram office today?"

"It's Sunday in the land of the Pope. What do you think?" The doctor looked thoughtful.

"What if there's an emergency?" asked Stella.

"We've got telephones. This isn't the Serengeti."

Stella looked around at the small apartment. "Do you have one?"

"Yes, I do and no, you can't use it," he said. "It takes effort to arrange a call to the US, and I'm not getting stuck with your overseas charges."

"We're good for it," said Nicky.

"You won't mind if I don't take your word for it, *Mr. Douglas Myna.*"

Stella crossed her arms. "What will you take?"

Dr. Davide's eyes roamed over Stella, calculating something, but she couldn't imagine what. The look wasn't suggestive or anything close to it, but Nicky didn't agree. He put his arm around her and squeezed her painfully to his side.

"I'll thank you not to look at my wife like that," he said.

"Don't blow your wig, kid," said Dr. Davide. "I'll take the coat. What is that? Lamb and fox?"

"Yes," said Stella, unbuttoning.

"No," said Nicky. "She needs that coat. You know she's sick."

"That's not my problem."

Nicky went stiff. "You are a bastard and a poor excuse for a doctor."

"Right on the first count and wrong on the second," he said.

"Fuck you."

Stella caught her breath. She'd never heard Nicky say that before. He was essentially an elegant man given to politeness. Unlike her family, where politeness was considered optional and a barrier to honesty.

"Just for that. Give me your coat, too," said the doctor, clearly relishing their predicament.

Nicky advanced on the doctor and towered over him, but, to Stella's surprise, the doctor, who was sixty pounds heavier and probably six inches shorter, didn't waver at all.

"Go ahead. Throw me out the window. It'll end my problems and give you a new one."

Nicky gritted his teeth. "I'm not going to throw you out the window."

"Then what's your plan, son? I'd really like to hear it."

Stella wormed her way between them. "Our plan is to give you our coats and to pay you as soon as possible."

Their eyes met, hers clear and blue, his bloodshot and brown, and a deal was struck.

"I like you, *Eulalie Myna*. I'm a sucker for a pretty face and a paycheck." He held out his hand and she gave him her coat with an involuntary shiver.

"Douglas, your coat," she said.

"This is insane," he replied.

"Insanity is nothing new."

Nicky took off his coat and gave it to the doctor, who inspected it and then said, "Off the rack. You don't strike me as an off the rack couple."

"Well, we are," said Nicky.

"This isn't worth much." He held out his hand. "I'll take the hat, too."

Stella shook her head. "No way. He needs that hat."

The doctor squinted at her. "More than you need me to lie?"

Nicky was so recognizable without a hat that Stella wasn't sure.

"It's fine." Nicky tossed him the hat and Dr. Davide examined it as if he expected to find something special inside. He was disappointed, glaring at Stella and noting her lack of rings and any other jewelry. "You're sure you're not Jews?"

"We're sure," said Nicky.

"Why do you care?" asked Stella. "You sent Dr. Salvatore to me yesterday."

"I didn't say I cared," said Dr. Davide. "Salvatore is a good doctor, almost as good as me."

Nicky snorted and the doctor showed an ounce of pride. "Scoff all you want, kid. You're looking at the best doctor you're likely to find outside of New York."

"I'm not entirely sure you *are* a doctor."

"I went to Harvard medical and trained at Johns Hopkins. So fuck you."

"You don't mind if I don't take your word for it," said Nicky.

The doctor chuckled. "Touché and get out."

They went to the stairs and Stella went first, gingerly stepping on the first questionable stair when Dr. Davide said, "Word to the wise. If you're not Jews, you need to prove it or you'll get hassled."

"How are we supposed to prove it?" asked Nicky.

"Well, you could pull down your pants."

Stella stopped and looked through the rotten spindles. "What in the world?"

He laughed. "That clinches it."

"Why would—"

"I'll tell you later, Stella," said Nicky, shooing her down.

"There's another option," said Dr. Davide.

"I think we've had enough of your ideas."

Stella went back up. "I haven't. What have you got?"

"Simple. Be a Catholic."

"I am a Catholic."

"Do you have a rosary and cross stashed somewhere?"

"I'm fresh out."

"Then my idea is that you buy them immediately, today, if possible," he said. "It'll help you get around."

"It's Sunday," said Nicky.

He glugged down the rest of his bottle. "I know people."

"I bet," said Stella. "Do you know anyone named Sorkine?"

He squinted at her and rolled the name around in his thick head. "No. Who is it?"

"Never mind. You're as useless as you look."

Dr. Davide chuckled. The comment seemed to cheer him up a bit and he told them about a woman who sold trinkets at the train station. Maria made it her habit to be at the station when certain trains arrived to solicit business. The way he said "solicit" made Stella nervous, but she didn't know why. She didn't really care what business Maria was in, if she had what they needed.

"Fine," said Nicky.

"I have a train schedule. There's one from Milan coming in. They usually have a few first-class carriages. She likes those, but I don't know for certain she'll be there."

"How much will it cost us?"

"I'll take whatever you've got when I come to Vittoria this afternoon," said Dr. Davide. "You better have at least 500 lira."

"Can you look at her feet now?" asked Nicky, frowning as Stella winched when she shifted her weight.

He spread his arms wide, showing off his yellowed pit stains. "Does it look like I'm doctoring right now? Sofia gives me dinner in exchange for seeing her guests and keeping my mouth shut about it."

"You're all heart."

"I was. Now I'm all booze." He gave Nicky a crinkled slip of paper. "You can make the eleven out of Milan, if you hurry."

They didn't hurry. Not down the stairs. That didn't seem prudent. When Stella stepped into the water on the first floor, she felt the cold up into her molars. It hadn't bothered her when she had her coat on. The warmth of her fur warded off quite a bit. Dr. Davide really was a horrible person, but she supposed they were lucky he didn't take the umbrella, as well. He was capable of it, to be sure.

"Alright," said Nicky, pausing outside and opening the umbrella. "I don't know about the train station idea. God knows what that bastard is up to."

"We should go. It's the train station. How bad can it be?"

"I wish you hadn't said that."

She smiled up at him. How handsome he looked under the black umbrella with the remains of a bruise on his chiseled jaw. Nicky could've been the hero in a thrilling movie and she would've found the whole thing romantic if her feet weren't turning into blocks of ice. "I think it's a good idea and I do miss my cross."

"I don't think you want a cross purchased from a...woman in the train station."

"God doesn't care where it came from."

He let out a sigh.

"We can get a better one later when we have money again," she said, doubting that she'd want to. Every penny counted. That was now printed on her very soul.

"Your money," he said.

"Sure. Why not?" She eyed him, daring him to say the wrong thing, even though she wasn't sure what the right thing was.

"I don't know, Stella darling, I really don't."

"There's nothing wrong with my money," she said.

"Okay. Fine. What's your job?"

"I'm a brewer's apprentice."

To her surprise, he cupped her cheek and kissed her full on the mouth with warm, insistent lips. "Of course, you are."

"You're not mad?"

"You keep telling me that you're a Bled. What else would you be but a brewer?"

"People call Uncle Josiah a rascal and a reprobate."

He kissed her again. "I'm relieved you're neither of those."

"Also, an addled-minded nincompoop. That came from a judge."

"A judge? What the—oh, never mind. Let's go to Santa Lucia and get this over with."

He turned, but Stella held his arm. "You're really not mad?"

"Stella, my wife is standing in front of me, shivering with torn up feet. I'm not mad. Your job is the least of my concerns."

The rest of the truth burst out of her. "I have 5000 dollars."

Nicky whistled. "That's a tidy sum."

"We can use your money, if you can think of a way to get to it," she said.

"It's all our money and if we keep dealing with that doctor, we're going to need a lot of it."

# CHAPTER 7

$\mathcal{N}$icky insisted they splurge on a water taxi to the train station, since they were both shivering and now had a plan for getting some funds. When they got on the boat, Nicky told the captain straight out that they weren't Jews, which appeased him, but, when it came to Nicky's request that he wait for them to come back out of the station, doubt was all over the man. He looked at their coatless, rain-splattered clothes and obviously thought there was something a matter with them. He just couldn't decide what.

He tapped his palm. "Money now."

"Later," said Nicky.

"Now."

"We have to meet someone," said Stella, doing her best to look appealing with chattering teeth.

"Now."

Nicky took his wallet out and held up a bill. "Now." Then he pulled out another bill. "Later."

The man grimaced. "You hurry."

"We will. We will." Nicky got out and lifted Stella over the side to carry her across the flooded piazza in front of the Santa Lucia station.

"Is it deeper?" she asked.

"Yes." He didn't elaborate and that wasn't a good sign.

When he set her down on the dry top stair, his pants were splashed up to the knee.

"I'm sorry," she said. "I could've stayed on the boat."

"I wasn't leaving you there. Did you see the way he was looking at you?"

"No."

"I'm glad." Nicky took her hand and they ran through the station as a train started to pull in. It was a fancy, silver affair, puffing smoke and making a tremendous racket. The train must've meant money, because there were several porters on the platform and a few people hawking trinkets. Nothing like the number that had been there earlier in the month when they'd left Venice, but a lot more than when they'd arrived a couple of days ago.

"What do you think she looks like?" asked Stella.

"Disreputable, I assume."

"She might not."

He gave her a look and they started walking past the platforms. One train was loading, but there weren't any women hanging about. Nicky tried asking a porter, but he didn't speak English and couldn't be bothered to try and understand Stella's rudimentary French. He shooed them away in a huff and they returned to the other platform, where the silver train was coming to a halt.

"There she is," said Stella, pointing at a woman who stood expectantly next to the newsman's stand they'd gone to when they arrived. And she did look reputable in Stella's opinion, except for the brassy blond hair that clearly wasn't natural. She wore a well-fitted navy-blue coat and hat, had pretty silver shoes with rhinestone buckles, and carried a small case, the kind that one might sell trinkets out of.

"She's a passenger," said Nicky.

"I don't think so. She's got a pair of galoshes tucked behind her and the newspaperman isn't too happy about her standing there."

The man scowled at the woman and said something, which she ignored.

Nicky shrugged. "All right. Let's give her a try."

They dashed past the engine and down the platform, startling the woman so that she backed up into the wall, dropping her case, which popped open to reveal necklaces with crosses, rosaries, engagement rings, watches, and some earrings.

Nicky reached for the jewelry, trying to help, but she screeched and slapped his hands.

"So sorry, Maria," said Stella. "Dr. Davide sent us."

She, instantly, went calm and businesslike. "Davide?"

"Yes. He said you might have a cross and rosary for me."

Maria stuffed her wares back in her case and looked them up and down, obviously finding them wanting, and Stella had to agree. If anyone was disreputable, it was them.

"You have money?" she asked.

"Yes."

She opened the case with a smile. "This is a nice rosary. My uncle make out of the olive wood."

It was nice, beautiful beads and a simple cross with a lovely swirling in the wood. She showed them other ones, but none were so elegant. The crosses were another story. Stella preferred a small gold one, nothing garish, and Maria's selection took garish to another level. They were huge, the size of a half dollar and covered in fake red stones and filigree.

Stella picked out the least obnoxious and asked, "How much?"

Maria thought for a moment. "1000 lira."

Nicky laughed. "I'll give you fifty for both."

The woman snorted in derision and countered with 850. Back and forth they went and Stella lost interest. A jewelry purchase had never been so boring. All she cared about was how hard it would be to pry out the cheap stones and clip off the filigree to get it to something that didn't scream tacky.

She turned away as the passengers began exiting the train and exclaiming at the pouring rain as if they didn't know. There were a lot more people on that train than on theirs. Maybe someone told them it would stop *domani* and they expected to find a dry Venice. The porters rushed around, searching for umbrellas for the demanding passengers, and Stella rolled her eyes. They could survive a little wet. She could. She did. She was.

Nicky and Maria raised their voices and the woman wasn't the least bit intimidated by him. She was getting mad. A flush was coming up her neck to color her cheeks. Then she eased her coat back to expose a nicely-rounded shoulder and voluptuous breasts, sweetening the deal as she puckered and licked her lips.

"It is worth a few more lira. I promise," said Maria.

Apparently, she'd forgotten Stella was there or maybe she didn't care as long as it got results. Stella stared in surprise. No one she knew would do that. Sure flirting happened with skirts short and décolletages low. But this was a whole other animal and it dawned on Stella that Maria's "soliciting" might be about more than jewelry. She wasn't exactly sure how ladies of the evening worked or what exactly they did, but it seemed train stations were where they did it.

Maria caught Stella evaluating her and in frustration yanked her coat back up. If Nicky had even noticed what she was trying, it didn't show. He kept on about quality and price. Stella suspected that Maria thought his quality talk might be about her and Stella smiled, which only provoked her to raise the price another fifty.

"I'll give you a hundred," said Nicky.

"Hundred and fifty," said Maria.

Back and forth again and a shout got Stella's attention. The voice was French and familiar. She scanned the complaining passengers and saw Monsieur Volcot speaking to an elderly woman who was refusing to get off the train. Stella couldn't tell if she wanted him to make the rain stop or wanted an umbrella. Her umbrage was completely overboard so it could very well be the rain, which showed no signs of abating. Monsieur Volcot tried to reason with the woman and then looked up at someone behind her. Something in Monsieur Volcot changed. While he was deferential when talking to the old lady, his body easy, his movements loose, when he spoke to whoever was behind her, he got stiff to the point of rigid and a familiar thrill of fear went through Stella. She squeezed Nicky's arm before she left and walked toward the train. She was shivering. Was it the cold and wet or was it this feeling of fear coming over her in waves?

The first thing she saw was the tip of a very shiny black boot. Her chest got tight. She couldn't breathe. She didn't want to breathe. It couldn't be him. Not yet.

Stella edged sideways, trying to see and not be seen. He came into view in profile. *Oberführer* Peiper in his black SS uniform, his hat pulled low and a grimace of familiar anger on his face as he waited to get off the train. Stella stood there for a moment, frozen in shock and horror, dozens of thoughts racing through her head.

Then a reasonable thought popped up. Stay calm and walk away like nothing is wrong. So she turned around, ducking behind an irate couple and their huge pile of luggage to casually walk back to Nicky.

She gently touched his arm. "We need to go. Just pay the woman."

"This is extortion. This stuff isn't even worth the hundred I'm offering and she's raised the price to two hundred."

"I don't care. Pay her," said Stella.

"I know I've been patient with your work and your family, but I am still your husband. The man of the house, if that means anything to you."

It didn't, but Stella said, "It does, but please just pay her."

Behind them came an outraged howl and then a screech of pain. They turned to see the crowd scattering and the old lady spread-eagle on the platform at Monsieur Volcot's feet. Walking off the train was Peiper followed by a boy of about thirteen carrying a small case and wearing a delighted smirk. Peiper slipped on a pair of black gloves and stepped over the old woman, who appeared to be unconscious as Monsieur Volcot dropped to his knees to attend her.

"Oh my God," whispered Nicky.

"Pay her," said Stella.

They turned back to Maria who was now wearing a smirk similar to the boy's. Nicky opened his wallet to pull out the 150, but she didn't give him the chance. She snatched the wallet and waved it in the air, "*Achtung! Achtung! Juden! Juden!*"

Everyone on the platform turned to look, including Peiper.

Instantly, he saw Nicky's shining blond head and his eyes lit up with malicious glee. Maria turned with the wallet to dash past Stella, who, on instinct, grabbed the case and twisted it out of Maria's hand.

Stella pointed at Maria. "Thief! Thief!"

Nicky grabbed Stella's hand and they ran through the crowd with Maria howling with rage behind them and Peiper shoving people out of his way. Passengers screamed and Stella didn't need to look to know he'd pulled a gun. The panic announced it.

The pain in her feet turned to fire as they pounded on the floor and she couldn't go any faster. They'd never make it.

"Stop!" yelled Peiper. "I'll fire!"

He would, too, and it didn't matter who got in the way, but they kept running, dodging around luggage carts and abandoned bags, hearing him get closer by the intensity of the screams. They got to the station doors and Nicky shoved Stella through. She stumbled into the driving rain, turning in time to see Nicky face Peiper and his pistol. He didn't freeze or hesitate. He picked up a luggage cart and threw it at Peiper. The thing was huge and Stella caught a glimpse of Peiper's eyes as it came hurdling through the air at him. He panicked, firing wildly before being hit and driven to the floor.

Nicky ran out the door, tossed Stella over his shoulder, and dashed through the flooded piazza, his long legs being a distinct advantage. He high-stepped over the water using his full length without Stella's short little legs holding him back and jumped over the side of the taxi, startling their captain.

The man protested as Nicky dumped Stella and went for the wheel. The men grappled for control of the boat, rocking it wildly. Stella rammed into the side and almost went over. She dropped Maria's case and saw Peiper limp out of the station with the boy. He pointed and the boy dropped his case, running for them full tilt, a gun in his young hand.

"We have to go. Right now!" said Stella.

"I know." Nicky punched the captain in the jaw with little to no effect. The man punched him back in the stomach and Nicky went double. The captain cried out in triumph and then he saw the boy wading through the water with the gun pointed at them. Luckily, he wasn't tall so it was slow going, and, in frustration, he fired at them. The bullet ripped into the cabin and Stella screamed. The captain froze and Nicky socked him again.

They grappled, going down onto the deck, and Stella squeezed past them to get in the captain's chair. She'd never driven a boat before. But how hard could it be? She turned the key and the engine roared to life. She grabbed the wheel and pushed the lever on the right. They jolted forward and there was a terrible cracking sound. They were tied to the dock.

"Nicky, get the rope!"

The boy was almost on them, but a carabinieri was running for him, tall and much faster. He shouted at the boy and raised his weapon. The boy hesitated and the carabinieri tackled him. A huge splash went up and the boy and the carabinieri went under a wave. Peiper was coming, slower with blood running down his face, but he was coming.

"Nicky!" yelled Stella.

"I'm trying." He picked up the case and swung it. It cracked the captain upside the head and he went down long enough for Nicky to get to the rope. He yanked it off the pylon and Stella shoved the lever forward again. The boat lurched forward wildly and sideswiped the taxi in front of them as they raced from the dock. Stella looked back and Peiper was fighting with a second carabinieri.

Their captain struggled to his feet and he was volcanically angry. He leapt at the helm and Nicky grabbed him around the chest in a bear hug. "Turn around!" Nicky yelled through clenched teeth.

"What?" she yelled, trying to avoid a collision with a boat piled with crates.

"Turn! Around!"

She turned but not around, barely missing a vaporetto. The canal curved to the right and got significantly wider. In the distance, a large container ship spewed black smoke. They were leaving Venice and heading out into the Lido.

"Turn!" yelled Nicky.

"I am!" She yanked the wheel to the right, the engine screamed and made a disturbing, grinding noise as they spun in the water. They narrowly missed the vaporetto again and Stella got them through a gauntlet of boats. The taxi sped back past the train station and Stella saw Peiper climbing on a boat, a larger one, unfortunately pointed in their direction.

"He's got a boat!" she yelled.

"God damn swell." Nicky took a glancing blow to the head and gave one in return. "Turn, Stella, turn!"

He couldn't mean turn around again, but, in her panic, Stella yanked the wheel and they carved a curve in the water, cutting off a private boat that pegged them in the stern, and shocked Peiper who was coming up hard from behind. He tried to hit them, but missed and hit the private boat, slicing it in half.

"What in the hell are you doing?" yelled Nicky.

"You said turn!"

He pointed at a side canal. "Turn there."

The captain punched him in the chest and Nicky turned a shade of red that panicked Stella again, but she held it. Peiper cleared the wreckage and was heading for them. The canal Nicky wanted was small and crowded with docked boats. Big enough for Peiper? She smiled. No.

Stella throttled back and turned. She went too wide and managed to miss, bumping into several pylons. She looked back to see if they were badly damaged in time to see Nicky toss the captain overboard into the Grand Canal. She worked the throttle and wheel until they got in the smaller canal. She was too slow. Much too slow. Peiper had turned and was heading straight for them.

Nicky lurched into the helm. "I'll take it."

"Just shoot him!"

"With what? I didn't bring the pistol. Did you?"

She hadn't. Of course, she hadn't. They didn't expect to shoot anyone in Venice. "He's coming."

"He can't. It's too crow—"

A huge crash exploded behind them and he was coming, bulldozing his way through the smaller boats like Tinker Toys, his eyes fixed on them.

"I can't believe it," said Nicky under his breath. They raced down the canal, but the engine was sputtering and they seemed lower in the water.

"Are we sinking?" asked Stella, pushing the throttle but not getting faster.

Nicky sat in the other seat. "I think so. I can take the wheel."

"He's catching up."

"I know how to drive a boat."

"I'm driving a boat right now."

"We're sinking."

"I'm turning!" Stella saw another canal and tried to do a better job. She failed and they hit two boats and a pylon, but they did get into the canal.

"Let me drive. I grew up yachting," yelled Nicky.

"This isn't a yacht!"

"Stella!"

"There's the Grand Canal again!" She looked back and Peiper was bearing down on them. "Where should we go?"

"Let me have the wheel."

They raced out into the Grand Canal, barely missing the stern of the same vaporetto.

"We'll go there," she said, pointing at another small canal.

"I know where we are. Give me the wheel."

Stella gritted her teeth and got out of the seat. They couldn't get past each other and, in that few seconds they were tangled up, they sideswiped another boat and the engine popped. Stella looked back, a plume of black smoke funneled up between the looming Venetian townhouses.

Nicky maneuvered into the small canal, but Peiper would be on them in fifteen seconds.

"Get out!" yelled Nicky.

Stella grabbed Maria's case and got poised to jump. Nicky came out of the helm. The boat bumped a pylon, he grabbed her around the waist, and leapt onto the walkway next to the canal. A bullet pinged off the building, shattering the masonry and making Stella scream. Nicky dropped her and took her hand before taking off, dragging her along behind him. She looked back and Peiper rammed the taxi, demolishing it. They ran onto a bridge as Peiper jumped onto the walkway and started running full out with a pistol in hand.

Another shot ricocheted off the corner of a building as they ducked into an alley. Nicky took lefts and rights. He seemed to have a plan, but Stella had no idea what it was. Everything looked the same in that relentless rain. All the buildings ancient and worn with wrought-iron balconies, no balconies, fresh plaster, no plaster, big doors, small doors. A flooded street there. A dry one here. Everything unique, but also the same in a blur of wet and fear.

"Yes," said Nicky, whipping her around through a door and banging her into a wall covered in stacks of books and papers bound together with twine. Nicky slammed the door shut and turned the hefty iron key in the lock. A resounding grind and click made it through the rain pounding on their heads. Stella stared at the door. It wasn't very thick, despite the incredibly large lock. Nicky pressed his ear against the door and listened. Then his shoulders relaxed and he turned. "He passed us."

Stella spun in a circle, shielding her eyes from the rain. "What is this place?"

All the walls in the small alley were covered in stack after stack of books and paper, exposed to the elements and molding dreadfully.

"I was here yesterday asking about the Sorkines."

"But what about these books?" she asked.

"As near as I can tell they collect old paper and send it to be milled again."

"What now? We can't stay here all day." And she didn't want to. That place was like the saddest library in the world. All those thoughts committed to paper allowed to disintegrate felt like a crime.

With that a woman came in the door at the end of the alley and screamed, dropped her load of paper into a large puddle. Nicky held up his hands and tried to calm her, but she backed away screeching.

He ran at her and clapped a big hand over her mouth. "Come on, Stella."

The door with the huge lock rattled and the unmistakable sound of German anger rose behind it. Stella squeezed past Nicky and the woman, dashing into a bookshop, small and ordinary with two choices. Out the front door or up the stairs. That was probably a dead end, but—

Nicky released the woman, who burst out screaming again. He grabbed Stella's hand and yanked her out the door. He hesitated, his tall frame pulsing with indecision. He looked up, saw something and dragged Stella to the right. They ran down the narrow streets and ended up heading toward a canal at the end, but as soon as Nicky emerged on the walkway, a shot rang out and her husband was knocked sideways, falling to his knees.

Stella dragged Nicky out of the open and another shot barely missed his foot. Men shouted in Italian. One German voice yelled back. Nicky scrambled to his feet with his hand pressed to his hip. Blood seeped through his fingers and he collapsed against the wall. "Go. Run."

"Are you crazy?" asked Stella, pulling his free arm over her shoulder. "Come on."

"No. Go."

She didn't respond. She dragged him along until he started moving and they got into another extremely narrow alley. "Where are we going?"

"Father Girotti's church." He grimaced. "Go straight."

They wound through a maze of passages and lost the yelling for a moment. Stella inadvertently stumbled into the open and Peiper's voice rang out. They were at the canal again. The SS officer was surrounded by Italians, outraged and trying to get his weapon.

"Hurry," said Nicky. "Come on."

He managed to pull her out of sight and do a kind of hopping run into another alley and then another and Stella found herself hopelessly lost. But then they were in the church's flooded courtyard. Nicky hopped up the steps and she grabbed the door handle, praying to anyone who would listen to please let it be open.

It was and Nicky hopped inside, his galoshes making horrid wet squelching noises that echoed off the old walls and came back at them like an accusation.

Father Girotti stood in the center aisle, holding a stack of papers. He spun around and his mouth fell open. Stella slammed the door shut and looked for a key in the lock, but there wasn't one.

"Father," gasped Nicky. "Help."

The priest dropped his papers and ran to Nicky's side. "What happened to you?"

"We have to hide," said Stella. "The SS. He's here."

Father Girotti paled. "Where?"

"Right behind us."

He looked around in a panic. The back of the church was too far. Stella spotted a confessional that she hadn't noticed before. It was terribly old-fashioned with a center compartment for the priest to be concealed in and kneelers on either side for the penitents. Her heart quelled at the very idea. It must be some kind of sin, but Father Girotti saw it, too, and started for it instantly. "Inside the chamber. Quickly now."

The Father opened the lower wooden partition and Stella pulled back the curtain. They shoved Nicky inside and Stella squashed in with him.

"Do not speak," said Father Girotti.

Stella nodded, unable to speak just then anyway. He closed the partition and drew the curtain. She heard him pad away and Nicky leaned heavily back against the wall before sliding down to sit on the bench. Stella stood with her arms wrapped around Maria's case, shivering uncontrollably, imagining the worst. Peiper would come in and shoot Father Girotti. She would've gotten a priest killed. There was no coming back from that. Absolutely unforgivable. What would Mother say, assuming she ever saw her again.

Nicky's hand ran up her leg and rested on her hip, squeezing it and somehow giving her strength. The man had been shot and there he was comforting her as he fought to control his ragged breath.

The sound of a door banging open echoed through the church and Father Girotti exclaimed. The hard, sharp raps of heavy boots reverberated on the marble floor and Peiper demanded something in German. Stella recognized "man" and "woman." Beyond that, his words were lost in a rant that Father Girotti responded to in confused Italian.

"A man and a woman came in here," Peiper yelled at the priest, switching to English. "Where are they?"

Father Girotti responded, once again, in Italian, sounding utterly confused and even a bit feeble. Stella had to smile over her clenched teeth. The good Father was quite an actor.

"I know they came in here!"

The priest responded the same way, but now his voice was added to. Footsteps ran through the church and the young priest's voice asked something in Italian. The two holy men went back and forth. Stella could feel Peiper seething. He yelled. He demanded. The priests countered in Italian. Then more voices came. Women, speaking Italian.

Stella couldn't resist. She delicately pulled a tiny portion of the curtain aside and peeked out into the nave. Peiper had been surrounded by the two priests and a passel of nuns. The nuns, in particular, weren't happy. They raised their hands in lamentation. One held out a bible and looked as though she might hit Peiper with it. Unlike Mavis, Stella had always had a great affection for nuns. Cousins Lidija and Paloma were Carmelites. They were lovely and spent, Stella suspected, a good deal of their time praying for her mother, in particular, and the Bleds, in general. Sister Paloma wrote wonderful, witty letters about her sisters and their cloistered life. She was nothing like the nuns Mavis described in her native Ireland. Mavis would walk five blocks to avoid having contact with a nun, despite Stella's assurances that no sister was going to whip out a ruler and hit her on the back of the head. Mavis said Stella didn't understand, having never attended school in a traditional sense and she was right. Stella got tutors and governesses, not angry nuns with weaponry.

But now, peeking out into that old church, she could see what Mavis saw. Those nuns were taking no guff off an intimidating SS officer with a pistol. Their habits flapped as they waved their arms and got in front of the priests and herded Peiper backward toward the door like a flock of oversized bats bent on feeding. He kept yelling in English and German, but it got him nowhere. The sisters had him backed up against the door and then outside in a matter of minutes. Then the tallest sister, an imperious lady with the kind of face Stella could easily see behind a brandished ruler, pulled out a large key and locked the door. "*Basta! Sei un idiota tedesco!*" she yelled at the door and then sped back to the priests as if on wheels and gave them a good talking to before she gathered her fellow sisters and they sped off down the nave, disappearing. A door slammed, but the priests didn't move for a moment, frozen in shock. If Stella had known nuns could get rid of the SS, she'd have found some earlier.

"It's fine," she whispered and Nicky let out a low groan, dropping his hand.

Footsteps came racing over and Father Girotti jerked back the curtain. "He's gone. You're safe."

Stella clasped his hand and pressed it to her heart. "I can't thank you enough, Father. Nicky, did you hear that?"

Nicky didn't answer and she turned to find her husband slumped against the wall of the confessional, unconscious with a pool of blood under his feet.

# CHAPTER 8

"*C*lose the door, Mrs. Myna," said Father Girotti.

Stella quickly closed the door behind them and the priests carried Nicky through the office and down a short hall into a small antechamber with a couple of cots and a wash basin.

"I can walk," said Nicky.

"Yes, I know," said the priest without letting Nicky take his arm from over his shoulders. "But now you will lie down and we will look to your injury."

They forced Nicky to lie down and roll over, revealing the large bloody spot on his hip and buttock. There were two holes in his pants. Two. Stella's legs went weak. He'd been shot twice.

"Let me see," she said.

"Perhaps…you should go," said the priest. "The area."

"He's my husband, Father."

"But you are so young."

"I was, but not so much anymore." Stella knelt by the cot and rolled Nicky on his back, reaching for his belt buckle.

"What do you think you're doing?" he asked, batting her hands away.

"Taking off your pants."

"I don't think so. Get Dr. Salvatore. I don't want you seeing this."

Stella rolled her eyes. "It can't be as bad as Oliver."

"Who is this Oliver?" asked Father Girotti.

"A friend," said Nicky. "Sort of. Can you get Dr. Salvatore?"

"Dr. Davide is closer." He spoke to Father Giuseppe and the young priest went for the door.

"Not him," said Stella. "That old scoundrel is the reason we're in this fix."

"You saw Davide?"

Nicky started to speak, but gritted his teeth, grasping at Stella's hands and holding them so tight she thought the bones would snap. "Dr. Salvatore, please, Father," she said, gasping herself.

Father Giuseppe rushed out and Father Girotti locked the door behind him. "Tell me what happened."

They unbuckled Nicky's pants and slid them down to expose his bloody briefs while Stella told him about the doctor and his fabulous idea of going to Maria at the train station.

"He took your coats," marveled the Father, "in this weather."

"He said we'd get them back. We didn't have much choice." Stella pushed Nicky onto his side, cringing when he groaned in pain. She pulled down the briefs and found two bloody holes. Compared to Oliver and the gash on his shoulder, it was almost a relief.

"Do you have a towel?" she asked and he gave her the cloth from the washbasin and she wiped the blood away. The holes refilled quickly but not like Oliver's gash. Nothing could be as bloody as that.

"How bad is it?" Nicky tried to look over his shoulder.

"Honestly, not too bad, but it must hurt something awful." Stella pressed the towel to the wounds and his shivering got worse. "We have to get him out of these wet clothes."

"Please sit down, Mrs. Myna," said Father Girotti.

Stella sat on the other cot and watched as the priest helped Nicky off with his jacket, tie, and shirt, all completely soaked. She saw Father Girotti noting the bruises and the ribs that stuck out too much. Then he covered Nicky up and turned to her. "You're limping."

"Am I?" she said lightly.

He knelt at her feet. "We must take off these boots."

"I don't think you want to see my feet."

"I'm certain that you are right." He pulled off her boots but had no reaction to the wet and pink-stained bandages. He unwound the fabric and let it fall with a slap on the floor.

"Oh, Stella," said Nicky. "How could you run?"

"I don't know. I just did."

The men were clearly horrified, but Stella wasn't. Her feet had looked worse and she chose to concentrate on that.

Father Girotti put a blanket around her shoulders. "I must get help for you."

"Isn't Dr. Salvatore coming?"

"I believe so, but you need…to get those wet clothes off and I can't."

She patted his hand. "I'm fine, Father. Don't worry about me."

"I sent you to Dr. Davide and he sent you…" His face flushed. "That foul creature. That Maria." He turned on his heels and said, "I will come back with help."

He left and Nicky said, "Are you all right? How much do they hurt?"

Stella wiggled her toes and remembered a time when she was worried they would rot and fall off. "Not that bad. They feel a lot better getting out of those boots."

"Stella, we have to face the facts."

She stiffened. She knew what was coming and it wasn't happening. It just wasn't. They owed Abel. He was in prison. Swollen feet didn't change that. "My feet will be fine. They just need a soaking. That's all."

He tried to roll on his side to face her but couldn't manage it. With a gasp, he went back to his front and stared down at the cot's cotton ticking. "We have to leave as soon as possible. There are ships in the harbor. We can book passage."

"To where?"

"Anywhere. We have to leave."

"I'm not getting on some random ship."

"Then we can take a train to Genoa and book passage on the Italian Line. Straight to New York," said Nicky.

"I'm not leaving before we find the Sorkines," said Stella at her most stubborn.

"Stella."

"No. Abel is in that awful place. I'm sure this is a picnic compared to that."

"I've been shot," said Nicky. "Peiper shot me. It's just luck that he didn't hit me in the head."

"I know that. What do you think will happen to the Sorkines if they go to Vienna and start asking after us? He tried to nab them in Paris and just missed."

"He's after *us*."

"For now, maybe," she said.

"What do you mean?"

"Roger saw the train schedule at their apartment. He figured out they were going to Italy. Maybe Peiper did, too. He's here now."

"Because he thinks we have the book. We should go and lead him away from them."

Stella crossed her arms. "And how do you propose we do that? Hand out flyers at the train station? 'Newsflash! Nicky and Stella have gone to wherever, follow them and leave other people alone.'"

"Don't be ridiculous."

"Same to you," she said. "We have to warn them and hope Peiper doesn't catch their scent."

He tried to sit up and cringed. "We can't. Look at us."

The same feeling Stella had in Vienna came over her again. She had to do it and she didn't care if it made sense. She couldn't see Nicky lying on that bed or her damaged feet. She only saw Abel being pulled into that boxcar. If the Nazis didn't discover who he was and Uncle Josiah got him out safe, what would they tell him? *It was hard, so we didn't do it?* What would she tell her father? Uncle Josiah? What would she tell herself if something happened because she gave up?

"You can go if you want to," she said.

"We're leaving and that's it," he said.

"Before we even try?"

"I tried, Stella. I searched the ghetto. They weren't there."

She wiggled her frigid toes. It might've been her imagination, but they looked better already. "We haven't gone to our old hotel yet."

"You can't walk."

Stella jolted to her feet, ignoring the stabbing pain, and said, "I've been walking. I've been running."

The door opened and Father Girotti hustled in with his arms outstretched. "Are you all right, Mrs. Myna?"

"Never better," she said, pointing at Nicky. "I'm not quitting. Bleds aren't quitters."

Nicky rolled over, grimacing hideously. "You can't be a Bled right now."

"I can't be anything else."

"Be a Lawrence. Be sensible."

"Uncle Josiah says sensible people don't change the world."

"He got arrested for being naked in the Trevi Fountain. I'm not listening to him. What would your father want? What would he want his only daughter to do?"

Stella sat down and the cot practically buckled in protest. "He wouldn't be afraid. Father went to war, too, you know. He was in France with Uncle Josiah," she said, but, in truth, she didn't know what Aleksej Bled would say.

Unlike Uncle Josiah, whose emotions and motives were ever at the surface, her father was inscrutable. As the designated heir to the company, he had defied his father and went to war with his brothers. They could all have been killed. Grandmother had been certain that was what was going to happen. Being in the army meant rules, but they were Bleds and unlikely to play by rules that they themselves had not defined. Grandmother thought at least one would be shot for disobeying orders, but the trio had survived.

Then when prohibition happened, Stella's father broke every law, bootlegging in the Ozarks and running speakeasies, while outwardly appearing to be the very model of conservatism. In contrast, this was also the man who wouldn't let her go to a regular school, fearing she would pick up "bad influences" and insisted her skirts be unfashionably long. But, then again, he let her work in the brewery with men who looked as though they could've spent time in Alcatraz. They hadn't. Perhaps that was the important point to remember.

"Darling, please."

"I don't care." The thought startled Stella. She didn't care what her father would do or want. He wasn't there. Abel wasn't his friend. He wasn't to blame. "I'm going to try. I have to try or I'll always regret it."

"What are you talking of?" asked Father Girotti.

"Our friend's family," she said. "I'm not giving up."

The Father held out his hand to her and helped her to her feet. "I never thought you would. Come into my office. Sister Claudia will help you."

Nicky grabbed her hand as she walked by. "Please, Stella, how could I face your father or worse your mother, if something happened to you? We have a choice this time."

The look on his face made her heart hurt. She hadn't thought of that, of his position. But he was wrong, there was no choice, not for her.

Stella squeezed his hand and said, "I'll think about it."

Nicky dropped her hand and looked away. He knew the truth.

Father Girotti didn't say anything. He just opened the door and ushered her down the hall to his office where they found a middle-aged nun, who'd managed to cram herself in a corner between two bookshelves and looked as though she might make a run for it.

He closed the door and said, "Mrs. Myna, this is Sister Claudia. You can trust her. She knows everything I know. More, perhaps, as she is German."

"Hello, Sister," said Stella.

Sister Claudia didn't answer. She did shake a little.

"The sister is a shy person, but she will help you with your clothes." He indicated a pile of fabric on his desk. "From our donations. I'm sure you can find something to get you back to the Vittoria."

Stella had to smile. Donated clothes for the poor, no doubt. Her mother would faint dead away. "Thank you, Father. I appreciate your help."

Someone knocked on the door and Father Girotti let in Father Giuseppe and Dr. Salvatore, who rushed over to her and made her sit down. "What have you been doing? Not resting, I see."

"It couldn't be helped," said Stella. "They are better."

"They would be better still if you would stop walking."

"I'm not the problem. Ni…Douglas has been shot."

The doctor spun around. "Why didn't you tell me this? Where is he?"

"It's only the buttocks, doctor," said Stella. "When do you think—"

The doctor ran out with the priests and she didn't get to ask when he'd be up and walking. In hindsight, it was a disgraceful question. Nicky had to heal. He'd walk when he was ready.

"Well, Sister, it's you and me," she said to the petrified nun.

She didn't answer so Stella stood up with a wince. The nun put up her hand and whispered, "I'll help you."

"Oh, you speak English. Thank goodness. I've been trying to learn Italian and German, but I can't get a moment to study."

Sister Claudia touched her with one finger and said, "Please sit."

"So you're German?"

"Yes." She peeked at Stella and began looking through the clothes.

"So you know what Father Girotti knows. About the von Bodmanns?"

She held up a skirt that would've fit two Stellas and then some. "Yes."

"Did you know about that family coming in on our train? The ones that Father Giuseppe met?"

"Yes." Another skirt was rejected.

"A German shot my husband."

"Yes."

"But you're helping me and the Jews?"

"Yes." She found a skirt that looked reasonable and offered it to Stella. She got to her feet and, ever so hesitantly, the shy nun helped her unzip her skirt and step out of it. Stella took off her jacket and blouse, but then was undecided. Her brassiere was soaked as well. Putting dry clothes on over it didn't make any sense. She would've asked Sister Claudia about a brassiere, but she was afraid the poor lady would pass out at the word.

"Do you have something I can dry off with?" she asked.

The sister gave her a cloth. "I'm going to take my… off. You might want to look away." She needn't have said anything. Sister Claudia certainly wasn't going to look.

Stella took off her brassiere and panties and squeezed the panties out in the cloth. Since they were silk they'd dry quickly and Stella wasn't quite ready to go without panties.

She put her damp ones back on and got dressed. "Sister?"

"Yes."

"It's very dangerous to defy the Nazis."

"I know this."

Stella finished dressing in a baggy cotton blouse and a sweater with several holes. The skirt hung on her hipbones but stayed up and she'd never felt so warm and grateful. "Thank you. I feel so much better."

The nun nodded and backed away. "I will hang these in my cell to dry. I have a small fire."

"Thank you."

She reached for the angel wing and Stella said, "That SS, he would hurt you to get to me."

The nun looked at the floor. "Yes."

"Why are you helping me then? You don't seem like the kind of person who would."

She backed out of the office, pulled the door to, and whispered through the crack. "It is God's will." The nun closed the door and Stella had the distinct impression that Sister Claudia would never lay eyes on her again, if she could help it.

Stella rooted through the clothes in search of socks. "God's will," she said to herself. "Maybe I should try that with Nicky."

"Mrs. Myna," called out Father Girotti. "May I come in?"

"Yes, of course."

The Father came in and looked her over. "It is not your style, but you are dry."

Stella grinned at him. "Dry is better than style."

"I found this in the lost clothing box." He held up a woolen coat, brown, serviceable, and extremely drab. "No one donates socks, so I brought you a pair of mine."

"Perfect." Stella kissed his cheek. "I think you might be a saint. Sister Claudia, too."

He blushed at her affection and said, "She makes most people nervous."

"Why? She's perfectly lovely."

The priest smiled the biggest smile at her. "You can see that? Most can't. She's so nervous and shy."

"She's helping us. I'm hardly going to criticize, but I'd like to know why she's doing it," said Stella. "She was rather terrified of me."

"Sister Claudia is rather terrified of everyone," he said.

"But not the Nazis?"

"She's especially terrified of them and she has good reason."

Stella tried on the coat, big but not bad. "Why? Has she got a price on her head?"

"As a matter of fact, she does."

Stella gaped at him. "That little nun? What could she possibly have done?"

"There was a man, a social democrat. He was printing an anti-fascist newspaper and they came to arrest him so he ran. Sister Claudia hid him at her convent. Word got out and she helped several people to escape, arranging for false papers and lying to officials. The bishop found out what she was doing and ordered her out of Germany just ahead of an arrest warrant."

"They put a bounty on her for that?"

"She went back."

"To do what?"

"She heard that a dear friend and her husband were to be arrested. She went to take the children away to safety."

"Jews?"

137

"Communists."

"Did she get the children?" asked Stella, her mouth going dry.

He smiled. "Yes and the bishop wasn't a happy man. She dressed as a Benedictine nun and smuggled her friend out as a fellow sister and the children as orphans going to Assisi."

"The husband?"

"He died during what the Nazis called questioning. Once they realized who it was that had robbed them of their other prize, Sister Claudia got a price on her head. She will never go home again," he said softly.

"Are you sure about that?" asked Stella.

"She knows it would be madness. You see, she has false papers, too."

"We're all a bit mad, don't you think?"

He took her face in his hands and kissed her forehead. "Some more than others, I think."

# CHAPTER 9

*N*icky lay on the cot, eyes closed with two bandages on his buttocks. He looked for all the world like he was having a nice rest, but, for a moment, Stella feared he'd died, he was so relaxed.

"Ah, Mrs. Myna," said Dr. Salvatore and Nicky's eyes fluttered. "You're looking…warmer."

"I am and my feet are feeling better, too," she said, although it wasn't strictly true. They were nice and cozy in Father Girotti's socks and that *was* better, in a sense.

"Sit down and I will see," said the doctor.

"How's Douglas?"

"Douglas is fine," said Nicky. "Just a flesh wound."

"Really? That's a relief," said Stella.

"Is it? I had the impression you didn't care whether it was serious or not."

"Of course, I care."

"But it changes nothing," he said.

"Well…" Stella was struck with the worse déjà vous ever. But then she remembered. It wasn't déjà vous. It was reality. Her parents had the same conversation about one of the brewery's scheduled new releases and her mother's birthday party. "It changes everything."

"You don't say?"

"I do say," said Stella, determined that she was not her father and, more importantly, Nicky was not her long-suffering mother.

"Good," said Nicky. "Are we done, doc?"

"We are," said Dr. Salvatore. "There will be much swelling and pain, but I believe you will heal quickly."

"So did you...dig the bullets out?" asked Stella.

"Out of what?" asked Nicky.

She waved at his rear. "Your bottom."

The doctor chuckled. "He's got a blighty wound."

Nicky rolled over and sat up. He wavered, clutching onto the cot for support. "That stuff you gave me is something else. What's a blighty?"

"It's a British phrase my father taught me. It means you get to leave the trenches and go home."

Nicky looked at Stella and she did her best not to set her teeth and look as stubborn as she felt.

"So I'm good to walk." He tried to stand and failed. Stella rushed over and insisted he lie back down. Nicky agreed, giving her a loopy smile.

"I thought he was fine?" she asked.

"He is. I gave him the last of my Eukadol. I'm afraid you'll have to do without, Mrs. Myna."

"I don't need it." Stella looked at Father Girotti. "Can he borrow some clothes from the donations, too?"

"Of course." He went out and returned with a stack of clothes and Sister Claudia, who quickly set down a basin of hot water and rushed out.

"Was it something I said?" asked Nicky.

"No," said Stella. "That's how she is."

"Poor little nun."

"She's more than that," said Stella softly.

"Yes, she is," said Father Girotti. "And she brought me some news. When will Douglas be able to walk, Dr. Salvatore?"

"Now, if he's careful. There was quite a bit of blood loss and, with the Eukadol, he'll be woozy." He looked at Stella. "I recommend he stay in bed for a minimum of three days."

"I want to be on a train tomorrow," said Nicky.

The doctor shook his head. "It will be much too painful. I'm afraid you're stuck in Venice."

"I'm not stuck I'm…" Nicky trailed off mid-sentence and went to sleep.

"What's your news?" asked Stella.

"Are you Irish?"

She frowned. That was a question she'd never been asked before. "No. Why?"

"I thought maybe you have the luck of the Irish."

Stella raised an eyebrow and Dr. Salvatore put her on the other cot to soak her feet. "I'm lucky? I hadn't noticed."

"Your SS officer has been arrested."

She clasped her hands together like a child waiting at a merry-go-round. "Are you sure?"

"Is he a thin brunet, medium height, wearing a black uniform with the skull and crossbones?"

"Sounds about right."

"He was arrested on multiple charges after the citizens of our ancient islands captured him."

The Father laughed and told her the story that had come to the nuns. News traveled fast in Venice and the sisters, while being very devout, were the tiniest bit gossipy and liked to hear the latest. A washerwoman had come directly to tell them about a German officer gone wild, stealing boats and crashing them into water taxis, firing a gun randomly, and frightening everyone half to death. Several men spotted Peiper, in his distinctive uniform, leaving the church court-yard. They threw oars at him, knocking him down and grabbing his weapon. When they found out just how many boats Peiper wrecked, he may have been kicked repeatedly. Venetians took boats very seriously.

"What about us?" asked Stella before biting her lip.

"No one saw Douglas get hit. They didn't mention either of you."

"Well, we stole the first water taxi and Douglas beat up the captain. He's sure to report it."

"I'm sure he will, but the officer is getting blamed for his water taxi being destroyed and the rest of the damage."

"Someone else must've seen us at the train station and what started it. Maria, for one, was there," she said. "She signaled to Peiper when she saw him."

The men exchanged a look that was both dark and a touch relieved.

"What?" she asked.

"You understand that we've been assisting people who want to leave Germany and Austria?"

"Yes, of course. So?"

"So some of those people aren't coming with proper papers," said Dr. Salvatore.

"I know. That's why we came to you."

"Some are considered criminals by the Reich," said Father Girotti.

"What's that got to do with Maria?" she asked.

It had a lot to do with Maria. Some of the people Father Girotti and the Jewish community were helping made it to Venice, but no farther. They were unexpectedly arrested and sent back to Germany. No one knew why those people were found out and others weren't.

"Did you see her at the platform on the day you arrived?" asked Dr. Salvatore.

"No, but it was pouring and I wasn't looking." She inhaled sharply. "The Goldenbergs. Bartali knows about them. Have they been arrested?"

"No, no. We sent them to Rome yesterday, but they may have been arrested there," said Father Girotti.

"Will you find out?"

"Eventually."

"Why did they have to get fake papers anyway?" asked Stella. "The Nazis hate them. Why don't they just let them leave?"

Dr. Salvatore lifted Stella's foot out of the water and looked closely at the toes. Stella suspected it was so he didn't have to look her in the eyes. He said nothing and after a moment, Father Girotti said softly, "It is not a question of leaving as much as where to go. They must have permission to come here or any other country."

"It is becoming increasingly difficult," said Dr. Salvatore.

Stella remembered Nicky saying that the United States wasn't taking Jews, but, frankly, she had been more concerned about Abel at that moment. Nicky could worry about the whole situation. He could think about the politics and policies. She could only think about the individuals that she knew, the faces she couldn't forget. The Goldenbergs were in that number now.

"Will they arrest them for being Jewish, like in Vienna, or just for the papers?" she asked.

"The papers are the excuse. Being Jewish is the reason," said Father Girotti.

"If they want to go to the States, maybe my family can help."

"Your family? Do they have influence?"

Nicky's eyes flew open. "No, no. We don't, but we can write our congressman and ask questions."

"Yes…we'll write. Maybe we can sponsor them. That helps, doesn't it?" said Stella quickly.

Neither man reacted to their odd interaction. Father Girotti had seen their passports. He had probably connected them to Bled Brewing, but he said nothing. The doctor didn't know their real names and Stella meant to keep it that way, for his sake as well as theirs.

"Don't concern yourself at this moment, Mrs. Myna. Until we know how the Goldenbergs are, there is nothing to do." Dr. Salvatore looked up at her, his intelligence shining through and telling her she had nothing to fear from him.

"I'm sure they made it fine." Nicky tossed off the blanket and struggled to sit up with Father Girotti's help. "We should go."

"A few more minutes," said Dr. Salvatore.

"Eulalie can do another soak back at the hotel," said Nicky. "Presumably, Dr. Davide is still coming to see her."

"You're forgetting something," said Father Girotti.

"I don't think so."

"Your passports."

Nicky slapped his forehead. "I completely forgot."

"Getting shot is a pretty good excuse," said Stella.

"Not in our present situation."

No one remarked on the "present situation" and Dr. Salvatore examined Stella's other foot. Father Girotti excused himself and Stella asked, "What are you going to do about Maria?"

"Do about her?"

"She's ratting on your people. Probably for cash."

"I believe so."

"Then you have to do something."

Dr. Salvatore looked back questioningly at Nicky, who smiled wanly, and Stella realized how very pale he was.

"My wife is always very keen to do something," he said.

"There is nothing to do," said the doctor, placing Stella's foot back in the water.

"She's a thief. Isn't that against the law?" asked Stella.

"Maria is many things, most of them illegal. The law isn't concerned with her."

Stella crossed her arms and Nicky gave her a warning look, but she didn't care. That woman had turned them in to the SS and for what? A few lousy lira. There had to be a way to punish her, a quick trip into a canal, at the very least.

"Darling?" asked Nicky. "What are you thinking?"

"I want to hurt her," said Stella.

"You already have."

"Have you?" asked Dr. Salvatore.

Stella drummed her fingers on the cot. "No. She's not in jail and she still has her front teeth."

The men chuckled and Dr. Salvatore said, "I think Maria has made an enemy for life."

"And she'll pay for it," said Nicky. "More than she already has."

"How has she paid for it?" demanded Stella. "How?"

"You stole her case."

Father Girotti came in with a stack of clothing under his arm. "You stole something, Mrs. Myna? This must be the first time." His eyes twinkled at her and she tilted down her chin, fluttering her eyes innocently. "Of course, Father."

"What did you take?" asked Dr. Salvatore as he stood up and stretched his back.

Stella scanned the room and saw the case next to the door, where she must've dropped it. She didn't remember that. She only remembered seeing Nicky's bloody pants and the fear that went through her. "There it is. Maria grabbed…Douglas's wallet and I took her case. She deserved it."

Father Girotti laid down the clothes next to Nicky and said, "Maria's case?" He exchanged a look with the doctor. "Perhaps it can help us."

"I don't think so," said Stella. "It's just her collection of tacky crosses and rosaries."

Dr. Salvatore got the case and opened it next to Stella. "They might be useful for us as well as you." He went through the case, pulling out more than just religious items. She had simple jewelry, such as earrings and some cheap rings. He lifted up the bottom of the case and smiled at Stella.

"What?" she asked, leaning over to see what he'd discovered.

He held up a small black ledger.

Nicky grinned. "Her account book. That could be extremely useful."

Stella didn't see how. So she kept track of her sales. Maria was a businesswoman, of a sort, and accounts were necessary. "So we can find out how many of," she held up a particularly garish cross, "these she sold. So what?"

Dr. Salvatore leafed through the book. He was smiling and trying very hard not to. "You are right, Mr. Myna. This will help us, if only we are willing to use it."

Stella snatched the book out of his hands. "I'm willing. Let me see." She opened the book and found as she suspected, rows of numbers, some addition, some subtraction. Her rudimentary Italian revealed that Maria was rather meticulous. She noted everything, bread, coffees, and the occasional chocolate.

"Please do not look at that," said Dr. Salvatore, his gentle voice tense, and he tried to take it back.

"Hold on now." Stella shifted it out of his reach. "What's so secret?"

"Don't worry yourself, darling," said Nicky as he examined a pair of pants.

"The last time you said that Vienna was about to be set ablaze, so, if you don't mind, I will worry."

Father Girotti helped Nicky get dressed and Stella thumbed through the book. Numbers, numbers, addresses. Numbers, numbers, names. Initials, men presumably. On the third time through, she saw it. Just a small entry, what appeared to be a date, a V with a number and a time, 6:48. Across from that were little hashmarks, one crooked, two straight, and three small ones.

Stella looked closer. There were more of these peculiar entries, but not many. None were exactly the same, but they had the same format and below them was another number with a plus, which seemed to correspond to the number of hashmarks. Two hashmarks equaled seventy-five. Four was 150 and so forth. But there wasn't always a number underneath.

"I've got it," she announced, but none of the men were pleased. They were flustered and didn't seem to know what to do with their hands. "What's wrong with you? I said I've got it. What was our train number?"

Nicky slipped on a jacket with holes in the elbows and refused to look up. "What was that?"

"Our train. What was the number?"

"Oh, um...2491." He looked up finally. "Why?"

Stella checked the ledger. Their train wasn't listed, but fifteen days before P2701 was listed with two crooked hashmarks and below it seventy-five. "Father did you have someone come to you about two weeks ago. Two people on train 2701?"

The priest stopped fussing over Nicky's jacket and froze. "Yes. How did you know this?"

"It's in the book and I think Maria got paid seventy-five lira for them. Were they arrested?" she asked.

He sat next to her and she showed him the entries. Then the priest stood up and walked across the room. His face changed completely, losing all its humanity and becoming dark to the point of ugliness. Nicky, for his part, looked relieved. That is, until he saw Father Girotti's face. "They were arrested then."

"Yes. Almost immediately," said Dr. Salvatore, who was packing up his bag and keeping his head down.

"What will happen to them?" asked Stella.

"They were sent back to Germany. They left without paying the tax that had been levied on them," said Father Girotti. "They will have to pay or be left in prison to rot."

"How much will it be?" asked Nicky.

"Everything they have, in every bank account they have."

The word "everything" echoed in Stella's ears and she looked back at the book. Maria turned in some people, but others got away. Maria was very orderly. She had a schedule. Sometimes she was at the station and sometimes she wasn't. But what about the lack of lira on some entries?

She looked through and found one of those. "How about the same train in August? Looks like a lot of people. Six."

Father Girotti shook his head. "No. I don't think so. Doctor?"

"The Strauss family came," he said. "But they had the proper papers. They have gone to Naples now."

"That's it. That's why Maria didn't get paid," said Stella, pointing at the page. "Sometimes she has an entry, but there's no number underneath."

Nicky plucked the book out of Stella's hands. "Very good. You've cracked it."

"Hey." Stella jolted to her feet. "Give that back. I'm not done."

"You're done, darling. You did it."

The way he said it rankled. Like she was a little girl who'd won a prize and ought to be satisfied with a sweet.

"Give that back. There's a pattern."

He tried to push her back, but she wouldn't go. "Please, your feet."

"My feet are better than your butt. Give it to me." She stepped out of the water, Nicky turned to keep the book away from her, and gasped in pain.

"Mr. Myna, please," said Father Girotti. "Your injury."

Nicky bent over, pressing his hand to his wound, and Stella easily recaptured Maria's book. "Serves you right."

"For God's sake, Stella. I'm trying to protect you."

A zing went through her and she shouted, "Then try remembering my name."

Nicky's eyes went wide for a second and then his mask came firmly down. "I know your name, Eulalie."

Father Girotti smiled at his feet and Dr. Salvatore flushed with embarrassment at Nicky's lapse.

"Oh, really. I'm terribly impressed that you remember it now," said Stella. "You didn't marry her. You married me."

"I know that."

"Good." She started to tuck the little book in her handbag, but Nicky stopped her.

"What are you doing?" asked the priest.

"I'm going to figure out Maria's schedule, Father, and when I do, you can have your people avoid her. Easy as pie."

"You can do that?" asked the doctor.

"I learned schedules from my father. There are patterns to people. I had to learn how to schedule workers at the right times. If someone was sick, it changed. If equipment was being installed, it changed. Maria isn't always at the station. She does other things."

The men looked nervously at the floor.

"Why do you insist that I'm completely ignorant of the world?" Stella stomped her foot and pain rocketed up her leg, making her leg buckle. Dr. Salvatore grabbed her and lowered her back to the cot. "You must be more careful."

"You must stop looking at me like I'm a child. I understand what Maria is."

He flushed to the tips of his ears as he smeared her feet with thick honey and then bandaged them, rolling the socks up over what looked like man-sized feet when he got done. None of them would say anything and Nicky refused to sit down. "We have to go and we're not taking that book."

"You don't think I can figure out her pattern," said Stella. "You have no faith in me."

"I do, but it's evidence of what happened today. If Bartali gets ahold—"

"He won't."

Father Girotti held out his hand. "He might arrest you or search your room. Please give it to me."

Stella reluctantly handed it over. "Will you look for a pattern?"

"I'll try."

She quickly explained how she'd do it with a chart noting days, times, trains, and number of first-class carriages.

"Surely first class isn't important."

"It is. Dr. Davide said she liked when there were multiple first-class carriages," said Stella. "That's her target for...you know."

The men made faces and Nicky said, "You don't know anything about...what she does."

"I know she's pretty and has the right kind of clothes. Maybe she wouldn't fit in in first class, but she's not far off."

Father Girotti shook his head. "She's not that kind of person at all. I would think third class. We should look at trains with mostly those cars."

Stella laughed. "Forget that. Maria is pretty and well-dressed in a hussy sort of way. If she worked in a bakery, you'd think she was pretty."

The men harrumphed and agreed at long last and, once that was done, Stella started in on things like Maria's rent and when that had to be paid.

"I believe her sister may be—"

A soft knock stopped the priest and he opened the door to find young Jacopo standing there, shifting from foot to foot with his eyes darting around.

"Ah, Jacopo," said Father Girotti, shaking the boy's hand.

Jacopo gave him a small packet and an Italian songbook. Then, without a word, the boy darted off. The priest closed the door and opened the packet. He handed Nicky two well-worn Canadian passports and held up their red US passports. "Would you like me to keep these for the moment?"

"I'll take them, Father," said Nicky.

"No," said Stella. "They're safer here. We might get searched. And keep the songbook. You never know, I might want to buy it again."

Nicky hesitated but agreed. He looked through the Canadian passports and smiled. "These are very good. I'd never know they aren't real. How does Alberto do it?"

"He was a master bookbinder in addition to owning his bookshop. Paper was his business," said Dr. Salvatore.

"What about the stamp on the photos? You'd never know it wasn't original."

The doctor glanced at the passports. "I believe he made his own stamp. He carved it out of rubber."

"He's a genius."

"I agree, but now we must get you back to the hotel and into bed."

Nicky limped toward the door, barely moving his right leg.

"People are going to notice that," said Stella.

"What?" he asked.

"Your limp. It must hurt terribly."

Nicky frowned and looked down. "Actually, it doesn't. It's stiff and aches, but mostly I'm tired and lightheaded."

"When the Eukadol wears off, you will be in very much pain," said Dr. Salvatore. "That is why you should go now."

"Wait," said Father Girotti. "You should know I sent a message to Dr. Davide."

"What on Earth for?" asked Nicky. "I hope you didn't tell him where we are."

The priest's face was still thunderous. "I reminded him what he owes me and the church."

"And what is that?" asked Stella. "It better be good."

"He owes me his life."

"No insult intended, Father," said Nicky, "but I don't think he's that fond of his life."

"Yes, but he didn't want it to end," he said.

Stella crossed her arms. "He sent us to Maria. He's probably in on it."

Father Girotti shook his head. "Davide's sins are many, but that is not one of them."

"You'd be in a position to know?" asked Nicky.

"I would, but I will say no more."

"I still don't trust him."

Stella retrieved her boots from where they'd been tossed in a corner. "It's good enough for me." Stella slipped on her damp boots and smiled. Not too bad. Not bad at all. She could search Venice on her own. Three days in bed for Nicky should be enough time.

"I don't like that smile," said Nicky.

"You should," she said. "My feet feel good."

"I seriously doubt that."

"Doubt all you want. It's the truth." She turned to Father Girotti. "So what do you expect Dr. Davide to do?"

"I expect him to do what his wife would want."

"He's married?" asked Nicky, clearly aghast.

"He was. The lady passed away some time ago. Her death broke him in every way possible. He remains in Venice, her favorite city and where she died, as penance for not being able to save her." The priest went to Maria's case and riffled through the contents. "Ah, yes. This one will do." He held up the crucifix Stella had initially chosen, but it seemed uglier and more garish in the humble room. And worse, it was very obviously something that Maria would sell.

"I don't think so, Father," she said. "Someone might recognize it."

The doctor nodded. "I agree and it does not suit you either. Let me see."

He took the cross and chain, examining the filigree and stones before asking, "Do you mind if I change it?"

"Not at all. Please do," she said and the doctor went to work, using the tools of his trade pulled out of the depths of his doctor's bag. He used a pair of scissors to nip off the filigreed edges and a stout needle to pry out the red stones. They went flying around the room and skittered across the stone floor to be lost in the cracks. Then he used a rather frightening pair of pliers to cut the cross down to a smaller size. Stella didn't want to think about what that tool might be used for on a human being.

"How do you like it now?" he asked with a pleased smile.

Stella took it. "It's almost elegant and, more importantly, nothing like the way it was before." She kissed his cheek. "Thank you. What do you think about the rosaries? They are nice, but are they too distinctive?"

Father Girotti reached in his pocket and came out with a plain, simple rosary of wooden beads and a rough cross. "Take this with my blessing. It is common enough not to be noticed."

Stella took it and pressed it to her chest where Abel's book had once been. "I don't know why you are so kind to us."

"It is my duty and my privilege. I may need to ask a favor of you someday."

"Please do, Father," said Nicky. "There's no way we'd refuse."

"You may come to regret that statement."

"Maybe, but that won't change it."

Father Girotti smiled and nodded as a gentle knock sounded on the door. He opened it and the altar boy, Pietro, stood there with a big smile on his round, happy face. He had a load in his arms. "I have a letter from Dr. Davide, Father Girotti."

"And our coats," said Stella, rushing over to unburden the boy. "Thank you." She kissed Pietro on the forehead.

"I still say that doctor is a nasty piece of work, but I'm happy your note worked." Nicky put on his coat, covering up his ragged clothes and donned his now battered fedora, pulling it low to conceal his hair.

Stella put on her fur and asked, "So what does the note say, Father?"

Father Girotti frowned and appeared to read Dr. Davide's message twice.

"Does he apologize for sending us to Maria?" asked Nicky.

"Or for taking our coats?"

"It is not in Dr. Davide's nature to apologize directly, but he has a suggestion."

"I hope he's suggested to himself that he jump in a canal headfirst."

The priest folded the letter and put it in his pocket. "Dr. Davide only jumps headfirst into a bottle."

"Let's have it then."

Like Dr. Davide's suggestion about Stella having a cross, this new idea had merit. Unfortunately, it depended heavily on him and they were not inclined to trust the doctor. He thought that Nicky must hide his wound at all costs and claim that he had an illness that would keep others at bay while he healed.

"And what illness am I supposed to have?" asked Nicky.

"Cholera."

Stella's mouth fell open as did Nicky's. Dr. Salvatore's did not. He nodded and agreed. "Yes, that will be the best solution and could be true, considering the flood."

"What's the flood got to do with it?" asked Nicky.

"Our water supply, our sanitation is affected. You could easily become ill, if you drink the wrong water."

Nicky buttoned his coat. "One more reason to leave immediately."

"There have been no reports of illnesses," said Dr. Salvatore quickly. "I believe you are safe."

"But you think people will buy that I have cholera? Come on, doc." Nicky spread his arms. "Do I look ill?"

The men stayed silent and Stella had to be the one to say, "You've looked better."

"Well, I was shot."

"And we have to cover it up. You are very pale and…" she trailed off.

"What, Eulalie? Say it."

"Frail-looking. You were thin but getting better. Now you're back to gaunt."

He turned to Father Girotti. "Do I look that bad?"

"You do not look like a well man. People will ask questions. Dr. Davide is correct. You need a reason that is not a gunshot to keep people away."

"But I tell you it hardly hurts."

"It will and soon."

Nicky looked at Stella and she said, "I think you have cholera."

"But it's crazy. No one gets cholera anymore," he said.

The doctor raised his hands. "No, no. It happens. We had many deaths in 1911."

"That was a lifetime ago before the war. And what happens when I don't die?"

The doctor chuckled. "You don't have to die. Dr. Davide will give you injections."

"Wait. What?" Nicky went paler still. "One injection was quite enough."

The men went back and forth about cholera, but Stella couldn't see what the fuss was about. It was a good idea and a few pretend punctures seemed a small price to pay for their safety. Nicky wasn't happy with his symptoms though. Diarrhea and vomiting wasn't dignified. Nobody claimed it was, but it did give him an excellent excuse to not walk normally.

"Oh, for heaven's sake." Stella put on her cross and tucked it under her bulky sweater. She was beginning to like the rough wool. She'd been cold so often and for so long, the coziness was lovely, even if it came with a hint of wet dog and holes. "You have cholera. Let's go before you can't walk. I'm not going to be carrying you on these feet."

"What about the flu?" asked Nicky.

"That comes with diarrhea as well," said Dr. Salvatore.

"What doesn't?"

"Syphilis."

"Doctor, please be serious," said Nicky as Stella stifled a yawn.

"I'm seriously tired. Please, Douglas. Let's go."

Nicky set his jaw. How anyone that attractive could resemble Winston Churchill in any way was beyond her comprehension. "There has to be another way or maybe we get on a train right now."

"You can't and I won't," she said.

"Please."

"No. I'm not leaving my books or my pin. Honestly, you're worse than Millicent when it's time for her bath."

The Winston look got worse. "I don't like it."

"You don't have to, but you've been through worse or so I suspect," said Stella with a warning in her eye.

That got Nicky moving. Dr. Salvatore left and Father Girotti tucked Maria's box away under one of the cots. "You are ready?"

Nicky winced as he took a step. "I have to be. Darling?"

"I'm fine." Stella hooked Nicky's arm over her shoulder and he surprised her by consenting to lean on her. They went through the hallways, seeing no one but Sister Claudia, who smiled shyly at them before ducking her head and giving her a bundle of her clothes. That woman was brave as brave could be. Seeing her, Stella knew she could do it. She could be brave like Sister Claudia or Uncle Josiah without the crazy.

They left from a side door right on the canal and found a small boat there waiting in the never-ending rain.

"When will this stop?" asked Nicky as he straightened up, attempting to walk normally for the benefit of any onlookers. The grimace on his face showed how much it cost him.

"*Domani*," said Father Girotti.

"I'm starting to think that means never." Nicky stepped on the boat with the help of the captain, a man Father Girotti called his dear friend.

"Father?" asked Stella, squinting in the rain.

"Yes?"

"How long will the SS be in jail?"

"That is hard to say. The people are very angry, but our carabinieri have many obligations."

"I see." When Nicky was inside the cabin and well out of hearing range, she said, "There's something else you should know, Father."

"I fear what you are going to tell me."

155

"I don't know if you should or not," said Stella. "The SS officer. He wasn't alone. He had a boy with him."

The priest's face grew dark again. "He brought a child on his hunt for you? What kind of man is he?"

"The worst kind, but, Father, this boy, he wasn't just a bystander. He chased us at the station with a gun. You need to be wary." She described the boy as best she could and Father Girotti nodded grimly and helped her into the boat.

"He is not a child then, this boy," said the priest, pressing her hand between his. "You believe he is one of them."

"I saw his face, Father. He is someone to fear."

# CHAPTER 10

The boat puttered down the narrow canal around the submerged boat below Stella and Nicky's window to the Vittoria's small dock. It only took a mere ten minutes to get there, but Nicky was already in more pain. He insisted on standing and clung to the edge of a shelf in the cabin, occasionally spasming and gritting his teeth. Stella tried to support him, but he wouldn't have it. All he would say was, "We're leaving."

Stella kept nodding and agreeing, but her handsome husband wasn't fooled. Between spasms, he eyed her, looking for dissent, but she was careful to keep her eyes wide and worried when she was thinking about how soon she could get out and find their old hotel. Maybe the carabinieri would keep Peiper in jail overnight or even a couple of days before the Reich intervened. Even if they didn't, Stella felt sure she could get around Venice more easily on her own. She was small and unobtrusive. Nicky made every room seem smaller, just by being in it.

The captain eased the boat up to the pylons and looped a rope around one. He leaned over and waved them out of the cabin.

"We're here," she said, wrapping his arm over her shoulders and holding him by the waist. "Just take it slow."

"Let go," he got out between clenched teeth. "I can do it."

"You've got cholera so you can't."

"I don't like it."

"Do you have a better idea?"

He spasmed in response.

"I thought not. Besides, Dr. Davide is going to come here, saying you have cholera and we have to play along."

"Re…dic…u…lous."

She maneuvered him out the door and the captain took over, manhandling Nicky over to the dock. They were happily sheltered from the rain by a wide overhang, but the canal water was high and washing up against the door up a good four inches.

"Oh, no. They've really flooded now."

The captain grinned at her, showing all his gapped teeth, and letting out a litany of Italian that Stella couldn't begin to follow. He rattled the doorknob and banged on the door. Then he grinned again, holding his large, rough hand out in the rain.

"*Domani?*" asked Stella.

He belly-laughed and clapped her on the back, swinging Nicky around wildly. "*Sì, sì. Domani.*"

"I think I'm going to throw up," whispered Nicky.

The captain saw his face turn grey and pounded on the door until a little window halfway up opened and a brown eye peered out at them.

"It's the Mynas! Let us in!" yelled Stella and the door shuddered and clanked.

Sofia pulled opened the door while standing in a pool of water. It turned out the hotel was a couple steps up and still dry. "Come in. Come in."

The captain half-dragged half-carried Nicky in and up the stairs before tipping his hat to Stella and heading back out the door into the deluge. Stella grabbed Nicky before his legs buckled and Sofia slammed the door, locking it with a heavy brass key.

"What has happened, Mrs. Myna? Your bambino? Is he okay?"

"Huh?"

Sofia raised an eyebrow.

"Oh, yes. That's fine. False alarm. But Douglas, he's very sick."

Nicky doubled over on cue. Just when Stella thought he was playing his part rather well, he vomited all over the floor.

"Good God, man," cried out Randolph, who'd turned the corner with Dolores. She clapped her hand over her mouth, spun around, and ran away. From the sound of it, she didn't get far before she followed suit.

"Dolores!" Randolph ran after her and Sofia stood there with her arms up, mouth open with shock.

"I'm sorry," muttered Nicky. "I have to lie down."

Sofia yelled for Antonio and sprang into action, hopping over the spreading pool and grabbing Nicky's flailing arm to support him before he collapsed. Antonio ran down the hall and stopped short.

"Can you get a bucket?" asked Stella. "I'll clean it up."

"No. No," said Sofia. "Antonio, help Mr. Myna."

Antonio took Nicky's arm and put it over his shoulder.

"I will send for Dr. Davide," said Sofia.

"Already here," growled Dr. Davide as he came sauntering down the hall, cleaned up and almost respectable in a worn-out grey suit and tie. "Now you've done it, Mr. Myna."

"Done what?" gasped Nicky.

"What tap did you drink from?"

They stared at the doctor and Stella couldn't think. The vomit stank and Nicky was growing heavier by the second.

"The tap. Where'd he drink the water from?" asked Dr. Davide. "I have to report it to the *polizia*."

"Oh. I…"

"Was it the one on the square by the church? It says non-potable. Can't you read?"

Stella met the doctor's stern eyes and his bushy brows shot up. "Yes, doctor. I think that's the one."

"Alright. Bring him to your room," he said, loudly. "This will mean an injection or two."

Randolph came down the other hall supporting the flushed Dolores. "What's wrong with him, doctor?"

"Bacteria. Possibly cholera or something like it."

"Cholera!"

Randolph looked ready to dump Dolores and run for it. Stella wanted to kick him, the coward.

"Don't panic. Unless you plan on drinking from that fountain, you'll be fine."

"We should move hotels though," said Randolph and Stella could see him calculating how fast they could escape.

"Suit yourself, but it's not catching," said Dr. Davide.

"You don't know," said Dolores.

The doctor turned on her, surprisingly fast for a bulky man in a tight suit. "As a matter a fact, ma'am, I do. Are you a medical doctor?"

"No, sir," said Dolores, meekly.

"Then quiet down and go back to your room. I'll see you shortly."

A happy smile flitted across her face at the prospect and Stella rolled her eyes. Who wanted to see a doctor? The woman was an odd duck. Stella could never see another doctor and be happy about it. Doctors meant poking, prodding, and pain. There were no two ways about that.

But, obviously, the Hutchinses didn't see it that way. They headed off while discussing temperatures and possible infection with something close to glee.

"Alright, Mr. Myna, let's get you in bed." Dr. Davide gave Stella his bag. Then he took over for her, supporting Nicky and quickly getting him around the vomit. Stella stood there for a moment, slowly realizing her heart was racing. She was practically panting.

Sofia took her arm. "Mrs. Myna, what happened?"

"He drank that water. We thought it was okay. I didn't see the sign until it was too late." She felt a twinge of guilt for lying to Sofia, who'd been so kind, but the less she knew the better.

"Did you have it?"

Stella shook her head. "I wasn't thirsty. But…" She got woozy and Sofia hooked her arm around Stella's waist.

"Let's get you to your room." She called out to Matteo who wandered into the hall and gave him several orders in Italian to which the boy was clearly horrified, but Sofia was having none of it. "He'll see to the mess."

"I'm so sorry."

"This happens when traveling."

"I never want to travel again then."

Sofia smiled and they came to the desk just as the double doors banged open and a large man, at least six feet, came barging in, carrying two suitcases and a briefcase. "Hello there," he called out in a British accent and the broad smile under his walrus mustache fell off his face. "No room at the inn?"

Sofia shook off her surprise. "Yes, sir. Have you a reservation?"

"I do. I do. I'm Mr. Leonard Bast, lately of London." He pushed a pair of small, round glasses up his reddish nose.

"You are two weeks, yes?"

"Unless this bloody awful rain keeps up," he said smiling cheerfully and showing off crooked, tobacco-stained teeth.

"It is said to stop tomorrow," said Sofia.

"Always *domani* in Italy." He chuckled and set down his bags with a thump. A small green one popped open and a typewriter fell out in a clanking heap. He muttered an obscenity and hurried to pack it back up.

"Mr. Bast, I must take Mrs. Myna to her room," said Sofia. "I will come back in a moment."

"Something wrong?" He squinted up at Stella and she got the funniest feeling looking down at him. Although everything about the man said jolly and merely inquisitive, there was a sharpness in his brown eyes that told her that he missed nothing.

"My husband is ill," said Stella. "Bad water."

"That happens, especially during a flood."

Sofia excused them and they edged past Mr. Bast and his bags. When they passed the von Bodmann room, Karolina poked her head out. "Is Bartali back?"

"No," said Sofia. "Do not worry."

Karolina's eyes softened. "Good. Rosa isn't well at all today."

"Dr. Davide is here. I will send him to her."

"Karolina!" called out Rosa.

Karolina glanced back and assured her sister before focusing on Stella. "Are you well? I hope the doctor isn't here about your feet."

"No. My husband is ill. Bad water."

"He didn't drink from one of those fountains, did he? They aren't sanitary. He could even contract a terrible illness." She lowered her voice. "Cholera is spread through water and with the flooding..."

"Yes," said Stella. "We know. But I'm sure he'll be fine. So who came?"

"Bartali the carabinieri. You would think he had something better to do," said Karolina.

Stella had completely forgotten about Bartali and did her best to look surprised, but she could tell that Sofia felt her tension. The lady quickly excused them after saying once again that she would send Dr. Davide to Rosa.

They went down the hall arms around each other and Stella was glad for the support.

"What did he say when we weren't here?" she whispered.

"He was angry, but I told him that you were ill and went to Dr. Davide."

"Did he believe you?"

Sofia shrugged. "One cannot tell with the carabinieri."

"He'll be back then."

"Maybe no. I must tell you that he went in your room."

Stella stopped walking, her mind wildly going through what had been in their room. Makeup case, her hat and Grandmother's pin. Her medicines, dictionaries, and *The Hobbit. The Hobbit,* Cyril's gift to her. Was her real name in it? No. She knew it wasn't, but the fear running through her made her question what she knew. But Gabriele's gun was under the mattress. If he found it...

"He...he can't do that. How can he do that?"

"He said that he thought you were Jews."

"So what if we were? That doesn't mean he can barge in and ransack the place."

"What is this 'ransack'?" asked Sofia.

"It means tear the place apart," said Stella.

Sofia shook her head. "I did not let him do this. But he went through your books and your cosmetics."

Stella's cheeks got hot. She never felt so invaded, so disrespected since the time Mother read her diary. It was the fake diary she kept in case Mother got nosy, but still it was an invasion.

"He can, if he wants to." Sofia urged her along. "It does not matter. He found nothing. You have nothing."

"That's suspicious though, isn't it?" asked Stella, picturing the carabinieri putting his grubby hands all over her things, and shivered with the very idea.

"He is suspicious, but you are fine now. You saw Father Girotti? Karolina said you asked her about him."

"We did. Everything's fine."

They arrived at the room and Stella opened it slowly so Nicky had time to cover up, but she needn't have bothered. He was already undressed and in bed with a thermometer in his mouth, looking grey and queasy. Dr. Davide looked up from rooting around his bag to say, "You two take the cake."

"I'll leave you now." Sofia hastily left and Stella marched across the room, mindless of the burning in her feet, and slapped the doctor across the face. "We take the cake? *We* take the cake?"

Dr. Davide stepped back, holding up his hands, and his bag fell off the chair. "What the hell do you think you're doing, you crazy broad?"

She slapped him again. Fast and without thinking. Uncle Josiah never taught her that, but she knew he'd bust with pride at the doctor's flaming cheek. "We could've been killed. That woman is a menace. She ought to be locked up. She ought to be—"

"Wait. Hold on. Maria? Are you talking about Maria? Didn't that SS shoot him?"

"Because of her. She flagged him down so he could come after us."

The doctor pushed past Stella and paced the room. "That God damn crazy whore."

Stella listened to him go on about blood money, Germany, and whores, comparing Maria unfavorably to canal rats and tuberculosis. Nicky put his hand over his eyes and said with the thermometer bobbing up and down, "Shut up, doc, please."

"Wait," said Stella. "You knew about Maria?"

Dr. Davide threw up his hands. "Of course, I knew. She makes her living in the train station. Rosaries don't pay enough for rent."

"I meant that she has a fondness for Germans."

He shrugged. "I wouldn't have said she was fond. Her father's German, but he abandoned her mother. I'm one of the few that know that. She wouldn't have told me, but she was delirious from a bad case of the measles. She nearly died."

"I wish she had," muttered Nicky.

Dr. Davide clenched his fists. "I won't be helping her again. You may get your wish."

"Let me get this straight," said Stella. "She's German and you sent us to her to buy a cross and rosary."

"She's Catholic."

"She can't be."

"She is and she has good merchandise or so I'm told," he said with a sly smile.

Nicky lifted his head off the pillow with considerable effort. "Doc, if I didn't want to throw up right now I'd sock you right in the kisser."

"Your old lady already took care of that." He rubbed his cheek dramatically. "So Maria's the one. I should've seen it. She will sell anything."

"Doc! So help me God. My wife is a lady and—" Nicky grew paler and his head dropped back.

Stella dashed over and yelled at the doctor to help, but he just scratched his wobbly chin.

"Do something," she demanded.

"There's nothing to do," he said finally. "He's lost blood and he feels rotten. Count on that for a while. Change the dressings twice a day.

Keep him moving. Around the room is enough. Hopefully, no infection will set in."

"Can't you give him some Prontosil?"

"I did." Dr. Davide clapped his hands together. "Let's talk cash. I believe I will need 5000 now."

"We haven't got that and you know it," said Stella.

"Didn't have time to call home to Daddy? Fine." He held out his hand. "I'll take whatever you've got. I need a drink."

"You're the last person that needs a drink," said Nicky. "I, on the other hand, could use a bottle of bourbon."

"Nobody's drinking. Have you forgotten? Maria stole your wallet," said Stella. "We haven't got two cents to rub together."

The doctor groaned. "This just gets worse and worse. I might have to have it out with Maria."

"If you do, get my wallet back," said Nicky.

"If I did, I'd sell it for a shot." The doctor put a packet on the bed and closed his bag. "Aspirin. Take two and do not call me until you have my money."

"How will I know if it's infected?" asked Stella.

"Oh, you'll know." He pushed past her and said, "I'm serious about that money. Maria isn't the only one with low standards."

"I don't understand you at all," said Stella.

"Join the club." With that the doctor left and Nicky closed his eyes. "I thought he'd never leave."

In a strange way, Stella didn't want him to go. The minute he did, it was time for her to do something. Her. Not Nicky. Not anyone else. There was no one else. She had to get the money, but hadn't even the funds to telegram for it.

"Stella?" asked Nicky. "It will be fine. I'll be fine. In a couple of days, we'll get out of here."

She didn't want to disagree or point out the obvious issues with that plan so she went with something more palatable. "You need bourbon."

"I was kidding about that."

She grabbed the key off the dresser and said, "I'll be right back."

He pushed himself upright and looked like he might just jump out of bed to stop her, if he had to. "No. Absolutely not."

"The von Bodmann's have booze. I'm going to ask for a glass for you."

"No. I don't want it."

"Yes, you do."

"I don't need a drink and I don't want you to go…"

"Where? Where would I go? It's raining. The whole town is flooded. I haven't a dime to my name and my husband's been shot," said Stella.

"I don't think that means anything," said Nicky.

He was right. It didn't.

# CHAPTER 11

$\mathcal{W}$hiskey was wonderful. It was Stella's new favorite thing. All it took was one hefty glass of that luscious golden stuff, combined with a good amount of blood loss, and Nicky was out cold. Karolina had surprised her with an array of choices. The ladies liked their alcohol and preferred whiskey and scotch to bourbon or their native schnapps. When she said the drink was to help Nicky sleep, they were very generous. Rosa needed a tipple, she said, to sleep and whiskey was the most helpful.

While Nicky softly snored on the bed, Stella got her makeup case and took a reluctant look in the small mirror on the wall. She'd looked worse, but that was hardly a comfort.

Her hair had dried in odd, loopy curls and her nose was red and starting to run. That's what she needed. A cold. She was still bruised, but the redness did help to distract from it. She just looked like she was coming down with something, which she probably was.

Stella powdered her nose, once, and then twice for good measure. Then rouge, kohl around the eyes, and mascara. A little lipstick and she smiled. "I look like me."

"What?" Nicky slurred on the bed.

"Nothing." Stella finger combed her hair and put on her coat and hat. At least, her beautiful hat hadn't been completely destroyed, just the feather, and Grandmother's pin completed the illusion of a woman who wasn't dead broke and just shy of desperate. A quick glance out the window told her she might have a chance if she hurried. It wasn't too late, not yet.

She tucked the pistol, her new passport, and the train schedule in her pocket and kissed Nicky's forehead, leaving a perfect lip print of oxblood red. "I'm going to see about dinner. Be right back."

His eyes fluttered and she hustled out, just in case he decided to be coherent. She paused in the hall and looked at the key in her hand. Maybe locking it wasn't the best idea, but she couldn't have someone coming in while Nicky was out of it and taking a look. He wasn't wearing his briefs. It wouldn't take but a second to find the wound. Connecting the bullet wound to Peiper to the water taxi theft was just logical. Any fool could put it together and they'd end up in jail.

She bit her lip and locked the door, hoping it would be fine like it was when Florence locked Uncle Josiah in the pantry after a particularly bad bender on Armistice Day. He said he was celebrating, but it looked more like grief to Stella. When he glugged down half a bottle of wine, produced a pistol, and started yelling, "They should've shot me instead," Florence and Mother started taking it seriously. Then he blindfolded himself with his own shirt. Mother had to wrestle the pistol out of his hand as Florence shoved him in the pantry with the help of William the chauffeur and in spite of the voluminous complaints of Cook, who said he'd ruin her supplies.

When they opened the door thirty minutes later, they found him passed out covered in flour, sugar, and butter. Florence thought that he'd tried to bake himself and attempted to get him to a psychiatrist, but no one would have him. Cook was not amused and said he only needed a good beating.

At least, Nicky wasn't that drunk and they had no baking supplies to ruin. Fire was her only concern, but, in the continuing downpour, she figured any fire wouldn't last long.

"All right then," she whispered. "Here I go."

"What was that?"

Stella jumped and spun around to find the new guest coming down the hall.

"I'm sorry. I didn't mean to startle you," said Mr. Bast.

She put the key in her pocket. "It's fine. I just…it's been a long day."

"How is your husband?"

"Better. Sleeping in fact. Dr. Davide says he may only have a cholera-like illness."

He pushed his glasses up and looked her over. "Going out? It's still raining cats and dogs."

"Dr. Davide suggested a special tea for his stomach. I'm going to get it. He needs all the help he can get," said Stella, giving him one of her most winning smiles, but it didn't work.

He merely looked at her and frowned. "On a Sunday evening?"

"Cholera, or whatever this is, wasn't polite enough to wait for Monday, so Sunday night it is."

Something in him changed. Stella felt it, rather than saw it. Something about that pleased him and she was pleased, in turn, to have thought of it so quickly.

"Can't one of the staff go for you?" he asked.

"They're busy and it's not far." Stella plucked a street name out of the air. "Calle del Forno. I won't be long."

He smiled jovially. "Well, you've got the boots for it, but at this rate you may need a gondola."

"Let's hope not. "Mister," Stella paused for effect. "I'm sorry. I can't remember your name."

"Bast. Leonard Bast." He held out his hand. They shook and he kissed her hand. "I'm pleased to make such a lovely lady's acquaintance."

Bast, Stella thought. That really was his name. Mr. Leonard Bast. She'd heard the name before, but she couldn't place it, but it was right there, so close she could almost touch the memory.

"Thank you, Mr. Bast," she said. "I have to go. I don't want to be late for dinner."

He patted his bulging belly and chuckled. "I understand completely."

Stella rushed off making sure she didn't limp at all and then left by the front door, managing to avoid seeing anyone else. She opened the small umbrella she snagged from the coat rack, took a breath, and went left. She could've gone right, to the hotel, the luxe Bella Luna. They knew her and more importantly they knew their families, the Bleds and the Lawrences. That hotel had been at Nicky's mother's insistence. Their room had come with a butler, for crying out loud, which Abel had thought was hilarious. So hilarious, Nicky had threatened to get him a servant of his own.

Their butler, Daniel Burgess, was an ice-cold Englishman, at least until Nicky charmed him into sampling a new martini recipe he'd learned at Harry's Bar. It involved Angostura Bitters and one sniff kept Stella from sampling. After a night of martinis, Nicky and Daniel were fast friends. She could probably persuade him to lend her a few bucks for a telegram and then they'd be flush again.

But the wallet had to be the priority. Maria wanted the money, of course, but she might not know what else she had. Paul Boulard's card was in there. Nicky's card. Their wedding photo. If Maria gave that wallet to her Nazi contact or Peiper, their gooses would be well and truly cooked. They'd have wanted posters, if they didn't already. She might as well stick a knife right in her mother's heart. A drunk uncle in the pantry was bad enough. This would kill the saintly Francesqua Bled.

And then there was the Boulards. She couldn't bear to think about them. Peiper wasn't stupid. If he saw that card, that brand new card, and made even the slightest inquiry into who the Boulards were, he'd find out they were just in Paris and been seen at their hotel in the company of a couple beat-up Americans. Peiper would be after them. The Boulards weren't ready for that. Paul already thought they were going to die.

Stella increased her speed, splashing through roads that had become ponds and trying desperately to remember how to get to the train station. Keeping close to the Grand Canal was her only hope and it worked.

She came out of a small walkway right at the bridge where they'd abandoned the water taxi. On the other side of the canal, a group of men were struggling to pull the submerged boats out of the water, using another larger boat and a hoist fixed to the deck. From what she could tell, it wasn't going well. Even through the rain and passing boats, she could make out the cursing. To make it worse, she was pretty sure their captain was over there, standing in water up to his knees with a bruised face and defeat written all over him. Poor man. She'd done it again. Destruction wherever she went. If she could've done something for him, she would've. That boat was his livelihood. He probably had a family. Stella clenched her fists. She had to stop thinking about that. Later. When it was all over, she'd find out who he was and help.

That thought pushed the guilt into a neat, little box next to her heart. The place was getting quite crowded with thoughts she couldn't think, the harm she couldn't undo. She took a breath and sauntered over the bridge, swinging her hips, but keeping the umbrella low. It wouldn't do to skulk by like she was guilty of something. She had to be the old Stella, happy and carefree, some would say careless and they'd be right. So she was careless, disinterested in the world's problems and the men struggling in the water. She didn't see them. They didn't matter.

Stella got over the bridge and disappeared into the warren of buildings. If anyone had noticed her, they gave no sign of it and she didn't expect them to. She was different than the girl on the taxi. The captain probably couldn't have picked her out of a crowd.

Fifteen minutes later, she emerged at the Scalzi bridge next to the train station. The sun was going down and the lights in the windows were a warm glowing yellow. The rain had lightened up to a drizzle and, through it, Stella saw the romance of Venice that she'd forgotten. The old palazzos became elegant, elderly ladies in the dim light that helpfully hid what they wanted to hide, but the romance couldn't diminish her nerves. She splashed through the walkway, swallowing them down, only to find the train station more alive than she'd ever seen it. Carabinieri and *polizia* both were gathered in clumps on the steps and she nearly turned around.

But her legs kept walking with a mind of their own and she came onto the piazza, joining the other tourists and keeping the old Stella as her shield. They wouldn't recognize her and if they questioned her she'd have Mavis's accent at its most incomprehensible.

But no one questioned her. She did get glances and second glances, but the kind that she was used to having, admiration and interest. Her hat was fabulous and the netting obscured her eyes, so people saw the style, not the girl wearing it.

Inside the station were more soggy tourists fleeing the rain that didn't stop *"domani"* and they weren't happy about it. It was easy to stroll around and blend in. The train from Geneva that Dr. Davide said had several first-class carriages for Maria to target hadn't arrived yet, so she had fifteen minutes to spare.

After walking through the entire station twice, Stella found a niche next to a column where she could watch the train come in. She waited with rising frustration. Maria hadn't appeared and a deep weight started pressing down on Stella. Of course, Maria didn't show. Stella had her merchandise and she had nothing to sell, except herself, Stella thought with repugnance. How Maria could do that was beyond her comprehension. As desperate as Stella had been before finding the Boulards, she never considered that. It hadn't crossed her mind. Perhaps she hadn't been desperate enough, but Maria seemed all right. Nice clothes, her cheeks full, hair shiny. She wasn't starving. But perhaps that was why.

A train whistle blew and Stella stepped out of her cubby to see the train far down the track. The tourists gathered on the platform and the next thing she knew vendors were all over the place, swarming over the crowd to hawk their wares. Questionable-smelling dried sausages hung from poles, pastries on platters, rugs, beads, and maps came at the tourists with surprising ferocity. They were much worse than before Vienna and Stella thought it was bad then. The letting up of the rain must've brought them out in droves to make up for days of lost sales, but she didn't think they'd get far. The miserable tourists didn't want to spend another nickel on Venice and Stella could imagine all the tales of how much they hated the canal city when they got back home. She couldn't blame them. If all you saw of Venice was a continual downpour, flooded streets, and drowned rats, you wouldn't remember it fondly. The weather had been intermittently nice before Vienna, but Stella could barely remember the sun shining, and being dry outside was a distant, almost unreachable memory.

The crowd stepped back, moving as one, when the train chugged into the station, blowing its whistle and grinding the brakes. Before it had even come to a complete stop, people were clambering onto the steps and it became a comedy of thrown elbows, dropped luggage popping open and spilling unmentionables, and conductors getting bowled over and literally tossed out of the way and onto the platform. People tried to get off, but there was no hope.

Stella turned away from the disagreeable display, her eyes searching for Maria through the increasing madness as more people and vendors rushed into the station. A vaporetto must've arrived and what had been chaotic became a mob scene. Stella couldn't see Maria's distinctive brassy blond hair, but, with so many umbrellas up and everyone wearing hats, it was hard to tell if she really wasn't there, trying to make a buck like all the other vendors.

A hand lighted on her shoulder and Stella jumped a foot.

"Mrs. Myna," whispered a voice.

She turned and looking down at her was Father Giuseppe, his young, handsome face crinkled in concern. He said something in rapid Italian, but, even if she was fluent, she couldn't have heard it well enough over the din to understand.

She shook her head and he jabbed his hand at the exit.

"No," she said. "I can't go."

He tried to push her out and she pulled him to her. "Maria. I have to find Maria."

Father Giuseppe took a sharp breath and glanced around at the pressing crowd. Then he made a motion like empty hands and said, *"No rosari."*

He thought Maria wouldn't be there as she had nothing to sell and Stella smiled at his sweetness. She wouldn't disabuse him of that notion, not that she could. How in the world could she gesture about what Maria could sell?

Instead, she mimicked a wallet and said, "Mr. Myna's. I need it."

He frowned and she could see him wondering why. Then he pulled out a handful of coins and tried to press them on her.

"No, no. I need the wallet."

He attempted to put the coins in her hand, but she refused. She couldn't take money from the church. Taking from Maria was one thing. The church was wholly different. The priest looked back at the insanity on the platform and muttered something that might've been profane as he was jostled forward into Stella. He blushed at being pressed against her and started pushing her toward the door. *"No Maria. Vai, ora."*

She refused to go and pointed at the train. The passengers were managing to force their way off with the help of the *polizia* and porters. Father Giuseppe hesitated, but he went for the train, looking for some poor refugees, and Stella was torn. She needed Maria to be there, but that wasn't good for Father Giuseppe's people. She hadn't had time to figure out the woman's pattern from her book yet, but that had to happen and soon.

But what Stella wanted didn't matter. She looked and looked, not finding Maria. The woman would be easy to miss in that crazy crowd and she found her mind thinking about what she had to do next. The thought of begging for help and money from Daniel Burgess was embarrassing and she regretted not taking the priest's coins. She supposed she could go after him and ask. He was still there, having pushed his way to a third-class carriage where he was questioning a conductor. The man nodded and then looked behind him.

The men stepped aside and a young woman with weary, frightened eyes and an infant on her shoulder squeezed onto the platform. Father Giuseppe shielded her and they made their way through the crowd slowly. Stella took another look, going up on her tiptoes, but she didn't see Maria anywhere, so she decided to go ahead and borrow from the priest. Just borrow. That was okay. The money would go back and then some.

Stella stepped out into the crush and was swept up toward the train. She pushed back and when she looked for the priest and his charge, she was startled to see his brown eyes trained on her as he looked over his shoulder. Then he jerked his head forward, ducked down behind a man hawking maps, and disappeared from her sight. If it hadn't been for his charge's green hat, she would've lost him all together. They were moving through the crowd much faster and Stella's stomach got the worst sinking feeling.

And then she saw her. Maria standing in her old spot next to the newspaperman's stand and scanning the crowd. Father Giuseppe would be directly in front of her in another fifteen feet. The crowd was pushing them closer. She would see them, a priest in a crowd of tourists, he stood out with his uncovered head and stark white collar. Maria couldn't miss him and she didn't.

Maria's eyes lit up and Stella could practically see the dollar signs in them as she craned her neck to try and see who the priest was with. Stella took a breath and charged through the crowd, elbows swinging and using the sharp point of her umbrella to great effect. People yelped and jumped away. Stella was on Maria in seconds and the woman didn't see her coming. Stella cracked her upside the head with her umbrella and Maria went down with a screech.

"*Scusi, scusi,*" called out Stella, using Sofia's accent.

She had Maria down against the wall. She was dressed for business in a tight red dress with a high slit and low, sequined décolletage. No coat. No place to hide Nicky's wallet, except a cheap handbag. Stella lunged for it and they tussled over the bag, each with a hand on the strap.

"*Ladra! Ladra!*" yelled Maria and Stella shoved the umbrella in her face. The strap broke and she tumbled back into the crowd. Dazed, Maria lunged after her, grabbing her arm. Stella tried to shake her off and their eyes met. It took a split second, but Maria recognized her. She smiled. "*Ladr—*"

Stella smacked her with the umbrella and screamed, "Help! Help! She tried to steal my handbag! *Polizia!*"

The crowd had thinned a little and a *polizia* spotted them instantly. He ran over as Maria yelled, "*Ladra! Lei è il ladro!*"

"Help! Help!" Stella waved at the *polizia* frantically. Maria sneered and tightened her grip.

The *polizia* got to them and seized both their arms. Maria yelled at him in Italian, aggressively complaining and spewing spittle. Stella watched and then widened her blue eyes, got tearful, and said, in what Uncle Josiah called her little kitten voice, "Sir, she tried to steal my bag. Can't you help me, please?"

The *polizia* looked them over, Maria in her harlot on parade outfit and Stella in her fur and pricey hat with its long pin and pearl, not noticing that she actually had two handbags clutched to her chest. A tear rolled down Stella's cheek and he let go of her, turning on Maria to yell, "*Lascia stare i turisti, puttana!*"

With his back turned, Stella dashed for the exit, jostling the map vendor into the sausage vendor. The two collided and their wares flew into the air along with bellows of outrage. Stella got hit with several sausages and tripped on one. She caught herself before falling and ran for the exit past a group of confused carabinieri coming in to see what all the fuss was about. She got past them and through the doorway. Something hit her, ramming her sideways into the door itself. Glass shattered and someone was at her, grabbing at her hands. She shoved at them and found herself in a fight with a boy about her height. She dropped the umbrella and held fast to Maria's handbag. He yanked it back, pulling Stella off her feet and tumbling backward into a couple entering the station. They fell back against the stone archway, exclaiming in Dutch. The boy didn't let go. He was small, but a good deal stronger than he looked. Stella tried to twist the handbag out of his grip. He glared at her with such ferocity that she almost let go. There was nothing but hate in his eyes and he grunted in oddly-accented German, "*Lass los, Schlampe.*"

It was Peiper's companion, the boy who'd chased them. Stella's heart seized in her chest and she violently twisted the handbag the other way. The clasp broke open and the bag ripped, spilling the contents out onto the stone steps. A mirror shattered, lipsticks rolled down the steps into the water and Nicky's wallet hit the step with a wet slap. She shoved the remains of the handbag in the boy's face, snapped up the wallet, and ran across the steps, splashing through the water and shoving people out of the way.

She reached the end of the station and darted into an alley between it and a church, but the boy grabbed her from behind and rammed her into the wall of the church.

"Where is it?" he yelled, his voice deeper than she expected and his infuriated face level with hers.

"I don't know what you're talking about."

"The diary! Where is it?" He had an accent. Scottish.

"It's gone. I lost it," said Stella, trying to break away, but he stepped on her foot and she doubled up in pain.

"You are lying. You have it."

She tried to tuck the wallet away in her coat, but he saw and ripped it out of her hands. "What is this?"

"Nothing." She spat in his face. He relaxed his grip for a second and she was able to wrestle it away from him. He blocked her way and she spun around, running for the Grand Canal. The boy was on her heels. She ran into the water, trying to get to the Scalzi bridge, but the water slowed her too much and he caught up. They tumbled forward. She went down on her knees with him on her back. He would get Nicky's wallet. He would give it to Peiper.

Stella slung the wallet out into the canal where it skipped over a wave and then was enveloped by another. The boy jumped up and almost bowled her over running to the edge of the walkway. "*Scheisse!*"

He balled up his fists and then reached into his bulging pocket, pulling out a pistol. Stella ran at him, shoving him as he turned and the boy fell into the canal with barely a splash. Stella turned and dashed for the bridge, running past a man who calmly stood there leaning on the railing. He had obviously seen the whole thing, and didn't care. That was good, but there was something about him, the way he stood, the way he watched. It was only a second, but Stella's panicked mind said she knew him. Tall, thin, stylish, white teeth, not Italian went through her head as she darted through the people coming onto the bridge, but then she pushed thoughts of him away. She didn't know him. A stranger in Venice. He didn't matter and she lost herself in the warren of old streets as soon as she could.

# CHAPTER 12

Stella stood off to the side of the Hotel Bella Luna at a total loss. She'd gone for the hotel because that was in her head when she shoved Peiper's boy in the canal and, to her surprise, she'd found it. Easily, as it turned out. Once she got in the San Polo section, things started to look familiar and there she was, standing outside what was probably the most expensive hotel in Venice and she couldn't go in.

She'd expected to simply trot up to the concierge and ask for Daniel or the management. They might even recognize her. It hadn't been very long and the hotel only had twenty-four suites. But she couldn't do that now. She was soaked to the knees from the boy knocking her down and the rain had kicked up to finish the job. The hotel was elegant and even stuffy with its Tiepolo frescos and gleaming marble floors. Stella could confidently compare herself unfavorably to those drowned rats. The staff might toss her headfirst into the canal on sight and ask questions later. They did seem like the type. Now that she thought about it, it probably wasn't a good idea for the whole staff to know she was back in Venice anyway. She didn't want them talking. Word got around.

Maybe she should go back to the Vittoria. Her main mission had been accomplished. The wallet was gone and the Boulards safe. She could come back tomorrow, but she was shaking from the cold and her right foot was burning. An unwelcome thought appeared in her mind. Could she make it back without help? Her heart said yes, of course. Her body wasn't so sure.

"There's more than one way to skin a cat," she said to herself through chattering teeth, a saying that Mavis favored, but that Stella always loathed. It made her feel bad for cats and she liked cats. Cats liked her as much as people and people generally liked her a lot. All people. She turned on her soggy heels and went for the service entrance, a plain door recessed deep in the side of the hotel. Abel had insisted on using that entrance rather than the ostentatious front door as he reminded them he was a servant of sorts. Nicky didn't hold with that and he used the service entrance, too, dragging an embarrassed Stella along behind them, apologizing for barging in. She knew, apparently better than Nicky, that most places like the Bella Luna liked the separation between the served and the servant, positions must be maintained and upheld. But the Bella Luna staff surprised her. They didn't mind a couple of gauche Americans using their halls. Of course, Nicky could charm the stern off a librarian and he worked his magic on the chef de cuisine, a fancy little Frenchman who blushed whenever he saw her husband. If there were any objections to them, Chef Brazier saw to it they were silenced. Stella had enjoyed being in the vast kitchen and watching the staff create. She'd never spent any time in the kitchen at home so the whipping of meringues was a revelation. They even let her have a go. She was terrible and they laughed.

Stella stood at the door inside a ring of sandbags, smelling the heavenly scents and desperately wanting to go inside. But she wasn't a guest now and barging in would garner unwanted attention. Plus, she didn't have her charming Nicky to smile at the chef so she took a breath and knocked.

It took three tries before someone came, a harried young woman in a maid's uniform, not one of the kitchen staff that she knew somewhat. "*Sì?*" she barked at Stella and then wrinkled her wide nose in distaste at the pool forming at her feet.

"Is Chef Brazier here?" she asked.

"No."

Stella couldn't remember any other names. Her mind was blank. "How about someone from the kitchen staff? The ones that make the meringues?"

"No." The woman shooed at her. "You are soaked. Go away."

"I can't. Daniel Burgess? Is he here? He's a butler. He knows me. Please."

The woman was surprised at the name and looked Stella over. "You know Daniel?" she asked with a raised eyebrow.

"Yes. He was our butler when we stayed here," said Stella.

"You?" she scoffed. Stella's fur was so wet it didn't look expensive anymore and the maid tried to close the door.

Stella slapped her hand on the wood and held it back. "Get Daniel."

The maid thought about it and held out her hand. Stella stared at the callused palm briefly and said, "Please."

The woman shook her hand and eyed Stella. Pay her to get Daniel? She couldn't pay for a cup of coffee. "I haven't got any money." She reached in her pockets to turn them inside out and found the pistol and her passport but something was jangling there. Coins.

Stella pulled out a fist full of lira coins in astonishment. Father Giuseppe, that sweetheart, must've slipped them in there. Tears pricked at her eyes and she gave the woman several coins, which apparently satisfied her, but then she asked, "Who is calling?"

Stella swallowed and thought for a moment. "Tell him it's Nicky's wife, who doesn't like Angostura Bitters."

"No one likes Angostura Bitters, but I will tell him." She closed the door and Stella reached down and slipped off a boot to check the damage. It wasn't so bad, only a little wet, but Dr. Salvatore wouldn't be happy. She tried the right boot and was dismayed to see blood had soaked through the sock. The old split must've opened up. No wonder it was stinging so much.

Before she could shove it back in the boot, the door opened and

Daniel Burgess, in full English disdaining mode, eyed her without an ounce of recognition. "Yes?"

Stella willed her teeth not to chatter and shoved her bloody foot back in the boot. "Don't you remember me, Daniel? I didn't take you for forgetful. It's only been a couple of weeks."

Daniel's mouth fell open at the sound of her voice and the ice melted. "Mrs. Lawrence?"

"Yes, it's me. I need some help."

He stared at her and then stepped outside, closing the door. "Mrs. Lawrence. I...what are you doing here? Didn't you go to Vienna?"

"Oh, we went all right." Her teeth started chattering with renewed fury.

He looked past her. "Where is Mr. Lawrence?"

"He's fine. I need some help, Daniel." Then she remembered she wasn't supposed to use his first name. "Burgess, I mean. Can you help me?"

"You're shaking and wet. Why didn't you come to the front? You're a guest."

"I'm not a guest. I can't be a guest. Please listen. There's been an incident and I need some help."

"Yes, of course." He opened the door and tried to usher her inside.

"No," she said. "Can you just let me borrow some money? Not a lot. I'm good for it."

"*You* need to borrow money from *me?*"

"I wouldn't ask if it wasn't important. We had a...an accident and I have to contact my family in the States."

"Are you hurt? I will call a doctor. Won't you come in? I can't have you of all people standing out in the cold," said Daniel.

"No. The less people know I was here, the better. Can you keep it to yourself?"

"Yes, of course."

"Do you have any money?"

"Not very much, but what I have is yours." He opened the door. "You have to get out of the cold."

"I only need to send a telegram to my family. How much is that? I don't even know," said Stella.

"It depends on how many words," he said.

"A few. I really don't know, Burgess."

"I'm not your butler now. Please call me Daniel."

"Thank you. I'm happy to," said Stella. "Where is the telegram office? Is it open?"

"It will be for me," he said. "Won't you please come in?"

"No, I—" Her teeth chattered so hard she couldn't finish the sentence.

Daniel looked like he might pat her arm, but his innate reserve held him back. "One moment, Mrs. Lawrence." He ducked inside and returned a minute later, wearing his overcoat and carrying a large golfing umbrella. "If you won't come in the hotel, please come to my flat. It's very close."

Stella didn't want to go to his flat. She wanted to send the telegram and get back to Nicky, but she was so cold and exhausted her brain shut off and she allowed him to lead her away down a few streets and into a narrow house. On the third floor, Daniel opened a door so short he had to stoop to get inside and he waved her into an extremely small flat. It was one room with a kitchen, sitting room, and bedroom all in one. Despite Daniel's prim and proper comportment, it was a god-awful mess with something on every surface and dishes piled in the tiny sink and table.

"I apologize for the mess. I wasn't expecting visitors," he said, hurrying to clean off the settee that he apparently used as a book shelf.

"Don't worry. I've seen worse," said Stella, thinking of the streets in Vienna, beds and blood, books and debris.

"You're still shaking. Let me take your coat." He took off her coat and wrapped her in a wool blanket before he started the kettle. "My mother would insist that you need tea, so I will, too."

"Tea would be wonderful," she said relaxing into the settee.

He got a pad and paper. "I will take your telegram to the office on San Silvestro. What do you want to say?"

Stella rubbed her hands together and pondered the question. She needed money and she needed to be anonymous. "I need money wired. Can I have it sent to you?"

"Me?" Daniel couldn't have been more surprised if she'd kissed him on the lips.

"Yes. I don't want anyone to know I'm here in Venice," she said.

"But shouldn't your family know?"

"They'll understand."

Daniel didn't look as though he bought that.

"I trust you. Will you accept the money for me?"

"Yes, of course, I will, but I don't understand. If you're in trouble, the *polizia*—"

"I don't want the *polizia*. Please just do what I ask. I'll make it worth your while."

He stiffened.

"I'm not trying to insult you, Daniel. I know you're very loyal. This is just so important."

His feathers smoothed. "I will do as you ask and have the money wired to me, but I don't understand why."

"I'll explain when it's all over."

"Will that be soon?"

She said yes, but the answer was no. She felt in her bones that it was far, far from over.

"What do you wish to say?" he asked, his pencil poised above the pad.

"To Patrick Mullanphy of…" Stella didn't know Patrick's address and she had to think. "Of Dogtown in St. Louis."

"Not your family, Mrs. Lawrence?" asked Daniel.

"No. Patrick Mullanphy. I know. He owns Mullanphy Motor Works. Send it there. That's in Dogtown, too."

"Dogtown?" he asked with a hint of a sneer.

"It's an Irish area. The name will help, since I don't have the address."

His mouth twitched, but he asked, "What would you like to say to Mr. Mullanphy?"

Stella tried to think of something endearing that Patrick would recognize and understand instantly. She smiled. "Say this. Dear Paddy Astaire. Please send a month's pocket money to Mr. Daniel Burgess of the Bella Luna. Much love, Miss Myna." She paused. "You should add your bank particulars."

"What does that mean?" he asked.

"He'll know or rather he'll know who will know."

"Is this Patrick a dancer like Fred Astaire?"

"His sister says no. It's an inside joke."

Daniel shook his head confused. "And pocket money? Isn't that a few pence?"

"Not my pocket money. Father says mine adds up to a Studebaker every two weeks."

"That's astonishing."

"I didn't think so before, but I do now." Her teeth began to chatter again and she gathered the blanket tighter around her shoulders.

"You're still cold," said Daniel. "Let me get your tea. Milk? Sugar?"

"Milk, please."

He made up her tea, a strong basic blend that warmed her middle but not her toes. "Can you go to the telegraph office now? I really should get back."

"Where are you staying?"

"I'd rather not say. It's better for you and us."

He sipped his own tea and Stella could see a fight going on inside him. It was an awkward situation to be sure. Daniel didn't feel he could tell her what to do, but he was older and a man. Those things came with authority or, at least, men thought they did.

"Go ahead."

Daniel jerked to attention. "Go ahead with what, Mrs. Lawrence?"

"First of all, call me Stella. I think we're well past the formalities," she said.

"I can't. It's not in me," he said with a smile but he was still at attention.

"Very well. Then say what you want to say. I know there's something."

"It would be inappropriate for me to express an opinion," said the butler who looked every inch like he thought he was standing in front of the queen, not a wretched eighteen-year-old American with no right to order him to lift a finger.

"Remember, you're not my servant anymore and Nicky saw you as a friend, like Abel."

"Is he with you?"

She glanced away at a stack of *True Detective Mysteries* magazines and said, "Nicky? Yes, of course, he is."

"I meant Abel. We got on quite well and I'd like to see him again."

"He's not here."

Daniel paused and she heard him sip his tea. Stella didn't look back until she'd cleared Abel's image from her mind. "Can you go now? It's getting late."

"The tea hasn't helped. You're still shivering," he said, putting down his cup and getting some towels out of a cupboard under the sink.

"I'm fine, really."

He swallowed hard. "Mrs. Lawrence, I insist you take off your boots."

"You insist, do you?"

He swallowed again and years of training went straight out the window. "I do."

"Fine." She reached a shaky hand for her left foot, but he intervened and did it for her, wordlessly taking off her boots, rolling down the wet socks and then, with a glance at her resigned face, he unwound the bandages and dropped them onto the wooden floor. He didn't grimace or recoil as much as he might've wanted to.

"It's all right," she said. "They're a lot better."

"Better?" he asked. "This is better?"

"It is."

"You're bleeding and your feet…I've never…what happened to you, Mrs. Lawrence?"

The kindness, the concern from a man she barely knew was

almost too much. She turned away to the magazines again and read a headline, "Death Trap and the Girl with the Green Eyes."

"Mrs. Lawrence?"

"Stella," she said. "Please."

He took a breath and she looked at him. "Stella," he said. "What happened?"

"We had an accident."

"With your feet?"

"Things happened in Vienna," she said with a shrug and a smile.

His face changed with the word *Vienna* and she wished she hadn't said it. He didn't need to know or think about it. He wrapped her feet gently in the towels and stood up. "Of course. You were in Vienna when those…things occurred. But surely you and Mr. Lawrence—"

"Nicky."

"Um…yes, Nicky. Wouldn't you have been away from all that?" asked Daniel.

"No one was away from it." She put her hand on his arm and saw him stiffen. That was too far for him and she removed it. "Please don't be worried about it. We just need some money and it will be fine."

He grabbed his overcoat and hastily put it on. "Yes. I'll go right now. Please drink your tea and rest. I won't be a moment."

Stella leaned back and smiled. "I will."

He opened the door but then stopped, looking at her from around the edge. "Stella?"

"Yes?"

"Where's Abel?" he asked.

"You don't want to know."

He nodded and left, not locking her in, and she settled back with her cup pressed to her lower lip, saying over and over again, "It will be fine. It will be fine."

It seemed like only a minute had gone by when someone took the cup out of Stella's hands and her eyes fluttered open. "Daniel?"

"I'm back, Mrs. Lawrence, I mean, Stella." Daniel stood over her with her cup in his hands and a frown on his face.

"What's wrong? Wouldn't they open for you?"

Someone else lifted her foot and she jerked upright to find a man sitting on a small stool in front of her and looking at her battered foot. "Good evening, Mrs. Lawrence."

She yanked her foot away. "Burgess! How could you?"

"You need a doctor, Mrs. Lawrence, Stella, Mrs. Lawrence. I don't know, but you need a doctor," said Daniel, red-faced and more than a little panicked himself.

"He did the right thing," said the man in a faint Scottish accent.

"Says you," said Stella. "How do I know who *you* are?"

The man, elderly with silver hair and small, round glasses perched on his bulbous, hair-filled nose, gently set down her foot and pulled a card out of his breast pocket.

Dr. Irving Spooner
Doctor and Surgeon
English and Italian spoken
San Polo 42

Stella glared up at Daniel as she slapped the card against her leg. "How do you know him?"

"Dr. Spooner is my personal physician and the Bella Luna house physician," said Daniel. "I can vouch for his character."

"I don't need a doctor. I have a doctor."

Dr. Spooner reached for her foot again, giving her a stern squint that made her relent and let him have it.

"Let me guess," he said, eyeing her left foot and then her right from all angles, "Dr. Davide?"

"Maybe."

Daniel let out an outraged snort. "Mrs. Lawrence, that man is a disgrace. He's a drunk and a lech."

"I told you to call me Stella and I meant it. Also, I'm well aware of Davide's character," she said, calmly. "Dr. Spooner? What is your opinion?"

"Your feet are in terrible shape."

"About Dr. Davide."

He directed Daniel to fill a pan with hot water and began digging through his oversized black bag. "Davide is a drunk and a lech. He is also an excellent doctor when sober, which is rare."

"You can't return to him," said Daniel. "You need good, reliable care. Your feet…"

Dr. Spooner took the pan, dumped a series of preparations and potions in it that smelled exactly like Dr. Salvatore's mixture, and dunked her feet in it. The stinging warmth made her jump and then sigh.

"This isn't your first medicinal bath," said the doctor.

"No."

"I assume you were given Prontosil."

"Twice."

"But you didn't stay off your feet?"

She shook her head and he prepared a syringe. "You require another dose and I want you to tell me exactly what happened to your feet."

He gave her the shot, which hurt more than she remembered, but she didn't open up about the injuries. There wasn't any point. It wouldn't change anything.

"Mrs. Lawrence, you need me to understand what has happened." The doctor's small hazel eyes bored into her, but she shook her head. He glanced over at Daniel. "Can you step out for a moment?"

Daniel didn't like it, but he left the flat.

When the door had firmly closed, Dr. Spooner said, "Mrs. Lawrence, I can't make you tell me what happened to you, but it is in your best interest to do so."

"I doubt it," said Stella, crossing her arms.

He explained that he knew from her reaction to the soak that she had seen Dr. Salvatore, who was particularly good with wound care. This was illegal as he assumed from the cross around her neck that she wasn't Jewish.

"I have nothing to say." She tried to give him back his card.

He snapped his bag shut. "You need it. If anyone comes calling, show it to them and say I'm your doctor." He glanced at the door. "I know what Salvatore and Davide are involved in."

Stella merely watched him with indifference.

"And if you are involved with the two of them, you are in serious trouble."

She said nothing.

"Where do you think Salvatore gets his medications? Who do you think is signing the backdated birth certificates?"

"I don't know what you're talking about," said Stella.

"Ask Father Girotti." He smiled at her expression. "I thought so."

"I have nothing to say."

"But," he said with emphasis, "I will have to say something if someone asks me about you."

"Okay."

"And what shall I say? That I've treated Mrs. Stella Bled Lawrence of the Bled Brewing family? Or perhaps something else?"

Stella met his eyes and her chest got unbearably tight. He knew her name. He could say it...or could he? "Do you believe in keeping your patients' secrets?"

"Yes. I believe in doctor-patient confidentiality and I will not disclose anything you say to me in private."

"Even my name?" she asked.

The doctor raised his eyebrows and clasped his hands over his bag. "Strictly speaking, your name isn't confidential. Unless it has a bearing on your health in some way."

"And if it did?"

"I would keep it confidential, but I can't confirm that you are my patient in that case."

"What if I were to be using another name? Would you confirm that?"

Dr. Spooner didn't answer. He got a couple of little pots out of his bags and mixed them together in a small bowl before applying the glop to her feet.

"Why honey?" asked Stella. "And what's the other stuff?"

"Honey fights infection and is very good for healing wounds." He held up the other little pot. "This is a mixture of arnica, calendula, and aloe vera. All good for burns."

"I don't have a burn."

"You do, in a manner of speaking. I'm sure Dr. Salvatore used something similar."

"He did."

"Sal is a good man." Dr. Spooner got a bundle of bandages out of his bag, dried her feet, and wrapped them up tight.

"You didn't answer my question, doctor," said Stella. "Would you confirm a different name for me?"

He thought for a moment and then nodded. "I believe I would, if you said it was necessary for your health."

There was nothing for it but to go ahead. "My name is Eulalie Myna. My husband is Douglas Myna. We're Canadians. My feet had a reaction to the canal water and nothing else."

"You haven't had frost bite, for instance?" he asked with a sly smile.

"Certainly not."

He held out his hand and they shook. "I'm very pleased to meet you, Mrs. Douglas Myna. Would you like to give me your current address?"

"I think not."

He nodded, dried out her boots, and helped her slip them on. "I recommend that you stay off your feet."

"I'll try," said Stella, giving him her most winning smile.

He sighed. "But you won't. The young never listen."

Stella looked at his card and then tucked it away. "If someone calls you, would you confirm that my husband is suffering from cholera?"

His eyebrows jutted up. "There hasn't been an outbreak of cholera here since 1911."

"But it's possible that he could have it." She pointed at her feet. "Look what the water did to my feet."

"Your feet were already damaged."

She sighed and leaned back. "So you won't do it?"

The doctor mulled it over. "Who diagnosed cholera?"

"Dr. Davide and Dr. Salvatore decided on it."

"May I ask what your husband is really suffering from?" he asked.

Stella wrinkled her little nose in a way she knew was charming, particularly to men, and he chuckled in response. "I guess not. We will leave it at cholera, but I think it would be best to say a cholera-like illness."

"Perfect. That's what Dr. Davide said." She grinned at him. "One more thing, doctor."

"I feared you'd say that."

"Have you treated or met anyone named Sorkine?" Stella asked.

He thought for a moment. "Man or a woman?"

"One of each."

"No, I'm sorry. Are they injured?" he asked.

"Not that I know of. We're trying to find them."

Dr. Spooner adjusted his glasses and chose his words carefully. "Maybe you can trust me to say why."

Stella leaned forward, putting her hands on his. "It's not a matter of trust. If you really know Father Girotti, you should understand why."

"You're very young to have so many secrets."

She thought of the Goldenbergs on the train with their children and the young woman and her infant. "I'm not so young."

"From where I am, you are a child. I will keep an eye out for these mysterious Sorkines." He got up and called out, "Daniel, come back in!"

Daniel rushed in with a pipe clamped between his teeth and two lines between his eyes. "How is she?"

"Eulalie? Oh, she's fine, young, and healthy. She had an unfortunate reaction to the canal water, but she'll recover well and quickly."

"Canal water?" He pointed at her feet. "That can't be canal water. Her feet...they're lumpy."

The doctor put on his overcoat and hat. "There is an abundance of nasty contaminates in that water right now." He looked down at Stella. "Eulalie, you should count yourself lucky that it wasn't worse."

"Yes, Dr. Spooner," said Stella demurely and he smiled at her with his eyes, not just his mouth.

"Who's Eulalie?" asked Daniel, looking around the room as if he expected another woman to jump out at him.

The doctor picked up his bag and patted the butler's shoulder. "Your friend, Eulalie Myna, wife of Douglas Myna. If you need anything, Mrs. Myna, don't hesitate to call."

"But I haven't paid you," said Stella. "I can't right—"

"It's well in hand. Daniel has taken care of my fee. Have a restful evening." He left and Daniel stared down at her bewildered. "Eulalie Myna."

"Yes, like on the telegram," she said. "Tell me you sent it."

"Yes, I did. But..."

She held out her hand and he pulled her to her feet. "I'll explain when it's all over."

"You said that before, but I'm starting to doubt it."

"I don't blame you, but will you call me Eulalie and forget Stella was ever here?"

"I suppose I will, if Dr. Spooner is," said Daniel. "How will I find you? Where are you staying?"

"I can't say, but don't worry, I'll come back to get the money." Stella put on her coat and hat, soggy as they were.

"What...what if you don't come back?" he asked.

She held out the few coins she had left from Father Giuseppe. "This is all the money I have. I will definitely be back."

"I wish you'd tell me what's happened, so I can help you."

"You are helping me. And I will ask one more thing of you."

"Anything, Mrs. ...Stella...Eulalie."

She chuckled and said, "Can you find out if anyone has been to the Bella Luna looking for us?"

"You you or you Mrs. Myna?"

"The real us or Abel. It's important," she said. "Their name is Sorkine and we need to find them as soon as possible."

"I'll ask and see what I can find out." He got his pad and pencil. "How do you spell that?"

She spelled their names and said, "Nicky and I are very grateful and if you ever want to come to the States, you know who to call."

He smiled so big that a dimple popped out on his left cheek. Stella didn't know he had a dimple before that moment he was so reserved. "Do you think Nicky needs a butler?"

"I don't think so, but I'm sure something can be worked out."

"I'll hold you to that."

She smiled and gave him a swift kiss on his dimple before he could object and become all stiff and formal. "I hope you will."

# CHAPTER 13

*N*icky slept on, breathing deeply without being bothered at all by grey morning light coming in from the window. It still wasn't *"domani"* and Stella looked out at the rain, aching for home like she hadn't since they'd gotten back to Venice. She had to get out and go, but it was the last thing she wanted to do. She longed to call out for her mother and be answered. To have someone come in and take over. Mother and Florence were so good at illness, even Mavis knew her way around a sickbed, but Stella didn't.

When she'd gotten back from seeing Daniel, Stella had felt sure things were about to go better, but then she'd seen Nicky, ghostly pale and moaning with pain. Stella couldn't soothe him and the aspirin wasn't helping since he couldn't hold it down. She read to him from *The Jungle Book* in a vain attempt to distract him until Sofia brought them dinner in their room, but he'd eaten almost nothing and then thrown it up. Around midnight, Sofia brought in a tin of something called *Brioschi*. She mixed a spoonful in a glass of water and insisted he drink the bubbly mixture.

It soothed his stomach and he only threw up once more when she'd insisted on changing his bandage, angering him into a rage when she had to roll him over. His buttock was insanely swollen, but he didn't want to sleep on his front. The battle had gone on all night with him insisting he couldn't sleep on his face and her saying he obviously couldn't sleep on his back.

Finally, in the early morning hours, he consented to roll over and fallen into a sleep that bordered on comatose. Stella didn't know what time it was, but now was her chance to get out, go back to the hotel, and see if the money had materialized, but she was so tired she could barely find the strength to stand at the window, looking out at the dismal rain. They were running out of time, if they hadn't already. Only the thought of the Sorkines ending up in Peiper's hateful hands could motivate her to move.

"Get dressed," she said to herself and she picked her skirt and Father Girotti's socks from the radiator. They'd finished drying, but her coat was still damp and her poor hat would never be the same. It's lovely swooping feather had been totally destroyed by the last rain with no hope of recovery. It was silly to mourn a hat when there were so many other things to worry about, but Stella was sad. Amelie Boulard gave her that hat and she felt guilty for wrecking it along with her nice, red suit. She was getting good at loss and that wasn't something a person should be good at.

She forced herself to put on Father Girotti's socks. Her feet were better again, but it was only a matter of time and the thought depressed her more than the hat. Now the big decision. What to wear? Her red suit was rumpled and, frankly, looked worse than the donation clothes the priest had given her, but those clothes weren't suitable. She had to go to breakfast where the fit and holes were sure to be noticed, so she decided on the suit as bad as it was. She could claim the lost luggage and say she was going out to shop. That would work.

The suit went on and it took a bit of effort. Having dried funny, it now pinched and pulled in strange places. Stella finger-combed her curls and got them to behave before powdering her nose and applying the rest of her makeup. At least that seemed like her and maybe they wouldn't notice the suit as much, if she smiled and charmed.

She'd just about convinced herself that was a real possibility when there was a soft knock on the door.

"Mrs. Myna, are you up?" called out Sofia.

Stella went for the door, reaching for the lever when another knock came, a terrific banging and her heart shot up into her throat. Peiper. Just like Vienna. She looked back at Nicky sleeping and the small window. There was nowhere to go. No way to go.

More banging echoed through the room and then a gruff, Italian voice yelled, "Answer the door!"

Bartali. Was she going to be arrested for stealing Maria's bag or pushing that boy into the canal or something else? It'd been a busy few days and he had plenty to choose from. She just had to keep him away from Nicky. Arrested or not, that was the most important thing.

"Mrs. Myna, please open the door," said Sofia.

Stella took a breath and unlocked the door, peeking out with her finger to her lips. "Quiet. You'll wake my husband."

Bartali, his uniform even grubbier than before, glared at her, fists on his hips. "Your husband that has the cholera?"

"That's right. I just got him to sleep. He's very ill. What do you want?"

He shoved the door and it whacked into Stella's chest. "Let me see this sick man."

"He is very sick," said Sofia. "Dr. Davide—"

"Davide will say anything for a price."

"He's a very good doctor."

Bartali grabbed Stella by the wrist and dragged her into the hall, ordering one of his men to go in. The man shifted from foot to foot and didn't budge. He said something in Italian and Stella caught the word *cholera*.

He was ordered in again, but he refused.

"What do you want?" asked Stella. "I've been up all night."

"You're a Jew and it is illegal for Dr. Davide to treat you."

"I am not and, no, it isn't."

He got in her face and the smell of fish and sweaty armpits washed over her. "You ran from me yesterday. I know you did. You're hiding something. You're a Jew from Germany."

"I'm a Catholic Canadian," said Stella, refusing to look away and reaching up for her cross. He saw the gesture, grinned, and ripped open her blouse. "I knew—"

Sofia screamed and smacked at his hands. "Stop that. She is my guest and a foreigner."

Bartali stepped back, looking at the cross in consternation. "I know you are lying."

"She is Catholic," said Sofia. "She went to mass yesterday. I sent her to Father Girotti or will you doubt the word of a man of God, too?"

The carabinieri glared at Stella. "I want your passports."

"Why are you bothering us?" asked Stella. "We're tourists. This is a tourism city."

"Show me your passports," he said with a knowing smile, but Stella smiled right back. "Let me get them."

She went in the room, got the passports, and something equally important. When she walked out again, she said, "Do you still doubt my husband is ill?"

"Very much."

She handed the other carabinieri a bucket and whipped off the towel. The smell of vomit flowed up and the man gagged. "My husband has a cholera or a cholera-like illness from *your* water."

Bartali put the towel back and said, "According to the drunken Davide." He tried to push his way past Stella, but she stood her ground and shoved the passports at him.

He looked through them, his face growing red and his jowls shaking.

"Please go," said Stella, using the voice her mother used on Uncle Josiah, a combination of weary anger and downright disgust. "I've had enough."

"Davide is no proof of illness. He can be bought."

"Why would I want to buy him? For what purpose?" Stella reached in her pocket. She didn't want to do it and it could go wrong, but she needed him to leave and hopefully never come back. "Can Dr. Spooner be bought?"

"You've seen Spooner?" he scoffed.

She held up the card. "I have. Feel free to question him. I under-stand he'll be at the Hotel Bella Luna today."

"Dr. Spooner only treats certain patients." By that, he meant rich patients and Stella had to think fast.

"I'm lucky then. He owed a friend of mine a favor," she said, straightening her blouse. "Perhaps you'd like to rip open his clothes and question him. He'll be happy to answer your questions."

"Will he?"

"He will."

They were toe to toe and Stella felt like *she* would throw up and that it showed on her face. But the carabinieri blinked and stepped back. "I will be speaking to Dr. Spooner."

"Do that."

He looked ready to go in the room in spite of it all and Stella's knees shook. She couldn't stop him from pulling back the covers and seeing the bloody bandage. He didn't know about Maria or the boy. If he did, he would've said so. But that wound would connect them to Peiper. He had to know about the shooting.

Bartali watched her carefully, a little smile flickered on his face, and moved in closer, saying, "I know you're hiding something."

"I'm trying to hide that you disgust me," said Stella. "How am I doing?"

Bartali growled as Randolph Hutchins turned the corner and saw them. The American rushed up, saying, "How is Mr. Myna? Is there anything I can do?" The American gave the carabinieri a funny look like a man like him ought not be allowed in hotels and continued on, "Dolores was up half the night worrying about an outbreak."

"Outbreak?" asked Bartali.

"Of cholera. Her husband has it. I've never seen anything like it."

Bartali eyed him critically. "You believe Mr. Myna is ill?"

"Believe it? The man vomited right in front of us. My wife hasn't quite recovered from seeing that herself. A man like Mr. Myna would have to be on death's door to do that. What is that terrible smell?"

"Vomit," said Stella. "They wanted proof."

Randolph recoiled. "You wanted proof of cholera? They're Canadians. Canadians don't lie. They're Canadian."

Bartali flipped open a little green notebook. "Who are you?"

"Who am I? Who am I?" asked Randolph in complete umbrage. "I am Randolph Hutchins of Des Moines, Iowa. An American. Make sure you write that down. American."

Bartali's mouth twitched. Stella couldn't see what he wrote down, but she doubted it was American in capital letters.

"You have a passport?"

"I do," said Randolph, becoming more imperious by the moment.

"Give it to me," said Bartali.

"Why? I've done nothing."

"I am a representative of the Italian government. I do not have to give a reason."

Randolph put his fists on his hips. "Oh, you don't, don't you? If this is how you treat tourists that bring in buckets of money, it's no wonder this city is sinking into the mud."

"Give me your passport."

"I'll give you my passport. Right in the kisser. Didn't you hear me? I'm an American. I have rights." Randolph's outrage echoed around the hall and Stella couldn't stop watching. The carabinieri was holding his ground, but she'd have put good money on Randolph.

"Darling?" called out Nicky from the room and the men stopped. His voice was weak and tremulous. On hearing it, Randolph caught fire and stuck his finger in Bartali's face. "And that's the man you think isn't sick? He'll probably end up in the hospital, if you even have one in this swamp you call a wonder of the world. When's it going to stop raining?"

"*Domani*," said Bartali, automatically.

"*Domani? Domani?* All I hear is *domani*. What does that even mean? Never?"

Stella leaned over to the other carabinieri and tapped the bucket saying, "How about you dump that for me? I've got a sick man to care for."

He may not have understood her words, but he got the meaning, and he wasn't happy. Sofia cheerfully directed him toward the bathroom with a sly wink at Stella and herded the hapless officer away. Stella ducked back in the room and closed the door, putting her back to it, finally allowing herself to breathe as heavily as she liked.

Nicky looked at her from the bed and struggled to get up. He tossed off the blanket and revealed that his bandage was less bloody than she expected. "What's going on?"

"Nothing. It's fine."

"Who's yelling?"

She pushed him back down and lifted the bandage. "Looks pretty good." She said it like she really knew something about healing bullet wounds but being cheerful and convincing was half the battle or so she told herself.

"Don't change the subject," said Nicky.

"I'm not."

"Who is yelling? Sounds American and—"

She quickly told him about Randolph and Bartali, but instead of being relieved as she had expected he tried to roll over saying, "We have to get out today. This morning, if possible."

"It is not possible and you know it," said Stella.

"You still want to stay? You are obsessed with the Sorkines."

"I am not." That might well be true, but she could hardly admit it. "We might need money to get out. Have you thought about that?"

The angry voices faded in the hall and he settled down, propping himself up on his elbows. "I've been thinking. What about Daniel Burgess at the Bella Luna? I'm sure he'd let us borrow a few bucks to telegram."

Stella sat on the edge of the bed and tugged on her galoshes. "Great minds think alike."

"Is that where you think you're going?" he asked.

Stella swallowed a tart reply. He had been shot after all, so she'd save it for later when he was walking. "I *think* I'm going to breakfast. And I *know* I went to see Daniel last night."

Nicky jerked to the side and then gasped in pain.

"Don't do that. You'll aggravate it."

"You're aggravating me. You can't go to the Bella Luna on your own."

"That's a shocking statement seeing as I already did." She stood up, popped a couple of aspirin in her mouth, and washed them down with some of the whiskey left in the glass. "Yuck. That's horrid."

"Stella!"

She slammed down the glass and turned on him. "What do you want me to do? Sit by your bedside, dabbing at your forehead like a good little nurse? We have things to do."

"We, not you."

"There's no *we* right now. It's all me and I took care of it." She whipped the bandage off his rear, picked up the whiskey glass, and tossed the remains on his butt. "Look. There's another thing taken care of."

"Are you crazy?"

"I'm a Bled. We're all crazy. Haven't you heard?"

He drew back in shock. "Stella, what is—"

"Look at me and you had better listen, Mr. Nicolas Lawrence of the New York Lawrences. I'm going to breakfast and then I'm going to see if my father replied to the telegram Daniel sent. If there's money, I'm going to get it. Understand?"

He stared at her. His expression was unreadable and she didn't know if she'd gone too far. But she quickly realized that she didn't care if she had.

She hid the bloody bandage behind the wardrobe and got out a new one, placing it gently on his swollen rear, and covering him to the waist. "That'll hold you for a while. Do you want me to send a telegram to your parents?"

"No."

Not one word of explanation. What kind of family had she married into?

"They might be worried," she said.

Nicky didn't reply, watching her with that damn blankness in his eyes and it infuriated her.

She took a breath and asked, "Do you want something to eat?"

"No."

"Drink?"

"No."

"Well then, I'm off. Wish me luck," said Stella, picking up her coat and handbag, tucking her Italian dictionary inside.

"Stella." Nicky had turned his head to the window and it felt as if he'd retreated to a distant place far from her.

"Yes?"

"They'll have released Peiper by now. If Maria's given him my wallet…"

She put her hand on the door lever. "Don't worry about that. I stole it back and threw it in the Grand Canal."

He was quiet for a moment and then said, "Our wedding picture was in there."

She looked back, but his face was still turned away.

"I know," she said, deciding not to say why she did it. That would only upset him more.

He didn't respond and she went into the hall and closed the door, locking it and then putting her hand over her mouth, blinking back the tears that wanted to come streaming down her cheeks. But she couldn't cry. There simply wasn't time.

The breakfast room was full up and Stella almost didn't go in, but she needed coffee like she'd never needed coffee before. She hoped it would wake her up and a little bucking up wouldn't go amiss. Uncle Josiah called whiskey liquid courage. Her liquid courage came with sugar and cream. Whiskey burned and sterilized wounds. She'd take coffee every day of the week.

"Mrs. Myna," called out Randolph from his table. "How are you?"

Stella hung her coat on the rack and walked over smiling. "I'm fine and Douglas is a bit better, I think."

"I can't believe that awful man," said Dolores. "Imagine wanting to disturb a sick man in his bed. Unbelievable."

"It is, but Randolph was wonderfully helpful."

Dolores patted her husband's hand. "He can be a real firebrand when riled. I could hear him all the way down in our room."

Randolph smiled smugly. "I put the servant back in public servant."

Stella struggled to keep her nose from wrinkling in distaste. The man *had* done her a bigger favor than he knew.

"You did. Thank you." She looked around and all the two-person tables were full. Only three seats were available and they were at the four-person table where Mr. Bast had taken up residence with stacks of paper and, more astonishingly, his typewriter. The portly Englishman was scribbling on a notepad and chewing on a sausage the size of a bratwurst without cutting it.

Randolph leaned over to Stella and whispered, "I can sit with him, if you like, and you can sit with Dolores."

"I wouldn't dream of it," she answered. "Sit with your wife. I'm only going to get something quick and go out shopping."

"Shopping?" Dolores's eyes lit up.

"Nothing exciting I'm afraid," said Stella, quickly. "I have to replace the things in our lost luggage. Nicky is badly in need of pajamas. He'll feel much better when he has some." She excused herself and marched over to Mr. Bast, whose sausage was now a nub on the end of his two-pronged fork.

"Excuse me," she said.

He coughed, dropped his sausage on his plate, and struggled to get up.

"No, no, Mr. Bast. I just wanted to know if I could join you. There are no other spaces free."

Mr. Bast pounded his chest and gestured to the chair opposite him. He hastily cleared the papers and coughed again. "I'm sorry, Mrs. Myna. How inconsiderate of me. Please, do sit down."

Stella sat, hiding her reluctance and asked Antonio for coffee when he came over to ask what she wanted. "It's no trouble. I just need some coffee to start the day."

"And a dreary day it is." He smiled at her from under his walrus mustache and a wave of déjà vu came over Stella. She didn't know him from Adam, but he felt so familiar.

"Mrs. Myna?" he asked. "Are you feeling well?"

"Sorry. I'm just tired. My husband. It was a bad night."

"I imagine so. If I may ask, when will he be better?"

"Doctor says a couple of days."

"And will you go then or stay to tour the city?" he asked.

"In this rain?" she scoffed to change the subject.

He laughed and speared another sausage. "Haven't you heard? It will stop *domani*."

They laughed together and then Stella got up to fill a plate with rolls and jam. She didn't want to eat, but thought it would look odd if she didn't.

"So where will you go?" he asked companionably.

Why did he have to ask questions? Stella's brain was murky, even after the coffee and she wasn't sure she could get her story right.

"Oh, I don't know. Douglas will have a plan. He does love to travel." She glanced around at the papers and typewriter. "You're clearly not touring. Why are you in Venice?"

"As a matter of fact, I am touring. Professionally, that is."

"Professionally?"

Mr. Leonard Bast was a travel writer of some repute. He wrote under several pseudonyms that he wasn't allowed to reveal. Stella pelted him with questions and kept him well away from asking her a single thing. Why Venice? What was his favorite city? Favorite museum? Had he been to the Vatican, etcetera?

When she paused to finish her roll, he saw his chance and he took it. "So where did you grow up, Mrs. Myna? Your accent, I can't quite place it."

Stella chewed, not too slowly, she hoped, and tried to form an answer that wouldn't prompt more questions, but what popped out wasn't what she planned at all. "Prince Edward Island." She'd wanted to say some place that no one could possibly be familiar with like Witless Bay or Moose Jaw. Stella had once come across her uncles planning a trip to Canada for the brewery. They were in their cups and having a grand time deciding where they should visit. Uncle Nicolai thought it would be fitting for Uncle Josiah to visit Witless Bay or Sober Island, but Uncle Josiah thought Spread Eagle Lake or Big Beaver was more his style, not that Stella would ever have chosen one of Josiah's favorites. That was just asking for interest as was Prince Edward Island.

Mr. Bast threw up his hands. "Prince Edward Island. I know it well. What town or should I say village?"

Stella almost said Avonlea. It was right there on the tip of her tongue, but she saved it at the last second and spat out the second town she remembered so well from *Anne of Green Gables* Carmody.

He smoothed his mustache and said, "Of *Anne of Green Gables* fame?"

She had to go with it though she wasn't even sure if the town was real. Avonlea wasn't. "That's the one. It's much less interesting than people think. Not like living in London. Where do you live exactly? I've read about London so many times, but I've never been."

Was she talking too fast? It felt like she was, but if Mr. Bast noticed he gave no sign of it.

"Well, I've moved around as you might expect for a writer. I came from Hertfordshire originally."

Stella got the funniest feeling when Mr. Bast said, Hertfordshire and she wanted to dash away, but Antonio came over and, without asking, refilled Stella's coffee cup. Now she couldn't escape. She had to drink it. "You said, 'lately of London'. Do you live in London now?"

"Yes, I did say that. Good memory. First, I lived in Wickham Place, but I've moved once again to Camelia Road."

The funny feeling got worse, like a memory that she couldn't quite recall and wouldn't be pleasant if she did.

"Do you know Camelia Road?" asked Mr. Bast softly.

"I don't believe so." Stella swilled the coffee and burnt her tongue. "Do you like it?"

"It's a basement flat and it suits me."

She looked up and found him watching her rather intently. "A basement suits you? Why is that?"

"I like feet, Mrs. Myna," he said. "I find them fascinating."

"Feet?" asked Stella, genuinely astonished.

"Yes, indeed. Feet tell you so much about a person. Where they're going. Where they've been." He stuck out his leg and pointed his fork at his heavy brown shoe, a lace up that was of good quality but well worn. "Take my foot for example, Mrs. Myna. What does it tell you?"

"I have no idea what your shoe says." She smiled and swallowed more burning coffee.

"Come now. You're an intelligent lady of the world. Look at that shoe."

Dolores waved at them and Stella could've kissed her. "I know," she said. "It says you need new shoes."

"Dolores!" said Randolph.

"He asked."

Mr. Bast laughed. "Indeed, I did and she's right. I do, but why do I, Mrs. Myna?"

Stella bit her lip, for once not trying to look charming but managing it anyway. "Well, the soles are worn. Because you walk a lot for your work?"

He swung his fork and held it like a trophy. "And there you go. I'm a man with sensible, worn out shoes, which must mean..."

Stella laughed. "That you're sensible and work for a living."

Dolores stuck out a foot, which was clad in a black leather pump with silk laces and a floppy bow. "What about mine?"

"That shoe, Mrs. Hutchins, says you don't like to walk and you choose fashion over practicality."

"Amen," said Randolph.

The entire room laughed and all the shoes were duly discussed. Stella excused herself and tried to get out before they made it to her oversized galoshes, but, naturally, she didn't make it three feet.

"How about Eulalie's feet?" asked Dolores, still laughing.

Stella was obliged to wait while Mr. Bast pondered her feet and she decided that perhaps the best thing wasn't to look ashamed or pained, but to be a doll as Florence would've said.

She flung her handbag over her shoulder and sauntered back

across the breakfast room, mimicking Katherine Hepburn's voice. "Here reflecting the spirit of the fall season is a Venice original. There's nothing like water damage to enhance the chic design of this once lovely suit." She turned and thrust out a hip to wails of laughter. "And for that one extra touch, our girl has added black, oversized galoshes meant for men, but, ladies, oh so stylish."

Stella posed by the coat rack before bowing and laughing along. She thought she saw Mr. Bast wiping his eyes and took it as a compliment. Sofia came racing in. "What is occurring? Mrs. Myna? Has there been a spill?"

"Just on me," said Stella, garnering more laughter.

"I don't understand." Sofia started examining Stella, getting even more laughter.

"It's okay, Sofia. It's a joke. We were joking."

"About the weather, yes?" she asked.

"The weather is a big joke," said Mr. Bast. "And as for Mrs. Myna's foot attire, I'd say *she* cares less for fashion than moisture level or...the flooding has ruined all her shoes."

"The second one," proclaimed Dolores.

Stella plucked her coat off the rack and said, "If I had my choice, I'd be wearing Dolores's shoes hands-down."

Dolores blew her a kiss. "Thank you, Eulalie. See, Randolph!"

Stella dashed down the hall, stopped at the front doors, and then rethought. She turned to Matteo at the desk and gave him a high-wattage smile. The boy shrank back instead of smiling and Stella wished Peiper's boy was more like him. That murderous little gutter-snipe wasn't afraid of her or anyone.

"*Signora?*" asked Matteo.

"I need a boat."

Matteo tilted his head. "Boat?"

"Taxi." She patted her chest. "I need a taxi."

"*Sì. Sì.*" He took her to the dock door and took a heavy rain slicker off a peg.

"No, no. You don't have to take me," she said. "A taxi."

Sofia came down the hall, wiping her own eyes with her apron. "Mrs. Myna is very funny. But what are you doing?"

"I was asking for a taxi."

She spoke to Matteo and they came to an agreement. Sofia smiled indulgently and nodded yes to the boy. Matteo went splashing into the water and out the door.

"He wants to take you in the hotel boat. This is right for you, yes?" asked Sofia.

Stella got a funny queasy feeling, but she ignored it. "Yes, of course, but I don't want to bother him or you, for that matter."

"It is no trouble. He will go for the linens and the market for the fish, too."

Stella offered to pay, since she had some money to indulge in a ride, but Sofia waved the coins away. "It is nothing. Where do you go?"

Finally, something she knew. "The vaporetto stop at San Silvestro."

Sofia frowned. "You go to see the doctor?"

"Yes, that's it. The doctor and some other things. I won't be long."

Matteo called in the door and Sofia told him Stella's destination. He looked as puzzled as she did, but he grabbed an umbrella for Stella and helped her down the steps into the water. They splashed over the little dock and into a small craft, just big enough for four people in the cabin if they stood up and put the cargo on the back. Matteo settled her into a seat and they eased away from the dock. Stella relaxed on the hard seat. Life was good when you didn't have to walk.

# CHAPTER 14

*M*atteo helped her out onto the dock near the vaporetto stop. She thanked him in her rudimentary Italian and he blushed before jumping back in the boat, "*Ci vediamo.*"

Stella watched Matteo do an expert turn in the canal and considered her options. She could go to the telegraph office, Daniel's flat, or the hotel. There was no point in going to the hotel or the flat if her father hadn't gotten the message. There'd be no money to get. So the telegraph office it was. She knew the location, a little shop off Campo di San Silvestro. She'd been there with Abel several times to send telegrams to her parents. Nicky had been irritated enough with the frequent trips not to go with them. He just didn't understand telegrams flying back and forth over the Atlantic. The memory made her sad, but even with those little snits, they'd been happy. She hadn't known how lucky she was. She hadn't appreciated the money or the walking without pain or even the beauty of the city. There had been so much beauty then.

She turned around to orient herself and saw Matteo still there, idling across the canal and watching her. She waved and she could've sworn he blushed again before motoring off. Maybe Sofia had told him to keep an eye on her. It wouldn't be surprising. People seemed to think her fragile. But it didn't matter what Matteo thought or Sofia. She wasn't close to fragile. Maybe once but not anymore.

Now she saw the buildings and their beauty rising around her, not even her umbrella and the incessant rain blinded her to it. She smiled and headed off down the street and made it to the square in minutes. It was as she remembered, except flooded, of course. The water was a foot deep and people were plowing through it and chatting like it was normal.

Stella followed suit and made her way across the square past the ancient white marble well in the middle, smiling at a group of small boys who'd taken up residence and made it a kind of fort with umbrellas and tarps. They peeked out at her warily with their fingers turned into pistols looking for pirates or whatever boys look for before they notice girls. She waved and they shushed her. It was all a big secret.

A lady with a big bosom stood in a doorway, smoking a cigarette and wearing uglier boots than Stella, laughing and shaking her head. She aimed a pistol finger and the boys shrieked, retreating into their hideout. Fun in the middle of a mess. Stella smiled all the way over to the telegraph office and was glad she'd been there before. The sign wasn't big and making it grey on a grey building wasn't the best idea. If Abel hadn't known the way, it would've taken forever to find *"Poste e Telegrafo"* on the big square. It was like they didn't want you to find it and the man in the doorway wasn't happy that she did.

He was balanced on some sandbags and holding a hose that spewed water out into the square. He grimaced with a cigarette clamped in his teeth, looking her over and not missing a thing. Her fur was of particular interest. It had to go. He wasn't likely to forget it or her.

*"Buongiorno, signore,"* she said, hoping that he didn't care about her origins. Stella was in no mood to convince him that she wasn't a Jew or that it shouldn't matter if she was..

He eyed her for a few more seconds and then nodded but didn't move aside. She sighed and got out her dictionary, remembering another thing she hadn't appreciated before, Abel and his fluent Italian.

It took a second, but she got out, *"Telegramma per me."*

The man gave her a worn-out tourists-make-me-tired look and stepped aside, yelling behind him. *"Elena! Telegramma per turista."*

*"Turista? Che turista?"* yelled a woman.

*"Turista! Turista!"* he yelled back and waved Stella in impatiently.

She climbed up over the sandbags and stepped into the little office that was the same as before, except there was a wooden table in the middle, six inches deep in water. It had some sort of motor on it, making a terrible racket and belching smoke. It seemed to be sucking the water off the floor with several hoses but wasn't making fast work of it.

There were sandbags around the perimeter to protect the little post office boxes and a young woman leaned on the counter in the back in the alcove. Stella didn't recognize her. Before the office had been run by a mother and grandmother team, who fought constantly, and Stella was relieved they weren't there to either recognize her or yell.

This new woman was about Stella's age with beautiful long hair flowing down her shoulders in silky coils. Behind her, equipment was stacked to the ceiling and Stella wondered if they were operating. The girl waved at her shyly and Stella splashed over with her dictionary ready.

*"Buongiorno,"* she said, raising her voice to be heard over the racket. *"Telegramma?"*

*"Sì, sì.* What is your name?" she asked.

Stella leaned on the counter. "You speak English. I'm so happy."

The girl laughed. "I speak a little English."

"You speak a lot of English, but let's not quibble."

"What is *quibble*? I do not know this word."

"It's means argue, but that doesn't matter," said Stella, taking a second to appreciate her good fortune. "My name is Miss Myna. Do you have a telegram from the States for me?"

"Ah, yes, Miss Myna," she said happily. "I have it."

Stella could've cried.

"But you are not happy?"

"I'm very happy. Can I have it?" she asked, itching to read her father's words.

"Have you the passport?" the girl asked.

Stella handed over her passport and it was duly glanced at. She handed the passport back and gave her a slender envelope that Stella instinctively pressed to her chest.

"Do you want send a telegram?" asked Elena.

"Yes. I'm sure I do."

The motor behind her sputtered and gave up, causing the man to curse and toss down his hose.

"*Grazie Dio*," exclaimed Elena, getting her a hateful look in response. "My father, he is mad at the rain, but the rain it comes. No one can stop it."

"It will stop eventually," said Stella.

Elena nodded solemnly. "*Domani*. Tomorrow it will stop."

"I'm sure." Stella looked at the envelope and smiled. Patrick and her father had understood. The message was addressed to Miss Myna and was sent by Patrick. No mention of the Bled name thankfully. She slit open the envelope with her fingernail and held her breath as she unfolded the thin paper.

Dear beloved Miss Myna,

Funds sent. Pocket money. Josiah well. Mother frantic.

Return home immediately. Proceed to Genoa. The Italian Line. Tickets waiting.

Love, Father

Stella read the telegram three times and it made her heart hurt. The money was good, but that was the best of it.

"You send reply?" asked Elena.

She read it a fourth time and thought for a moment. "No. Not right now. You are open all day?"

"We close at noon to 1430 for *riposo*."

"Oh, right. I forgot." Stella looked at her father's words. She had to reply, but what could she say? Uncle Josiah was okay. Thank goodness. But Abel wasn't. Father would've said so if he was. And Mother. She'd completely forgotten about keeping it from her. If Patrick went to the house instead of the brewery, Mother would've read the telegram and known something was terribly wrong and, perhaps even worse, she realized Father knew and didn't tell her. To top it off, they couldn't proceed to Genoa or anywhere else. It was a struggle to get Nicky to the bathroom just then.

"You have message now?" asked Elena.

"No. I'll be back."

Elena nodded and Stella tucked the telegram in her handbag to join the growing collection. She splashed to the door, past the motor and Elena's father who was cursing and trying to start it by pulling a cord so hard Stella was surprised it didn't snap off, but then she turned around, splashing back.

"Elena?"

The girl returned to the window. "You send now?"

"No. I need some new clothes. Can you recommend a shop?"

"For you?"

"And my husband. Nothing fancy."

"To wear now?"

Stella nodded emphatically. "Off the rack."

Elena looked confused, but gave her directions to a shop, Venezia Augusto, that was close by. She even drew her a map.

"I almost forgot," said Stella. "Have you received any telegrams for a couple named Sorkine?"

"Sor…"

"Sorkine." Stella wrote it on the map and Elena shook her head.

"Can you describe?" she asked.

Stella couldn't and she could only suppose they were French. "They might be speaking French or have a French accent."

"No French in many weeks."

Stella sighed. But at least there was the money. That was a good thing. She must remember that and not the rest.

"Thank you." She splashed back out as the motor growled to life and spewed out a cloud of noxious smoke. Elena started yelling and Stella climbed over the sandbags into the square. The boys in the fortress were still on the well, but beyond them were two *polizia* huddled in a doorway next to the tall tower.

Stella caught her breath and turned the other way, doing her best to casually walk away. Her umbrella helped. It was a perfect shield. Everybody and their mother had a black umbrella and she made it out of the square without being noticed. There was no reason to think they were looking for her, but no reason not to either. Suddenly, Venice felt full of enemies, as Germany had, and she hurried away toward Daniel's flat, once again longing for the safety of home, but home as it had been. Now Father would be furious and Mother hysterical. Still, she preferred that to New York and the chilly Lawrences. If Nicky's parents knew anything had happened, they probably just had a glass of wine and called a lawyer to look into it, if that. Maybe that was ungenerous, but Stella wasn't feeling very generous. Nicky didn't care to send them a telegram reassuring them. She wasn't sure if that said more about him or them. Either way it wasn't a good sign and she made up her mind right there on the streets of Venice that she wasn't living in New York with those people. Her people would work to save Abel. His? Who knows.

Stella tried Daniel's flat first in hopes she wouldn't have to bother with the hotel, but he wasn't home. Butlers were on duty twenty-four hours a day when they had guests and he was probably overseeing their breakfast, arranging tours, or seeing to a million other details that a demanding guest might require. Daniel had said that she and Nicky were so self-sufficient it was like being on holiday. She got the feeling that other guests weren't quite so relaxing.

Going to the hotel wasn't ideal, not in her current state, and with Peiper out looking for them. It wouldn't be hard to find out where they'd stayed before and she expected him to show up and bang on the desk before the day was out. Daniel would keep quiet about seeing her, but there was no reason anyone else should.

She'd have go to the service entrance again and tip someone to find Daniel. It wasn't ideal, but nothing was anymore.

Even less ideal was her arrival. The hotel was abuzz with delivery people bringing everything from fish to flowers. She could scarcely squeeze through the door much less get anyone's attention. Stella had never been down there during delivery time. Night was fairly quiet, especially after dinner. Morning was a madhouse. People jostled her out of the way, pushing and yelling in Italian and sometimes French. Everyone was tremendously busy. Water covered the floors, dripping off coats, boxes, and umbrellas. Maids were trying to mop. Cooks were inspecting produce. Papers were passed back and forth with much yelling. Waiters pushed through, carrying enormous trays covered in silver cloches. One slipped and went down. Dishes flew everywhere. Hollandaise hit the wall and a chef hit the waiter.

Stella squeezed by and went for the stairs, not to go up but to hide out of the way until it calmed down. It didn't. It just kept going. She was about to give up when a white chef's jacket appeared in front of her. She stepped back and bumped into the wall. A man crouched and yelled in her face, wagging a finger, and demanding something, but she had no idea what.

"I'm looking for Daniel Burgess!" she finally yelled back.

He stopped mid-yell and stepped back to get a look at her. "Madam Lawrence?"

Stella didn't know whether to be relieved or not. "Yes," she said hesitantly.

"It is me, Serge, the sous chef." He patted his chest. "I taught you the meringue."

"Yes, of course, Serge. I just…"

He took her hand and kissed it the way only a Frenchman would, with style and aplomb. "I frightened you. I made a mistake. We do not allow people from the street to wander in." He looked at her ridiculous boots, making it plain that he meant riffraff, not people.

"I know and I'm sorry to intrude, but I'm looking for Daniel Burgess. Have you seen him today?"

"I have not. But what are you doing here? Do you not go to Greece?" he asked.

Greece. Stella went blank for a second and then she remembered that they hadn't told everyone about the change in plans. "We did and now we're back."

"Your fur." He waved at the matted black lamb. "You are not wearing a hat. What terrible thing has happened to you?"

Trust Serge to take a lack of hat as a sign of tragedy, but he wasn't wrong.

She smiled at him, tilting her chin down and batting her eyelashes. "It got wet. Everything's wet."

He threw up his hands. "This rain. It never stops."

"*Domani*," someone yelled and Serge made a rude gesture in return. "Here let me escort you upstairs. Mr. Lawrence? He is in your old suite?"

She pulled away. "No. Please. I just need to see Daniel."

He bent low over her. "You are here for Daniel? You have the… passion for the butler?"

"For God's sake, no. Can you send for him? He's done me a favor and I need to see him."

"But you come in the servant's hall?"

"Yes."

Serge thought for a second and then snapped his fingers. A busboy rushed up and he said, "Bring me Daniel Burgess."

The boy looked back and forth between the chef and Stella.

"Burgess now!" yelled Serge and the boy ran away.

"You're terrifying," said Stella.

He bowed. "Thank you. I run a good kitchen."

Stella didn't disagree, but she had no idea how beautifully prepared dishes came out of that insanity.

"I must return. Wait here." Serge ran off dodging crates of tomatoes and a dolly stacked with boxes of wine. No one else seemed to notice her. Maybe they didn't have a moment to notice. She could hear Serge yelling somewhere in the depths of the kitchen while she waited, thinking about the telegram. No reply came to her, except maybe a lie. She could say they were going to Genoa. It would soothe Mother but not for long and then it would be worse.

She was about to get it out again when Daniel ran down the stairs in a panic. "What are you doing here?"

"Looking for you. I've had a telegram from my father. Do you have the money?"

Daniel looked over his shoulder and led her into the depths of the servants' domain, taking her into a small room stacked with linens where two elderly ladies were ironing napkins. He asked them to leave and they did but not without giving scornful looks. They would probably tell everyone Daniel had one of *those* women in the linen closet, but Stella couldn't have cared less.

"The carabinieri are looking for you. Did you know that?" he demanded.

Stella went cold. "When?"

"This morning."

"Are they gone?"

"Yes. I nearly fainted when I heard them ask for you and Nicky."

"What did they say?"

Daniel paced in front of her. "They wanted to know if you were staying here."

Stella sighed in relief. "That's all?"

"No, that's not all. They said you stole a water taxi, Nicky beat up the captain, and threw him overboard. That can't be true."

"Well…"

"Mrs. Lawrence. They want to arrest you. They say you're wanted in Germany for theft."

"That is *not* true. Did they happen to mention that we stole that taxi because a Nazi was shooting at us?" she asked.

"That was about you?" he asked astonished.

"I thought they'd skip over that."

"Why was he shooting at you?"

"It's a long story," she said. "Do you have the money?"

He stopped pacing and stood in front of her, fists on his hips. "I don't know if I should give it to you."

"We're not criminals, not exactly. We couldn't just let him shoot us, could we?" asked Stella.

"But if someone's trying to hurt you, wouldn't you be safer in custody? The carabinieri can protect you and call the American embassy for you."

"Are you kidding? No. We'd be fish in a barrel."

"Mrs. Lawrence."

"Stella."

"Stella, you stole that man's taxi. That is a crime."

She took Daniel's hands and used every ounce of charm she possessed. "But we didn't destroy that boat. That was the SS officer and he did it on purpose. He shot Nicky and, if you don't help us, he'll finish the job."

Daniel blanched. "He shot Nicky. That wasn't in the paper. When? How? Is he…"

"He's okay. It's a flesh wound. Hurts like hell, but it's healing fast."

"He's seen a doctor?"

"Yes."

"Why is this SS trying to kill you?" asked Daniel.

"Like I said, it's a long story and it won't help you to know it. Please give me the money. I promise I'll explain everything someday."

Daniel squeezed her hands and, for a moment, she thought he'd refuse, but he let go and reached in his breast pocket withdrawing his wallet. "Your father sent 5000 dollars."

She smiled and clutched her handbag to her chest. "I knew he'd come through."

"That's more than a Studebaker. You could buy a house for that."

"Yes. Do you have it?"

Daniel did have it. Some of it. The bank didn't have 5000 dollars in dollars. They only had 1500 and he got that in hundred-dollar bills. He got another thousand in lira, thinking they would need it. Stella took the wad of bills and stuffed it in her handbag, making it fat and lumpy.

"Thank you so much, Daniel. You don't know how much you've done for us."

"What about the rest?" he asked uneasily.

"We'll worry about that later. Tell me about the carabinieri."

There wasn't a heck of a lot to tell. An officer, not Bartali, had come asking about them, but he wasn't, to Daniel's mind, terribly interested in the case or maybe he didn't believe that they would be stupid enough to come back to the same hotel. He did insist that Stella and Nicky were crazed criminals and had to be found immediately. To that, the staff had laughed in his face. The hotel manager argued and said they could not possibly be the people he was looking for. When the carabinieri claimed that he knew for a fact that they were, the manager informed him that Stella was heir to the Bled brewing fortune and Nicky was heir to United Shipping and Steel. The Lawrences were on their honeymoon. They'd hardly be going around stealing boats. That set the officer back on his heels. Apparently, he hadn't been informed of exactly who he was searching for.

The manager saw Daniel lurking around and he was brought over for questioning. Daniel said he hadn't seen them since they left earlier in the month. The carabinieri wanted to know where they went and before Daniel could answer, the manager had promptly said, "Greece."

"I guess no one told him about our change in plans," said Stella. "But I'm sure Abel told the concierge about Vienna. He changed our tickets. And Nicky told our waiter the night before we left and our porter. Lots of people knew. The maids. Practically everyone, except the kitchen staff. No one contradicted him?"

"They wouldn't, not if they value their jobs. Also, you and Nicky were well-liked. The carabinieri are not."

"But they might tell the Sorkines?"

"Unless Signore Blanca was standing there, yes, they would," said Daniel. "I, also, confirmed your trip to Greece. I said you were touring several islands before returning to the States."

Stella looked down. That had been the plan. The plan she changed.

"What is it, Stella?" asked Daniel.

"I wish we'd gone to Greece."

He reached out to touch her shoulder but couldn't quite make himself do it. His training was too ingrained. She could've used a hug, a fatherly shoulder.

"Stella?"

She smiled. That was something. He used her name without hesitating. "I'm fine."

"Vienna was very bad then?"

"It was the beginning of very bad."

"What did your father say?"

"He says to come home."

Daniel breathed a sigh of relief. "Quite right. Go home and forget."

"Did you ask around about the Sorkines?"

He did, but no one had seen them or been asking about them.

"Thanks for trying," she said.

"My pleasure."

Someone knocked on the door and Daniel answered in Italian. "The ladies need to finish their work."

She nodded. What to do now? She had two days to find the Sorkines. Then Nicky would be able to leave and she couldn't possibly refuse to go. But maybe it didn't matter, if she didn't find them in two days, she wasn't going to find them. And if she couldn't find them, maybe they wouldn't be able to find out where Abel had really gone. There was some comfort in that.

"Daniel, how many hotels are there like the Bella Luna?" she asked.

He put his nose in the air and was every inch the snotty butler. "None."

"Oh, come on. If we hadn't come here, where might we go? Lots of money to spend."

"You mean where might this couple be looking for you?"

"That's it exactly."

It hurt his pride to admit there were several hotels that might, just might, come close to the Bella Luna standard. She had him write the names on her father's telegram, five in all. "Alright. Which ones are below that?"

He drew back. "Below the Bella Luna and those five? You would never go to a hotel below the luxury class." He paused. "Where are you now? You never said."

"It doesn't matter." She couldn't help but smile. The Vittoria wasn't within spitting distance of the Bella Luna and it was perfectly fine, lovely in its own way. "Remember the Sorkines might not know which hotels are the standard."

His nose went farther up. "What kind of people are they?"

"Abel's people, his family."

He came crashing back to reality. "I forgot."

"I know you did and they are fine people. They live in the Marais district in Paris. A nice building, but not…"

"The Bella Luna sort."

She hated to admit that. It was so snotty. "That's it. Where would they go?"

He gave her five hotels that might suit. Not surprisingly, the Vittoria wasn't on the list.

The ladies knocked again, now complaining loudly. Daniel ushered her out and took her speedily through a back way and let her out a small side door that was so ill-used it had rust on the hinges and complained something fierce when he forced it open.

"Thank you, Daniel."

"About the money," he said.

"Don't worry. It's fine."

"It's not my money. I wouldn't presume to leave it in my account."

"I'll be back and if I'm not, consider it a tip."

He went stiff with indignation. "I do not need a tip to help you. It is my honor to serve."

"You're a hard man to please, Daniel Burgess." She kissed his stony cheek. "I like that about you."

"If Abel's people come, what should I do? How do I contact you?"

"Do me a favor, if they come and you talk to them, give them a message for me," said Stella.

"Of course. What is the message?"

She thought about it for a moment and then the image appeared in her mind. Gutenberg's portrait of his beloved wife. "Tell them that Stella Bled Lawrence said Nissa is safe and not to look for her anymore."

"Nissa is a person?"

"Yes. Just tell them. They'll understand."

"What if they ask about Abel?" he asked.

"I don't know if they will ask," she said.

"If they are Abel's family and he is connected to this Nissa person, they will ask, and I believe you most likely owe them an explanation," said the butler who served people and knew people.

"You're right and they might keep looking if I don't say."

"Is he somewhere they can't go?"

"He's somewhere I'm trying to keep them from going," said Stella. For some reason, this information was hard to give up, harder than saying Nicky had been shot, harder than being hungry, harder than begging their butler for help and money, but she had to say it. They had to know.

"Abel was sent to Dachau," she whispered.

"What's Dachau?" he asked, puzzled.

"It's a kind of prison. They sent the Jews in Vienna there." She could see Abel being pulled back into the boxcar. Uncle Josiah hadn't found him. He wasn't safe and it was her fault.

"This information will scare them?"

"It will hurt them. It hurts me."

He nodded. "But he may have already been released. They can't keep those people locked up forever."

"Says who?" asked Stella. "The United States? England? No one has done anything about the Kristallnacht."

"It's impractical and what purpose does it serve? None. Mark my words, Abel has been released and is looking for you right now."

He really believed that. Probably the whole world thought it, too, but they didn't really care as long as there wasn't another war.

"There's going to be another war," she said softly to herself more than Daniel.

"No. It won't happen. Chamberlain has avoided it. Hitler has what he wanted. He signed the agreement. Peace in our time." Daniel smiled. He believed in Chamberlain and she let him.

"Thank you again."

"Where are you going? To check the hotels?"

Stella opened her umbrella and stepped out into a deep puddle. "To telegram my father."

"To tell him you're coming home?"

"Yes." If she was going to lie to her father, she might as well lie to Daniel.

# CHAPTER 15

*S*tella hurried away from the hotel, composing the telegram in her head. Maybe she wouldn't lie. Maybe she would just do what Father had done. He hadn't said what had happened with Abel. She wouldn't say they were leaving. She wouldn't mention it at all. A simple "Thank you," and "All is well," would do to calm her mother down, if she didn't think too hard about it.

First, she'd do the shopping. When she had clothes she could go to those hotels and fit in. She could pay for water taxis now, so it wouldn't take that long. Half the hotels today and the rest tomorrow. If she didn't find them, she'd start on the telegraph offices. There had to be more than one.

A kind of peace came over her, a plan could do that, but she needed a map. Then she remembered she had one. For the first time, she had a destination and knew exactly how to get there, in Venice, no less. That was a miracle and deserving of appreciation, all on its own.

She pulled out her father's telegram with Daniel's list and Elena's map to the shop. She'd helpfully marked the Grand Canal and the square on it for reference. Stella found one of the marked crossroads and ended up at the shop without getting lost. It was just a little place, like the Vittoria, not what Daniel would've considered up to standard at all. But the dresses, while cheap, were stylish and had all the right bells and whistles.

Stella opened the door, smiling at her good fortune, and a little bell made her jump. A lady came out of the back wearing a smock and smoking a long cigarette. Her painted-on brows shot up when she saw Stella, hatless, in her soggy fur coat and ill-fitting, ugly galoshes. The woman's mouth frowned, but her eyes were calculating. Was she a Jew? Probably. How much money did she have left? Not much.

Stella absolutely had to get another coat. She'd chosen the fur because of its distinctive style. That was now a liability.

The woman waited, taking a long drag on her cigarette before asking something in rapid Italian that Stella didn't quite catch.

Stella pulled out her dictionary, cobbling together enough sentences to get her point and flush finances across in an Irish accent. The woman smiled, relieved. She understood completely and they found they didn't need to talk. Fashion was a common language. A wrinkled nose was enough to say no. A tapped chin, a yes. The lady, whose name Stella never knew, did a speedy measure of Stella's proportions, tapped her lips twice, and it was off to the races. Stella bought two suits, five dresses, a new, rather spectacular, green swing coat, and then they got to shoes. Stella refused to try them on, not wanting to reveal her feet. The lady shrugged and wrapped up shoes to match everything, plus panties, bras, stockings and new garters. Stella got herself and Nicky pajamas and then got him two new suits, an overcoat, and shoes. The lady looked like it was Christmas. Stella imagined she didn't sell that much in a week or maybe two weeks. So what if the clothes weren't the highest quality? Stella decided that was to her advantage. Peiper would be looking for Stella Bled of the Paris ateliers. Miss Myna was a different character altogether. She wore off the rack and silk wasn't her mainstay.

They finished with hats, sensible ones that were more about covering the head than making people look at it. Perfect. It did take a little dictionary work to explain that she wanted to wear one dress, a pretty little emerald shirt dress with a matching hat and the new coat, but she didn't want to wear the shoes. This was bizarre, Stella had to admit. The road outside was dry, but she managed to say that her hotel was flooded and the lady understood, although it obviously pained her not to see her work complete. They did have fun trading words. Stella pleased her by getting the accent perfect, eliciting clapping and Stella bowed. The language was starting to come to her, like putting together the little model train tracks that it was her job to assemble under the Christmas tree every year. Soon, the train would be chugging away and she wouldn't need a dictionary for every sentence.

After she'd changed clothes and had the extreme pleasure of putting on something brand new, the lady boxed up her purchases, her fur, and wrecked red suit to be delivered to the Vittoria and Stella paid her, peeling off crisp bills and adding a generous tip. So generous that she got kisses on her cheeks and what she thought was an invitation to come back anytime.

Stella stepped out of the shop and opened her umbrella. For the first time, she truly felt like Eulalie Myna. She'd put on another skin, it fit, and she liked it. This other girl took care of things, got money, and figured it out. This was good. This was right.

Like most good things, that lovely feeling didn't last long enough. Stella followed Elena's map back to the square intent on her telegram. She wasn't paying attention. She was happy, not thinking, and she didn't notice until it was almost too late.

Elena's father was still standing in the doorway of the telegraph shop, holding the hose and smoking, his face dark, his teeth bared. The motor chugged away behind him and wisps of black smoke snaked out of the top of the doorway.

He saw her when she reached the well, and his eyes lit up but not in a welcoming way. He gave a little shake of his head. She kept walking trying to remember the Italian she'd just added to her repertoire. But then he took his cigarette out of his mouth and flicked the ashes at her, a big fat go-away, if there ever was one.

Shocked, Stella stopped directly in front of Elena's father. He stepped into the middle of the doorway and waved her away, saying nothing.

Why? What was going on? It wasn't *riposo* yet.

Then she saw someone behind him through the gap and she leaned to the side to get a better look. Uniforms. The ordinary carabinieri uniform and another, the distinctive black of the SS. Stella couldn't breathe. How could he be there? Of all places. There. Right where she was going.

Stella turned quickly to the right and went into the first little alley she saw. She didn't think. She walked, taking as many turns as possible, and found herself lost. She was afraid to keep going and she was afraid to stop going. What if she ended up back on the square? What if she ran into Peiper on accident? What if Elena told Peiper about her? No, her father warned Stella away. Sofia and Daniel had said the people weren't overly fond of the carabinieri and they probably knew Peiper was the SS that was shooting up the streets of Venice and wrecking their beloved boats. That wouldn't win him any popularity contests either. Besides, she was Eulalie Myna with a Canadian passport, not half of an American couple named Bled Lawrence.

She turned a corner and at the end of the street were two carabinieri, her worst nightmare. No. Not quite. She didn't recognize them, not that she necessarily would. Men in uniform were sadly similar, but she couldn't turn tail. That would be the height of suspicious. So she became what her mother always warned against, a girl who flirted with strange men. That was supposed to be a black mark against one's character that could never be washed away, although Stella could never see why. All men were strangers until you met them. And the two at the end of the street, walking rapidly toward her, were prime candidates for flirting, young, handsome, and they'd noticed her in a big way.

Stella swung her hips and smiled, tilting her chin down and her umbrella back so that they might see her better. It could be a big mistake, but every instinct she had said to do it. She was wearing Italian clothes. She could be an Italian girl.

"*Ciao, signorina,*" said the one closest to her. He had stunning green eyes and Stella breathed a sigh of relief. She would've remembered him.

"*Ciao, signore*," she said in the shop lady's accent and moved to the side to pass them.

Both men paused and her chest tightened, but there was no recognition in their eyes. The other man, dumpy but with a lovely smile, said, "*Hai tempo per un caffè, signorina?*"

Stella caught the words for time and coffee. Just enough, along with the flirty smiles, to understand and she said almost without thinking, "*No mi dispiace.*" She heard that plenty in the shop when she asked for certain items the lady didn't have, silk stockings, for instance, and rayon was the only option.

The men made sad faces and she said with her little wave, "*Ci vediamo.*" She hoped it was the right thing. Antonio used it kindly and so had Matteo.

The carabinieri nodded enthusiastically and the green-eyed one winked. She passed them and felt their eyes on her as she walked away. It wasn't a wholly unpleasant experience to be watched. She liked being a pretty girl again and to be seen, not skulking around hoping to get by unnoticed.

She turned the corner, took a breath, and got out Elena's map again. It was useless with where she'd ended up, but she thought she could hear boat engines over the drizzle and she went in that direction, smiling at everyone she passed. She could do it. She could be Italian in limited doses and it seemed as big an accomplishment as getting the money.

Stella emerged onto the Grand Canal as she was hoping to, but in the last part she wanted. She'd gotten turned around at some point and was back at the San Silvestro vaporetto stop. There were a couple of carabinieri loitering in a doorway, smoking and drinking out of tiny espresso cups. They didn't look her way and several people were rushing onto the dock and Stella decided to go ahead and blend in with them. The vaporetto chugged down the Grand Canal and would be there in moments. She could get away from the carabinieri and back to Nicky quickly, if she was willing to chance it. She and the other six people on the dock looked the same, hunkered down with black umbrellas and old galoshes. She could do it. They'd never notice her.

The vaporetto cut its engine and coasted up to the dock. Before it even stopped the passengers were rushing aboard to get out of the rain and Stella followed suit. She stepped onto the boat and passengers came at her, trying to get off. She grabbed the edge of the guardrail to keep from being knocked back and several men came up behind her. Her stomach knotted as she folded her umbrella, reluctantly, and got through the small crowd to the other side of the bus, keeping her back to the entrance. No one asked for a ticket and or appeared to be selling them so she did her best to look like an old hand at vaporetto riding and examined her nails. The men, who came on behind her, smelled of sweat and espresso and were blowing out huge amounts of rancid smoke. Stella dared to glance back and caught a glimpse of a uniform.

Of course, it was the carabinieri. What had she been thinking?

But the men still weren't paying any attention to her. They were belly-aching about something. That was understandable in any language. She didn't pay much mind until she heard "Gestapo". They had to mean Peiper. According to Nicky, the Gestapo wasn't the same thing as the SS, but what they did sounded pretty much the same to Stella. Besides, how many Nazis were running around Venice irritating the carabinieri anyway?

"*Che palle!*" exclaimed one man and the other agreed.

The vaporetto pulled up to another stop, the Rialto bridge. She couldn't move. She should get off, get away, but somehow she couldn't. She had to hear what they said. If they mentioned the hotel or the Sorkines, she had to be there to hear it.

"*A chi importa di una ragazza americana? Può cercarla, se la vuole.*"

The other man responded to the affirmative with what Stella took to be cursing. *Americana.* That had to be her, not Nicky.

The vaporetto jolted forward and Stella cursed to herself. The engine was so loud she could barely make out what they were saying, but it didn't seem significant. No mention of the Sorkines, their hotel, Dr. Davide, or Father Girotti.

Then she cursed herself. She should've studied last night instead of lying in bed listening to Nicky groan. That was useless. She needed Italian. Maybe she could've found out why they happened to be at the telegraph office. That was quite a coincidence, but it could be nothing. She was going to check all the other offices for the Sorkines. Maybe Peiper was doing the same, looking for her. It was logical.

The men continued to crab for a couple more stops and then switched to lunch. At least, that's what Stella thought with all the talk mentioning fish and pasta. They may have been talking about their wives cooking for all she knew, but it wasn't about Peiper or her, unless they were calling her *branzino*.

When the water bus pulled up to the San Stae stop, she took a breath, turned and pushed between the men, keeping her head down, and saying, "*Scusi. Scusi.*"

The men parted and kept talking, not really seeing her at all. Stella stepped off the boat, opened her umbrella, and casually walked away, splashing onto the piazza in front of the church they'd been so unwelcome in. But she didn't go far, just far enough to see if they were getting off, too. They weren't and when the vaporetto started up again, Stella waited a moment after it left to return to the dock and peek around the edge of the building. When it was well enough away, she dashed out onto the dock.

They didn't go far. The next stop was the nearest to the ghetto. It'd take some walking, but they have to get off if they wanted to go to there. Stella squinted and wished for binoculars. People got off, but the umbrellas blocked everything. She thought she saw the carabinieri get off, but it was far enough away that she couldn't be certain.

She turned around and went as fast as she could across the piazza. The water was deeper and threatening to come up over the edges of her boots, if she wasn't careful. The church now had sandbags piled against the doors, making it even less friendly than before. She carefully trod down the water filled alley beside it and found herself at the Vittoria's backdoor in the tiny alley in record time. It was locked and she knocked, making a concerted effort not to pound on the door, even though her feet were freezing and she'd begun to worry that she'd been gone too long. Nicky might've gotten up. Someone could've seen his wound.

After a long, drawn-out minute, Antonio came. He opened the door with a smile and Stella's knees went weak. Smiles were good. Well, they were good when the SS wasn't smiling them anyway.

"*Ciao, bella,*" he exclaimed, taking in her new clothes.

"*Ciao,* Antonio."

Sofia came around the corner. "You've been shopping, yes? The green is lovely on you."

She led her into the main hallway and Stella closed the umbrella, depositing in the bin.

"Thank you. I found a little shop and they were very helpful," she said. "How is Mr. Myna? Have you checked on him by chance?"

"He is better," she said. "Dr. Davide is with him now."

Sofia was smiling, but her eyes were serious.

"Such service," said Stella.

"Yes, I fear this will be costly."

Stella patted her bulging handbag. "Not to worry. I'm happy to pay for good care."

Sofia relaxed and Stella left her at the desk, walking down the hall past several guests with a smile and in no particular hurry.

The room door was unlocked and she went in, continuing to smile. It didn't last but a moment. "What is that smell?"

"Me." Dr. Davide was stretched out in the chair with his arms behind his head, revealing large sweat stains. "I've had a long day."

"I imagine all of your days are long." Stella turned to Nicky and was surprised to see him sitting up. "You're better."

"He gave me a shot," said Nicky. "A big one."

"Eukadol?"

"Beats me."

She looked at the doctor and he nodded. "I found him trying to get dressed, not resting."

Nicky plucked at the covers and wouldn't look at her. "I was going to the bathroom."

"He was going to look for you," said Dr. Davide. "Some nursemaid you are."

Stella unbuttoned her new coat and hung it in the wardrobe. "I'm a fine nursemaid. I got the money to pay you."

He slapped his hands together and rubbed them furiously. Stella waited for him to salivate, but it didn't get that far. "All of it?"

"Yes, all of it."

He gave her the once over. "Nice rags. Those'll get you through."

Nicky blinked at her, bleary-eyed. "You went shopping before you came back?"

"We needed clothes." She jerked a thumb at Davide. "Ask him."

"You two looked like you'd been through hell and I know hell," said Dr. Davide. "Nose is good now, too. How are the feet?"

"You care?"

"You paying me?"

"Yes."

"Then I care."

"Better. I saw another doctor."

Dr. Davide put his hands behind his head again. "I heard. Spooner's a good man."

"How did you know?" she asked.

"He told me."

Stella put her handbag on the side table and sat on the bed, putting her hand to Nicky's forehead. No fever. That was good. "Why on Earth would he tell you?"

"Fifty lira," said Dr. Davide.

"Are you serious?"

He sneered at her and pulled a flask out of his breast pocket. "If you've got my 2000 lira, what's another fifty?"

"That's not the point," she said. "What is wrong with you?"

He took a long drink and offered her the flask. "I've got bills to pay like everyone else."

"What would you charge me for a drink?" asked Stella.

"On the house."

Nicky reached out. "I'll take it." He leaned too far and Stella had to pull him upright again.

"No, sir," said the doctor. "You don't mix medications. You want to know the purpose of the good Dr. Spooner's call or not?"

Stella was suddenly tired. She could've laid down beside Nicky and gone right to sleep. "Fine. Why did he call?"

"He got a friendly little visit from the carabinieri this morning, except it wasn't so friendly. Spooner got smacked around for a while." For the first time, Dr. Davide's expression wasn't one of greed or smarmy indifference. Stella couldn't quite read it, but there was some kind of pain there.

"The carabinieri beat up some doctor?" asked Nicky, becoming alert.

"Not too bad," said Dr. Davide. "Call it a little official motivation."

"I can't believe they hurt him." Stella stood up and turned to the wall. There she went again, making a victim where there wasn't one before.

"Believe it. That's how the carabinieri work, saves time."

"Is he okay?" she asked.

"He's fine. You want to know what they asked him?"

She did and it was worth the fifty bucks. Bartali had shown up at the doctor's house, asking for confirmation about Stella's name and religion. Dr. Spooner confirmed that she was Eulalie Myna and a Catholic, and got a few good smacks just to make sure. Bartali was frustrated. He didn't believe she was who she said she was. He didn't believe that Nicky had cholera, or anything like it either, but he had nothing to prove it.

"Why does he care so much?" asked Nicky. "I don't understand. We've done nothing to him."

"Bartali got himself in a little trouble last year. Now he's down at the bottom of the barrel and trying to claw himself back up. Lucky for you," said Dr. Davide with little smile.

"Why's it lucky?" slurred Nicky. "He's been on us since we got here. I call that damn unlucky."

The doctor kicked his feet up on the bed. "Because Bartali is on the outs. Low man on the totem pole. Dangling on the bottom rung. He's the—"

"We get it," said Stella. "Bartali's a loser, but that's not helping us."

Dr. Davide drained the flask. "Ah, but it is. Bartali beat the stuffing out of Colonello Costa's cousin last year. Put the boy in the hospital for a month. He got stripped of four ranks and is persona non grata."

"So what?" asked Stella, turning around. "He's still a carabinieri. He's still beating people up."

He yawned and shook a couple of drops out of the flask onto his tongue. "He got put on the job nobody wants, finding Jews and hassling them. That's why he's here bothering Sofia's guests on a daily basis. She's known for turning a blind eye to refugees."

"How does that help us?" asked Nicky.

"Because Bartali's on the Jews, nobody talks to him and I mean nobody. Jews have been marrying Italians forever. Most everybody is friends with a Jew or has a Jewish brother-in-law, including the higher ups in the carabinieri. Bartali wasn't popular before. Now, he may as well throw himself off the Rialto." Dr. Davide shook his flask at Stella. "On the downside, he thinks you're his ticket out of purgatory."

"Us?" asked Stella. "Even if we were Jews, how would that help him? He hassles Jews all the time."

The doctor stood up. "I need whiskey."

Stella went over and pushed him back down. "No, you don't. Why does Bartali think arresting us would help him?"

"Sofia keeps a nice bottle. I could use a drink. You have the money or so you say."

Stella put her hands on her hips. "Tell me. Now."

He stroked the bristles on his chin and looked up at her. "Bartali may be a bastard, but he's not stupid. He's on to you."

"On to us?" asked Nicky warily.

"We all know you're not Canadians that lost your luggage. Something's going on with you and Bartali can smell it. You're lucky the muckety-mucks don't tell him squat."

Nicky got stiff and all the muscles popped out on his torso. "What would they tell him?"

Dr. Davide laughed. "That the SS officer who shot up our precious little island isn't just crazy. He's after someone specific, a couple of pretty Americans named Lawrence that just so happen to look a hell of a lot like you two."

# CHAPTER 16

Stella pulled off her galoshes and stabbed her new hat with her precious pin. Dr. Davide was paid up for both his work and his silence. It hadn't taken the doctor long to figure out who they really were. The carabinieri, who were in the know, had been going to every high-priced hotel in Venice asking for Nicolas and Stella Lawrence. That was the bad news. The good news was how they were described; young, beautiful, and wealthy Americans. The Venetians, not overly fond of the carabinieri to begin with, weren't buying it. According to Dr. Davide, the hotels were pushing back. A Bled of the Bled brewing family stole something in Germany and then came to Venice and stole a water taxi? A couple of places laughed. Others downright thought they were lying for some nefarious purpose as they'd been known to do. The reaction was worse when Peiper was there. Everyone knew what he'd done and people wouldn't tell him the time of day. Mussolini might have admired Hitler, but the Venetians weren't enthralled and they didn't like some SS coming down and demanding information as if they belonged to Germany. They weren't Austrians and they told Peiper to get lost.

Dr. Davide was amazingly well-connected for a drunk, but Stella shouldn't have been surprised. Uncle Josiah tended to know everyone who was fond of whiskey and a good time. Dr. Davide wasn't so fond of a good time as he was discreet and cheap. He treated things that had to be kept from wives and lied on demand. The doctor was always ready for a drink and a card game. Being rather bad at the latter made him welcome in most places.

"We have to leave, Stella," said Nicky.

"And you're in shape for travel?"

"I am." His head lolled to the left. "I will be."

She bit her lip and crossed her arms. "How does it feel?"

"Doesn't feel like anything."

Stella checked her own bandages and they were a tiny bit damp so she undid Dr. Spooner's good work and checked her feet. Not bad. Not bad at all. They were nearly normal-sized and the splits were closing up. Taking Matteo's ride and the vaporetto had certainly helped.

"What are you doing?" he asked.

"Putting my bandages back on," she said.

"Why?"

"I'm going out."

Nicky tossed off the covers and fell over in a heap. "Out...of the question. I will not allow it."

Stella pushed him back upright and tucked him in. "To get lunch. You want to eat, don't you?"

He gazed at her, unblinking.

"What?" she asked.

"Where are you going?"

"To get lunch."

"You're going to search for the Sorkines."

A soft knock startled them both. Stella waited for a demand from Bartali, but nothing happened. She went to the door and found Antonio standing there, smiling with another man, who was piled so high with boxes she could only see a damp mop of hair over the top.

"*Grazie. Grazie,*" said Stella. "Douglas, our clothes are here."

"Swell," said Nicky.

"It is swell," she shot over her shoulder. "Come in, Antonio."

The men weren't anxious to enter a sickroom, but they did, quickly unloading their boxes on the bed beside Nicky and retreating twice as fast. Stella had to chase them down to give them a tip. Antonio tried to refuse, but she insisted. It felt too good to be able to thank him properly to let it go.

Back in the room, Nicky was snooping through the boxes. "How much did you buy? The whole store?"

"Not quite, but who knows when I'll be able to shop again," she said.

"I know. When we get back to the States."

"Whenever that is."

"If we leave early tomorrow, we can get to Genoa in time to find a ship and leave the next day."

Stella ignored that and sifted through the boxes in search of Nicky's clothes. Predictably, they were on the bottom. "I got you pajamas."

"I want to talk about leaving," he said.

She flipped back the covers. "So talk."

He tried to cover up. "Stop that."

"I've seen it all before and you needed pajamas. I got them. Is there nothing that will please you?" She reached over to help him up and he grabbed her arm.

"Stella, we have to leave. You heard Dr. Davide. It's only a matter of time before Bartali hears about who Peiper is looking for. It's a miracle he hasn't already."

"We deserve a miracle, so it's fine by me."

"That's not the point. As soon as he puts it together, we will be arrested for boat theft and whatever Peiper has cooked up."

"What's he going to cook up?" she asked.

"You stole his plane for one," said Nicky.

Stella grinned at him. "It was just a little plane."

"He'll have us back in Germany before we know what's happened. We will go to prison."

Stella got him standing, checked the new bandage that Dr. Davide had put on, and offered new briefs. Nicky agreed reluctantly. Stella didn't know why, unless it was just to be stubborn, which was a distinct possibility. He had that bulldog look again.

She helped him into the pajamas and he laid down with a sigh. "I didn't know cotton could feel so good."

"I guess I did something right," said Stella as she hung up her dresses.

"You do a lot right, but you can't do this."

"Because?"

"For God's sake, because it's crazy. Because I say so."

"Don't start that husband thing again." She hung up his new suits. They looked nice and the tailoring wasn't bad.

"I'm not starting anything," said Nicky. "But this can't go on."

Stella managed to wedge her feet in a new pair of shoes, but just barely. The bandages made her feet so fat. Back to the galoshes. "What about lunch? Can you eat?"

"I don't want to eat. I want you to say you're not going out."

"Do you think they do chicken soup here?"

"It would have fish in it. Everything has fish in it," he said. "I'm serious, Stella."

She tucked him in. "I promise that I'm only going to see about food for you."

"Promise you won't leave the hotel until I can leave with you."

Stella kissed his forehead and then both his cheeks. "No."

"No?"

"Would you rather I lied?"

Nicky looked like that wasn't a terrible idea, but he said, "I can't stop you."

"Why would you want to? Abel's your friend, too. We're doing this for him. Don't forget I'm the one that landed him in Dachau."

"He could've refused to go to Vienna."

"Abel wouldn't refuse me anymore than you would've," said Stella, eliciting a funny look from Nicky. "What?"

"Nothing," he said, pulling her close. "Abel wouldn't want to risk you. He'd be the first to say, 'No. Don't do it.'"

"We're talking about his family here, so I wouldn't be so sure about that."

He took her face in his hands. "I am sure. He would not want anything to happen to you." He had a look in his eye that made her stomach flip. "And I think you know that."

Stella pulled back. "I'm risking me. I belong to me."

"Because I screwed up our vows."

She laughed. "You didn't screw up. I was never going to obey, whether I vowed it or not. My mother doesn't." She was rewarded with his mouth dropping open and it was very satisfying.

"Are we talking about the same woman?" he asked.

"Francesqua Bled. Yes. My mother doesn't obey my father. Don't confuse demure with weak."

"I didn't say she was weak."

"But you thought it because you don't know her, not really, and there's a lot of her in me," said Stella.

"I thought you were all Bled," he said.

"I'm all me." She walked to the door. "Soup?"

The bulldog look vanished. "How long do you plan to be gone?"

"I really am just getting you something to eat."

"You know what I mean."

How long was a good question. Even in Stella's stubborn resolve to find the Sorkines, she knew there was a point in which it became too much. She just wasn't at that point yet.

"I have a list of hotels that Daniel gave me. Likely places that people like us might stay," she said.

"How many?" he asked with a bit of hope in his eyes.

"Ten in total. I'll do as many as I can today."

"And then what?"

"I'll go to the telegram offices. How many do you think there are?" she asked.

Nicky thought about it. "Five or six, maybe. I can't tell you how much I want to do this and leave you here."

"It's better this way." Stella smiled and touched up her lipstick.

He crossed his arms. "How do you figure?"

"Because you're you and you're always you, even when you're Douglas Myna."

Nicky shook his head. "That shot has me thick as a brick wall."

"You're not thick. You're Nicky Lawrence. We can't disguise that; tall, blond, unbearably handsome."

"You're Stella Bled Lawrence."

"Not today. Today I was Italian. A carabinieri asked me for a date. He had no idea I wasn't a local girl." She spun around, belling out her skirt.

"You got asked on a date?" Nicky looked about ready to jump out of bed and pound someone.

She laughed. "I said no. When I go to the hotels, I'll be French, English, or Dutch." She gave him a trial run in her Dutch girl persona and he smiled.

"That's good. Very good, but you still have those blue eyes, that face."

"But I'm Dutch and wearing middle-class clothes. They're looking for a wealthy American couple and I don't have a big blond man with me. He'll expect us to be together."

"He might know that he shot me."

"The Italians don't, so I think we're safe."

Nicky watched her and then said, "Don't do a German accent. They'll lump you in with Peiper."

She dashed back to the bed and kissed his forehead again. She would've kissed him on the lips, but, as much as she loved him, the vomit scent nixed that. "It'll be fine. I can do it."

"You can do anything, but Bartali isn't a fool. This is going to come together for him."

"I'll be as fast as possible."

He took her hand and kissed it. "When it's done we leave."

She agreed and she meant it. She really did.

"Looks like I'm going to be here for a while on my own," said Nicky.

Stella went back to the door. "You'll sleep."

"Not the whole time. Do you think Sofia has any books in English?" Nicky held up *The Jungle Book* that he'd finished reading.

"Maybe, but I know someone who definitely does."

He flipped to the ex libris. "Let me guess. The Ladners?"

"Bingo."

Sofia was way ahead of Stella. She'd had her cook make something she called, *Pastina*.

The cook ladled up a bowl and Stella had her doubts. The kitchen smelled like fish and there was a pile of fish bones that was getting dumped in an enormous pot next to the little pot that the cook dipped into.

"*Pastina* is for the sick, yes." Sofia dropped two triangles of parmesan cheese in the center of a clear broth with tiny pieces of pasta floating around in it. "He will be well. This is my grandmother's recipe. She fix everything with it."

"You should give it to Rosa von Bodmann," said Stella.

Sofia pointed at a tray on the work table. "I am. The poor lady is very ill today."

"Can I take it? I would like to borrow a new book for Douglas. He's a bit better and getting bored."

The cook finished the trays and Stella loaded them on a cart, covered in cloches to keep them warm. Stella hadn't thought she was hungry until the cheese hit the hot soup. The smell was intoxicating and it was definitely chicken, not fish, so she got a bowl for herself, too.

She wheeled the cart down the hall, half expecting to see Bartali lurking around although Sofia swore he'd gone. She didn't say that she was very worried, but she was, reminding Stella it wasn't only about her and Nicky, the Sorkines, and Abel. Other people had been caught in the crossfire before and Sofia could easily be the next one.

Stella knocked on the von Bodmann's door and Karolina answered timidly, her eyes red as her hair. "Mrs. Myna, I didn't expect to see you today. We heard about your poor husband."

"He's better actually. I was getting his lunch and I've brought yours. May I bring it in?" asked Stella.

She opened the door and the smell of liniment washed over Stella. The smell wasn't unpleasant but it spoke of how ill Rosa was. That and Karolina's slumped shoulders. All her energy had vanished and she was a different woman. If not for her size and hair, Stella would scarcely have recognized her.

"Yes, please," she said. "Can you put it on the bed? Rosa will not mind."

Rosa didn't mind. She lay back on the pillows, smaller than ever, her mouth sagging open as she slept an uneasy sleep.

"Thank you," said Karolina.

"I was wondering if I could borrow a book for Douglas," said Stella, setting down *The Jungle Book* on the Kipling stack. "He's bored and restless."

Karolina lit up. Books, her salvation, came to the rescue, giving her a touch of the vitality that Stella missed. "Yes, of course. What is to his taste?"

Stella was stumped. The only thing she'd seen Nicky read, other than the Kipling, was newspapers. "I really don't know."

"Our English authors are in the original English or does he read in French or German?" asked Karolina.

"Let's stick with English."

She led Stella over to the window where stacks of books blocked a good deal of the light. Stella recognized some, running her fingers over familiar spines of *The Murder of Roger Ackroyd*, *Gone with the Wind*, *Pride and Prejudice*, *Rob Roy*, and *Stamboul Train*. Then she got to E.M. Forster. The ladies had all his novels in lovely burgundy with gilt lettering. Forster was her mother's favorite and Stella had read them all. He was good for a lazy Sunday with the wind howling outside, quiet and comforting, not Nicky's style at all, but her hand kept going back to *Howard's End*.

"If I might interject," said Karolina, "that is not a book for a young man."

"No?" asked Stella, her mind in the story. It had been a couple years since she read it. Who were the characters? She smiled. "Margaret Schlegel was fantastic."

"You've read it then?" asked Karolina.

"Yes. My mother loved Margaret and she felt so badly for," —she tapped the spine— "what was the mother's name? The one that died."

Karolina took her hand and squeezed, comforting them both. "Ruth. Ruth Wilcox."

"She was lovely, but she had a very trying husband."

"She did. But don't we all?"

They smiled together.

"Look here," said Karolina. "This is a book for your husband." She put a slim volume in her hands and Stella tore her eyes away from *Howard's End*.

"*The Great Gatsby*?" she asked. "Never heard of it."

"That's a shame. It's a great effort and, may I say, very American."

Stella looked over the cover, a beautiful work of art. Eyes blazing in the sky above a fairground or carnival. That was enough to sell it. "You don't mind if I borrow it?"

"Not at all. Books are for reading, not sitting on a shelf forgotten. My husband liked this book very much. I will be happy to have yours read it."

Stella opened the cover and found, as she feared she would, the beautiful ex libris of Max Ladner. "Karolina, you have to take this out. Please. I beg you."

"No. I will not. And you must promise me that you won't either."

"It's just a bookplate."

"No. It is what I have left."

Stella promised and took *The Great Gatsby*. She turned to go and Rosa opened her eyes. She tried to speak, but wasn't able to get the words out. The hint of vitality went right out of Karolina.

"Has Dr. Davide been by?" asked Stella.

"Yes..."

Stella raised an eyebrow.

"He is a very good doctor, but sometimes…"

"He drinks."

A whoosh of breath burst out of her. "Yes. I do not mean to sound ungrateful. He is kind to come."

"What about Dr. Salvatore?" asked Stella.

"He cannot. The carabinieri, he is watching him and we aren't Jews."

Stella wasn't sure what to say. They were Jews. She'd have bet the farm on it, but it hardly mattered.

"I heard…Bartali." Karolina puffed up to her normal height and balled up her fists, like she was getting ready for a fight.

"What did you hear?"

"He said to the other carabinieri that you lied to him."

Stella laughed. "You'd think he'd be used to it."

"You said you went to another doctor and he didn't believe you."

Rosa was watching from the bed and she couldn't lie, not to them, not with Rosa's life so tenuous. "I didn't lie about that. I saw Dr. Irving Spooner."

"He is the doctor for the rich and the tourists?" asked Karolina.

"I think so. We didn't really discuss his practice. He's British," said Stella.

"This doctor treated you? He didn't ask any questions?"

"He did, but it was fine. He knows Dr. Davide and Dr. Salvatore. Something about birth certificates."

The ladies exchanged a glance and Karolina said, "Will you ask him to come to Rosa? We can pay, but you mustn't tell him who we are."

"I don't really know who you are," she said with a wink. "Why didn't you ask Dr. Davide? He was just here."

Karolina's strength faded and she wrung her hands, looking down. "I didn't want to insult him. He's done so much and he didn't have to take the chance. Others wouldn't."

"I'm sure he was well-paid." Stella couldn't keep the sarcasm out of her voice and Karolina looked up sharply. "Oh, no. You misunderstand him."

"I don't think so. He's wringing us out for every nickel."

"Not Dr. Davide," whispered Rosa. "He's a truly kind person."

"Dr. Davide?" asked Stella. "Fat, drunk, bald? He just charged me fifty lira for some information he got for free."

"He must've had a good reason," said Karolina stoutly.

"If you say so."

Karolina took Stella's hand. "Will you ask Dr. Spooner to come? I would not ask you, but Rosa is so much worse and Dr. Davide says he can't do anything."

Stella didn't know what to say. She certainly couldn't mention that Dr. Spooner had already been smacked around on account of knowing her. She didn't want them to be afraid. They were already scared enough. He probably wouldn't come, but the ladies were looking at her with such hope she had a moment of weakness and said yes. She'd ask, but she couldn't guarantee anything.

Karolina thanked her profusely to the point that Stella was embarrassed, knowing it was probably pointless.

Rosa raised a weak and shaking hand. She whispered something, but Stella wasn't sure any words came out.

Karolina bent over her, putting her ear close.

"Oh yes." She smiled at Stella and seemed to find something happy in that room filled with illness and fear. "My sister would like to show you something she thinks that you will appreciate."

"A book?" asked Stella. "I think you must have all the good ones."

"We do, but it's not exactly a book," Karolina whispered.

"You've piqued my interest. My father is a collector of many things, mainly art, but rare editions are favorites, too."

"This is the rarest edition." Karolina held out her hand and, with Stella's help, she got down on her knees to dig around under the bed. She pulled out boxes of books until she found a heavy, rectangular box made of oak and filled with less interesting books, like reading primers and tattered music books.

Stella couldn't imagine why the ladies lugged those to Italy, unless they were purely sentimental. Karolina passed the ordinary books to

Stella and she stacked them on a pile of Thomas Mann's work, including the one about Venice.

"Here it is," said Karolina as she pulled another box out of the first box. This one was fine and made of rosewood with inlaid flowers, dragons, birds, and vines. She handed the box up to Stella and hoisted herself up to her feet. Rosa held out her hands as much as she was able. Karolina put the box on her lap and helped her to open the lid. Stella couldn't see what was inside, but the ladies were clearly enthralled. "This was my husband's prize possession."

"Max?" asked Stella.

"Yes. Max was my husband. He was Rosa's brother."

Rosa tapped the box and Karolina lifted a thick roll out. It was wrapped in fine, white linen and it took a minute or so to unwrap. When Karolina revealed Max's prize possession, Stella couldn't speak. It looked like...but it couldn't be.

"Do you know what it is?" asked Karolina. "We thought maybe you would. You have that look about you."

"Do I?" whispered Stella. "What look is that?'

"That you have seen treasures and love them dearly."

She nodded. "Is that...a Ripley Scroll?"

The ladies smiled broadly, even Rosa, who barely had the energy to blink.

"Yes, it is. Would you like to see it?" asked Karolina.

"Very much. My father showed me pictures once, but I've never seen a real one."

"I am not surprised," she said. "There are only twenty-four scrolls in existence." Karolina explained that Max's grandfather had purchased the scroll in the last century while visiting England and it was, other than Gutenberg's diary, the most wondrous thing Stella had ever seen. She and Karolina unrolled it but not to its full length, which she said was over twelve feet. It was the illustrated version of George Ripley's work, a noted alchemist, and gave instructions on making the elixir of life.

"It's done on vellum and painted by Leonard Smethley in around 1620."

Stella had to hold herself back from touching the fantastic images of dragons, a creature half-human half-lizard, nude men, along with the confusing instructions that had something to do with a magical toad, the sun, and a bird with a human head. The colors were wonderfully bright and the whole thing preserved like it had rarely seen the light of day, which Stella imagined it hadn't.

"Thank you," she whispered. "It's wonderful."

Rosa lifted her hand and Stella kissed it.

Karolina began rolling it back up carefully, the vellum making little snaps and cracks.

"I'm afraid I have to go, although I hate to," said Stella. "I have so many questions. I assume Max studied it."

"He did. It was in many ways his life's work." Karolina wrapped the scroll back in its linen. "But you go now, give Douglas his soup, it will be here when you have more time."

Rosa whispered something and Karolina went over to listen. "She wants to know when you are leaving Venice and where you will go when you leave." She shrugged. "I don't know why it's important. Do you mind saying?"

"Not at all. I think we may leave as early as tomorrow and Douglas wants to go straight to New York, but I don't know what we'll do."

Rosa touched Karolina's hand and the ladies whispered back and forth. Rosa got more agitated than Stella thought she was capable of.

"What's wrong?" she asked.

"Nothing, dear," said Karolina. "She's just very tired."

That didn't look accurate to Stella from the frown on Rosa's pale face, but she let it go and excused herself. She went into the hall, bumping right into Mr. Bast, lumbering down the passage with his typewriter and a stack of files.

"You look like the cat that got the cream," he said jovially, but then paused. "Perhaps it was bad cream."

"No, Mr. Bast. It's fine. Excuse me." She kept the book pressed to her chest and hurried off down the hall. He was watching her, that odd Mr. Leonard Bast, and, for the first time, she didn't like it.

# CHAPTER 17

*O*nce Nicky had eaten his soup, Stella slipped out. He wouldn't be happy, but it had to happen. He'd regained his normal coloring and was healing remarkably fast. Only Dr. Davide's shot of Eukadol kept him in bed. Stella would be lucky to get another day of rest out of him.

The first hotel was a bust and the second and the eighth. On the way to the ninth, a swanky affair off St. Mark's Square, Stella passed a little shop selling glasses. On a whim, she went in just as they were trying to close. A smile and a flash of cash got her through the door. So far her accents had been going off without a hitch, but she did look the same every time. Glasses could change that. Through a bit of back and forth, she got the confused clerk to sell her a pair with plain glass lenses he had sitting in the window for display. She said it was a joke she was playing on her husband. The clerk's response indicated she was too pretty for glasses and she wondered what she was supposed to do if she actually couldn't see. Be blind?

He sold them to her for a discount and asked her where she was from in Ireland. Stella picked Dublin since she was using Mavis's accent, but she could've said Cork or Belfast. He wouldn't have known the difference. He was too busy looking at her décolletage. But it occurred to her that broadening her Irish accents could be helpful. She knew Mavis so well; her accent was easy. Michael, the boy that delivered from the green grocer, was Irish. His accent was different. Mavis turned up her nose at him, saying he was shanty Irish, whatever that meant.

The clerk opened the door for Stella quietly asking if she would like a coffee. She said that she wished she could but had to get back to her hotel. He didn't press and gave her a little bag with her glasses, ushering her out into the darkening street. The rain pounded on her umbrella and she splashed into St. Mark's Square to get her bearings. The square was wide awake and alive with people. Stella hadn't encountered so many tourists since they'd arrived. Probably because most of them were there. People were actually sitting at Caffè Florian, sipping overpriced coffee under the gallery with water up around their ankles. Stella had to give it to them. They weren't letting the rain beat them, but it was beating her. There'd been a lot of walking and her feet were aching, her coat was damp, and, worse of all, she had nothing to show for it. Stella was starting to think it was pointless. The Sorkines probably had more sense than she did and had left Venice.

Stella walked across the flooded square on a wooden walkway that was just above the water line and found the street to the next hotel, Hotel Barocci. That hotel was so swanky they had a walkway built off the one on the square that led right to their door. A double layer of sandbags was piled up in a half moon to protect the ornate entrance which was entirely dry.

She put on her new glasses as she approached and felt instantly unattractive. They were not good-looking glasses, if that even existed. These were particularly bad in heavy, black, round frames that were so close to her eyes that her lashes knocked against the lenses every time she blinked. But they did make her look different. They were the kind of glasses that took over a face, which was exactly what she needed.

She stepped down off the walkway with the help of the doorman. He asked if he could help her in Italian. She could now understand that question, she'd heard it so many times, and she responded in her English accent, saying she just needed to go to the front desk to ask about a guest. He opened the door for her and she went into the grand atrium of a former palace with a double staircase that couldn't have been more overdone if it tried. Two clerks stood directly across from her at a desk that made Napoleon's tomb look humble. They greeted her simultaneously with polite smiles.

Stella asked them if a couple named Sorkine had been in looking for anyone in the last three days. She couldn't say they were looking for Bleds or Lawrences since the carabinieri were looking for them. The last thing she needed was for someone to put those puzzle pieces together. And by now, she had the description down pat, French, middle-aged, and well-dressed, but not wealthy and that worked for every hotel so far.

As Stella expected, they said no and when pressed they did call the manager, who also said no.

"Who are these people?" asked the woman.

It wasn't an unusual question and Stella had a quick response that they were friends of the family that they were supposed to meet at St. Mark's, but they hadn't shown up. She knew their hotel was right off the square and she thought that might be the one.

Both clerks nodded and apologized, but the manager got a little squinty. He was thinking and Stella didn't like it.

"I'll leave you to it then. Sorry to disturb," she said.

"You don't have a son, do you?" he asked as she turned.

Stella laughed. "Do I look old enough to have a son?"

The woman blushed and quickly said, "We are not asking your age, ma'am."

"I should hope not. One never asks a lady's age."

The manager was undaunted by the embarrassed look the woman gave him. "What was the name of these people again?"

"Sorkine."

He frowned. "They are French you said."

"May I ask what you are thinking?" asked Stella, trying to stay calm.

"Do you have a younger brother here perhaps?"

She didn't know what made her say it, but she replied, "I have a cousin. Why?"

"There was a boy asking for a couple earlier today, but he was German and he said the name differently."

"That would be Hans," she said as calmly as possible. Her heart was thumping and she could hear it in her ears. "He's helping us look for them. How did he say the name?"

He imitated the boy's accent and he said the name the German way. The boy pronounced every letter, making it a three-syllable name where the French way was two. The endings were totally different. If you didn't know it was the same name...

Stella laughed. "I told him how to say it, but he doesn't listen."

The clerks smiled and the manager said, "Boys have their own minds. He, also, said that some Americans were looking for the French couple and wanted to know if they had been here, but that is not you." He squinted at her again.

Stella thought her heart stopped beating for a few seconds. "Our other cousins are looking as well. They are American. Have they been here?"

He looked at the clerks and they shook their heads. "I think not."

"Perhaps our cousins decided not to come, on account of the rain," said Stella.

"The rain will stop tomorrow."

"I'm sure," she said. "I apologize for troubling you twice."

The clerks urged her not to worry and she left, feeling awkward as she walked away. Every step felt stiff and unnatural. She had to get out and breathe. Get out and think.

The doorman opened the door and helped her back onto the platform. She turned automatically to the Gritti Palace, her last stop, and whipped off her glasses, stuffing them in her handbag. That boy looking for the Sorkines had to be Peiper's boy. Peiper had wised up. He sent the boy, a less threatening person, if you didn't know him as Stella did.

"I suppose it had to happen," she said to herself as she reached a piazza at the end of the walkway. She stepped off, down into the flood without a care to the splashing and got the hem of her coat wet. So Peiper had figured out why they'd come to Venice. She should've expected that. He wasn't stupid. Then she smiled. Or maybe he was. That fool still believed they had the book and that the Sorkines' presence in Venice confirmed it. It would never occur to him they'd be looking for Abel's family to protect them and that the ultimate prize was long gone. Yes. He was a fool. He thought they were clever enough to evade him, but not to change the plan. If they hadn't run into the Boulards, they could've mailed the book to someone while they were in Paris or simply gotten off the train in Milan or Verona and done it.

She went to the end of the piazza and looked for a taxi in the small canal, but it wasn't that well-traveled and all she found was a gondolier, dejectedly puffing on a cigarette under an enormous umbrella that covered both him and the cushioned seat. Gondola wasn't exactly a speedy way to travel, but it was easier on the feet.

"*Buonasera!*" she called out and he jumped in surprise.

"*Buonasera, bellissima,*" he said and then a jumble of Italian she was too tired to understand.

She used her English accent to ask for the Gritti Palace and he helped her aboard after a small negotiation for the price. Stella got him down to half, using a combination of batting eyes and pleas of poverty. He gave her the enormous umbrella and closed hers before guiding the gondola under the low bridge. Thankfully, he didn't sing. Her mind couldn't have stood it. She had to decide what to do next beyond the Gritti Palace. She had no faith that she'd get lucky this time and Peiper's boy was in the neighborhood. If there was a lead to be found, he might've gotten it first. The two of them must've been missing each other all day. She didn't know what she would've done if she'd come face to face with that brat again. There were always canals nearby, but she wasn't sure she would be given another chance to push him in. Who was he anyway, this boy of Peiper's? Surely not his son. What kind of man would take his child to hunt people and give him a gun no less? No. He couldn't be Peiper's son. That was too low, even for a Nazi.

The gondolier turned them onto another small canal and Stella thought about Nicky. Peiper was getting closer and he'd want to leave immediately. What would Peiper do, if they left? He was exceptionally good at tracking them. Would he follow? No, she thought he wouldn't. Since he knew the Sorkines were there, he'd think they'd handed off the book and go after the Sorkines with everything he had. If Peiper didn't nab them, the Sorkines would eventually end up at the Bella Luna. Maybe Daniel would give them her message or maybe he wouldn't and someone would say Vienna to them. It would all be for nothing. Peiper would chase the Sorkines the way he chased them. Relentless. She couldn't think what to do. All the options were ridiculously bad.

They left the calm small canal and merged with the Grand Canal, nearly at the mouth where it met the sea. The waves were high and slopped over the side of the gondola, rocking them violently side to side and Stella began to think she ought to have walked, her feet be damned. But it was only a few minutes, and they banged against a dock made specially for gondolas. The gondolier leapt onto the dock and looped a length of rope around a pylon before helping her out. They exchanged umbrellas and she paid him with a hefty tip for keeping them upright. He kissed her hand and was back in the gondola in less than thirty seconds, poling away from her.

She turned around and found the palace's wide street completely empty. When Stella had been there before it teemed with people. Sidewalk cafes were packed and vendors sang and sold postcards and other bric-a-brac. Now it was a ghost town and it made Stella nervous after the buzz of St. Mark's.

She waded through the water to the surprisingly discreet entrance, put on her glasses, and opened it herself. Inside, it was much the same as the last hotel and two almost identical clerks smiled at her from behind yet another atrocious desk. She went through the same questions and answers, but this time she asked if her cousin, Hans, had been by. She pronounced Sorkine as he would, but they hadn't seen

Peiper's boy, and no one had come by looking for anyone, except the carabinieri. The word *carabinieri* got just the slightest hint of a frown. The clerks were well-trained, but they didn't like officials coming in and, without a doubt, making obnoxious demands. They didn't mention Peiper so he'd learned he wasn't helpful in the search and her heart smiled at the frustration that must cause him.

"Who were they looking for?" Stella asked in her Irish lilt.

"Americans." That got a bit of a sneer, too. "They think rich Americans are hiding here after they stole a taxi. They have no sense, only fists."

"I wouldn't think that if they could stay here, they'd need to steal."

The clerks laughed and the man leaned over the desk conspiratorially. "I think they are asking for the German."

"There's a German looking for Americans?" Stella's eyes went wide with wonder and curiosity.

"They say the Americans steal from the German. What would they steal? Ugly clothes? Bad food? Stupid."

"That is very odd."

The other clerk leaned over, too. "They let the German out of the jail so he can look for the Americans. I heard one of the carabinieri, a Colonello Costa, talk of it. Fools. The German is the one who steals."

"What did he steal?" asked Stella as if she didn't know.

"A boat," they said together and went on to describe pretty accurately what happened. There was some passing mention of Peiper chasing someone that they supposed were the Americans, but they were forgiven since the German wrecked at least two boats and was firing a gun.

"Did anyone get hurt?" she asked.

They thought not. The captain of the first boat, the one being chased, got what they called a roughing up and a dunk in the canal, but he was okay. Their feeling was that a man who let his boat get taken deserved what he got.

Stella thanked them for their help and left with the tiniest sense of relief. The captain really was fine and nobody wanted to help Peiper. She must be grateful for that and that her list was done. No more hotels. She was supposed to start on the telegraph offices, but it was getting late and she promised to go to Dr. Spooner for Rosa. She hadn't been near his office or the Bella Luna all afternoon and she wasn't close then either, but she had to go.

She turned around and returned to the Gritti Palace. The clerks were gossiping and smiled to see her. She asked for the nearest telegraph office, saying she needed to send word that she hadn't found their cousins. They gave her directions and said to hurry because they would be closing soon. She hadn't thought of that and rushed out into the night.

The telegraph office was closed and no amount of banging on the door got them to open up. Stella supposed they couldn't stay open all the time, but it was annoying just the same. She turned around, took off her glasses, and went back to the Grand Canal. There was a vaporetto stop there and she hoped they were still running. She'd spent too much on taxis and, after paying Dr. Davide, her lira was getting low.

The vaporetto pulled up and this time she bought a ticket, using her Italian accent, just to see how it would go over. The man didn't question it and, if she understood him correctly, he liked her green coat. She went to the back of the bus and stood under a light to check her dictionary. He did like her coat.

She went through the handy phrases at the back as the vaporetto churned through the waves, stopping at stop after stop. She swayed with the other passengers and no one paid her any mind, other than a few looks from the men boarding. They didn't approach her, thankfully, but it might be good to have a wedding ring to guard against such things. As soon as she thought that, she felt terribly guilty about Nicky. She hadn't thought she needed a ring because she was married. She needed a ring to use as protection, a disguise. This wasn't a good thing, not that it would stop her. Later she could worry about the niceties. Right then it was important to get where she was going.

The vaporetto, at long last, pulled up at the San Silvestro stop. Things always take forever when you're in a hurry and Stella was in a hurry to get her miserable task over with. She should've gone earlier, but she'd given herself excuses. None of the hotels on the list were nearby. Dr. Spooner would be with a patient or at the hotel attending a guest. The real reason was that she dreaded facing him and wouldn't have done it, if it weren't for Rosa.

Now she regretted her excuses. She should've gone first thing and gotten it over with, even though he was bound to say no. The hotels had taken nearly six hours. Stella hadn't realized it until the sun started to go down and by then she was nowhere near San Polo. Karolina would think she'd forgotten or didn't care. She did care and she rushed through the streets as fast as the water would let her.

Dr. Spooner had a little map printed on the back of his card and she followed it to number forty-two on a little street covered with wrought-iron balconies and vines growing up the walls. The doctor's door was a faded blue, set in stone with a Moorish peak at the top and a brass knob in the middle. There wasn't a knocker or bell that Stella could see, but there was a small brass plate confirming she had the right place.

Dr. Irving Spooner
Doctor and Surgeon

Stella took a breath and steeled herself for what Dr. Spooner would say or, perhaps worse, what his wife would say. She'd seen what interrogations looked like and her eyes filled when she thought about the doctor and his kindness to her.

It was no use waiting. Waiting wouldn't heal him or change it. She knocked on the rough old paint and a minute later a miniature door in the door opened at eye level and a woman about Dr. Spooner's age looked out at her with large brown, inquisitive eyes.

"*Buonasera, signorina. Posso aiutarla?*"

"*Buonasera, signora.*" Stella checked her dictionary. "*Il dottore è qui?*"

The lady frowned. "*Non sei italiano?*"

Stella couldn't think. It was basically no and Italian. She didn't speak Italian?

"I'm sorry. Do you speak English?" she asked.

The lady smiled. "Yes, of course. You are not Italian?"

Stella frowned and a thrill of fear went through her. "Was my Italian that bad?"

"No, no. The accent, it was perfect. It was only that you looked down to read it. I was confused. Are you a patient of the doctor?"

"Yes, I am," said Stella, relief washed over her but was quickly replaced with fear. "Is he here? Is he okay?"

She frowned. "Yes. My husband is here. You have an appointment. I was not aware of this."

"No. I don't, but I only need a moment of his time."

"Your name?"

Stella hesitated. If she gave her name, he might not see her and she wouldn't blame him. But what else could she do? "It's Eulalie Myna."

The lady closed the little door and Stella waited, not so patiently, watching the water drip off the points of her umbrella.

Then the door opened and the lady welcomed her in with a wide smile. "Please come in, Mrs. Myna. The doctor is in his office and he will be happy to see you."

"Really?"

She frowned again. "Yes. You are surprised?"

"Well, it's late and he must be tired," Stella said quickly.

"It is not late for a doctor," she said. "I am his wife, Gloria. May I take your coat, hat, and umbrella?"

"Yes. Thank you."

Gloria helped her out of her coat and admired her hat pin. "This is beautiful. A, how do you say, family…"

"It's an heirloom," said Stella. "My great grandmother's."

"This pin was made in Italy, I think."

"Maybe. I don't know."

Gloria smiled. "It is beautiful and strong like Italian women and this mark here." She pointed at a tiny mark in the silver next to the pearl, "it is from Florence."

"It's my good luck charm," said Stella. "But it hasn't worked so well here."

"Maybe it has and you don't see the luck." Gloria put her hat with the pin on a side table next to the coat rack. "Come this way."

They walked over glossy wood floors through a maze of interconnected rooms to the back of the house. Stella caught the scent of a pipe as Gloria stopped at a room and knocked on the door.

"*Sì?*" asked Dr. Spooner and Gloria answered him in Italian.

The door flew open and Dr. Spooner stood there, astonished, in his shirtsleeves with a pipe clamped between his teeth. His nose was swollen and badly bruised. There was a touch of blood in his nostrils and the side of his face was purple.

"Mrs. Myna would like to speak to you." Gloria looked back and forth between them and a different kind of frown came over her face. "What is this? What is wrong?"

"Nothing," he said. "I'm just surprised. I didn't expect you, Mrs. Myna."

"I know. I'm sorry. I promised a friend that I'd come talk to you. I know you probably can't help her, but I said I'd try."

"Come in, please." Dr. Spooner waved her in to a chair in front of his desk. "I hope I can help."

Stella sat down and Gloria asked, "May I offer you a drink? Aperitif? Wine?"

"Thank you, but I shouldn't."

"It is the correct time of day and I have Montepulciano. You will like," she said.

"I'm sure I would, but I haven't eaten since—"

Gloria threw up her hands. "You are hungry. I will get you something."

"No, no," said Stella to no avail. Gloria rushed off and Dr. Spooner sat down behind his desk. "Now you've done it."

"I was trying to be polite."

"You've told an Italian grandmother that you are hungry. It is like"
—he snapped his fingers— "this rain. She will feed you. She is
unstoppable."

"I didn't mean to—"

"Hurry. Tell me why you are here. Gloria is unstoppable with food
and also fast. Are you all right? Your husband?"

"We're fine. What about you? Your face."

He waved the question away. "Never mind me. Go on."

"There's another patient, like I said. She's very ill and her sister
wants a second opinion. I told her I would ask you to come see her. I
understand if you can't."

"Who was the first opinion?" he asked.

"Dr. Davide. He says there's nothing he can do, but he was drunk
today."

He nodded and said nothing.

Stella sat back. She expected a refusal, but it would be hard to tell
the ladies. Karolina loved Rosa so very much. "I understand."

"I will come, but I must be careful. Since the *Leggi Razziali* were
passed, the carabinieri have been getting more and more difficult."

Stella braced herself. "But are you okay?"

"It's nothing."

"Dr. Davide told me that Bartali visited you."

He touched his nose. "That man is desperate to get at Davide and
through him, Dr. Salvatore."

"How bad was it?" she asked.

"Why do you keep looking at my hands?"

Stella shook her head. "No reason. Please tell me."

Gloria marched in the room and plunked down a wine bottle and a
trio of glasses. "Yes. Tell her about that *stronzino* Bartali. I want to hear
this."

"Gloria, my love, I—"

"*Basta!*" She uncorked the wine and tossed the cork over her shoulder. "I know you did not walk into a door. People do not walk into
doors. You walk into a fist."

"It's not what you think," he said, turning red to the tips of his ears.

Gloria poured the wine in big heavy glugs. "Who are these people you ask my husband to help? Jews? Always with the Jews."

"I..."

"You are not a Jew," said Gloria. It wasn't a question.

"No. How did you know?" Stella asked.

She pointed at the beet red doctor. "He knows better than to tell a Jew to come here." She tried to hand Stella a glass, but she refused.

"You are against the Jews?" she asked, trying to contain her anger and frustration. How could this lovely woman hate people she didn't even know?

"I am against my husband getting smacked in the face," said Gloria. "Let Salvatore take care of his people."

"He can't do what needs to be done," said Dr. Spooner.

Gloria sputtered. "Birth certificates, baptisms! It is all lies. People should be who they are."

"They can't." He gulped down half his glass. "You see what is happening."

"I see it will happen to us."

"It won't."

Gloria poured him more wine. "It will. I know you treat the Jews. You think I don't know. I know." She turned on Stella. "You know this is illegal. Why you ask this of him?"

Stella leaned back as far as she could get from the doctor's enraged wife. "I'm sorry."

"You lie to me."

"Me?" she said in astonishment.

"You lie. You say you are his patient. You come here to make him criminal. He will be arrested. Do you want this to happen?"

Dr. Spooner stood up and carried his wine glass around the desk. "Of course, she doesn't. She is my patient."

Gloria threw up her hands. "You think I am stupid. You have the nose, the bruises on your face. What does this girl have? Not even a cold."

He gave Stella a look and she pulled off one of her galoshes to reveal her fat foot with the bandages sticking out of the sock. "Dr. Spooner treated my feet."

Gloria crossed her arms. "What happened to your feet? You stub your toe?"

"Actually" —Stella sighed. She might as well say it— "I have frostbite and the flood water got on them. I don't know. It did something to them."

She remained unconvinced. "A pretty girl like you has frostbite?"

"Pretty has nothing to do with it."

Gloria gave her husband a sideways glance. "Pretty always has something to do with it."

The doctor flushed again and took a drink of wine before squatting in front of Stella. His knees popped and cracked, but he took no notice of Stella's wincing. "May I?"

"Sure," she said. "Why not?"

He took off the sock and unwound the bandage, showing off all the ugly lumpy skin and the healing splits. Gloria jolted to her feet. "*Mio Dio!*"

Stella held out her foot and admired it. "Actually, it looks a lot better. I think I can wear normal shoes soon."

"This is better?"

The doctor crackled and popped his way to standing again. "It is. Believe it or not. She's a fast healer."

Gloria forced a wine glass into Stella's hands. "You drink this now. You need wine."

"Um...well, I still haven't—"

"Food. Yes. You are hungry." Gloria ran out and Stella obediently drank. It was very good and she did like it.

Dr. Spooner went to the door and peeked out. "All right. Quick. Where is this woman?"

Stella hesitated.

"You have to tell me or I can't come see her."

"What about Gloria?"

He looked out again. "I'll come tomorrow after I check in at Bella Luna when I'm seeing my other patients."

"Hotel al Ponte Vittoria."

He smiled. "Sofia's hotel. I should've guessed. Bartali knows you're there?"

"Unfortunately. He's been accusing us of being Jews and of not being Jews. I don't know which he'd prefer. He's crazy." She started to rebandage her foot, but he insisted on soaking them.

"Bartali doesn't care what you are as long as you give him Davide, Salvatore, and even better me." Dr. Spooner unwrapped Stella's other foot and examined it. Then he got a basin and filled it with water as he explained the situation. The new laws had some exemptions. If a person had converted by a certain date, they weren't subject to the new laws, for instance. The exemption Gloria referred to was about babies. If a child was born and baptized before the laws took effect, they weren't Jewish and thus protected. Parents, desperate to keep their children from being barred from schools and jobs in the future were having their children baptized. Father Girotti and Father Giuseppe were giving people fake baptismal certificates. Dr. Davide and Dr. Salvatore were backdating new births to before the cutoff so parents could take advantage of the exception.

"What's that got to do with you?" asked Stella, wincing as he lowered her feet into the hot water.

"I've changed a few of the certificates. Usually for the Catholic mothers when the father is Jewish, but sometimes I see patients that I'm not allowed to treat anymore, but I'm their doctor. I have always been their doctor."

"And Gloria doesn't want you to do it?"

"She doesn't want any trouble."

"But you do it anyway?"

He shrugged. "A man has to do what a man has to do."

Stella patted his hand. "And women, too."

"Does your father know you aren't coming home?" he asked.

"I didn't get a chance to telegram him, but I will."

He swirled the water with his finger. "I hope so. I'm a father. I know how worried a father can get."

"It's not my father I'm worried about. He'll be fine. My mother, on the other hand, is a different story. She used to be quite wild as a girl, but you'd never know it now. She's the only Bled known for being quiet, calm, and never ever putting a foot wrong. I was supposed to behave myself and follow the rules. I didn't and here I am. She's probably in hysterics."

"Another reason to go home immediately." Dr. Spooner lifted her foot out of the water.

"I will."

"When?"

Stella laughed. "You are a father, aren't you? I will when I've done what I came to do."

Gloria bustled in with a tray piled high with salads, a risotto, and thick hunks of bread. Stella was planning on refusing, but she couldn't. The smell of the risotto made her mouth water. She ate while Dr. Spooner coated her feet in a new kind of liniment and bandaged them.

After drinking her glass of very nice wine, she insisted on leaving. The doctor said he had to work on some patient notes and Gloria walked her to the door.

"I heard you talking about your mother," she said. "She is worried about you."

"She is, but worrying is practically her profession. I think she enjoys it."

"My husband wants you to go home to America."

"He does and I will."

Gloria got her coat and hat, helping her on with them before she paused at the door, holding her umbrella hostage. "Don't come here again. My husband's heart, it is too big. He won't refuse you and he cannot be arrested. He's not as strong as he seems."

"I don't think I'll have to," said Stella.

Gloria held her arm tightly, her large eyes afraid. "You should go home to your mother. Telegram her so she will not worry. Think of your mother."

"I am. Believe me."

She didn't believe her. Stella could tell.

# CHAPTER 18

"What are you doing?" Stella ran down the hall and hooked Nicky's arm over her shoulders. "You're supposed to be in bed."

"Bathroom." He pulled his arm away and kept walking, slowly, but he was walking. "I couldn't stand my own breath anymore."

"Why are you wearing a coat?"

"You didn't buy a robe and the one we have is too small."

"Oh, right. I'm sorry. I didn't think of it." Stella opened the door and he went in, limping to the bed. She closed the door and took off her hat, stabbing the crown with Great Grandmother's pin.

"I still hate that thing." Nicky dropped his coat on the end of the bed and laid down on his good side.

"Do you?" She rolled the pearl between her fingers. "I think it's my good luck charm."

"Let's not talk about luck. I can barely walk to the bathroom."

"I think you look great. You were barely limping." She sat down and pulled off her boots. "I have to tell you something and you're not going to like it."

"Same here," said Nicky, his blue eyes boring into her.

"What happened? Did Bartali come back?"

He tossed Karolina's book in her lap. "I read it."

"Did you like it? Karolina said it was very American."

"Why did you pick that out?"

She leaned back and flexed her toes. It felt wonderful to be able to do that without burning pain. "I didn't." She looked up and he was eyeing her in a way she'd never seen before. It was chilling.

"You didn't pick out that book?" he asked.

She picked it up. "No. Karolina did. Was it that bad?"

He slumped back on the bed. "You haven't read it?"

"No. What's it about?" Stella climbed onto the bed. She would've straddled him, if it wouldn't have hurt him so much.

"It's about a wealthy man in the twenties."

"Is he blond?"

"Probably."

"Tall?"

"Yes."

She grinned. "It's you."

"He's in love with a woman he can never have."

She crawled up beside him and snuggled into his shoulder. "Not you. I hope." Then she sat up. "What were you thinking?"

"I don't know."

"You do."

"It doesn't matter. You didn't pick it out," he said.

Stella leaned over and she kissed him. "And what was she like, this woman he can't have?"

"Daisy. She's not worth it," he said, smiling.

She pushed back and slapped him on his chest. "You devil."

He pulled her close, kissing her like he hadn't since Paris. "Don't you forget it."

Nicky's kisses were almost enough to make her forget. Almost.

"I have to tell you what I found out," she said, breathless as he worked his way down her neck.

"If it's a reason not to leave tomorrow, I don't want to hear," he said.

"Tomorrow? It hasn't been three days."

"You saw me walking. I can go and we're going."

Stella sat up and pushed him back onto the pillows. "Peiper knows why we're here."

He grimaced and made for her neck again. "That makes no difference."

She pushed him back a second time. "It does. Peiper has that kid going around to the swank hotels, asking about the Sorkines. He might find them before us. He'll try to use them to get the book."

"Well, it won't work, will it? He'll find that out if he gets a chance to try it." Nicky put his hands behind his head. "So he's using the kid, huh? Interesting strategy."

"The local population hasn't exactly warmed to Peiper and the kid is convincingly innocent. People are talking to him."

"He must be Peiper's son."

"I don't think so. He must be one of the kids from that club you talked about."

"The Hitler Jugend? It's just a club for sports and get them ready to join the party."

"Maybe it's not," said Stella. "Nobody, not even Peiper, would bring their child to do this job. Besides, there's something wrong with that boy."

"What do you mean?" Nicky asked. "Did something else happen?"

Stella bit her lip and regretted saying anything.

"You have to tell me now." Nicky clenched his muscles so tight, Stella was afraid he'd open up his wounds.

"Okay but try to stay calm."

"If I was going to be calm, you would've already told me."

Stella sighed and told him about Maria and how she got the wallet. Nicky went paler than when he'd been vomiting and tried to get out of bed. "We have got to pack and leave in the morning. That kid could've killed you."

"This is not news."

"It is to me. I didn't know they'd seen you again. If anything, this will make Peiper more obsessed with us," said Nicky. "Pack your bags. We leave in the morning."

Stella laid back on the bed. "Good luck with that."

"Are we seriously going to argue about this again?"

"Nope."

"No?"

"No," she said. "I'm not packing because I can't."

"Because you're as obsessed with the Sorkines as Peiper is with us," he said.

She stretched out and yawned. "Because I have no bags to pack."

Nicky stood there at a loss for a second. "God damn it. Did you do that on purpose?"

"No, but I would've, if I'd thought of it," she said.

He stared at her and then threw up his hands. "What's your plan, Stella? Stay here until kingdom come? Until Peiper arrests us or worse?"

"He knows we're looking for the Sorkines and that they're looking for us. We can't just leave them to that jackal. We led him here."

"You don't know that," he said. "Peiper might've known where they went all along and finding us was an accident."

"It doesn't matter how it happened. If we leave, he'll think we gave them the book," she said.

"So what? They don't have it and, might I remind you, they aren't wanted by the Reich. We are."

"Anything could happen. We just don't know."

"That's right. We don't, so we're leaving," he said.

"I have to try," she said. "Just a little while longer."

He laid back down on the bed. "I'll give you some time tomorrow, but that's it."

"Says who?"

Nicky grabbed her handbag off the side table and pulled five hundred dollars out. "Says me. I don't care where we go, but we're not staying here."

"Oh, yeah?"

"Yeah and I'm completely willing to hire Antonio and Matteo to truss you up like a turkey and toss you on a train. Don't test me on this, Stella. I'll do it."

She sat up and looked at him. He would. He really would.

"Okay. Fine. I need to get the rest of our money from Daniel and check the telegraph offices."

"And then we go," he said.

"What if I get a lead?"

"You won't. Venice seems like a small place, but it's not. You've gone to the top hotels and struck out. You won't find them."

"But if I get a lead, I have to see about it." Stella leaned over and kissed him. "Please try to understand."

"I do, but if you can't get it done by, say, two o'clock tomorrow, then it's not getting done," he said.

"Why two?" Stella asked. "That's early."

"It's not that early and there are always trains at two."

She shook her head. "It's not enough time. Abel—"

"I care about Abel as much as you. But this is beyond what he would expect. You know that, right?"

She met his eyes and she did know. "All right. Fine. By two, I have to find them or get a lead."

Nicky's eye twitched, but he asked, "If you don't, you'll be on that train?"

"I will, but be prepared to be wrong. I'm going to find a way."

"Nope. Never going to happen."

"Want to bet?" She grinned at him.

He ran a finger up her thigh. "What do you have in mind?"

"I bet St. Louis. You bet New York." She rubbed her hands together. This would solve it. And she would win, if she had to be out the door at five in the morning, going door-to-door.

"What does that mean?" he asked, suddenly suspicious.

"If I find the Sorkines or a lead, we live in St. Louis. If you win, we live in New York."

He laughed. "I don't need to bet that. We were always going to live in New York."

She stared at him, flinty-eyed. "What gave you that impression?"

"I work in New York. United Shipping and Steel is in New York."

"Bled Brewing is in St. Louis." She held out her hand. "Do we have a bet?"

He rolled his eyed. "Fine. It's your funeral."

"I'm going to hold you to this," said Stella.

Nicky yanked her over to him. "I'm very worried." He began kissing her in earnest and sliding her dress up over her garter.

"You do feel better."

"Yes, I do."

Before it could go any further, a soft knock came from the door. "Mr. Myna," called out Sofia. "I have the dinner."

"Perfect timing," groaned Nicky and Stella slid off the bed, laughing. She answered the door and Sofia rolled in a cart with two dinners on it.

"Thank you so much, Sofia."

"You are welcome," she said. "Mr. Myna, you look much better."

"I am," he said, "and I'm sorry to say that we will be leaving you tomorrow."

She looked at Stella. "Yes?"

Stella shrugged. "That's what he thinks."

"We need luggage," said Nicky. "Can you recommend a decent shop?"

"Yes, of course. Bagagli du Venezia has good pieces."

"Perfect," said Stella.

"Is there anything else I can get you?" Sofia asked.

Stella went to the wardrobe and pulled out her fur coat. "Can you have this cleaned?"

She took the matted coat and said, "It is very good quality to have survived so well."

"Like us," said Nicky with a grin.

"Subtle," said Stella.

"I thought so. Sofia, do you know if there's a train leaving tomorrow at two?"

Sofia nodded. "Yes. I believe it is to Rome, but I am not sure."

"It doesn't matter. We are going to be on that train."

Sofia looked at Stella again and Nicky eased himself up to sitting. "Why are you looking at her? I'm telling you we're leaving."

"We will see, Mr. Myna." Sofia left, smiling.

"She's on my side," said Stella.

"There's only one side," he said.

Stella crossed her arms. "Yours."

"Ours. Let's eat. I'm starving."

He was starving. Dinner was a seafood risotto and he ate both his portion and Stella's, since she'd already eaten at Dr. Spooner's house. Then he polished off the bread and cheese, but Stella wouldn't give up her slice of almond cake.

When they were done, she yawned and closed her eyes, but Nicky got up, groaning slightly, and went to the window. "I can't believe it's still raining."

"I can't believe you're not asleep."

"I slept half the day. I'm antsy," he said. "Maybe I'll go out for a little walk. Dr. Davide said it was good for me to walk."

That woke Stella up. "You can't be walking around. You've got cholera."

He grinned. "I'm over it."

"You still limp. How about that?"

He screwed up his face and admitted that was a problem.

"How about I go get you another book from Karolina? I have to tell them Dr. Spooner is coming tomorrow anyway."

"What have they got in English? I need something to put me to sleep."

She yawned and put on her boots, hoping that no one would be out and about. It was pretty odd to be tromping around in galoshes if you weren't going outside. "Not a tremendous number of authors." She said the first name that popped into her head. "E.M. Forster." Why did she think of him? She greatly preferred Jane Austen and Agatha Christie.

"What does he write?" asked Nicky.

"Literary. Mother loves him."

Nicky groaned, "You're killing me."

"You wanted something to put you to sleep and *Howard's End* isn't exactly boring," said Stella.

He eyed her. "You've read this one then?"

"Yes, I have and there's no hidden meaning, if that's what you're thinking."

He plucked a crumb off her dessert plate and popped it in his mouth. "What's it about?"

"There are all these intersecting characters and it all comes together in a rather explosive way in the end."

"But what's it about?" he asked.

She sighed and sat down, trying to think. *Howard's End. Howard's End.* "There are these two sisters, Margaret and Helen, and they met this family. I can't remember the name. Helen falls in love with one of the sons and—"

"Let me stop you right there. Is this a romantic story? Lots of longing and star-crossed lovers?"

"Well, a little, but it's really about class. Margaret and Helen are middle-class and artistic. The family they meet..." Stella trailed off. There was that feeling again. The feeling that something was right there and she could almost reach it.

"Stella?" asked Nicky. "What's wrong?"

"Nothing. I just...I can't remember something."

"About the book?"

"I don't know."

Nicky captured another crumb and said, "Keep telling me about it. Maybe it will come."

She picked up Karolina's books so she could return them and stroked the spines. "They, Margaret and Helen, meet this other family and they're rich. That's right, the Wilcoxes. They have this house and it's a whole thing about who should have the house."

"Not exactly a class war," said Nicky. "I'm going to sleep already."

"Well, that's not all. There's this clerk. He's—" Stella jolted up. "Oh, my God."

"What?"

"Mr. Bast!" She ran for the door.

"Isn't that the writer?" asked Nicky as she whipped open the door. "I'll be right back."

"Wait!"

But she didn't wait. She closed the door and hurried down through the halls to the von Bodmann's room. She's knocked softly, although she wanted to pound.

"Yes?" asked Karolina without opening the door.

"It's me…Eulalie," said Stella. "Can I see your copy of *Howard's End*?"

She opened the door. "Of course. Is something the matter?"

"Yes. Maybe. I don't know." She pushed the books into Karolina's hands and rushed over to the window to yank *Howard's End* off the window sill. She flipped through the pages and found it immediately and it was exactly as she remembered. Mr. Leonard Bast, right there on the page.

"May I ask what is the matter?" asked Karolina.

"Mr. Leonard Bast," she said.

"Yes. The writer. He writes the travel books. He told me."

Stella held up the book. "Mr. Leonard Bast is a character in *Howard's End*."

Rosa shifted in the bed and coughed before whispering. "Perhaps he was named after the character. He is a good character."

Karolina shook her head. "He's too old."

"Or the character was named after him," whispered Rosa.

"Please rest, dear," said Karolina. "You must not get excited."

"I'm sorry to bother you both," said Stella, still looking through the book. "But it's not that either. Mr. Bast told me where he lives in London and when he told me…"

"What?" asked Karolina.

"I don't know I just felt funny about it."

"Doesn't he live in London?"

"He does, but he was very particular about where he lived. He told me the exact names of the streets. Most people would just say London and that would be it. He said—oh, I don't remember. It didn't seem that important at the time."

Rosa raised her withered hand. "Leonard Bast the character" —she took a ragged breath— "lived at…"

"Don't try," said Karolina. "It doesn't matter where a character lived."

"It does," said Stella. "The Mr. Leonard Bast that is in this hotel isn't who he says he is."

"Look in the book."

"I will. I am." Stella peered at the pages, scanning for Mr. Bast and his homes. It wasn't a huge book, but it was still difficult.

Rosa took a deep breath and said, "Camelia Road."

"That's it," said Stella. "That's where he says he lives and before that…it was Wickham Place."

Karolina went to Rosa and took her hand, white as the sick woman. "What does this mean?"

"That's in the book, right? Wickham Place?"

The ladies nodded.

Stella leaned against the books and pressed *Howard's End* to her chest. "It can't be a coincidence. He told me purposefully. He wanted me to know or notice or something."

Rosa trembled. "He…is the SS."

"What?"

"Sofia told us that there is an SS in town. He shoots at people," said Karolina.

She shook her head. "No, it's not him."

"How do you know?"

Their eyes met.

"I know. You'll have to trust me on that."

Rosa took a deep painful breath and whispered, "The Nazis are looking for us."

"Why? Because you're Jewish?" Stella asked.

"It does not matter," said Karolina. "But there is a warrant for our arrest and a reward. Are you very sure? We would have to go and quickly."

Stella bit her lip and thought back to all the conversations she had with Mr. Bast. She knew accents and she'd detected nothing strange about it, but he said he was originally from Hertfordshire. What did that sound like? Similar to London and how many accents did London have? It was a big city.

"Have you talked with him, Karolina?" she asked.

"Yes," she said, the tremble still in her voice.

"Well, you're German. Does he sound German to you?"

Mr. Bast sounded like an Englishman to Karolina. She got no hint that he was from her country. Stella went over it in her mind. Mavis was from Dublin and she could always tell where a fellow Irishman was from by their accent. It didn't take three words before she knew.

"Mr. Bast in the book was from Hertfordshire, wasn't he?" she asked.

Rosa didn't try to speak. She only nodded and a tear rolled down her cheek.

"Try not to worry. I don't think he's German," said Stella. "I don't hear it in his voice or the way he speaks. More importantly, neither do you."

"But what if you are wrong?" asked Karolina.

"I'm not," said Stella confidently. "I don't know who he is, but if he was here trying to catch you or me, what would be the point in hanging about and waiting. We're here. He's seen us."

Karolina relaxed, leaning on the bed and breathing out before kissing Rosa's cheek. "Then who is he?"

"I don't know, but if he was going to do something, I think he would've done it by now," said Stella.

"Then we don't need to worry."

Stella agreed, but there was every reason to worry, for her anyway. She thought about how he was always around her, smiling and asking questions. "I almost forgot. I have good news to temper this situation with Mr. Bast."

"You went to the doctor?" Karolina squeezed Rosa's hand.

"I did and he will come tomorrow as soon as he has time."

She rushed over to Stella, pulling her into her bosom. "Thank you. Thank you. Not that we aren't grateful for everything Dr. Davide has done for us."

"I understand. A second opinion is a good idea," said Stella when she managed to escape Karolina's happy embrace. "Can I still borrow a book?"

"Yes, yes. What do you want? More by the American, Fitzgerald?"

"I think not." Stella plucked a book off the shelf and accepted more hugs before going back to their room.

Nicky was up, stiffly pacing back and forth. "That took a while."

"You know how ladies are," she said. "Lie down. This is crazy. You'll make it worse."

"I won't. It's not even bleeding anymore. Besides, I was bored. Did you get me *Howard's End*?"

Stella handed him the tome she picked out.

"*Ivanhoe?*"

She kissed his cheek. "For my white knight."

# CHAPTER 19

*T*he next morning Stella stepped out of the little oval bathtub and exfoliated herself with her rough towel. With her skin red and still hot from the bath, she dried her hair as much as she could and combed it into waves. There wasn't a hairdryer and that would have to do.

She tossed everything back into her sponge bag and hurried back to the room in an effort to get out before Nicky woke up. She wasn't too concerned. It was early and she didn't expect him to stir for at least another hour.

She was very wrong on that score. She opened the door to the room and there was Nicky dressed, combed, and dapper in his Italian clothes, but not looking remotely Italian. No amount of clothing could manage that.

"What in the world?" she asked.

"You think you're so smart," he said, "but I'm on to you."

"On to me?" Stella tossed her sponge bag on the chair and went to pick out a dress. "Go back to bed. I'll bring you breakfast."

"Not a chance. I'm going with you today."

She peeked around the wardrobe door to see if he was serious. He was.

"You're going to walk to a bunch of telegraph offices?"

"And the luggage store. Don't forget the luggage store."

"I haven't." She chose a blue dress that brought out the color of her eyes and slipped it on. "Do you imagine that you're going to carry that luggage back?"

"I might at that," he said while chasing around his new shoes with his toes, unable to bend over to put them on.

"Right. I'm sure that will happen."

"Are you being mean to me?" he asked with a twinkle in his eyes. "A man who was shot and has heroically gotten out of bed to escort you around town."

"How about you heroically bend over and put on your shoes, all by yourself?" asked Stella, twinkling herself.

"You *are* mean."

"And I'm right. You can't be running around. You can barely be walking."

"I'm going," said Nicky, the bulldog look back, full force.

"You'll slow me down."

He got a shoe on, not tied mind you, but it was on. "I'm going to slow you down? Your feet look worse than my rear."

Her hands went automatically to her hips. "Show it to me and we'll see about that."

"No."

"That's what I thought," said Stella. "You're staying here."

He chased his other shoe around. "That's not happening. Accept it."

The tone of his voice said she had no hope of winning an argument and it wasn't like she could force him back into bed. Even with a bullet wound, he'd win that fight.

"So what's your plan, gimpy?"

"That's Mr. Gimpy to you, Mrs. Gimpy," said Nicky. "My plan is breakfast and then a water taxi."

"Breakfast? We don't have time for breakfast."

"We're injured and we have to eat." He stared down at his feet and tried to lift his foot, which looked as painful as bending over.

Stella stopped him and tied his shoes. "You're only doing this so you can watch me."

"I want you to get on that train and I'll do whatever it takes. Now when do they start breakfast in this joint?"

"Seven I think, but I can't go." She pointed at her head. "Wet hair."

"Not a problem. You got wet in the rain."

"Before breakfast?" said Stella. "I don't think so and, besides, it's finally *domani*."

He limped to the window. "I can't believe it. The sun. I see the sun coming up."

"It's a sign."

"We don't believe in signs."

"Why not?" she asked. "We believe in luck."

Nicky looked back out the window. "You believe in luck. I believe in getting out of here while we still can."

"We will."

"You didn't happen to buy a watch, did you?" he asked.

"Sorry."

"Add that to the list today. But first, breakfast."

"Now we have to buy a watch?" groaned Stella. "We really can't do breakfast."

"We can and will." He slipped his jacket on and buttoned it. "Not bad. Not bad at all. Do I look Italian?"

"Northern Italian, as in mostly Swiss."

"I'll take it. Get dressed. I'm starving."

Stella couldn't figure out how to escape the room without him so she complied and finished getting dressed. When they walked down to the breakfast room, she was shocked at how late it was. Nearly seven. She really did need a watch.

"Good morning," called out Mr. Bast from his usual table, typewriter in place with stacks of paper all around. "Mr. Myna, it's good to see you up and about. Better, I take it."

"Yes, very. It must've been the cholera-like illness the doctor spoke of." Nicky was all ease and friendliness, but Stella couldn't breathe. She hadn't given Mr. Bast another thought since she put his name and details together with *Howard's End* and had simply hoped never to see him again. Why was he always up? Always there?

"Mrs. Myna, are you feeling well yourself?" asked Mr. Bast.

"Oh, yes. I'm just surprised to see you here so early. Sofia's not even serving breakfast yet."

On cue, Sofia hustled in with a large pot of coffee. "I will have breakfast in a moment." She pulled out a chair for Nicky. "Please, Mr. Myna, you should be resting."

Nicky limped over and winced as he sat. Sofia said nothing, but Mr. Bast was watching closely.

"You're limping, Mr. Myna. Have you had an accident?"

"I…" Nicky trailed off and Stella quickly picked up the sentence, "fell. When he was getting sick he fell and hurt his leg pretty bad."

It might've been Stella's imagination, but she could've sworn a hint of a smile flickered below Mr. Bast's mustache and it annoyed her. She got a couple of coffee cups and asked offhandedly, "How's your book coming?"

"Very well indeed," he said.

She gave Nicky a cup and then walked over. "May I?" Without waiting for permission, she picked up a stack of paper and began reading about Museo Correr. It read like a travel book and a good one, at that.

"What do you think, Mrs. Myna?"

"Very good." She picked up another stack and read a chapter on the five synagogues in the Cannaregio. He seemed like a travel writer. He even had ink stains on his fingers and the manuscript wasn't fake. Mr. Bast had sections on Borano, Murano, the Doge's Palace, rail travel, water taxis, and hotels. It wasn't fake, but what about that name. It was fake without a doubt. She wanted to ask him right then and there, but Nicky didn't know. It would only upset him. If she'd mentioned it last night, they'd probably be on a train at that very moment.

Mr. Bast's eyes crinkled. "Something you'd like to ask me, Mrs. Myna?"

"How did you get started in the business? Are your parents writers?"

He seemed vaguely disappointed, but went on to spin a tail about traveling as a youth and having no interest in staying put in Hertfordshire. Stella felt sure he mentioned that name for her benefit. The way he looked at her when he said it, like he was testing her, gauging her response in some way.

Sofia brought back a breakfast of phenomenal proportions, saying that a man recovering from a bad illness needed very much food. They had eggs cooked in spicy tomato sauce, hunks of thick peasant bread, and pastry after pastry. Nicky's eyes began to droop and Stella got her hopes up. But then Nicky casually said to Sofia, "We will be checking out today. When is checkout time?"

"Eleven," said Sofia.

Nicky tapped his long fingers on his cup. "I don't think we'll be back in time. We'll have to check out this morning before we go."

Stella glanced at Mr. Bast, who was pouring over a map. If he was surprised, he didn't show it.

"We have to come back," said Stella. "We have to pack."

"Sofia," said Nicky, giving their host a broad smile. "I'd like to be on that train we discussed, is there any way you could pack for us?"

"Douglas," said Stella. "That's not her job and we don't have luggage yet."

"We'll have it sent here immediately." His gaze was flinty. He meant to have her on that train. "I will be happy to pay you for your time and effort, Sofia. I've been so ill. I really want to see a little of Venice and then head straight home. You understand."

Sofia nodded with a sharp glance at Stella. "Yes, I do. You've had a terrible time and I regret that our city wasn't at its best for you."

Nicky laughed. "More reason to come back." He stood up with hardly a wince and held out his hand to Stella. "Time to shop."

She took it reluctantly. For the first time in her life, she didn't want to shop. "Yes. All right."

"So you're going," said Mr. Bast, getting his bulk out of the chair. He shook hands with Nicky and then took Stella's hand. "I'm sad to see you go. I suspect that your travels are more interesting than most. Perhaps you could've given me a few tips." His eyes bored into hers.

"I seriously doubt that," she said, her heart starting to pound in her chest. "You're a professional."

"I am, indeed," he said. "Some would say the best."

"It was nice to meet you, *Mr. Leonard Bast.*"

That elicited a smile, so big his mustache went into his nose showing his yellowed teeth that were crooked all the way round. "I'm sure we'll meet again, Mrs. Myna."

"It's a big world, Mr. Bast," she said. "I wouldn't count on it."

He kissed her hand and said in a low voice, "I would and you should."

Stella didn't know if that was a threat or a promise. Maybe a little of both. Either way, she got out of there in a hurry and hustled Nicky down the hall at his top speed.

"What was that about?" asked Nicky.

"I think he has a crush on me."

"He's not the only one," he said with a grin.

A half an hour later, they were climbing into a water taxi at the hotel's little dock and marveling at the sunshine.

"It's a whole different city," said Nicky.

"Everything's been washed clean and it makes me want to stay," said Stella with her most charming smile.

"You would want to stay if it looked like the Newark port."

"What's wrong with Newark's port?"

"Put it this way, I'm surprised I haven't gotten cholera just by walking through it."

"Nice."

"Some of the dock workers look like they bite and have rabies."

Stella stifled a laugh and then smacked his arm. "You're trying to distract me, you skunk."

The captain gestured for them to go into the small cabin, but Nicky indicated that he'd rather stand. The captain shrugged and said, "You go...?"

"Rialto," said Nicky.

"First?" asked Stella.

"I'm going to buy you a watch."

"We need luggage."

"That, too."

The captain pulled away from the dock and Stella had to twist around and grab onto the wind screen. As they pulled away, she caught a glimpse of a face peering out a small window at them. Mr. Leonard Bast. Her stomach flipped and she got weak-kneed all the sudden.

"Are you all right?" asked Nicky.

"Fine. Just afraid we won't find them."

He hugged her close. "I've made my peace with that. We tried. Abel would never ask for more. He wouldn't have asked for this much."

"I haven't given up."

"Believe me I know."

"I'm going to win our bet."

He groaned and hugged her tighter. "I know you think so and I hate for you to be disappointed."

Stella said nothing and, instead, enjoyed the beauty of Venice that was now totally different with blue skies. The pinks, greens, and even the grey buildings look brighter, happier. The Grand Canal teemed with boats and the vaporettos were packed with passengers. It was a new day and a new city.

"It feels weird not to have an umbrella," said Stella.

"Pretty soon you'll have real shoes on."

She looked down at the galoshes and found that she was sort of attached to them, ugly though they were. "I'm keeping them."

"What for?"

"You never know."

The taxi cut his engine and they glided up to a dock next to a gondola stand that already had a line of tourists waiting. The water was still over the edge of the canal and a couple of inches deep on the walkway, but no one seemed to mind. Nicky paid the captain and helped Stella out. He was limping slightly, but it was getting better the more he moved.

"This way," he said. "I think Sofia's luggage shop is on the other side of the canal."

They worked their way through the crowds and found the shop at the foot of the bridge. It wasn't open yet, so Nicky insisted on coffee. A long coffee. Then another. Stella was about to jump out of her skin. They had so much to do.

Finally, she dragged a protesting Nicky out of the cafe and into the shop. He started touching all the pieces, comparing leather quality and grain. Stella kept picking sets and he kept shaking his head. Before she knew it, it was ten o'clock.

"Buy the brown set," she said.

He stepped back. "Dark or light?"

"Either one. I don't care."

"Light will show less dings, but the dark is more attractive."

"It doesn't matter. Just pick one."

Since when did Nicky care about luggage? His own luggage for their honeymoon looked like it had been dropped off a truck and then run over. His mother tried to make him buy a new set, but he refused.

"It matters. We're going to have this stuff for a long time."

"Are we? Fine. Get the light. It's prettier."

He nodded. "The light. Matching straps or contrasting?"

It was everything Stella could do not to yell. "Matching."

"Are you—"

"Yes. Get matching."

"All right. All right. Keep your hair on," said Nicky. "How many pieces do you think?"

Stella stomped her foot, radiating pain up her leg. "We only need two each."

"Two? We can't buy only two. It's a set."

In the end, Stella agreed because she feared they'd never get out of there if she didn't. They got suitcases, trunks, and hatboxes. Twelve pieces in all. They hadn't come to Europe with so much luggage and her mother had been packing for every contingency, except the one that actually happened.

"What are we going to do with all this luggage? What I bought can't fill half of it."

"Think of it as our souvenir." Nicky took her hand and rubbed where her rings should've been. "We're leaving this continent with less than we came with."

She sighed and agreed to go get watches next, if he hurried. He didn't.

"I remember a shop down a little alley." Nicky led the way and they found the shop and little was right. It was only slightly larger than their hotel room, but had a nice selection of new and used watches. Stella quickly found a used Cortébert watch that was a bargain, but Nicky puttered about trying on practically every watch they had.

"Hurry up," she said.

"I am."

"You're not."

Then he tried on a watch that he'd already tried and did a lengthy bit of admiring with Stella rolling her eyes at him. She knew what he was doing and it wouldn't work. She paid the lady for her watch and marched to the door.

"Wait," he said. "Where are you going?"

"Cagier men than you have tried this. I'm leaving."

"What men?"

"Cyril Welk with the cheese in Paris."

Nicky darkened. "I know you are not comparing me to that bastard."

"If the shoe fits. You're trying to keep me busy so I don't have time to search for them."

"I am not."

"So you've suddenly developed an interest in hat boxes? Really?"

"I want you to have what you need."

"I need to go to the nearest telegram office. That's what I need." She shoved open the door and the little brass bell nearly fell off its tether.

"Wait a minute!" Nicky yelled, but she was out the door and down the street with the list of telegraph offices in her hand. There were six on the island, according to Sofia. That wasn't too many to get done, but they were spread out. San Salvador was probably the closest. Stella headed for the main thoroughfare while unfolding Sofia's map. Yes, there it was. A fifteen-minute walk.

"St—Eulalie!" yelled Nicky. The pain in his voice made her pause and then stop, tapping her galosh on the stone impatiently.

"Are you out of your mind?" Nicky hobbled. "You can't go off on your own."

She turned around and glared up at him. "I'm checking the telegraph offices. I don't care what you say."

Nicky swallowed hard and leaned on the nearest building, a pink one that had actually been painted in the last decade. "I'm not trying to stop you."

"Oh, yeah? Check your watch."

He did. It was eleven already. "It's not that late."

She stared at him and it was her big husband that had to look away. "Are you going to help me or not?" she asked.

"I am helping you."

"By slowing me down?"

"Peiper's here in this city right now," said Nicky. "He could find you before you find them."

"You mean us."

"I mean you. I love you. I don't care what happens to me or anyone else. To hell with them. My job, my most important job, is to take care of you."

"I've been taking care of myself and you, in case you haven't noticed."

Nicky took off his hat and ran his hands through his hair. "Your father pulled me aside before our wedding and told me to take care of you. He said that you have every trait that makes the Bleds succeed, but that those are the same ones that make them crazy."

"He said that?" she asked.

287

"I'm sorry, but he did," said Nicky, looking unrepentant. "I thought he was wrong, and I—why are you smiling?"

"Father *does* want me to succeed him at the brewery. I was never sure. Now I am."

"*That's* what you got out of what he said?"

"Yes and it's wonderful." She kissed his cheek.

He took her by the shoulders. "Your father thinks you might...be like Uncle Josiah or Elias?"

"Or my great grandmother Leonie or Cousin Alfonz?"

"What did they do?" he asked.

She wrinkled her nose. "You don't want to know and it doesn't matter. I'm myself and not any of them. Are we doing this or not?"

Nicky threw up his hands. "Do you promise me that we will be on that train?"

"I promise, unless we get a lead, of course." She held up the list and ripped it in half. "Which half do you want?"

"We're going together."

She explained that they didn't have time to get to the offices and get the money and return the clothes to Father Girotti. He'd forgotten about the money and the clothes, even though he'd seen them rolled up under her arm.

"Do you think we have to give the clothes back?" he asked dubiously.

"I do. Other people need them and they're bound to be in worse circumstances than us."

"Still. We can send a generous donation when we get home. Surely, that would be more useful."

"What about our old passports?" Stella asked. "Don't we want those back?"

Nicky slapped his forehead. "I completely forgot. We have to have those."

"All right then. Pick a list," she said. "Any list."

He examined both, gauging which would keep her safe and he took the one with the offices farthest from the Santa Lucia train station. Stella was to go to Father Girotti and the ones around the station.

"Have it your way." She took the list and studied the map. "I think I'll get the passports first. I don't want to carry this bundle around. It's getting heavy already."

"Excellent idea. I'll go to Garibaldi."

"That's pretty far. Are you sure you want to walk that?" She pointed to it on the map. "It's way over there."

"I'll take a vaporetto. An hour round trip tops. Then I'll go to the Bella Luna and get the money."

"An hour? That's optimistic."

He pulled her to him and kissed her. "Now who's worrying about somebody getting to the train on time."

"Do you think you can?" she asked. "Because I won't leave without you."

"I'll make it. You worry about where you want to live in New York."

"Ha ha. Very funny. I can still find them."

He tweaked her hat. "We'll see." Then he tried to slip her Gabriele's pistol.

She pushed it back down in his pocket. "I don't want it."

"I'm not interested in want. Take it."

She pulled out the pocket in her new coat. "Too small."

Nicky looked at her handbag, also too small, and frowned. "I don't like it. You need a weapon."

"I have one. My ability to blend in. You, on the other hand, have never blended in your life."

He shoved the pistol back down and kissed her. "You have your lethal pin, I suppose."

"And I'm not afraid to use it."

Another kiss and they hurried off to the Rialto, getting on vaporettos going in opposite directions. A few more hours and it would all be done, one way or another.

# CHAPTER 20

Fifteen minutes later, Stella was at the dock beside Father Girotti's church, stepping out onto a damp walkway and able to thank the captain in flawless Italian. She was sure he never suspected. Her night studying had paid off and it didn't hurt that she said very little.

People passed by her, singing out *buongiorno* and smiling at her, sunny as the weather. Everything was different, not that the Venetians weren't friendly before. They were, but there was a restraint to it, a kind of acknowledgement that she wasn't one of them. It was small, so small that she didn't know it was there before. She couldn't hear it. Now that she did, she couldn't fail to notice all the other little differences. The women held themselves a certain way with a kind of pride and swing of the hips. Once Stella saw it, she could imitate the attitude and it gave her a satisfaction she'd never felt before. To blend and become, in an odd way, invisible was special.

She turned and went under the archway into the church's courtyard. A bunch of little boys were kicking a ball through the remaining water, cheering wildly. They were the first kids she'd seen since she'd encountered Peiper's boy and they were a whole different story.

Peiper's boy looked as though smiling was a foreign country and not to be trusted.

Stella glanced around nervously, remembering the hate. Maybe it was his youth, but something about that boy made him seem worse than Peiper as bad as he was. The boy was actually more like Gabriele Griese and that thought made her hurry into the church and down the nave as if she were being chased.

Stella knocked on the door to the dressing room. No one answered so she went in. The room had changed. No coats, boots, or umbrellas. Instead, there were stacks of crates stuffed with clothing, old dishes, and tins of food.

The office door at the far end was cracked open and soft, musical Italian voices floated out into the dressing room. Stella walked down, smiling. Although she couldn't follow exactly what they were saying, she knew that noise. It was as familiar to her as her mother's voice. Clinking china, scraping forks, talk of food, money, and children. The priests were hosting a charity meeting and the good ladies of the parish had turned out with their pastries and pocketbooks to decide what to do about fundraising and the donations.

Francesqua Bled had hosted a million and a half of those meetings. It wasn't unusual to have fifty ladies in the garden discussing how much money an orphanage in Arkansas needed to stay afloat. Stella loved those meetings. She was rarely called on to attend, since she was supposed to be studying, and fifty ladies was enough of a distraction that she was able to sneak out to the airfield or the brewery.

Stella paused at the door, trying to think of how to get Father Girotti out of there. Should she be Italian or Canadian? Maybe English was best.

She didn't get a chance to decide. The door opened and two portly ladies in black came out at top speed.

"*Buongiorno*," said Stella automatically and the ladies came at her in a rush of Italian, taking the rolled-up clothes and adding them to a stack of boxes next to the door. She couldn't get a word in edgewise. Stella recognized that, too. Whenever her mother's cadre of volunteers got a new recruit there was a whole lot of happiness. Those women didn't know what they were in for and neither did Stella.

The ladies herded her into the office and before she knew it, she was in a chair with a coffee cup in her hands and a chipped plate holding a slice of almond cake, a croissant, and five cookies. She must've looked hungry because she didn't say anything. She didn't have to. The group of ladies, ten in all, did it for her. When Stella looked up, she met the astonished eyes of Father Giuseppe. The poor man was wedged between two of the older ladies, who looked like they were force feeding him. He sat there with his shoulders up around his ears with a coffee cup halfway to his mouth.

"*Buongiorno*, Father Giuseppe," Stella said sweetly.

He nodded and took a sip, presumably too shocked to speak. The ladies took care of that and, luckily for Stella, they were talking over each other and she just kept nodding and stuffing herself with cake so she couldn't speak. She was able to nod correctly to being married and shake her head when she thought they asked if she had children. There was a lot of encouragement about bambinos. They pinched her cheeks and admired her curls. She was pretty sure they thought her babies would be beautiful.

Father Giuseppe just sat there totally useless. He never spoke and nodded so much she would've thought he didn't speak Italian either. She had to get out of there and quick. Time was going by way too quickly. She was on her third cup of coffee and her plate was nearly clean. If Stella knew them, and she was pretty sure she did, they'd be piling her up with more cake any second.

Stella forked the last bite in her mouth and swallowed without chewing. It hurt, but it was worth it.

One of the ladies saw and went for a tall cake with lemon filling and Stella made her move. "Father Giuseppe, *dov'è il bagno, per favore?*"

The ladies sucked in a breath and leaned back. Stella hadn't considered that going to the bathroom was a crime, but clearly ladies didn't go to the bathroom.

"*Scusi. Scusi.*" She had to save it, even Father Giuseppe was horrified. The man was blushing intensely.

She held up her sticky fingers and tapped them together, making a face. The ladies let out a collective breath and smiled understandingly. Several started to get up to take her to the bathroom, but Father Giuseppe finally came alive and insisted on taking her to Stella's relief. She didn't miss the knowing glances that zinged back and forth between the ladies. Little did they know how wrong they were.

Father Giuseppe opened the door to Father Girotti's office and ushered her inside, closing the door behind them. He leaned against the door and whispered something so fast she couldn't catch a word.

"*Scusi*, Father Giuseppe. *Passporte?*"

He went blank.

"American *passporte. Dov'è Father Girotti?*"

Father Giuseppe said he was gone. Something about ladies.

"*Dov'è passporte?*" she asked.

He clearly didn't know.

"Mr. Myna and I are leaving Venice. We're going today."

He shook his head and she was forced to get out her dictionary to cobble together an explanation.

Father Giuseppe understood, but he didn't know where they were. He took Stella by the shoulders and put her against the door to block any noisy ladies from coming in. There was a key in the lock, but no doubt the sharp ears in the next room would hear it turning and there would be talk. Forever.

The priest started going through drawers and then seemed to have an epiphany. He went to the floor to ceiling bookcase and hunted down a fat book with a French title. Once he opened it, Stella saw that it had been hollowed out and inside was a cache of money in several denominations, papers, and their passports. Father Giuseppe held them up in triumph and Stella patted her chest over her heart whispering, "*Grazie mille.*"

He gave her the passports. She tucked them away and stopped him from replacing the book.

"Here," she said, handing him a good deal of lira and dollars. "For the cause."

The priest tried to refuse, but Stella insisted. She couldn't think of the right words and could only say, *"Per Goldenbergs and per Ladners. Dalla Germania."*

He put his hand on his heart and bowed his head. *"Grazie, Signora Myna."* Then he took her to the other door and opened it, looking out briefly.

"It's okay," whispered Stella. "I can do it."

*"Sei sicuro de questo?"*

She wasn't sure what that meant, but she agreed to it and went out the door. Then she turned to kiss him on both cheeks before hurrying away in the warren of back hallways. She must've made a wrong turn because she ended up getting shunted out the door on the right side of the altar instead of the backdoor Father Girotti had sent them out. She considered turning around but decided that would take too long and there was a good chance she wouldn't do any better a second time. The church was empty anyway, except for a few people praying in the pews and they didn't pay her any attention.

Stella walked quickly down a side aisle, heading for the doors when three men burst in. They discussed something loudly for a second and then one, the youngest, dashed down the nave and ran into the cloak room. Stella stepped behind the pillar, listening as more people came into the church. Voices were raised and panicky, but she couldn't make out what was happening. They were talking so fast their words ran together in a jumble of fear. Then she heard the distinctive tones of the ladies and peeked out to see them flooding into the nave, throwing up their hands. Some were raising their fists. Her mother's volunteers never looked so feisty. Whatever it was, it was a cause for rage, not sorrow, and more and more people flooded through the front doors. She'd never get out that way.

Stella turned around and nearly yelped in surprise. Sister Claudia stood ten feet away as shocked as she was. The terrified nun hadn't gotten her wish to never see Stella again and she was acting so oddly someone was bound to notice her there, frozen with her mouth open. Stella walked over and quickly turned the nun around, hustling her to the door beside the altar.

When Stella closed the door behind them, Sister Claudia took a breath and whispered, "What are you doing here?"

"I came to return the clothes and get our passports. We're leaving."

"When?"

"Today at two." Stella checked her watch. "I have to go."

"Yes. Go. Go quickly." Sister Claudia took her by the hand and practically dragged her down the hall. Something about the way she did it was odd, even for Sister Claudia. Stella dug her heels in. "What's wrong?"

"Nothing. You will be late."

"I have a little time."

Sister Claudia shook, her pale hands fluttering against her black habit. "You must go."

Stella narrowed her eyes. "Tell me what happened."

"They can't find you here."

"They?"

Sister Claudia glanced around. "The carabinieri."

Stella shook a little herself. "Now you have to tell me what happened."

The little nun could barely speak she was so frightened. Father Girotti had been arrested by Bartali for something. She didn't know what, but she expected Bartali to invade the sanctity of the church at any moment to search for evidence.

"Can he do that?" Stella asked. It didn't seem right. She didn't think that priests could even be arrested.

"He will. He knows no bounds," Sister Claudia said. "Please if he finds you here…"

Stella took her by the arms. "If he finds *you* here."

The nun shook like a sapling in a summer storm. "God will protect me, if it is his will."

"Let's forget about his will for a minute and get out of here."

Sister Claudia became calm. "I cannot leave the church to hide, but you must go."

"Please," said Stella. "You have false papers. Bartali might notice."

"He might notice that one of my number are gone, too."

She had a point, but Stella wasn't ready to give up. "Just make yourself scarce. Go buy bread or visit the sick. That's not out of the normal, is it?"

Sister Claudia hesitated. "No, but…"

"What would Father Girotti want? You in jail with him? I don't think so."

She shook her head. "No. I will stay with my sisters and pray for the Father and the ladies."

"The ladies?" asked Stella.

"Father Girotti was visiting the sick when the German came."

All the air left Stella's lungs and Sister Claudia pulled her through the hallway, getting her to the outside door. "You will go now and leave Venice. No one can find you. They will know that the Father helped you."

She started to open the door and Stella found her voice. "Was anyone else arrested?"

"Yes." She fluttered her hands. "Go. Go away."

"I'm not leaving until you tell me."

"The doctor and some others. I don't know who they are." She pulled on the angel wing door handle, but Stella put her hand over the nun's. Her chest was tight and was getting tighter. Had she done it? Was it her fault? "Which doctor? Davide? Salvatore?"

"No, no. You don't know him. They arrested his wife, too. I don't know why."

Stella could barely keep from shouting. "Who is it?"

"The rich one for the tourists. You don't know him."

She could barely breathe. "Dr. Spooner?"

Sister Claudia's eyes went wide. "You know him? You have no money to pay him."

"I…I…we met through a friend." Daniel. They might've arrested Daniel. "It's us. It has to be us."

"You? No. This rich doctor, it is just bad luck that you know him."

"No, it's not. It can't be a coincidence. Where was he when he was arrested?"

She shook her head. "I don't know. It does not matter."

Stella squeezed the nun's hand. "Trust me. It matters."

"I don't know."

"Who was Father Girotti visiting?"

"A very sick lady. Word came that she was very bad and he went to her," said Sister Claudia. "Please go now."

Stella took a breath. "Was it Rosa von Bodmann?"

The nun began shaking so violently that her teeth chattered and she nodded with her hands clamped over her mouth.

"They were arrested at the Vittoria?"

Sister Claudia nodded.

If Peiper knew about Dr. Spooner and his wife, Father Girotti, and the Vittoria, he might know about Daniel or he would shortly. Nicky was going to see Daniel after the first telegraph office.

"I have to go." She hugged the nun fiercely, tears flooding her eyes. "I'm so sorry I did this to you."

Sister Claudia whispered in her ear, "You did not do this. The hunted are not responsible for the hunt."

"It is my fault. Please forgive me."

"You were born forgiven." She kissed Stella's cheek.

"A lot has happened since then."

"Then work for His forgiveness and you will be forgiven. Go now. Save yourself. I feel it is his will."

"What about you?" asked Stella.

"I know my place and it is here." Sister Claudia opened the door and Stella went out. She caught one glimpse of the little nun and she was smiling, serene and not shaking. Not one bit.

Stella paced on the dock for a good ten minutes before she flagged down a taxi. Venice was awake again after her damp slumber and absolutely everyone was on the move. Once she explained where she needed to go the captain turned his little craft around and headed for the Grand Canal, but it wasn't exactly the top speed Stella had requested. She wanted to yell, "*Rapido!*" at the poor man but knew it would do no good. The narrow canal was clogged with boats of every description from small personal crafts to big ones hauling produce.

She thought it would get better on the Grand Canal, but it didn't. A boat towing shipping containers was jackknifed in the middle, having barely avoided a collision with another smaller boat. Stella started to wish she'd run to the Bella Luna. It might've been faster and she was considering getting off and doing just that when the captain squeaked around the shipping container boat with inches to spare. He turned and grinned at her. She smiled and nodded while suppressing the yell that wanted to erupt from her throat.

Instead, she did the math in her head one more time. Nicky would take a minimum of fifty minutes round trip on the vaporettos, then he'd have to walk to the telegraph office and he wasn't exactly speedy. Assuming he found nothing out about the Sorkines, he'd be on to Bella Luna. That wasn't an hour. He wouldn't be there yet. She could head him off at the dock and decide what to do about Daniel. Sending a note to the butler didn't seem appropriate, but being seen at the hotel just then wasn't the best idea either. Would a note be enough? Would Daniel understand the danger? Stella could see Albert's hands. Roger's. Peiper was capable of anything. No. They would have to talk to Daniel themselves and convince him to leave with them or just plain leave.

The taxi got caught in another jam at the Rialto bridge and Stella very nearly jumped ship, but the captain got them through quickly with a combination of yelling and rude gestures, which were returned in kind. They zipped under the bridge and in just a few minutes, he turned onto a smaller canal and glided up to the grand hotel to drop her at the door.

She managed to direct him a little farther down so she could get off at the end of the Bella Luna's courtyard. The captain only shrugged and took her where she wanted to go. She paid him generously and he helped her out before heading back into the fray on the Grand Canal.

Stella made herself small beside the pillar at the end of the courtyard and watched the comings and goings at the hotel. She didn't remember it ever being that busy, but she probably just wasn't paying attention. Stella hadn't paid attention to much before Vienna. She felt like she'd been asleep and had been rudely awakened to find herself in a world that looked the same but definitely wasn't.

She kept checking her watch. Where was he? He should be there. Five more minutes. He still didn't come. Maybe she'd missed him. Could he have slipped by her? Come from a direction she didn't expect? Maybe.

Stella bit her lip and made up her mind. She'd go ahead and warn Daniel. Then she'd station herself at the service entrance. She doubted that Nicky'd go in the front. He was in pain, but he wasn't crazy. She dashed into the courtyard and splashed around the hotel. Maybe she could talk to Chef Brazier. He'd want to protect Nicky. He might be willing to spare someone to watch the front, just in case.

She turned the last corner and was relieved, then nervous to find the area empty and eerily quiet. Not a single delivery was coming in. No one was out having a cigarette, enjoying a moment in the sun. That seemed unusual, but it didn't stop her from heading for the recessed door, but the scream that came out of it did.

Stella froze and a second scream pierced the still of the courtyard, this one a high-pitched shriek, like a woman, but it wasn't a woman. Then other people were yelling, outraged and terrified. A man came stumbling out of the door and tripping over the sandbags. He was battered and bloody. Daniel. He fell to the flooded ground with a splash and Peiper was on top of him, screaming, "Where is he?"

Daniel sputtered, spewing blood in a wide arc.

"I know he was here!" Peiper kicked Daniel in the ribs, eliciting another shriek.

Several carabinieri came out with another man, Chef Brazier. He had bruises on his thin face, but he wasn't bleeding. Stella didn't recognize the carabinieri. Bartali wasn't there. Those men, they weren't happy, whether it was about what Peiper was doing or Daniel's not cooperating, she couldn't tell.

The hotel manager rushed out in a panic. "What do you want? I don't know what we have done."

Peiper turned on the manager and the man nearly went down he was so afraid. "I want Nicolas Lawrence."

"Mr. Lawrence checked out weeks ago. He's not here."

Peiper got in the man's face. "He was here this morning." Then he pointed at Chef Brazier. "He saw him and sent him to your butler."

"I don't know what you're talking about."

"I hope you don't," said a tall carabinieri that came out. He was obviously the highest ranking, going by the number of pins and medals on his uniform. "These Americans are dangerous criminals."

"The Lawrences aren't criminals. Mrs. Lawrence is a Bled of the Bled Brewery family."

The tall carabinieri turned to Peiper. "Is this true?"

"You've been ordered to cooperate with me fully," said Peiper, gesturing to the door. The boy came out. He had blood on his slender hands. "That woman attacked him. She tried to drown him in the Grand Canal."

"I don't understand," said the manager. "Mrs. Lawrence wouldn't hurt a child."

"I'm not a child!" screamed the boy and the manager shrank back.

The carabinieri were looking at their leader, doubt written all over them.

"Perhaps we should bring this man to our office and contact the embassy," said the tall carabinieri.

Peiper pulled out his weapon and pointed it at Daniel, who was on his knees, sobbing. "Where did he go?"

Daniel shook his head. "I don't know. I don't know."

"You gave him money." Peiper walked up to Daniel pointing his weapon at his shaking head. "Where did he go?"

"I don't know."

"Where is Stella Lawrence?"

"I don't know."

"She's not at her hotel. Where would she go?"

Daniel sobbed. "I don't know."

The tall carabinieri stepped up. "That is enough. If the man knew this information, he would've told you."

"It's not enough!" screamed Peiper. "Where are they?"

"Stop this." The carabinieri reached for the weapon and Peiper fired. Blood sprayed from Daniel's head and he fell backward into the water. Stella was screaming. She could hear it coming out of her but was powerless to stop it. The carabinieri fought with Peiper. Chef Brazier tried to break away. The boy. He turned. He saw her.

"There she is!" he yelled.

She turned and ran with more screams ringing out behind her.

# CHAPTER 21

*S*tella didn't get far. She reached the corner of the hotel and a hand reached out, snatching her off her feet. A man tried to bear hug her and drag her away, but she stomped on his foot. He bellowed and, when his grip relaxed for a split second, she threw her elbow back, connecting with his face. She got a glimpse of rage and blood before sprinting away.

She expected him to be hard on her heels and she ran as fast as her galoshes would allow. The man was big, not as tall as Nicky, but tall enough that he should be able to catch her easily, but she didn't hear splashing behind her. Instead, a scream in German burst out and echoed around the narrow passage she'd darted into.

"*Schieße!*" The voice was young, angry, and shocked. Peiper's boy.

Something had happened. She could get away.

Stella ran into a crowded street filled with shoppers, out for the first time in days. She tried to squeeze by them but ended up running headlong into baskets laden with fruit, bread, and cheese. People screamed at her, grabbing at her arms and handbag and shouting for the carabinieri. She didn't stop and shoved when she had to shove.

As she ran, a screech of pain burst out behind her. She glanced back and caught a glimpse of the boy bowling over an elderly woman and tumbling to his knees. Attention turned from Stella to him.

"Thank you," Stella whispered as she took a hard right and left the shopping street, leaving the shouts and complaints behind.

She had no idea where she was until she hit a small bridge. She remembered it and the small canal. It was directly behind the hotel. She could get to the Grand Canal now and maybe grab a taxi.

When she reached the other side, she heard a gasp. Looking over her shoulder as she ran she saw the boy hitting the bridge. The slippery little bastard had gotten away.

"*Halte sie auf!*" yelled a man. Peiper.

The boy came charging after her, but he was bloody and limping. Stella ran into a main street, darting this way and that, hoping that she was choosing wisely and not leading herself right back at them. Her lungs were burning the same as her feet, but she didn't stop or even slow down. She couldn't. The pain didn't matter.

Then she heard a clamor in the distance. Engines, whistles, and the general buzz of people. The Grand Canal. It had to be. She ran for the noise. There was safety in numbers. Perhaps she could get lost in the crowd.

She emerged onto Campo San Silvestro and found a little market had popped up. She weaved through the stalls and thought she had lost the boy and Peiper until she heard a shout of outrage behind her. She was careful this time not to shove or do anything to give herself away and ran through easily without a single applecart upset.

Running off the square, she was so close to the vaporetto stop she could hear the engine revving. Was the vaporetto coming in to the stop or leaving? Stella didn't know what she was hoping for. She just ran.

There it was. A vaporetto, pointing left and leaving the dock. Stella put on speed. She didn't think. Not one single thought went through her head. She just reacted, racing down to the end of the dock and jumping for the boat's gateway. She didn't notice the chain that had been strung across it and, when she jumped, she hit it. The chain took her out at the knees. She struck a passenger first and then the deck with her outstretched arms. Her push thrust the passenger, a sizable man, into the other passengers, taking them down like bowling pins. Everyone was screaming, including Stella. The pain seared through her arms and knees, but she scrambled to her feet, gasping and looking back. There he was, the boy, running on the dock. Just when she thought he couldn't possibly do anything to catch her, he launched himself at the side of the vaporetto.

The boy banged into the solid side but managed to grab onto the railing. He dangled off the side, yelling an odd collection of German and English curse words. Stella ran over, their eyes met and she had a moment. Just one small moment of doubt, but then she did what she never imagined she'd do to a child. She hammered his fingers with her fists. He screamed and slipped. She almost had him off. Almost. People grabbed her from behind, dragging her away.

"No!" she screamed. "He's dangerous!"

Stella got pulled off her feet as they dragged her backward and two men in work clothes hoisted the boy over the side. He collapsed onto the deck, screeching in rage and clutching his hands to his chest. Stella fought the people holding her and struggled to her feet. A woman rammed into her, screaming and pointing off the vaporetto. Behind them on the dock, Peiper yelled and pointed a pistol at them. Everyone went down. Everyone, except the boy. He jumped to his feet and pulled a small handgun. The passengers panicked, scrambling away from him and dragging Stella along in the crush.

Stella frantically looked for an escape, maybe off the bow. But that's where every other passenger was going. The door to the helm was open and people got shoved in with the captain. The engine revved to a painful level and the vaporetto turned sharply to the right. It was fast, so fast that people were thrown across the deck into the railing. Several went tumbling over, screaming into the canal. A huge impact listed the boat farther and Stella thought for a moment that the vaporetto would flip over. She slid across the deck, ramming into screaming people, not three feet from the boy, who fired into the ceiling, sending splinters raining down on them.

Then the vaporetto violently flipped back upright, throwing everyone from the railing to the deck. Stella fought to get on her feet, but two more impacts knocked her down. More people went over. The captain was hitting the horn. There was a tremendous grinding *bang* and black smoke flooded the deck. Someone screamed, *"Fuoco!"*

Stella didn't have a clue what that was, but from the panic that ensued she knew it wasn't a good thing. She scrambled for the opposite railing. The boy saw her and fired again. For a second, she thought he must've hit her. He was so close, not five feet. But a woman beside her screeched and collapsed. The workmen went for the boy, but he pointed his weapon at them. Stella reached the railing and looked out at a traffic jam of epic proportions. The vaporetto turning into the canal's traffic so suddenly had caused a chain reaction. It was a sea of accidents. Looking back she knew what *"Fuoco"* was. Fire. Flames were shooting off the back of the vaporetto and spewing the noxious black smoke. It rolled over them in waves. She could see the boy and then she couldn't.

Stella spotted Peiper climbing onto a boat and then another, using them as stepping stones to get to them. Behind him was another man and, if anything, he was angrier than Peiper. Blood coated the lower half of his face and his nose was crooked sideways. He had to be the man who grabbed her. Stella wasn't sure who she was more afraid of. All she knew was that she had to get off that boat.

She turned back and climbed over the railing. If she jumped far enough, she could make it onto the small deck of a taxi. If not, she'd be in the water.

"Please help me," she prayed as she took a flying leap.

Stella hit the bow of the taxi. It was wet and slippery. She would've slid right off if her arm hadn't hit the flood lamp on the tip of the bow. She grabbed it and kept herself out of the water. The captain was screaming at her. She got her feet under her and her galoshes came in handy. Their sticky rubber got her traction and she stood up in time to see the boy get to the vaporetto railing. He aimed his weapon at her and the captain stopped screaming at her and ducked. Stella leapt at the next boat deck and the boy fired. It struck the taxi or so she assumed from the captain's yelling. She leapt from boat to boat across the Grand Canal with the boy behind her, but he was slow, his leg injured. She kept moving, jumping this way and that. The boy fired again and again, missing her. She hoped, despite the screams, that he didn't hit anyone else, but she couldn't stop to look.

She reached a gondola with a crouching gondolier in the passenger cabin, leapt onto its bow, and ran down the length of it as the boy fired twice more, hitting a pylon and pinging off the gondola a foot ahead of her. She jumped from the gondola to the dock and ran down the length of it, searching for the exit. In her panic, she passed it and had to climb over the fencing and landed painfully on her hip. The boy fired again. The bullet splintered the fence and grazed her shoulder. She clamped a hand over the wound and clambered to her feet, running for a small alley, but it was the wrong way. She had to get to the train station. The Rialto. That was the closest bridge. It wasn't far. She could make it.

Stella ran through the warren of streets and back alleys, hoping she wasn't getting turned around. The boy was behind her. She could hear his gasping and the occasional screams he caused. She found a wider street and ran down it toward a bridge she knew. She bumped into the wall, gasping so hard she could barely get enough air. A boat's prow pulled up under the bridge. Maybe she could get on it, but she remembered there wasn't a dock. That was okay. She jumped before. She could do it again. She ran for the bridge, turning to the right of it with every intention of leaping on that boat. She didn't care where it was going as long as it was going away from that boy.

Almost there. Ten feet. Five. A head emerged over the top of the stone walkway. Peiper looked right at her, a smile in his eyes. Stella skidded to a halt so fast she fell backward to the ground. Scrambling to her feet, she turned to run back to another alley, but the boy was on her. He rammed her into a wall. She shoved his chest, but he had her by the collar with the pistol in her face. They rolled along the wall, fighting for control, until they were almost at the alley.

"Where is it?" the boy hissed at her through bloody teeth.

"I don't have it!"

Peiper screamed at them and they both looked. He was trying to climb onto the walkway but couldn't get a grip on the damp stone. A window flung open above them and a woman looked out. She screamed and more windows opened. The Italians were yelling. Stella didn't know what they were saying, but she had no doubt they would be coming to get the hated German boat thief.

"Where is it?"

"I don't have it!"

"*Sie hat es!*" yelled Peiper.

The boy stuck the pistol's muzzle under her chin, jamming it into her throat. His other hand searched around her body, paying particular attention to her breasts. They were eye to eye and she saw his expression change. She didn't have it and his disappointment was immense.

"Where is it?" he hissed.

"I don't have it. It's gone. Hidden. You'll never find it."

"You must have it."

Stella pushed her head forward, burying the barrel painfully in her throat, so that the tip of her nose touched his. "You were at our hotel. You must've searched it. You know we don't have it."

"*Haben Sie es?*" yelled Peiper.

"*Nein!*"

"*Töte sie!*"

The boy's eyes went wide and Stella looked at Peiper's malicious face that was now over the edge. He was smiling. "Kill her!"

"No," whispered Stella. "I don't have it. I don't."

"I have to get it."

"I can't give it to you. It's not in my power."

He wasn't going to do it. Shooting at her from a distance was one thing. Up close and in her face was different. She eased her free hand up. If she could just reach her hatpin.

"Shoot her now, Gerhard!"

"I…"

"The man has the diary. Her death will break him!"

Stella stared into his eyes and slid her hand up to her face. A few more inches. "He doesn't have it. I promise you he doesn't."

He believed her and relaxed his grip. Stella went for her pin. Peiper must've seen it.

"She killed Gabriele!" yelled Peiper. "Shoot her!"

The boy's face changed to something savage. "My mother," he hissed and pulled the trigger.

The pistol clicked. Nothing. Stella opened her eyes to see Gerhard's astonishment and a hand coming around the corner. Before she could react, a pistol butt cracked the boy on the temple and he went down without uttering a single syllable. Peiper screamed and the man with the bloody face grabbed Stella, dragging her around the corner and kicking the boy's pistol into the alley. He pushed her against the wall with a hand over her mouth and leaned over to fire at Peiper.

Peiper fired back but his shots were wild, up high, pinging off the third stories of the surrounding buildings or shattering against the stone walk. One lady bravely leaned out her window and winged a frying pan in Peiper's direction. Others followed suit and Stella was sure she saw a couple of bricks and a jam jar go by. From the sound of Peiper's yelling, something connected.

Several men ran down the alley armed with oars and some fish pikes. The man with the bloody face spoke in fluent Italian to them. She caught enough to know he was telling them that the German who stole the boat was shooting up their beloved city again and something about her, which they accepted readily. As he spoke, his Italian was perfect, but Stella instinctively knew he wasn't Italian. Something was just slightly off in his inflection.

The Italians discussed something quickly and the man kept his hand firmly over her mouth no matter how much she struggled and clawed at it. Then he leaned over and whispered, "Shut up and I'll let go."

Stella nodded and he released her before firing around the corner as the Italian men ran into the alley. Stella could only assume they were insane, but she didn't stick around to see what happened. The moment he released her face, she snaked down out of his grasp, scooped up the boy's pistol, and ran for it.

She only made it a short two blocks before he caught up with her, but instead of grabbing her and throwing her against a wall again, he took her hand and ran ahead, dragging her along behind him. He was fast, a real runner, and she could barely keep her feet. She kept trying to whack him with the pistol but couldn't make contact.

"Stop!" she yelled. "Let go."

After a few blocks, she managed to twist her arm out of his grasp and darted away down a side street. That time she didn't make it a whole block before he had her. She raised the pistol, but he easily pinned it to her side. "Mrs. Myna, please."

He towered over her, his nose at an unnatural angle with blood still slick on his chin, and his brown eyes met hers.

So familiar. The eyes. The hat. The wide expressive mouth filled with straight teeth. The man on the bridge. The one who'd watched her shove the boy, Gerhard, into the canal.

"Who are you?" she whispered.

He glanced around and tipped his hat, revealing a full crop of dark blond hair. "Don't you recognize me?" he asked in a British accent. "Not at all?"

"You were on the bridge the other night."

"Very good."

"But who are you?"

He smiled, crinkling his eyes, and a thrill of recognition went through her. But it couldn't be.

His accent changed, still British but different. "Mr. Leonard Bast, lately of London, at your service."

"But...how..." She couldn't understand what she was seeing. He *was* Mr. Bast the portly writer, but he'd lost fifty pounds and a mustache. Plus, he'd grown hair and gotten a set of lovely teeth.

"I'll explain later, but right now I need you to stop fighting me. We need to get you out of Venice immediately."

"We? Who are—"

"Lord Bickford sent me."

The name sparked a memory in Stella, but she couldn't place it. "But what about my husband? Douglas. He's Nicolas Lawrence."

"I know who you both are and I have every reason to think that he'll be at the station."

Should she trust this man? He wasn't anyone she knew. Even his name was a mystery. But what else could she do? She couldn't get away. She couldn't even raise her arm.

"What's your name?"

"Mrs. Lawrence, you disappoint me. Do you really expect me to tell you the truth?"

"I guess not."

"Then come on. Peiper may get past those men so we haven't much time to put some distance between us."

She went with him, thinking at the very least she'd make it to Santa Lucia. If she could just get there, she could think of something then. She shoved the small pistol in her pocket as they ran through a multitude of streets before reaching the Rialto bridge. But then he inexplicably stopped at a restaurant near the bridge and walked in, trailing Stella behind him. He spoke Italian and the owner rushed out to give them the most comfy chairs. His wife exclaimed over Mr. Bast's crooked nose, gave him a hot towel and ran off to make them tiny cups of espresso.

"What did you say to them?" whispered Stella.

"Hold on a moment." He opened the steaming towel, put it over his nose, and wrenched it straight with a grinding crack.

"Oh, my God."

Mr. Bast soaked up the blood streaming out of his nose. "That's better. Now tell me what you heard."

"Oh, my God," she said. "Your nose...oh, my God."

"I assure you that no one said that." He grinned at her with bloody teeth.

"I don't know."

He waited.

"Maybe that I'm your wife and a man did something. You mentioned a gun."

Mr. Bast smiled. "Very good. I said that the mad German had attacked us and asked for help. You are Italian by the way and so am I."

"Okay. Let's go. I have to get to the station."

He pointed at his still bloody face. "Do you want to attract attention?"

"No."

"Then give me a moment to blend back in." He wiped his face with the towel. Once his nose stopped bleeding and the crust of blood was gone, a slit below his lip started oozing again. The owner's wife rushed out, took the towel and gave him a new one. There was a short conversation about his scarf and coat. Then the lady took both into the back.

Bast smiled at Stella. ""They're very sympathetic."

"Nobody's crazy about Peiper."

Mr. Bast's face darkened and he pressed the fresh towel to the slit a second before the blood dripped off his chin. "I only wish I'd hit him."

"Maybe you did."

"No." He sounded certain, but Stella still had hope. Hope was essential in such situations.

"Let me see your shoulder," he said.

"Huh?" Stella looked over and saw a hole in her coat sleeve, but no blood. Once she looked, it hurt, and she wished she hadn't. "Oh, right. It's fine."

"He hit you, didn't he?" asked Bast.

Stella slid her hand under her coat to her shoulder. It was bloody, but nothing like his chin. "I think it's just a scratch."

He reached over and shifted her to the side. "Well, you've got two extra holes in that lovely new coat. Would you like me to take a look?"

"That will take extra time."

"Indeed."

"So no."

"Drink your espresso." He checked his watch. "We have time, but with the SS you learn to expect the unexpected."

"Tell me about it," said Stella. "How do you know what time I have to be there?"

"Most secrets aren't really secrets, if you know which keyhole to listen at."

"You eavesdropped on us?" This offended Stella, but she couldn't really say why. She'd done worse and imagined she would continue in that vein.

"Not this time, not that I'm above it." He leaned forward, grinning ear to ear. "There's not much that I'm above." He tilted his head to the side and became a bit perplexed. "I can't think of anything actually."

"Who are you?"

"We've been down this road."

Stella groaned and looked at her watch. "You are frustrating."

"You aren't the first to say so." He checked his bloody towel and then sipped his espresso, swishing it around to wash away the blood.

"Okay. Who's Lord Bickford? I know that name."

"I should say so. The Earl of Bickford is Albert Moore's father."

Her mouth dropped. "He sent you?"

"Not officially, but yes. The former ambassador knows what he's about."

"I don't know what that means."

"You will," he said.

"So he's not an ambassador anymore? What happened?"

Bast took a slow sip, considered something, and said, "His son and heir turned up nearly beaten to death by Nazi thugs. That has a way of shifting one's priorities."

"Albert made it back to England?" asked Stella.

"Yes. He did."

"Is he all right?"

"He's not dead. That's as much as I know."

Stella checked his eyes and decided that she couldn't tell if he really knew or not. In the end, it didn't matter. That was something she could not change. She downed her espresso in one gulp. "I'm ready. Let's go."

"Be patient."

She must've looked as antsy as she felt because he shook a finger at her. "Don't make a break for it. You need me."

Stella wrinkled her nose at him. She wasn't some incompetent boob. She could do things. She had done things. "Oh, you think so?"

Bast smiled and checked the towel again. The bleeding had slowed but not quite stopped. "As good as you are, I'm better."

"Good at what?"

He only smiled in response.

"Fine. Can we go?" she asked.

"Enough complaining, seeing as this is your fault."

She stiffened and got ready to bolt. "My fault? What do you know about it?"

"More than you imagine. I assure you. But I'm not talking about why you're here in Venice, I'm talking about my face."

Bast was the man that grabbed her by the hotel in a failed attempt to take her back inside. A member of Spanish royalty happened to be staying on the fifth floor and his plan was to have her seek refuge with him. Bast seemed to think that was something he could pull off and, from his expression, Stella believed him.

"But you fought me off. For someone so small, you are an effective fighter," he said.

"I wouldn't have stayed there. I have to get to Nicky."

He pondered her quietly for a moment. "Yes, I see that now."

"See what?" she asked.

The owner's wife came out with a wet cloth in a bowl, dry towels, and a little tin box. She pulled up a chair and they spoke in Italian. Then she checked his wound before cleaning it with the smelly solution in the bowl, dried it, and bandaged his face with a surprisingly discreet amount of cotton and tape.

When she was done, Bast's injury was obvious but not eye-catching. The owner came out with Bast's coat and scarf. Both were blood-free and only slightly damp. Bast thanked them profusely and paid them more than they thought he should, but he insisted. There were many cheek kisses and Bast took her hand to escort her out of the restaurant.

Once they were outside, he leaned over, "Take note. That is how it's done."

"I don't know what you mean. Please. I have to go."

"This is Italy. The trains are always late." He checked his watch. "You have thirty-five minutes as it is."

"You don't know Peiper," she said. "That might not be enough."

# CHAPTER 22

$S$tella and Bast walked swiftly through the streets toward the Rialto bridge, but then he led her to the right, instead of over.

"Where are we going?" he asked.

"We'll take a taxi. You made yourself quite an enemy, so you're right. We shouldn't chance it."

Bast quickly hired a taxi, using Italian, but with a different accent. Somehow he became someone else yet again. A jovial man with a ready smile, full of jokes that made their captain slap his leg. Stella went down into the small cabin, out of the wind, but she tried to listen. The new Italian accent was harder to understand, but she did gather that many of his jokes were about wives. She had the urge to kick him from behind and the captain looked back in time to see her expression. Then he laughed even more.

Stella told herself it was a good thing. It showed she heard and understood, making her more Italian, but she still wanted to kick Bast.

Another good thing was that particular captain. He excelled at getting around the heavy traffic in the Grand Canal, but then he turned off onto a side canal before the station. Bast must've sensed her unease because he gave her a thumbs-up behind the captain's back. Despite that, Stella's stomach tied itself into multiple knots and she couldn't stop looking at her watch. They were moving quickly, but the minutes were ticking away. She started praying for Nicky to be there, uninjured and unperturbed.

Then they turned into another smaller canal and slowed down. Stella couldn't hold herself back. She came out of the cabin. Bast said something to her in Italian, but she didn't try to understand. She could only think of the time and below that fear was sadness. She'd failed and people got hurt. As they slid over the placid water, she felt her whole body was nothing but a pillar of regrets. She couldn't remember what it was like to feel anything else. She would have to tell Nicky about Daniel. She would have to give him that pain. The thought was unbearable.

The captain said something and she looked up. Up ahead was the Santa Lucia station with not one but two trains chugging up. One of them could be the two o'clock, early for once, but instead of relief, all she felt was dread and increasing sadness.

Bast spoke to the captain and he drove to where the canal turned before turning around to drive them back to a small dock next to a park. They pulled up and Stella climbed out without waiting for a hand up. Bast chatted a little more with the captain and then paid him. He was in no hurry and Stella felt as if she was covered with the red ants Uncle Josiah had encountered in Texas.

He stepped onto the dock, took her hand, and waved as the boat pulled away.

"For heaven's sake, what are you doing? We have to go," she hissed.

"We have to be seen as Italian, Southern Italian in this case."

She dragged him toward the station. "I don't care how he sees us."

Bast yanked her back to his side, putting an arm around her waist. "Everything matters, Mrs. Lawrence. Absolutely everything."

"I don't know what you're talking about and I don't care." She tried to pull away, but he held her, tight as a mother losing a child.

"We have a half hour and then some. These trains are always late."

"I have to see if Nicky is here," said Stella.

"If he's not here, there's nothing we can do about it."

"I'm not leaving without him."

Bast didn't answer and she got a new feeling. He was having her on that train one way or another. She had to think of something quick.

"Forget it, Mrs. Lawrence," said Bast, walking her down the length of the park next to the tracks and the station. "I was tasked with keeping an eye on you and bringing you back safe and sound. That will happen."

"What about Nicky?" she asked but already knowing the answer.

"If I can get him, so much the better. He's not my priority."

"The ambassador told you that? I don't believe it."

"The earl is a player, but not the only one."

"What in the—"

He shushed her. "There's the door. You are Italian. Do you have your passport?"

She gritted her teeth, but said, "Yes."

They left the park and walked along a high brick wall to a narrow green door with a simple pull ring instead of a door knob.

"I won't leave without him," Stella said.

"You will and that's how he'd want it." Bast pulled open the door and they walked into the station far down the platform. The trains were coming to a halt and, like Bast, they were in no great hurry. The platform teemed with people, but something wasn't quite right. The food vendors and people selling trinkets that she remembered so well were back, moving through the crowd hawking their wares. The tourists and travelers were looking politely or turning away in annoyance as they usually did, but it wasn't the same. Bast felt it, too. He was stiff beside her. But if their bodies hadn't been locked together, she never would've known. His face was still relaxed and jovial. He greeted people and eased her through the crowd without missing a beat.

Then he stopped at a woman selling cheap necklaces with a bit of Murano glass dangling off the end. "Look at these," he whispered in her ear.

His grip stayed as tight as ever, so she looked, not knowing what else to do. Bast went up on his toes and scanned the crowd. He remained smiling, but she could see the intensity in his look.

Then he pulled out some lira and negotiated with the seller for a necklace. She caved easily and he flicked a glance at Stella. That's what was wrong. The sellers were there, but they weren't trying. There wasn't the usual obnoxious thrusting of their wares into the tourists' faces, the insistence that they buy. This time they looked as though they'd rather be somewhere else.

Bast paid the woman and she slipped away silently without urging another purchase. That was so odd. Stella looked back and saw the woman slip out the door they had entered, even though she had a full tray of jewelry.

Bast tapped a man on the shoulder and asked about the train that had now stopped. The man tossed an answer over his shoulder and rushed to get on, but he couldn't do it. People were trying to get off and the porters pushed him away. He wasn't the only one on the edge of panic. The whole row of cars had similar interactions going on. It wasn't the rain. That was over. It reminded Stella of Vienna with the furtive glances and atmosphere of dread.

She went up on her tiptoes. "What's going on?"

"I'm not certain," said Bast. "But neither of those trains are the two o'clock to Rome."

"It doesn't matter. I don't have a ticket anyway."

Bast scanned the platform, still jolly but squeezing her hand painfully. "Let's go to the counter and check the board."

They walked to the end of the train. Arriving tourists crowded around them, all smiles coming into a sunny Venice, none the wiser to whatever was going on. The tall doors to the station were wide open, but crowded. Stella kept looking for Nicky, but didn't see anyone so tall or nearly as blond. She checked the big station clock over the door. Twenty minutes. He had to be there, but it was such a mess, she might not see him until they got on the train whenever it showed up.

Bast guided her through the doors, jostling her left and right. When they got through, he whispered, "Pull down your hat."

He did the same and she brought down her brim as far as

possible. There was no need to ask twice. The station was packed with carabinieri and *polizia*, all carrying weapons and looking more intense than usual. People were giving them a wide berth and Bast followed suit, taking Stella to the ticket counter. He stopped a few feet away and looked up at the board listing the arrivals and departures. The two o'clock train to Rome was already flagged as late.

"We may have to get on another train," whispered Bast.

"Not without Nicky."

He looked her in the eyes and a hardness came over him. "I will get you out of here."

She looked back at the board. "What do you suggest? Verona to Munich or Trieste to Vienna?"

Bast's jovial expression stayed firmly in place. "I think we'll choose not to visit Herr Hitler today."

"I couldn't agree more."

They turned to the ticket counter and got run into by a group of school children rushing through. "*Scusi! Scusi!*" called out a woman, frantically herding them. More people rushed at them with looks of distaste or fear on their faces. Bast pulled Stella tight to his side again and fended off the crowd. They got in the short line and some shouts erupted from the door in Italian. Stella went up on her toes. It could be Nicky.

"Don't look," said Bast.

"What is it?"

"The carabinieri."

Stella got as stiff as Bast. "For us? Me?"

He glanced over and a flicker of something, a tiny little reaction, crossed his face. If she hadn't been looking at him so intensely, she wouldn't have seen it.

"What?" she asked.

"Nothing," said Bast. "Do not look."

Her heart hurt. The air in her lungs burned. "Is it Nicky?"

"No."

"Promise me."

Bast bent over and looked in her eyes. "It is not Nicky. I don't see him."

Right or wrong. She believed him. "Okay."

He squeezed her hand and stepped closer to the ticket window.

"I have money," she said, pulling her handbag from the crook of her arm.

"Never mind that."

"Don't forget a ticket for Nicky."

His smile grew larger. "I couldn't possibly."

He stepped up to the window and spoke to the grumpy woman behind the glass in Italian as a burst of yelling broke out behind them. Bast had to let go of her to get his wallet out and Stella turned toward the sound. The woman demanded a hefty sum, but Bast didn't answer. He reached for Stella instead. "Don't look."

She couldn't help it. To tell the truth, she didn't try to stop herself. A voice was raised. In German. A woman's voice. She knew it.

"Mrs. Lawrence," he growled, but she went anyway, pushing through the crowd toward the voice. People ran into her going the opposite direction away from the voice that had become wailing. With it was pleading and sobs of other voices, men and women. She couldn't stop going. She had to know.

A group of carabinieri surrounded several people with suitcases. They were talking to the carabinieri, but their pleas fell on deaf ears. Stella caught the words for hospital and doctor. When she got closer, she saw someone was on the floor. A woman. Her face lolled toward Stella and she gasped. Rosa. Rosa von Bodmann. Karolina was on her knees beside her, wailing. Two carabinieri pushed her out of the way and grabbed Rosa's arms, pulling her upright. Someone barked an order. They dropped the unconscious lady and her head hit the floor with a solid *thunk*. The carabinieri seized Karolina and dragged her away, her face stricken. Stella went for Rosa, but Bast wrestled her off her feet, carrying her backward through the horrified crowd. "You can't help her."

"It's Rosa von Bodmann. Let go."

"You can't help her. She's beyond help."

"She needs a doctor."

He tried to get her to the door to the platform, but so many people were streaming out, he couldn't make any headway. She could see Rosa laying there in a heap, a circle of people widening around her. No one was helping. No one was doing anything. Stella kicked back, connecting her heel with his shin. He gasped and let go, dropping her on her feet painfully. She ran for Rosa and dropped to her knees.

"Rosa?" She held the old lady's face between her hands. It was cold and clammy. "Rosa? Can you hear me?"

A face appeared in front of hers and Stella drew back in shock.

Bartali took her hands from Rosa. "She's dead." He looked up and said over her head, "Get her out of here now."

Bast lifted Stella off her feet.

"Rosa," she whispered, staring at the slack face of such a sweet person. "You killed her."

"Go now," said Bartali, looming over Rosa's body. "My men know her face."

Stella focused on him, pain bursting through her chest, an agony of unexpected grief. "Why don't you just arrest me? That's what you've wanted to do the whole time."

"Dr. Spooner's wife told us who you are," he sneered at her. "You could've saved me a lot of trouble."

"I don't understand."

"I'm not sending an American heiress to a camp. I don't care what that murdering German says."

"Why did you arrest Karolina and Rosa then? They're innocents."

Bartali sneered at her. "They're Jews."

"But—"

He leaned in close. "Let the Germans eat their own. It will be their undoing."

Bast pulled Stella back into his chest. "The world isn't going to allow that," she said.

"I don't know what world you're living in," said Bartali. "Get out of the station." The carabinieri turned on his heels and marched through the crowd that frantically made way for him.

Bast paused for a second and then spun Stella around toward the outside doors.

She fought him, writhing and twisting in his grasp. "No. He has Karolina."

He tightened his grip, whooshing the breath out of her lungs. "She's been arrested. It's done. Don't attract any more attention."

They went for the doors, weaving through other passengers, and Stella glanced back at Rosa's body between the multitude of legs passing by.

"Your train will be here in thirty minutes. Track one. Be on it," said someone with a different British accent than Bast.

Stella whipped her head around but only caught a glimpse of a man in a grey fedora melting into the crowd. Bast pushed her out of the door and the sun blinded her for a second. She dug in her heels at the edge of the first step.

"No. We have to do something."

"Keep walking," he said, forcing her down the steps onto the wet piazza. The water had receded, but it was still very wet. Bast didn't seem to care and plowed right into it, mindless of his fine leather shoes and pant legs.

"They'll take her to Germany."

"Yes. Do you want to go with her?"

"No, but—"

"Mrs. Lawrence, you have a price on your head," he said.

"Since when?"

"Since you slipped the net in Vienna. You're lucky Bartali has a deep hatred of Germans from the war."

"But—"

"Look for your husband. Do that. Find him and leave. There'll be a time for your weapons, but it isn't now."

He'd turned her left and they walked across the piazza toward the vaporetto stop and the expansive Scalzi bridge.

Stella scanned the tourists taking pictures and lining up in front of the vaporetto ticket booth. No one caught her eye. "Where are we going?"

"We'll take the street between the station and the church."

She nodded and kept looking as the next vaporetto pulled up and bumped the pylons. The tourists bunched up together, twittering anxiously and pouring over their maps. They were all surprisingly short, even with their hats. Bast turned her to skirt the long line and she looked over their heads at the bridge. It was crowded with people taking pictures and admiring the sunny view. She saw several blondes, but they were women.

Just as Bast turned her toward the end of the station, something caught her eye. Not a blond, but it was a head. A tall one, taller than anyone else, but it wasn't the head or its hat that attracted her attention. It was the way the man was moving. His head bobbed and jutted to the right sharply with every step.

She stopped walking.

"Mrs. Lawrence."

"Wait." She couldn't see his face. The man beside him had a hat that blocked her view. "I think…"

The man came over the crest of the bridge, clearing the glut of tourists.

"Nicky," Stella whispered and relief flooded her chest. "Thank God."

"Come with me now," said Bast.

She lowered her voice further. "It's Nicky."

Bast clutched her waist, but she pivoted and rolled herself out of his grip.

"Stop."

She didn't stop and he lunged for her. She slipped on the wet pavers, falling backward. Bast grabbed her wounded arm and she shrieked at the sudden pain. He tried to pull her up, but only succeeded in grabbing her wound a second time. She shrieked again and Nicky heard her. He ran down the rest of the bridge with a pair of suitcases in his hands.

"È lei!" a man yelled.

"Bloody hell," said Bast, yanking her upright and dragging her toward the bridge.

Two carabinieri came from the right, yelling and holding out weapons. Stella and Bast ran through the crowd coming off the bridge, dodging screaming tourists. Bast drew his weapon and people fell into the canal as they tried to get out of the way. Nicky saw them coming and dropped the suitcases. He spun around the two people with him and yelled, "Run!" They took off and he met Stella at the end of the bridge, taking her free hand.

Between the two men, Stella got yanked off her feet. Her galoshes were dragged off and her knees scraped on the ground.

"Stop!" she screamed.

They reached the crest of the bridge and Nicky looked back. "Holy shit!" He scooped her up and ran, his limp worsening with every step. The carabinieri yelled for them to stop and fired a warning shot over their heads. People scattered, so panicked they hit the stone railing and buckled, falling to their knees. One man hit it hard enough that he flipped over and went screaming into the canal.

At the end of the bridge, Nicky put Stella down and grabbed two people hesitating at the foot of the stairs. "Come on!"

They all ran left into the terrified crowd on a small piazza. Another shot rang out and everyone ducked, except for them.

"Boat!" yelled Bast.

They ran for a power boat at the end of the short dock. An astonished man stood at the helm with his mouth open and his hands on the wheel. Bast and Nicky leapt onto the boat and tossed him onto the walkway, where he rolled away and curled up in a protective ball.

"Get in!" yelled Nicky.

Stella and the people with Nicky tumbled on board as Bast took the wheel. He revved the engine and they pulled away from the dock into the traffic on the Grand Canal. The carabinieri were at the pylons. They both fired.

"Get down!" Bast didn't get down. He didn't even crouch.

Nicky forced Stella to her knees and covered her with his body behind Bast. "Who the hell is that?"

"Mr. Leonard Bast, lately of London." Stella glanced at the woman next to her. The one blue eye she could see was wide with terror. "Who are they?"

"The Sorkines!"

"Oh, my God!"

"I know!"

Bast jerked the boat starboard, screaming obscenities. They listed so far to the right they took on water and there was a grinding impact that nearly rolled them over. When the boat righted itself, Stella looked up to see another boat. They'd collided with a water taxi. It had a crumpled bow, but it was turning in a tight loop. At the wheel were two men fighting for control. Peiper and presumably the captain grappled with each other. Peiper pulled out his weapon and shot the man in the chest. He flipped over the side into the wake. Peiper righted the craft and came after them. Behind him was a *polizia* boat with a wailing siren. They almost ran over the man in the water, dodging to the right at the last moment.

Other boats were trying to get to the man and got in the way of the *polizia*. They were cut off. Bast deftly weaved past two large delivery boats, but Peiper was right behind them.

Nicky pulled out Gabriele's pistol and aimed with his arm bouncing around. He didn't fire.

"Shoot him!" yelled Bast.

"I can't!"

There were too many people and boats. No clear shot with such bad aim. Bast wove between a series of boats with Peiper right on their tail.

"Shoot him!" he yelled.

Nicky's arm couldn't hold steady. "I can't! I'll hit someone else!"

"Just do it!"

"He's slowing down!"

The woman beside Stella was shaking so hard she was vibrating the both of them. "Are you okay?"

Her eyes showed no understanding. Stella rubbed her back and tried to think of something, anything in French, but her mind was blank.

"I'm turning onto a side canal," yelled Bast. "It'll be clearer then."

"Hurry up!" yelled Nicky.

Stella got out from under Nicky's arm and went for Mrs. Sorkine. She was shaking more violently than ever.

"It's all right," said Stella. "It'll be fine."

But she didn't look at Stella. She was looking back. Stella turned. Mr. Sorkine was sitting behind them, upright, with an odd, fixed expression. Blood covered his white shirt and a drip ran out of the corner of his mouth.

Stella scrambled back to him.

"Get down!" yelled Nicky.

Mr. Sorkine fell to the side, but Stella had him. There was a hole under his breast bone. She pressed her hands to it and blood soaked them.

The woman was with her. "Raymond!"

"Hold on!" yelled Bast.

The boat did a screaming turn to port and Stella hit the low side of the boat. She and Mrs. Sorkine grabbed at whatever they could to stay aboard, but Mr. Sorkine tumbled over the side. Stella scrambled for him, grabbing at his feet as they slipped over the side, but she couldn't get a hold of him. Mrs. Sorkine screamed and dove for the side of the boat. Before Stella could stop her, she jumped in after her husband. Stella leapt for the back of the boat. She got her feet on the low seat and crouched to jump but was yanked backward, falling on her bottom.

"Are you insane?" yelled Nicky.

"They're overboard!" She clambered to the back of the boat.

"The *polizia* will get them!"

Nicky and Stella looked at the Sorkines in the water. Peiper's boat appeared at the entrance to the canal.

"Oh, my God," whispered Stella.

Nicky fired and kept firing until his weapon ran dry. It made no difference. They watched as Peiper aimed his boat for the Sorkines. He could've missed them easily, but he chose to hit them dead on and never flinched.

Behind Peiper, the *polizia* boat roared into view, cutting off another boat on the turn, but bypassing the Sorkines' area.

"They're stopping," said Stella.

Nicky pulled her down. "He isn't."

They went under a bridge and cut in and out around some small boats where those on board had enough sense to duck as they passed. Every window was open along the canal with people pointing. Peiper fired twice with his shots pinging off buildings harmlessly. Stella could see people screaming and ducking into houses and side streets, but it was soundless over the roar of the engine. With their voices muted, they seemed unreal and separate, not a part of Stella's world on the canal where Mr. Sorkine's blood stained her hands and the deck.

Bast dodged around a vaporetto stop and yelled at the panicked passengers in Italian.

"What did you say?" asked Nicky.

"Watch out for the mad German!"

"That's an understatement." Nicky pulled Stella against him as they crouched beside Bast. His face wasn't blank as she would've expected. He was grim and haunted.

"Turning!" yelled Bast as he cut their speed and aimed for the small side canal they'd been down before. Stella swallowed hard, but Peiper slowed down, too. Her last sight of him was the boat hitting several pylons at a hotel's dock. It might've been wishful thinking, but she thought she saw him slumped over the wheel. She'd never prayed for another's death before. She didn't think that was something a person would ever be driven to do, but she prayed that Peiper died and if he didn't, she prayed that he would suffer and never know another moment of joy.

They sped down the canal instead of doing the neat turn of the taxi driver. Bast just pulled up to the dock and said, "Get out and run."

Stella jumped out first with Nicky grabbing at her hand. "Where are we going?"

"The station." She knew where she was and checked her watch. They could make it on the train. Bast and Nicky caught up with her and they ran past the park, dodging a couple of tourists that were clearly lost and made it to the side door.

"Stop," said Bast and he banged the door shut as she tried to open it.

"What?" asked Stella.

"We need to straighten up. Fix your hats. Mrs. Lawrence, yours is barely hanging on by that enormous hatpin."

Stella felt Great grandmother's pin and was deeply grateful it was still there. She put her hat back on the top of her head and tilted it rakishly over one eye, straightened her coat, and was surprised to see her handbag dangling from her elbow. It was a stubborn thing and she suddenly felt very attached to it. "I'm not going to be presentable," she said, getting out her handkerchief.

The men smoothed themselves out and Bast said, "I think you look rather smart, not at all like you've been running for your life."

She held out her foot, still fat with bandages and sporting a bulky sock.

"Okay, maybe not."

Nicky eyed her foot and said, "There's nothing we can do about it. How are they? Can you walk?"

It seemed a silly thing to ask as she had just been running, but she appreciated the care with which he said it.

"I'm fine." She looked at Mr. Bast and asked, "Are you coming with us?"

"That's my job."

Nicky crossed his arms. "What is your job exactly?"

"We can get into that later. Lord Bickford sent me," said Mr. Bast.

"And we're supposed to trust you?"

"Given what just happened, I think so."

The men went back and forth, but Stella didn't listen. Her mind was too full of bodies. Her ears ringing with gunshots. Blood on her hands that her handkerchief couldn't begin to wipe away.

"Stella?" asked Nicky.

"Yes?"

"We're going in. You're going to stay between us. Maybe no one will notice your feet."

He leaned over and looked in her eyes. "Are you all right?"

The answer was no, but she said yes. Sometimes that's all you can say. It's what they need to hear.

Bast opened the door and they walked in the station. It was as busy as before and there was a train on Track One. People were hurriedly getting aboard, but not that many.

"I have to buy tickets," said Nicky.

"Already done," said Bast.

"What car?"

Stella didn't wait for the answer. She left them and walked down the length of the train.

"Wait," said Nicky.

She didn't wait. She dodged around passengers and a suspicious porter who certainly did notice her feet. He said something to her, but she ignored him. Next to one of the first-class cars stood Sofia.

# CHAPTER 23

Sofia had a porter and a pile of luggage on a cart beside her. Their luggage. The porter spoke to her anxiously and shrugged at a conductor on the train's step as she cried into a handkerchief in a quiet, very demure way that most people didn't notice.

Stella walked up and stood in front of the hotelier, unafraid and ready to hear what she had to say. She deserved it. "Sofia?"

"Mrs. ... Mrs. Myna." She looked up and wiped her face. "You came."

"I'm so sorry."

"You know?"

Stella couldn't speak. Yes, she knew, but she couldn't say it.

"The German that wrecked the taxi, he came to my hotel. He..." Sofia buried her face in her handkerchief.

Nicky and Bast joined them, quietly greeting Sofia and glancing around for Peiper. Bast showed the porter their tickets and a hefty tip got him to quickly load the luggage without any questions.

Nicky gently pushed Stella toward the steps, but she refused to go.

"I have to hear this," she said.

"We don't have time."

Sofia shuddered, lifting her tear-soaked face. "There isn't very much to say."

Bast took her arm and glancing around quickly. Then in an American accent that had a western twang, he said "Then it won't take long and you can say it onboard."

She took a look at this stranger and Stella held her breath but saw no sign of recognition. "Who are you?"

"William F. Cody, at your service. I'm a friend of the Mynas from back home."

Stella and Nicky smiled and nodded so Sofia let Bast guide her on board. The train was a hive of activity, but mostly with people gathering their last bits and pieces to get off. Their compartment was the third one down and sadly well-worn with thread-bare cloth seats and tarnished fittings. Stella and Sofia sat by the window, perching on the edge of their seats with their knees touching while the porter reached overhead to put the luggage on the racks and Nicky closed the shade.

Stella swallowed and asked, "Why were Karolina and Rosa arrested?"

Tears rolled down Sofia's cheeks. "I don't know. I don't know. They didn't do anything. Bartali, he always suspect them, but they did nothing."

"Tell me what happened?"

Urged on by Nicky and Bast, Sofia told the story quickly and, indeed, there wasn't much to say. Peiper showed up at the hotel with several carabinieri that morning after Stella and Nicky left. They accused Sofia of harboring fugitives, which she denied. They smacked her and Antonio around for a bit, but they refused to tell them anything. Then the German insisted on searching their room. Stella went cold, but she couldn't think of anything that would be a problem. She had their old passports and they had nothing else from their old lives that could give them away. She'd even thrown out Nicky's bandages. There wasn't anything to find.

"They tear apart your room," said Sofia. "The wardrobe, they pushed it over, and tore apart the bed. The German was so angry. He was screaming, asking me where you were. I said you went to shop. He didn't believe me."

"But what about Karolina and Rosa?" asked Nicky.

"I don't know what happened," she said. "The German was hitting me and Bartali came. He went in the room. I didn't hear what he and the other carabinieri said. I was so scared of the German."

"He's a nightmare," said Stella. "I don't blame you."

"You know this man?"

"Yes, but what happened then?"

From the way that Sofia told it, Bartali came out of their room angry and he fought with the other carabinieri about arresting important people. He said he wouldn't side with the dirty Germans against Americans.

"He said that?" asked Bast, thoughtfully.

"Yes and the German tried to punch Bartali, but the other carabinieri stopped him. They told Bartali he had his prize and to go get it. Then he go to Karolina and Rosa's room. That nice Dr. Spooner was there with Father Girotti. He arrested them all." Sofia buried her face in her hands as the train whistle blew. "What was in your room? What was it?"

"I don't know," said Stella at a loss.

The porters had left and Nicky helped Sofia to her feet. "Thank you for everything. I don't know how to thank you."

"Who are you really?" she asked. "Bartali wanted to protect you, but he dragged Karolina out of her room by her hair. I don't understand."

They were silent for a moment. The horror of it felt fiery on Stella's skin. They'd done that to Karolina somehow. But how?

"Didn't anyone stop them?" asked Stella. "How could anyone stand by and let that happen?"

"The Americans, they come. Mr. Hutchins, he got Karolina away and Bartali put gun on him."

Randolph and Dolores did their best to help Karolina and Rosa. Randolph said he would call the embassy, the New York Times, the Vatican. It made no difference. Bartali said he would arrest them for interfering. Then they dragged the old ladies out with Father Girotti and Dr. Spooner, who kept saying he was innocent. The German smacked him and said he could thank his stupid wife.

"What did she do?" asked Nicky.

"I don't know. He didn't say," said Sofia. "Then the German said to pack up everything in the von Bodmann's room. Mr. Hutchins said they were stealing and the German said it all belonged to the Reich and would fetch a pretty price."

"They got everything?" asked Stella.

Sofia nodded sadly, more tears rolling down her cheeks. "Yes. They took the scroll. Karolina made a mistake. She was wrong, and then it was too late."

"What scroll?" asked Bast.

The women ignored his question and Stella said, "What mistake? She didn't cause this. Clearly, we did."

"Rosa wanted to give the scroll to you to take away to America, but Karolina refused. She couldn't part with it and now it is gone, like her and Rosa."

The train whistle blew again and Bast led Sofia out, but Stella jumped up and stopped her. She opened her handbag and pulled out the passports, Abel's photos, and her cosmetics, then pressed the bag into Sofia's hands. "There was a man and woman with us. The man was shot and the German ran over them with a boat he stole. I don't know if they are alive or dead. Please take this money and help them if you can and…" —Stella wiped away a tear— "bury Rosa. Dr. Salvatore can help you find out how to do it."

Sofia pressed the handbag to her chest. "Then they were Jews."

"Yes."

"I didn't know for sure. So many are running."

Stella nodded and found she couldn't speak. Bast helped Sofia out of the door and she heard him telling her that it was best for her to go out the side door of the station so no one would see her. Stella didn't hear her reply, but she knew that Sofia wouldn't slip away. She would go to find out if Rosa's body was still in the station. Stella wanted to do that right now, but she couldn't. She'd caused Rosa's death somehow, but she couldn't do anything to help without risking everything she had left.

She turned around and saw Nicky sitting in her spot by the window, staring straight ahead. "Are you upset that I gave Sofia the money?"

He didn't look at her. "Is that who you think I am?"

"I'm sorry. I just...the way you're sitting there. I don't know anything."

"The money is fine. It won't be enough."

"It was a lot."

Nicky kept staring so hard at the other seat that Stella looked to make sure there wasn't anything there. But it was just worn fabric and buttons.

"Nicky?"

He didn't blink and she wondered if this was the stare Uncle Josiah described seeing during the war. The men coming out of the trenches would stare blankly at nothing but then jump at every little sound. Uncle Josiah found them unnerving and was very glad he wasn't in the infantry.

The train jerked and Stella stumbled sideways into the seat as it pulled away from the station, but Nicky didn't notice. Bast knocked on their compartment door and came in, closing it firmly behind him. "I told Sofia to get out of the station and stay away from Bartali, but I doubt she'll listen. Apparently, Rosa von Bodmann was dear to her."

Stella glanced up and let the tears roll down her cheeks. "I think she was dear to everyone who met her."

"I didn't have the pleasure," said Bast.

"It's your loss."

"I believe you, Mrs. Lawrence."

Now Stella and Nicky's knees were touching. He looked at her, but he wasn't seeing her. She had a feeling he wasn't seeing anything. She much preferred Sofia's raw grief.

"Take off your coat," said Bast. "I want to see to your shoulder."

It took a second but Nicky turned. "What happened to your shoulder?"

"The boy shot at me," said Stella.

Nicky shifted to her side and helped her off with her coat and jacket. The blood had dried and fixed the sleeve of her blouse to her arm. As Nicky looked at her arm, his mask of indifference cracked and she could see the agony underneath.

"It's fine really," said Stella. "I don't think it even hit the muscle."

"I will kill him," said Nicky, low and throaty.

"You won't. He's a child."

Bast sat down across from them. "Who was he?"

They shrugged in unison.

"You must have some idea."

"Peiper called him Gerhard," said Stella. "But I never saw him before Venice."

Nicky leaned toward Bast and asked, "How about you tell us who you are?"

"Besides your savior?"

Nicky's mouth twitched down into a grimace. "Besides that."

Bast flicked a glance at Stella.

"Albert's father sent him for us." She didn't know how to say that Bast was mainly sent for her. That wouldn't sit well with Nicky. It sure didn't sit well with her.

Nicky crossed his arms and sat back. "That doesn't tell me who you are."

Bast smiled. "I know."

"You work for the ambassador?"

"I work for His Majesty."

"You're military?"

Bast lifted a shoulder in a laconic shrug and then went out the door to speak to the conductor. He asked for some hot tea to be brought to them as the lady was ill. That grated on Stella. She wasn't ill. She was fine.

"I can go to the dining car to have tea."

"First of all, the tea is for your shoulder and second, you have no shoes," said Bast.

She looked down at the priest's dirty, wet socks. "We can fix that. Sofia packed our things."

The men looked up at the luggage and Stella realized it wasn't only theirs. There were other battered bags in addition to their expensive new ones. "Are those yours? How did you know we were leaving?"

"I'm a gifted listener. Once I heard Sofia would be packing for you, I asked her to send my things to the station to be put on the same train. I'm lucky she forgot about them in her distress so I didn't have to tell her who I am."

"She wasn't suspicious about you leaving so suddenly?" asked Stella as Nicky stood up and got the top most suitcase that looked a likely candidate for shoes.

He smiled. "People usually accept what you tell them."

"Not everyone."

They gave each other the same knowing glance that Stella observed between Nicky and Abel. She was now on the inside, but it wasn't as nice as she thought it would be

"No, not everyone," said Bast.

Nicky put the suitcase on the seat. "I don't think this one has shoes. It's too heavy."

"May as well check," said Stella.

The conductor knocked and Bast called out in his twang, "Hold on a minute." Then he draped his coat over Stella's feet and hers over her chest, concealing the blood.

"Good thinking," said Nicky.

"That's what I get paid for," said Bast. "Come in."

The conductor slid open the compartment door and Nicky took a loaded tray from him.

"Signora is unwell?" asked the conductor. "I bring the tea and my mother's cure for the stomach."

"Thank you very much," said Nicky. "What's the cure?"

"Ginger and lemon to put in the hot water. It will help the upset."

Nicky thanked him again and tipping him generously before closing the door. "That's lucky. Now we don't have to put Earl Grey on your arm."

"I am trained in wound care," said Bast. "Would you like me to take care of it?"

"Be my guest," said Nicky.

Bast dunked the heavy linen napkin in the hot water and pressed it to Stella's shoulder. "Does that sting?" he asked.

"Not really," she said. "Nicky, can you give me the suitcase?"

He balanced it on her knees and she popped the little brass clasps. Inside, she found her new pajamas stuffed in with her French and German dictionaries, *Babar*, *The Hobbit* and *Ivanhoe*. She ran her hands over the books and a fresh pain encircled her chest, swirling like a tornado and getting more and more violent.

"Interesting choices," said Bast.

Stella didn't answer. Her hand was on *Ivanhoe*.

"What is?" asked Nicky, leaning to look around the suitcase.

"Your books."

"Oh, right. Have you read them?"

"I have," said Bast. "Have you?"

Nicky frowned. "You sound doubtful."

"Your file didn't indicate an interest in either author."

"My file. I forgot about that." Nicky stood and put up the window shade, flooding the compartment with light. "You really know us."

"I do or rather I thought I did. You chose the books?"

Nicky gazed out the window. "No. Stella bought the children's book. One was a gift to her and the other..." He turned sharply. "Oh, my God."

Stella gripped *Ivanhoe* like she was about to fall and it was the only thing that could save her. "Yes."

Bast pressed the napkin to her shoulder again. "Did I miss something?"

Stella opened the cover to reveal the ex libris, the identification Karolina and Rosa refused to remove.

"Max Ladner," read Bast.

Nicky took the suitcase off her knees and tried to pry the book from her hands, but she wouldn't let go. "It's not your fault, Stella. You told them to strip it out. They wouldn't do it."

"Ah, this is what the German found in your room and gave to Bartali," said Bast.

"They wouldn't do it," Stella choked out. "It was their past. They didn't want to lose it."

"That was their choice," said Nicky.

"I should've made them." She could barely get it out. All that death because of her. Because of her insistence. Because of her weakness.

Bast peeled the silk from her shoulder and then deftly ripped the sleeve off. "I can tell you from experience that is a losing battle. They made their choice and they paid for it."

"How can you be so cold? Karolina and Rosa were lovely women. Innocent. They didn't know what they were choosing."

He pressed the napkin back over the two-inch slice on her shoulder. "They did. Those lovely ladies stole from the Reich. They knew what that meant. Enough to change their names and run for it."

The tornado got hot, pressing the breath out of her lungs. "It was their property." She pointed at the book. "Theirs."

"For the record, Mrs. Lawrence, I'm not cold. I couldn't do the work I do if I was. I'm logical."

"This is not logical. Their books don't belong to the Reich."

"They do if the Reich says they do." He laid down the bloody napkin and dried his hands on another one. "May I see it?"

With difficulty, she gave it to him. He examined the book for a moment and handed it back. "Did they have many similar volumes?"

"Yes. Their room was packed with books," she said.

"This is a first edition and signed. It has worth. The Reich needs money and they're also insatiable collectors. They are taking hordes of books, art, creative works of all kinds."

"They said there was a warrant out for their arrest," said Stella. "And a reward."

"But they can't just declare the von Bodmann property theirs," said Nicky.

"You underestimate them, Mr. Lawrence." Bast went on to tell them what probably happened. Max Ladner died and the Reich imposed a death tax on his widow, one that couldn't possibly be paid.

Therefore the ladies' property would be confiscated to pay the tax. He said it was insidious and quite common.

"That's evil," said Stella.

"Agreed."

"But that can't be why so many Jews are showing up with nothing," said Nicky. "It can't all be taxes."

"The Nazis are nothing if not creative," said Bast. "Particularly, if you have something they want. They'll charge huge amounts for visas to get out of the country so the target will have to sell. Their property will be valued well below market value and it will cost them everything to escape. Sometimes, people get arrested on trumped up charges and selling is the only way to get out of prison."

"And this is about books?" asked Nicky. "Just so they can burn them?"

Bast picked the fabric away from the wound and pressed the napkin back to Stella's shoulder. "There's a complex and organized system in place for books. They're funneling the best volumes into Hitler's personal library and the libraries of high-ranking officials. The rest will either be sold or put into libraries for the people," said Bast.

Stella thought of the diary, but that wasn't part of that plan. It was special. Its own particular target. "It wasn't only books."

"You mean the scroll Sofia mentioned?" asked Bast.

She told them about the Ripley Scroll in its box beneath Rosa's bed. The ancient scroll was now in the hands of the Reich. The thought of Hitler touching it, claiming such a precious object as his own at the cost of the ladies' lives made her ill enough to need the conductor's remedy.

Bast quickly made her a cup of steaming tea and pressed it into her hands like the good Englishman his accent proclaimed him to be. "They won't burn it, if that's what's concerning you."

"No?" asked Nicky.

"They do love a good bonfire, but that is always, absolutely always, for a purpose," said Bast.

"To put on a show."

"Yes and no. They're burning books that don't work for them. Books that don't agree with their Aryan ideal. They don't want those ideas out there. The scroll won't serve that purpose and they have an interest in the occult. It's a particular passion of Hitler's. Or it might be sold to fund the coming war. They won't burn it." Bast bandaged her shoulder with her sleeve and asked Nicky to find another jacket to cover it.

Nicky packed up the books into the first suitcase and found a jacket in another. While he was helping Stella put it on, Bast asked, "Now that we know about the ladies, who wants to tell me about the couple in the boat?"

Nicky put away the suitcases and looked out the window. He had the stare again and Stella could wait all day, but he wasn't going to answer. "Friends."

"Friends that you were searching for. But you didn't know what they looked like or where they were staying?"

Stella glanced at Nicky. He didn't move. "What makes you say that?"

"Mrs. Lawrence, I'm good at what I do and you know I wasn't alone in watching you."

"You weren't?" asked Nicky.

"No."

"Why didn't any of you help us?" asked Stella. "We could've used some help."

"That wasn't the mission," said Bast. "I was tasked to observe, evaluate the situation, and bring you in, if necessary. Who are the Sorkines?"

"Why don't you tell us, if you know so much?" Stella couldn't keep the bitterness out of her voice. It could've been different. Bast could've changed everything.

"I only know what I gathered in Venice."

"Go ahead. Lay it on us."

"You two decided to stay in Europe, with the SS looking for you, to search for a French couple whom you obviously don't know. The Sorkines were also looking for you, going from hotel to hotel asking about the wealthy Americans and where they went. At some point, the SS became aware of their presence and began a hunt for them as well. We saw no indication that the Sorkines were aware of the danger they were in."

Nicky stared out the window and Stella sipped her tea, burning her tongue, but she didn't mind. She deserved it.

"All right then," said Bast. "The couple was middle-aged and not wealthy. They have a daughter, but she wasn't with them. She attends university in France, but she isn't there at the moment. People do talk way too much to strangers." Bast waited for a minute and then continued. "They own an import business that is thriving and plan on expanding soon. Mr. Sorkine has a bad back. Mrs. Sorkine suffers from lumbago. They enquired repeatedly about your tour guide, Abel Herschmann, whom we believe was arrested in Vienna on November ninth or tenth."

Stella's hands were shaking. All she could see was Mrs. Sorkine's terrified blue eye looking at her. "That's enough."

"Tell me who they are."

They didn't answer so he continued in a monotonous voice that somehow felt ruthless. It was certainly unrelenting. "Since they have shown interest in your tour guide, they may be connected to him, not you. Possibly relatives, although Abel is Jewish and they are not. They're—"

"Dead," Nicky hissed at him. "They're dead. Nothing else matters. Don't you see that? I got them killed and that's it. Shut up about it."

Bast folded his hands in his lap. "The question remains."

"It doesn't."

"Who they are is why they're dead or most likely dead, as it were."

Nicky spat out what happened. He'd changed his mind about the order of the search, prioritizing the money before going out to the telegraph shop. He went straight to the Bella Luna to get it from Daniel and found out that the Sorkines had been there not an hour before. Daniel told them Stella's message, but they weren't satisfied. They insisted that they had to see Stella and Nicky before they left Venice. Daniel sent them back to their hotel near the Doge's Palace to wait to be contacted. Nicky went there and convinced them to leave the city immediately. It took some time. They didn't want to go. They thought they'd be safe staying where they were.

"If they'd ignored me, they'd be alive," he said.

"If I'd listened to you and left Venice, like you wanted, they'd be alive," said Stella. "It's my fault."

Nicky shook his head and turned back to the window. "I just hope that this doesn't touch Daniel. Getting involved with us can be a death sentence."

Stella held her breath and looked at Bast, who only nodded. Of course, he knew. He was there.

Nicky turned to Stella, his eyebrows jutting up. "What?"

She couldn't say it so Bast did it in that unfeeling factual way of his. "The SS Peiper shot Daniel Burgess when he wouldn't tell him where you were. He's dead."

Nicky didn't say anything. He banged open the compartment door and walked out.

Stella watched Nicky leave the first-class car, heading who knows where. She wanted to follow him. She wanted to change it. But there was no changing anything.

"Let him go, Mrs. Lawrence," said Bast. "He'll walk it off."

"I don't know about that."

He pulled a battered suitcase off the rack and sat with it on his knees. "He has to. Close the door. We need to talk."

"I don't know when he'll come back," said Stella.

Bast opened the suitcase and took out a pipe. He clamped it between his teeth and said, "He's not part of this conversation."

"Then I'm not interested."

"You will be. Close the door."

She didn't close the door. She didn't care. Nicky was probably headed for the club car. She'd wait until he'd had a drink and then go down. Whiskey was calming and he deserved a double.

"Don't you want to know why I was sent for you and not him?" asked Bast.

She looked back and nearly jumped out of her skin. Bast had transformed back into the old him, an overweight, myopic writer, sporting a mustache. He still had hair though.

"Impressed?" he asked with a smile.

"How did you do that?" she asked, closing the door.

He pointed at the suitcase. "Take a look."

Stella sat next to him and saw a collection of glasses, little pots, brushes, wigs, and what looked like skin. She looked closer at his face. He'd applied some of the skin to his face, creating a double chin and adding quite a bit of weight to his profile. But now she could see the edges between the real and fake.

"Obviously, were I to go out as Leonard Bast the writer, I'd finish the application to be seamless." He peeled off the chin and pulled a thick pad out from under his shirt that gave him an impressive belly.

She poked a bulbous skin-colored dome in the suitcase. "Is that your bald head?"

"It is. And this is all easier to master than you think."

"You forgot your mustache."

He chuckled and ripped off the fringe of hair on his upper lip. "A mirror is helpful."

"I don't understand. What does this have to do with you coming for me?"

It had everything to do with it. When Lord Bickford found out what happened to his son, he told the British government about Stella and Nicky and asked that they be quietly located and brought in. Bast's bosses at something called the SIS set about doing just that. Although they were unable to catch up to them since events were unfolding too quickly, they did get a rough idea of what happened from paid informants, opponents of the Reich, and newspapers. The fact that they were still alive and had not been run down by Peiper and his infinite resources intrigued them and they decided to wait and see what would happen next.

"How did you know we'd gone to Venice?"

Bast shrugged. "I was informed of my destination, not how we got the information."

Stella took a breath and held it before asking, "Is Abel alive?'

"I have no information on his situation."

She waited, but he wasn't going to say another thing about that. "What was the point of coming here? You didn't help us."

"I beg to differ," he said.

She crossed her arms and leaned back. "Not until the last minute."

"As per my instructions. I was to observe, evaluate, and bring you in, when and if necessary."

"Evaluate what?"

"Your abilities, your character and hopefully figure out how you escaped the SS," he said, pouring himself some tea. "Frankly, I had my doubts."

"That we escaped?" she asked incredulous.

"That it wasn't just luck."

"It was."

He smiled. "No, it wasn't. You have an interesting set of skills, Mrs. Lawrence."

The swirling tornado reformed around her chest and she could see the Sorkines in the water, the blood bursting from Daniel's skull. "Like the ability to get innocent people killed, I suppose."

"That is an unfortunate side effect, but hardly your fault," he said.

"I'm the reason. I wouldn't give up when Nicky wanted to. I wouldn't leave."

"You didn't kill anyone. Peiper made those choices, not you."

Stella stood up and went to the window, watching the sunny Italian countryside rush by. "I bring misfortune with me wherever I go."

"You are a natural mimic. A keen observer and imitator. I watched you transform into several different women and you did it without a mustache or a fat pad."

"I used glasses," she said.

"A nice touch, but you didn't need them. You can do it with the power of your personality."

"A fat lot of good it did me."

"We can use you."

She turned and looked at him lighting his pipe. "That's always been an ambition of mine, to be used."

"Make no mistake, Mrs. Lawrence. There is a war coming. Hitler's troops will be marching over Europe in a matter of months."

"That's got nothing to do with us," she said, wanting very much to believe it.

"If you think Peiper is bad, he's nothing compared with his leadership. They intend to wipe out the Jewish race."

"Don't be ridiculous."

"They've been very open about it. In Das Schwarze Korps last week they said, 'We root out criminals from our orderly state: with fire and sword. The result will be the certain and absolute end of Jewry in Germany; its complete annihilation!'"

"I don't know what you expect me to do about it," said Stella although she was shaken.

Bast closed his suitcase, having transformed back into the younger, thinner Bast, and put it on the shelf. "I wasn't to approach you until I was absolutely sure you would be able to do this."

"What? Be a spy? What makes you think that I would or could do that?"

"I *wasn't* sure until I heard the name Gabriele."

Apparently, Gabriele Griese's body had washed up several miles downriver from Paris. French Central Intelligence had identified her and passed the information on to the British. There'd been speculation that Nicky killed her, but it was felt more likely that a foreign operative, perhaps Czech or Polish, had done the deed. No one suspected Stella, except Peiper.

"Why do you care about her?" asked Stella. "She was horrible."

"I don't care about her. I care that you killed her."

"Why?"

"Because you have the ability to do it. That's essential in my line of work."

Stella frowned. "Wait a minute. You heard Peiper say that I killed Gabriele? You heard the whole thing?"

"I did and it was very illuminating as I said." Bast puffed on his pipe. He couldn't have looked more satisfied.

"Peiper said it to get that kid to kill me."

"Correct. He's a real bastard that Peiper."

She balled up her fists and yelled, "It worked. He pulled the trigger."

Bast jumped up, put a hand over her mouth, and forcibly sat her down. "Quiet, Mrs. Lawrence. It doesn't pay to lose oneself in anger."

She gritted her teeth. "You let him do it. I could be dead right now."

"Hardly."

"What in the world do you mean by that? He pulled the trigger."

"With no ammunition."

"That was dumb luck."

He chuckled and pulled the gun out of her coat pocket. "You think I don't know how many rounds of ammunition this Mauser holds? Or is it that you think I can't count?"

"You were taking a chance," she said.

"I don't take chances like that, particularly not with a valuable asset."

"So I'm an asset now?"

He blew out a ring of smoke and smiled. "We're all assets. Some are worth more than others. How old do you think Gabriele Griese was?"

"Not old enough to be that kid's mother," said Stella.

"That's my thought as well. Interesting, don't you think?"

"Not remotely." She turned back to the window.

"Now as to what happens next. I'm bringing you and Nicky to London. From there, I can't say exactly what will happen, but I believe that—"

"Please stop talking."

"There's training involved, quite intensive, but I doubt you'll have any difficulty."

"I'm not doing it," said Stella.

She heard him puff on his pipe again. The compartment filled with a blue haze and she opened the window, waving it out along with his words.

"I'm going to recommend language training. We usually recruit those who are already fluent, but I think we can turn you into a polyglot easily."

"Is there something wrong with your hearing?"

"Stella, may I call you Stella?"

"No."

"Mrs. Lawrence, what do you plan on doing instead?" he asked, mildly. "Go back to your old life? Host garden parties? Buy clothes?"

"I don't know. Leave me alone."

"What about Karolina? She's still alive," he said.

"Are you implying that you'll help her, if I do it?" she asked and the image of Rosa's head hitting the floor appeared in her mind and it would not leave.

"There are certain avenues that could be explored," said Bast.

"Then explore them and leave me alone." Stella put her head out the window and let the wind hit her in hopes that it would drive the pain away.

Bast joined her and whispered in her ear, "You have the ability to fight in the coming war, to be valuable, to take revenge for what has already happened."

"I can't change the past."

"But you can change the future. Isn't that the most important revenge?"

"I don't want revenge. I want to go home."

"What's it going to take, Mrs. Lawrence?"

"I'm just one person."

"As am I and look how I changed your future today." Bast blew a lungful of smoke out the window and the wind whipped it away to nothing. "How many people have to die to incite your wrath?"

"Nobody else is going to die."

"That's not true, Mrs. Lawrence," he said. "It's just not true."

# CHAPTER 24

*B*ast left them in London. He didn't expect to and Stella flattered herself to think he didn't wish to, if only to keep an ever watchful eye on her. The spy seemed to think something had changed in the five days it took them to get to the British Isles, but he was quite mistaken. Stella studied her dictionaries and her children's book to distract herself from the never-ending talk of the coming war, nothing more.

When Nicky returned from the club car, it was like he'd never left, like nothing had happened at all. He didn't wear his mask. He was the Nicky before Vienna, intensely interested in German troop movements and the possibility of Hitler pulling out of a non-aggression pact with Poland.

Stella did her best not to listen, but their words seeped in. Obviously, there would be a war. Stella had little doubt about that, but she didn't see how it helped to buy maps and pour over them as if they had troops themselves. When she tried to change the conversation, Nicky would say things like, "Don't worry. You'll be safe in Missouri," or "I'm just glad you'll be okay at home."

You. You. You.

He never said "we" or "I" when he mentioned Missouri, but it *was* always Missouri, even though she hadn't won their bet. He had found the Sorkines before the train so maybe he thought that counted, but she didn't think so and his words didn't give the comfort he intended. They only made her crouch over her books and ignore Bast's suggestive raising of his eyebrows.

They were never alone again, she and Bast, at least she had that to be grateful for. It was hard enough, keeping one's mind off things without his poking and prodding.

In Rome, Stella had seen a lady much like Rosa, small and delicate, but very much alive. The sight of that smiling woman put Stella back in Venice, back in the station, smelling the water from the canal and the greasy hot train engines on the platform. It felt like she was going crazy until she managed to force it away. At least she could make it go with practice and she had plenty of that. Anything could remind her and now she could make Mrs. Sorkine's eye go and Mr. Sorkine's bloody chest. And the boy yelling. And Karolina's agonized face. Daniel. Abel. She could press them down and away to look at later when they didn't make her feel heavy and lost. Bast might have a million reasons why she should do as he asked. But she had a million to go home. She couldn't think of a single reason why she, Stella Bled Lawrence, should stay.

When they arrived in Naples and went to find passage to Britain, she saw the schedules. If they waited a week, they could go directly to New York. She suggested this, but both Nicky and Bast insisted that they had to get her off the continent immediately and she hadn't the strength to fight them both. They'd found a ship to take them to London the next day.

Stella agreed to go, like she agreed to go to Naples in the first place, like she agreed to eat dinner and have her feet examined by a doctor who had no clue what to do about infection and frostbite. She agreed because she didn't care. She agreed because she knew what she was going to do before she got on that ship.

The telegraph office was a block from the small hotel they found near the Naples dock. Stella slipped away when Nicky got into the bath the next morning, hurrying away on mostly-healed feet that she'd stuffed into the adorable Italian shoes that would never be the same and with a pocket full of dollars that she'd liberated from Nicky's wallet.

The office clerk was surprised to see her standing there outside the door when he flipped the closed sign to open. He grimaced, making his shaggy grey brows come together to form one long brow, but he let her in. She was able to say what she needed in Italian and he rewarded her with a gaped-toothed smile. Two telegrams. Two attempts to save Karolina.

The first telegram was to her mother, who wouldn't be sleeping for worry and wringing her hands raw. At the very least, she could fix that.

Dearest Mother. All well and good. Going to England to tour.

Friend Karolina von Bodmann arrested and sent to Munich. Innocent and elderly. May be using name Karolina Ladner. She needs you. Please help. Will die in Dachau. Ask Red Cross to intervene.

Much love, Stella

Her mother had worked with the Red Cross for years, doing dozens of auctions and teas, jumble sales and cake walks to support everything from soup kitchens to clothing for poor youngsters. That had to count for something. Francesqua could be very persuasive and her army of ladies tenacious when riled.

And the second was addressed to Nicky's father at United Shipping and Steel.

Dear Father. Well and going to England. Please use influence to help friend, Karolina von Bodmann. May be under name Karolina Ladner.

Innocent and elderly. Arrested and sent to Munich. Will die in Dachau.

Forever grateful, Stella.


This would not make Nicky happy, but she decided to follow Uncle Josiah's tenets of doing what you want and apologizing later. Nicky's father had pull with the government and the Nazis had what they really cared about, the Ladner books and the Ripley scroll. They could let Karolina go with no cost to them. They might just do it, if Mr. Lawrence asked them. Or should she say Father. He wanted her to call him that and it grated. She had a father and quite a good one at that, but she humored Mr. Lawrence since she was the only person he seemed remotely interested in at the wedding. He always put down his papers when she came into a room and smiled. Nicky thought this was extraordinary as the old man, as he called him, cared little for anyone or anything except for the business. Nicky took it as a good sign and Stella decided to use it.

Maybe it wouldn't work. Maybe Mr. Lawrence wouldn't care about a plea from his new daughter-in-law, but, then again, maybe he would. She had to try and she knew Nicky wouldn't ask.

She rushed back to the hotel and Bast noticed that she'd been gone, but Nicky didn't. Bast didn't say anything. She never for a moment thought he would. He saw her and Nicky as very separate entities. In a way, he was right as Nicky had said nothing of consequence to her since he'd come back from the club car and had spent his nights with his back turned to her, sleeping so deeply she often feared he'd stopped breathing.

But he was, once again, his old self as he directed the porters to take their luggage onboard and then to their cabins. When Stella walked up the swaying gangplank to the ship, a small, rather rickety-looking rust bucket, she thought they would have a chance to talk during the voyage, but she spent the three-day passage vomiting and trying not to vomit. The ship couldn't weather a single wave without listing dramatically. Nicky lost what little weight he'd managed to gain and by the time they pulled into the London dockyard, he looked as though he might jump overboard and swim for it. Stella would've been right behind him, but she didn't think she had the strength to climb the railing much less hoist herself over.

Bast wasn't bothered by the unrelenting waves and only said that he'd gotten his sea legs long ago. He stood beside Stella, scanning the dock and ready to grab her, if she went down.

"How long?" she croaked as she clung to the railing and prayed for the ship to stop.

"Almost there."

Nicky tried to pat her back, but he wobbled and had to give up on the attempt. "I'm sorry."

"For what?" asked Stella. It was hardly his fault. They'd taken a ship to Europe without the slightest bit of seasickness. He couldn't have known.

"I didn't think our honeymoon could get worse." He leaned over the railing and vomited a thin stream of stomach acid over the side. "It has."

Stella couldn't make herself deny it. After everything they'd been through, that voyage was the worst. She'd been thinking about death for three days and if they didn't get off that ship soon she'd be ready for it.

They finally stopped moving and a swarm of men in crusty overalls rushed for the ship, yelling and moving machinery. Their calls were answered with insults and thick ropes thrown onto the dock.

"Now?" asked Stella.

Bast suppressed a smile and said, "We need a gangplank. Look out at the docklands. They're not moving. Concentrate on that."

He wasn't exactly correct on that point. The docks were alive with people and crates. It was a symphony of movement without any rhyme or reason that Stella could see. They weren't on a regular passenger ship and had docked among the cargo vessels. Stella could see everything from vats of olive oil to exotic birds passing by on the passage below them.

"Would you look at that," said Bast.

"The gangplank?" asked Nicky. "Where?"

Bast shook his head and pointed. Three long black cars were inching down the dock behind a truck piled high with fat bags of grain. "Something tells me this is where we part."

"Who is it?" Stella asked, but she didn't care. She was too busy looking for the gangplank.

"Government officials, unless I miss my guess," said Bast.

"For us?" asked Nicky.

"I doubt they're here for our cargo of lemons and olives."

"How did they know we were coming?"

Bast smiled.

A sailor came over and told them that their luggage was being unloaded and Stella watched their bags swing from a crane to be plopped on the dock. Several men pulled the pieces out of the thick netting and sent it back.

"There we go," said Bast and he helped Stella to the gangplank as it was secured to the decking. She forced herself to wait, shake hands with the captain, who kindly came to wish them well and once again apologize for the rough passage.

Then Nicky chivalrously put Stella in front of himself, although she could tell he wanted to run down the gangplank and never look back. She walked down, holding onto both ropes, her legs like rubber and aware she looked both ridiculous and awful at the same time.

At the end of the incredibly long gangplank stood four men in dark suits with serious expressions. They reminded her of Peiper and her stomach would've gone into knots, if it weren't already there.

"Mrs. Lawrence?" asked a man with an American accent.

"Yes," she managed to force out.

"Welcome to England."

Stella accepted his helping hand and stepped on the dock. She lurched sideways and grabbed onto a post. The dock was moving and she nearly vomited again.

"You've had a rough voyage then?" he asked.

"You have no idea."

Nicky came off with Bast and Stella kept ahold of the post while

353

listening. The men were from both the US embassy and the British Home Secretary. Nicky asked for their identification and they handed it over readily.

"Mrs. Lawrence, can I help you?" asked Mr. Rhodes, who said he was an attaché to the American ambassador.

"I'm fine," she said. "Why are you here?"

"Ambassador Kennedy requests along with His Majesty's government that you proceed to Bickford House at the invitation of the Earl of Bickford," said Mr. Rhodes and the British officials agreed. One handed an envelope to Bast, who quickly read the contents and handed it back.

"Why?" Nicky had already straightened up and looked as though he hadn't been vomiting ten minutes ago.

"I'm not privy to that information," said Mr. Rhodes. "I'm to accompany you and see to your needs, but I believe that it will be made clear to you upon arrival."

Nicky turned to Stella. "I promised you The Savoy."

The dock kept moving and Stella's eyesight was fuzzy at best. "I don't care as long as you don't put me on a ship."

"You couldn't pay me enough to get on another ship," said Nicky. "So I guess we'll go."

The men shook hands and the uniformed chauffeur came over from the first car and began loading their luggage, theirs, not Bast's.

"This *is* where I leave you," said Bast, shaking hands with Nicky. "May I say that if the rest of America is as resourceful as you two, the future will be different from what some imagine."

"Thank you for saving our bacon," said Nicky. "If there's anything I can do for you, I hope you know that I will do it."

"Unless I miss my guess, you're already going to do it."

Nicky smiled grimly. "You don't miss a trick, do you?"

"It's important that I don't." Bast shook Stella's hand and kissed it with aplomb. "Mrs. Lawrence, it's been a surprise and a pleasure meeting you."

"Glad *you* enjoyed it," she said.

"I'll be seeing you."

"*No*, you won't."

The chauffeur opened the door for her and then ran around to open the other side for Nicky. Bast helped Stella in and bent over saying quietly, "You can ignore the fire, Mrs. Lawrence, but that won't make it go out."

"There's no fire."

"You went to Venice and you stayed."

"I was trying to do the right thing," she said.

He smiled. "I know and you will again."

"You're wrong."

"We'll see." Bast closed the door and the chauffeur and Mr. Rhodes got in the front seat.

"How long to Bickford?" asked Nicky as the car started rolling.

Mr. Rhodes turned in his seat and said, "Less than two hours. Will you be all right, Mrs. Lawrence?"

"I think so," said Stella.

"There's a basket on the floor between you. I believe it has crackers in it. You might find those useful for the stomach."

Stella thanked him for the idea, but stared out the window instead. Suddenly, it felt like it wasn't over, and that was all she wanted.

# CHAPTER 25

The silent chauffeur drove through little villages with half-timbered houses and thickly thatched roofs, the country-side more beautiful and green than Stella would've thought given that it was December and frost tinged the windows. Once Stella's stomach stopped rolling, she was able to admire the beauty a little but not a lot. They were going to Bickford for a reason and she feared what that might be.

"Do you think Albert is there?" she asked after an hour and a half.

Nicky sat casually in the seat as if he had no worries at all and it made Stella feel very alone in her fears. "I would think he'd be in the hospital. Mr. Rhodes?"

"Yes?"

"Is Albert at Bickford House?" asked Nicky.

The attaché turned around, his forehead wrinkled. "Albert who?"

"Viscount Finley of Bickford House," said Stella.

Mr. Rhodes's eyes widened. "You know the Viscount?"

"We do," said Nicky. "Is he there?"

"I don't know. I heard the Viscount was in a terrible accident and barely survived. Beyond that, I have no idea. He's probably still in the hospital."

Stella and Nicky shared a glance. Mr. Rhodes knew nothing. An accident. Right.

"How do you know the Viscount?" asked Mr. Rhodes. "I believe he lives abroad."

"We met in Vienna," said Nicky, but he didn't elaborate.

"Vienna. What a lovely city."

"It was," said Stella. "I'm sure."

Mr. Rhodes frowned and started to say something, but the chauffeur said, "Ten minutes."

He turned the car onto a narrow lane, driving through a large, ornate gate and into a dense wood, emerging at a lake. The chauffeur slowed as they drove onto a stone bridge passing a couple of men with rakes on their shoulders and a maid in uniform on a bicycle. They all waved and smiled, so friendly and open. Stella found herself waving back, although she had to fake her smile.

"There we are," said Mr. Rhodes.

"Oh." Stella sat up. Across the lake was the grandest house she'd ever seen outside of Versailles or Fontainebleau. It was a wide expanse of dark stone with square turrets and windows galore. Jane Austen might've said it was perfectly picturesque. She only hoped it had a library equal to the view.

"The British call this a country pile," said Mr. Rhodes. "Looks like a pile of money to me."

Stella had been born in one mansion and grown up in another, but they were nothing in comparison. "This is a house?" she asked.

"Typical British sense of humor," said Rhodes. "What do you say, Thompson?"

"I quite agree," said the chauffeur shortly.

"When was it built?" asked Nicky.

"I don't know, but the family is an old one."

Stella stared at the beauty of the building and swans gliding across the semi-frozen lake. She'd forgotten such serenity existed. Her world had become small and full of the fire Bast mentioned. She sighed and sat back, feeling the fire recede like the light behind Bickford House.

Nicky reached for her and took her hand, like he hadn't in days. "It's like a palace."

Thompson surprised them by saying, "It had a queen, some would say."

"A queen?" asked Mr. Rhodes. "Which one?"

"Not a real queen. She was only thought of that way. Cecily Moore, Countess of Bickford. This is her house." The chilly chauffeur thawed under questioning as he drove off the bridge and down the long drive toward the back of the house. "She began building it after her first husband died and finished it while she was married to her second husband. He became the first Earl of Bickford. You can see her initials at the top."

They all craned their necks to see the initials done in stone on each rooftop. Stella smiled. Cecily wasn't shy. She wanted everyone to know this was her house.

"How do you know so much about the countess?" she asked.

"I grew up in the village. Lady Bickford was a source of pride. She was quite a woman. She and Bess of Hardwick vied for the title of wealthiest woman in Britain behind Queen Elizabeth, naturally."

Mr. Rhodes said something inane about how it must have been her husband's money and Thompson replied that the Bickfords had a talent for marrying well, which Rhodes misunderstood completely, and Stella stopped listening. She looked out at the gardens. They went on as far as the eye could see and appeared to have different influences. Some sections formal like the French and others more robust like the English.

The car turned to the back of the house and then into a main courtyard completely done in stone with an elaborate zigzagging staircase coming down from an enormous arched door. The courtyard was covered in more windows and Stella had the feeling they were being watched from every one.

Thompson glanced back at Stella. "Have you heard the rhyme about Bess of Hardwick's house?"

"No, I haven't."

"Hardwick Hall more glass than wall."

She smiled, feeling the fire recede further. "That would fit this house, too."

"The ladies competed for the most glass," he said, stopping the car at the foot of the stairs.

"Who won?" asked Nicky.

"It depends on who you ask."

Thompson got out and opened Stella's door, helping her before going over to assist Nicky. He'd gotten stiff on the drive and had to be pulled upright. While the men discussed Nicky's wound, which was healing well, Stella took a good look at the dark and quiet court-yard. She began to wonder if anyone was home. But just as that thought crossed her mind, the big doors opened and servants began coming out. Four men in dark suits went to the left stair and four women in plain but fashionable dresses with white aprons went to the right. They took their places, each on a stair, and then an older man and woman came out. He was much more formal in a suit that looked like a tux and the woman wore a dress with many pin tucks but no apron. They stood on either side of the door, stiff and decid-edly unfriendly.

Nicky came to Stella's side while Thompson opened the trunk.

"What do we do?" asked Stella.

"I have no idea," said Nicky.

Thompson leaned around the trunk and gave them their first smile. "Give them a minute. This is how they do it."

"Do it?" asked Stella.

"Receive guests."

She didn't know what to say to that and she didn't need to say anything because just then a woman came out. She was dressed in a kind of hunting outfit in tweed with trousers. Instead of being stiff, she smiled and waved. "There you are! The wait has been inter-minable." She rushed down the stairs, which was impressive consid-ering her substantial bulk. Once she'd cleared the servants, they followed her down the stairs at a dignified pace.

"Lady Bickford," whispered Thompson, setting down one of Stel-la's hatboxes.

She came at them with hands out. "I'm so pleased to see you here and all in one piece, too. I'm Agatha Bickford. Please call me Aggie."

They shook hands and Stella had to blink back tears of relief. Aggie radiated motherliness, but Stella found it hard to believe that she was Albert's mother. It would've taken three of Albert to make one of Aggie.

"I'm Nicky Lawrence and this is my wife, Stella Bled Lawrence," said Nicky, slightly taken aback at Aggie's friendliness.

Aggie shook his hand and kissed his cheek and then hugged Stella fiercely. "Thank goodness you're here. Your mother has been worried sick."

"Mother?" asked Stella. "You know each other?"

"We do now," said Aggie and she turned to Thompson. "And there you are. My favorite bad penny."

She hugged Thompson and gave him kisses on both cheeks before introducing her staff. There were so many names, Stella didn't try to absorb them.

"John, William, please see to the luggage," commanded Aggie before turning to Stella. "Let's go inside. You must be exhausted. So thin. Were you ill on the crossing?"

Aggie pelted her with questions as they went up the stairs, her arm around Stella's waist. "Smith?" she asked over her shoulder.

"Yes, ma'am," said the butler.

"Please send a telegram to Mrs. Bled informing her that Stella and Nicky have arrived safely."

"Yes, ma'am. Right away," he said.

They went through the doors and Stella nearly gasped. The hall was enormous and three tall stories high with tapestries, fireplaces, and dark woodwork covering every surface. And the artwork. Her father would be thrilled. There was a Velázquez in the corner. Two Gainsboroughs and a Sargent. Florence would like that.

Aggie squeezed her arm. "It is impressive, isn't it? Better than Hardwick, if I do say so myself. The earl will be down for dinner. You must go rest and change. Mrs. Hart will take you to your room."

Their hostess bustled away saying she had to change as she had been hunting in the park. Mrs. Hart smiled and led them to the stairs, a masterpiece that curved around the hall and seemed to be supported by nothing.

The footmen followed them to a beautiful guest room in what Mrs. Hart called the Daughter's Wing. It had lovely dark walls and a half tester bed twice as big as any normal bed. She showed them the bathroom and a young girl brought in a tray with tea and cookies. They were to dress for dinner at eight. And then she was gone.

"I forgot to ask about Albert," said Stella.

"I'm not surprised. It's overwhelming," said Nicky, beginning to strip. "You better hurry, if you're going to take a bath."

"I already did this morning."

"I think I'll have a soak then." Nicky went for the bath and Stella washed her face. She thought about putting on her powder and rouge, but couldn't work up the energy. Instead, she drank a cup of tea and ate several buttery cookies while picking out what to wear. She had nothing grand enough for Bickford House and settled on her green dress.

"I never would've thought Albert grew up in a place like this," said Nicky sinking deeper into the bath.

"Me either," said Stella. "His apartment was so small and simple."

"You should've taken a bath. This is heaven after sitting in that car."

"I'll be back in a minute."

Nicky jolted up and water splashed on the floor. "Where are you going?"

"To explore. Surely you don't think there's any danger here," said Stella.

"I don't think it's polite to wander around uninvited."

She rolled her eyes at him and went into the hall. It took fifteen minutes before she saw another living soul. Bickford House was like a huge empty museum and she'd just about given up hope when she ran into Smith the butler. He wasn't thrilled to find her out and about, but he wasn't unkind either.

"Is the viscount here?" she asked.

"Yes, ma'am."

"Can I see him?"

"You will have to ask her ladyship," said Smith. "Perhaps at dinner."

"I don't want to wait for dinner," said Stella. "Is he all right?"

Smith's stiffness relaxed a bit. "I believe the viscount is improving daily."

"Can I see him? I need to see him."

"I'm afraid—"

A small man in a three-piece suit with a watch chain dangling from the waistcoat pocket came around the corner and said, "That's all right, Smith. I'll take Mrs. Lawrence to see Albert."

Smith nodded and left silently.

The man held out his hand. "I'm Lord Bickford, please call me George. I believe you've met my wife, Aggie."

Stella took his shaking, exceedingly thin hand and said, "I have. Please call me Stella."

"Come this way. Albert is in the library." He led her through the house and stopped at a tall door carved with deer and pheasant. "You come with bad news, I assume."

"I'm afraid I do." She put a hand on his arm. "Thank you for sending Bast. We wouldn't have made it out of Venice without him."

"I don't know who Bast is, but you're welcome. I had feared that my friends had plans that diverted from my own."

"They did."

"But you're here."

"The plans came together."

"I hope you'll tell me all about it." The earl opened the door and they walked into a glorious two-story library. In front of the fireplace was a large armchair with a wheelchair parked beside it. Albert looked up and smiled. "I heard you were coming. I hardly believed it."

Stella had to swallow hard. Albert was painfully thin with dark shadows under his eyes and his arm in a cast. The bruises were fading, but he was missing several teeth and he wheezed slightly when he spoke. "Do I look that bad?"

"I'm just glad you're alive," said Stella, sitting in the chair across from him.

"I wasn't sure I would be for a time, but my mother got ahold of me and here I am." Albert smiled showing off the gaps in his teeth. Then the smile fell away. "Do you have something to tell me?"

"I do." Stella told him what happened in Venice. She wanted to do it in private, not at some dinner table with servants all around. "Did you know the Sorkines?"

"I did. They were lovely people." Albert wiped his eyes with a handkerchief. "Why would this SS do that? I don't understand."

The earl paced in front of the roaring fire and said, "I would like to know that as well."

Stella told them what happened in Vienna, about the package, and the chase across Europe, leaving out the gorier details.

"You've hidden this package then?" asked the earl.

"We have." She started to tell him what it was, but he held up a hand.

"Some things are better left unknown."

Albert turned away, trying to hide his sorrow, and the earl went to his son, putting a gentle hand on his shoulder. "Do you want to come to dinner tonight, Albert?"

"I don't think so. I'd rather stay here, if you don't mind." Albert didn't look at them and Stella questioned whether she should've told him about the Sorkines.

The earl led her out of the library and patted her back. "Don't worry. He's healing. It will only take time. Please don't say anything about your uncle though."

"My uncle?" asked Stella.

"Josiah Bled. He's coming here from the continent. Didn't you know?"

"I had no idea. What happened?"

Lord Bickford took her arm. "All I know is that he went to Munich, pulled every string he had, and now he's coming here. In fact, he should've been here already."

"Did he get Abel out?" Stella asked breathlessly.

"I hope so. The news out of Germany is getting worse by the day."

He stopped at the foot of the staircase. "Stella, this Bast person, what did he tell you?"

"Very little actually," she said.

"My contacts in government have expressed an interest in you after they found out you'd evaded the SS in Vienna and Paris."

"He told me that."

"And…"

"He wants me to work for your government." She didn't say be a spy. She didn't have to.

He pondered her for a moment. "You're thinking about his offer?"

"No."

He nodded, but said nothing.

"You think that's wrong?" she asked.

"I think you are extraordinary and we will need the extraordinary very soon."

"Everything I've done has hurt people."

"You survived and did what Abel asked. That shows a loyalty and resourcefulness beyond what anyone would expect."

"Look at what's already happened. I didn't tell Albert everything. The Sorkines are just the tip of the iceberg."

He nodded and the few hairs clinging to his scalp waved at her. "That's more true than either of us know. Now let's have dinner and wait for the arrival of your uncle. He's a man I'd like to meet."

"His reputation precedes him."

"It does indeed. Did he really get arrested with Abel in Rome while naked?"

She laughed in spite of herself. "He did."

They went into dinner and spent the time telling stories of family and folly. Stella kept looking at her watch with a growing feeling of dread in her stomach.

Josiah never came.

# CHAPTER 26

*W*hen Stella finally allowed her eyes to open the next morning, she saw Nicky at the foot of the bed tying his tie into a full Windsor knot.

"Where are you going so early?" she asked.

"Breakfast and it's not early. It's already nine," he said.

"Well, it feels early." She sat up and yawned. "Hold on. I'll be ready in a minute."

He adjusted his tie and put on his jacket. "Don't you remember? You're having breakfast in bed. It's tradition."

"I thought that was a joke."

"The British don't joke about tradition."

"What if I don't want to?" she asked.

"I don't think that's an option." Nicky came to the side of the bed and gave her a quick kiss. "Just relax and enjoy it."

She crossed her arms. "I want to know about Uncle Josiah."

"If there's any news, I'll come back up."

"Immediately?"

"I promise." He didn't meet her eyes as he said it and then limped to the door suspiciously fast.

"What's going on?" she asked as he reached for the doorknob.

"Nothing."

Stella frowned and flipped back the covers. "That's it. I'm coming."

He rushed back over and forcibly tucked her back in. "All right. All right. I'm going to discuss the situation with the earl."

"Which situation? We've got a few."

"Karolina and the Sorkines. He was going to call London first thing this morning. He may have news."

Stella settled back on her pillows. If the earl had news and hadn't sent for them, it would be bad, and she didn't mind waiting for that. "But if Josiah—"

"I'll come up immediately," he said and gave her another kiss, smiling.

A knock on the door interrupted them and Nicky went to answer it. The maid, Lizzie, stood in the hall bearing a tray. "Good morning," she said. "Is Mrs. Lawrence awake?"

He gestured for her to come in and smiled at the maid so warmly that Stella could almost see Lizzie's knees go weak. The rascal.

"She is," said Nicky. "And Lizzie, make sure she stays in bed."

Lizzie blushed and said, "Yes, sir. I will."

He went out and Lizzie came over to set the tray on the foot of the bed before plumping Stella's pillows and giving her the tray.

"Thank you," said Stella. "But I don't really understand why I can't eat downstairs."

"Her ladyship likes to preserve the ladies' traditions at Bickford."

"So it's not a British tradition then?"

Lizzie smiled shyly and poured Stella's coffee. "It was but not many do it anymore. Bickford has its own ways."

"How long have you been here?" asked Stella.

"Two years, ma'am."

"Do you like it here?"

"Very much and I was lucky to get the place. Not many estates have ladies' maids anymore." Lizzie finished putting a linen napkin on Stella's lap and then hesitated at the foot of the bed.

"Is something wrong?" Stella smiled at her. "Am I holding my cup incorrectly?"

"Yes, ma'am. I mean, no. You're doing it perfectly, just like her ladyship. It's just that…"

Stella raised her eyebrows.

"Her ladyship said you came from the continent." Lizzie twisted her apron. Then she caught herself doing it and smoothed it aggressively.

"I did. Why? Are you worried about the war?"

Lizzie twisted her apron again. "So it's true then? There will be a war. The earl has said so for a long time, but the prime minister said that we have peace for our time. There's a treaty, isn't there?"

Stella sipped her coffee to distract from the images racing through her head. "The earl is right. In my experience, the Nazis are relentless. They won't stop because of any treaty."

Lizzie slumped and smoothed her apron again.

"I'm sorry to tell you that, but I was in Germany and Austria. It's coming. I wish I could tell you something different."

"I thought you would say that, but I was hoping." She smiled tearfully. "My mother always says I have too much hope and not enough reality."

"I used to be like that. I wish I still was," said Stella.

"No, she's right. My brothers are going to sign up as soon as it happens. I just keep hoping that it won't."

"You're not the only one," said Stella. "I think all the world will be drawn in."

"All the world?"

"We were in Italy. It's starting there, too."

"Will Mr. Lawrence volunteer?" asked Lizzie.

Stella hadn't thought about that before. The States were so far away from Europe, but, of course, their allies were right next door to Germany. She nodded. "If America fights, I imagine he will. I can't bear to think about it."

"You don't think…that the viscount will go, do you?" asked Lizzie in a tremulous voice, avoiding Stella's eyes.

"I'm sure you would know better than I."

"Oh, no. We're barely acquainted."

Stella bent over her cup to keep from smiling.

"It's just that he's the heir and it's important to the family," said Lizzie quickly.

"Of course. Do you know his friend, Abel, by any chance?"

Lizzie clasped her hands together. "Oh, yes. He's a lovely person. The family has been worried sick. Was he really arrested? I can't imagine that he would do anything wrong or illegal."

"He was, but he didn't do anything wrong." Stella's heart began to hurt and the coffee didn't ward it off.

"The earl thinks we will find out where he is today."

"I hope so. Does Abel have any family that you know of? He told us his parents were gone, but maybe there's someone we don't know about," asked Stella.

Lizzie shook her head sadly. "I don't think so. Albert, I mean the viscount, always says we're all he has." She blushed again and practically ran out of the room, closing the door behind her.

Stella sipped her coffee but couldn't make herself eat anything. Where was Uncle Josiah? The earl brushed off the delay, but she could see he was as worried as she was. The last telegram he'd sent was from Munich, saying he was coming to Bickford immediately. That telegram was sent the day they left Naples. Three days ago and he was coming by train and ferry. He should've beat them by a day.

She set the tray aside and slid out of bed. It was taking too long. She couldn't wait anymore. Lizzie had laid out her clothes the night before and she quickly started dressing in her blue suit. If she had to go back to London, she wanted to be ready.

In the bathroom, she pushed her cosmetics aside and grabbed her brush. She'd gone to bed with a wet head and it had dried half flat and half in ringlets.

"Going somewhere?" Nicky appeared in the mirror behind her.

"I couldn't wait. What happened?" she asked with her brush pressed to her chest.

"Nothing. No word from Josiah."

"Why are you up here then? What did London say?"

"There's no news yet. I couldn't eat and found I wanted to be with you," said Nicky.

Stella spun around and pinned her hair back from her face so it would be ready for a hat.

"There's nothing for you to do," he said.

"You never know." She looked at him for confirmation and found him looking at her rather fearfully.

"I thought you said you didn't know anything about Uncle Josiah?" she asked.

"I don't."

"The Sorkines then."

"No. Nothing there either."

"Then what?"

He held out his hand and pulled her into the bedroom. "I have to talk to you about something."

She wrapped her arms around herself and waited.

"When Josiah comes, I want you to go back home with him," said Nicky.

"Where are you going to be?"

He blew out a breath and she could see him forcing himself to act casual. It wasn't working so well. "Here."

"Bickford? Why?"

It took a minute, but then he said, "I'm staying in England. I'm volunteering."

"Did Bast talk to you?" she asked.

"Bast?" he asked, frowning. "No. He's a spy of some sort. I'm joining the military."

Stella walked to the window and looked out at the lake. A man walked across the bridge in the beautiful sunshine. The lake was serene with swans gliding over placid water. There wasn't a war out there, only inside.

"Stella? Did you hear me?" he asked.

"I heard you."

"What are you thinking?"

She wasn't surprised, that much she knew, but she kept checking to make sure of it. No, no, she wasn't. When he'd come back from the club car he'd been so calm and settled. He'd decided then. He just didn't tell her and she was glad of it. The journey had been hard enough without that hanging on her heart.

Stella thought of Lizzie's face when she spoke of Albert and her brothers and wondered if her face looked like that now. "When?"

"As soon as it can be arranged," he said. "The earl will make some calls."

"Will they let you join their military? I didn't know Americans could do that."

He took her hand and grinned at her. "You forget. I'm Canadian."

"Be serious." Stella looked back out at the man, who'd gone off the road and headed to the edge of the lake.

"I am. I'll change my citizenship to Canadian."

She didn't know why that hurt her, but it did. They were Americans and she liked being who she was.

Nicky wrapped his arms around her and rested his chin on the top of her head. "It's the right thing, Stella."

"Is it for the Sorkines?"

"It's for me. I want to."

The man had stumbled into the water and then back up on the bank. The swans were racing over and not in a friendly way. Stella had always heard that swans were mean and watching them chase the man around the lake proved it was true.

Nicky chuckled. "Those swans sure hate him."

The man weaved back and forth, but he was too slow. The swans were right on his heels with their long necks outstretched, wings flapping.

Nicky squeezed her, beginning to laugh. "That fool better get it together."

The man jolted to the right and ran into the lake, slowing him down considerably.

"What in the world is wrong with him?"

The man made it out of the lake and ran full out toward Bickford

House. His hat flew off and the sun glinted on dark brown hair. A jolt went through Stella. "It's Uncle Josiah!"

"It's a man from the village. Josiah will come by—oh, for Christ's sake!"

The man ran past their window and looked up. It was Josiah Bled, war hero and millionaire playboy, running from a bevy of swans.

Nicky grabbed her hand and they ran out of the bedroom, only to crash into Aggie.

"Your uncle!"

"We know," said Stella.

They ran down the long stairs in time to see the footmen race out the front door armed with canes. They had to chase Josiah and the swans almost halfway around the lake before they caught up and gave the irate birds a few whacks and flung some bread into the lake.

"Those birds are a menace," said Aggie. "If I had my way, we'd have them for dinner."

"Why don't you?" asked Nicky.

"Tradition. There have been swans here since Bickford was built. I'm going to have to put up warning signs. They're getting worse. This happens at least once a week."

Stella watched as Uncle Josiah scooped up his hat, nearly falling on his face in the process. "Signs wouldn't help in this case," she said.

"Why not?"

"He's drunk."

Josiah Bled was drunk, but, in his defense, he'd stopped drinking at two in the morning and he thought that rather impressive. He got a lot of mileage out of his whiskey.

"I thought the walk would sober me up," he said, stretching out his muddy legs on the wide stone steps of Bickford House.

"When did you get to the village?" asked Aggie.

Uncle Josiah looked up at the countess sheepishly, a lock of wavy brown hair falling over one pale blue eye. "Noon. Yesterday."

"Noon?" burst out Stella. "Where have you been? We've been worried sick."

He chuckled. "You sound just like Francesqua."

Stella might've sounded like her mother, but she felt like no one she recognized. She wanted to cry, or scream, or throw a two-year-old's tantrum. Maybe all three at once.

Nicky came up behind her and wrapped his arms around her chest, probably fearing that she would smack her own uncle. It was a reasonable fear.

"What have you been doing?" he asked.

"I stopped for a drink at the pub," he said.

"Which one?" asked Aggie. The large lady was somewhere between enraged and amused. It was hard to say which way she'd go.

"How many are there?" asked Uncle Josiah and he fell over on the steps.

Aggie threw up her hands and went with amused. "You're a ridiculous creature. What are we going to do with you?"

"I don't know," he muttered with his handsome face squashed against the stone. "Ask Stella."

Everyone looked at her, including the footmen with their swan-smacking canes.

When she was sure she wasn't going to scream or hit, she peeled Nicky's arms off her and yanked her wayward uncle upright. He blinked at her bleary-eyed and burped. She'd seen him like that plenty of times, usually in times of celebration, not stress, but she'd never been the one to sober him up. That was her mother's department or Florence's.

"Sorry, sweetheart." He took her hand and pulled her down to the steps beside him. "It was a hard trip."

"I know all about hard trips," said Stella.

Aggie told the footmen to go back inside and tell the earl that Josiah Bled had arrived, but not to disturb the viscount.

When the young men's footsteps faded away and the doors closed, Uncle Josiah put his head in his hands and Stella put her hands over her heart. "Where's Abel?"

"I wasn't ready to come out here. Then a man recognized me. Bought me a drink."

"Did you find Abel?" asked Stella.

"I shouldn't have drank so much. I knew you were waiting. I couldn't..."

She pressed her heart so hard it hurt. "So you found him then."

He nodded.

"In Dachau?"

"Yes."

Aggie gasped and pressed her hands to her mouth. Nicky turned around and looked out over the lake. Only Stella looked at Josiah. "Is he dead?"

"Yes."

Aggie ran past them on the stairs and into the house, slamming the door behind her. A high-pitched wail came through the many windows, but Stella didn't join in. She didn't want to wail or scream or throw things. She was so angry she felt frozen in flames.

"Were you with him when it happened?"

Uncle Josiah looked at her, his eyes red-rimmed. "No. He was already dead by the time I got there."

"What happened?" asked Nicky without turning around.

"It doesn't matter."

"You're wrong. It does."

Uncle Josiah told them what he knew. Abel had died on the train to Dachau. He never made it inside the prison. He'd been beaten terribly and died of his injuries.

"Did you see the body?" asked Stella.

He pulled a knapsack off his back and opened it. "No. They'd already cremated him."

Stella looked inside the knapsack and saw a plain metal urn.

"I had to pay for his ashes and this crappy urn, if you can believe that," he said.

Nicky finally turned around, his face inscrutable. "How do you know it's him?"

Uncle Josiah told them that he didn't believe it at first. Abel was young and healthy. Why should he die? Uncle Josiah had seen plenty of men survive things that shouldn't be survived. Then the camp commandant produced Abel's wallet, passport, and two pictures he had with him. They had dried blood on them, but he still didn't believe it. Then the commandant had several prisoners brought in. They told him that Abel had died on the train and were clearly confused about why he was asking. Uncle Josiah didn't think they were lying. He believed them, not the commandant.

"Do you have Abel's things?" asked Stella. She didn't know why she asked. She didn't want to see Abel's blood.

Uncle Josiah pulled the wallet, passport, and the blood-stained photographs from the knapsack and gave them to her with shaking hands. The first picture was of her, sitting at a Parisian cafe, holding a glass of champagne and laughing. Stella couldn't remember that picture being taken, where they were or why she was laughing. That girl was so different from the one she now saw in the mirror, she wouldn't have recognized herself if it weren't for her great grandmother's hatpin piercing an outlandishly fashionable hat covered in frilly feathers. The other photo was a wedding photo, taken before the war, she recognized the couple and two of the people with them.

"They're his parents," said Josiah. "The names are on the back."

"And the Sorkines," said Stella, her fingers touching Abel's blood where it had stained the face of his mother. She was the pretty girl with the long braids in the picture Stella had upstairs. "They're dead, too."

Uncle Josiah put his arm around her shoulders. "It's not your fault, sweetheart."

"I know exactly whose fault it is." With that, Stella stood up and went into the house.

Stella hadn't cried yet and she didn't think she would. The anger was too great. Abel's life was over. He died alone in horrible pain because he had something the Nazis wanted. They went after what they wanted. It didn't matter if it was Gutenberg's diary or the Ripley scroll. And it would never be enough. They would always want more. They wanted everything.

She'd wandered around the formal gardens, walking through the French designs in the low hedges of hearts, arrows, flames, and tears. She got lost in the hedge maze and found her way out again. Got lost a second time and ended up by the center fountain. It would've rivaled Versailles' if it hadn't been drained for winter. She stood beside it, chilled to the bone, and the sight of the icy mermaids and seahorses made her colder.

Stella felt the temperature dropping as the sun dipped below the horizon and a few lazy snowflakes floated down to stick to the gravel. She should return to the house with its roaring fires and lap blankets. But she wanted to be cold. Maybe that could stop the painful burning inside.

Just as the snow picked up, she heard the sound of wheels on gravel. She turned and saw Albert in his wheelchair. He was slumped to the side and had Abel's urn resting on his red tartan lap blanket. Lizzie pushed the high wicker back, but her eyes were so swollen from crying it was a wonder she could see where they were going.

They stopped next to her and Albert put up his good hand. Lizzie took it and gave it a squeeze before dashing back to the house with fresh tears.

"I was thinking about putting him here," said Albert. "But I forgot that the water's gone. I had thought the lake, but those swans. They always chased him."

Stella couldn't think of anything to say and remained silent.

"Perhaps I should put him on the mantel in the library. He loved books. That's how we met, you know."

She swallowed and managed to say, "I didn't know."

"It was at Oxford in the Bodleian library. He was sitting at a table with the tallest stacks of books of anyone there. He was writing a paper on Hadrian's Wall. Construction and consequences, I believe. He had a book I needed and we struck up a conversation on building techniques. The librarian yelled at us." He smiled. "The first of many times. He was my closest friend. My only friend, besides my brothers."

For a second, Stella thought she might cry. She didn't, but the pain grew hotter.

"I think I'll put him in the library. He does have some family left and they might have an opinion on the lake or fountain. His cousin, Gaspard, is in Greece. He's only a distant cousin, but that's better than nothing. And Lucienne Sorkine. Maybe we can find out what happened to her."

Stella could feel him looking at her, but she couldn't look back. Not yet.

Albert took her hand. "What is your opinion?"

"I don't think I get to have one," she said.

"He was in love with you. Did you know that?"

A tear slipped down her cheek. "I think I did."

Albert squeezed her hand and then let go. She looked down and he had the urn nestled against his cast, tears were dripping down the metal. He was paying for the Nazis' greed and it made her more angry than ever.

"Do you want me to push you back to the house?" she asked.

He wiped his eyes with the sleeve of his jacket and then smeared the tears across the surface of the urn. "No. I'll stay here a while. Will you take the urn though? I'm getting him all wet." He smiled, stretching the scars on his cheek. "Abel would hate all this sniveling. For all his books, he preferred action to agony. Soon I'll have to think of something to do, now that the business is gone. He would if our positions were reversed."

She took the urn and held it to her chest. "You can worry about that when you're better."

"Yes," he said, looking out into the winter-dead garden. "When it's better."

Stella kissed the top of his head and turned around. The gravel crunched under foot. The urn icy cold and damp in her hands. At the top of the zigzagging stairs, the earl and Nicky watched her as she walked through the courtyard, all those windows, eyes upon her.

She stopped at the foot of the stairs and then she decided, just like that. It wasn't hard when it happened. It was so easy it felt like she'd decided long ago. She turned left, walking up the stairs to the earl.

"Call London," she said. "I'm not going home."

The End

# PREVIEW

## ONE CHILD IN BERLIN (STELLA BLED BOOK THREE)

*I*t was a gift from God. A sign of *his* bountiful mercy and because of it they would survive the Dachau internment camp and go on to fight for the inevitable defeat of the Nazis. Michael Haas could find no other explanation and he believed it with all his heart. His friend, Adam Stolowicki, did not.

Adam could not find God in Dachau and he had tried. He'd prayed for months, given service where he could, and looked for a sign that God knew he was there, that *they* were there. But after a year, he'd lost too much, including his name and profession along with his clothes, weight, and hair. Not to mention the friends, too many to count, who had died in ways he couldn't bear to remember.

There were days when he could not recall his real name and when he did, it seemed unimportant that he was Abel Herschmann, a historian and travel guide. He had become someone else entirely. If Michael had known, he would've said this was a gift, too. That the real Adam Stolowicki had died in that dirty, freezing boxcar so that Abel Herschmann might live to fulfill a purpose.

That was certainly what Jakob thought. The old man gave him Adam's name and instructed Abel on who he now was, a bricklayer from Warsaw and a communist. As far as Abel could tell, if God was in Dachau he took the form of an elderly man with gout and severe arthritis. It was Jakob who delivered the gift that Michael was so sure came from God.

"Do you hear them?" whispered Michael.

"No. Not yet," said Abel.

"Maybe we should start now."

"No. It will be suspicious if we go out early. They'll ask questions."

Michael nodded, his head rubbing against Abel's shoulder in the bunk they shared with three other men. The other men were recently arrived from Poland and were still sleeping, having talked late into the night about escape. They didn't yet understand there would be no escape. The SS guards would see to that and, if they didn't, their fellow prisoners would. An escapee left a death sentence for his fellows still in the barrack. Abel carried the scars of one man's failed attempt on his legs and buttocks, but he survived the beating well enough. Others hadn't.

Michael, who had already been weak from an illness, had gotten an infection. His legs were swollen and weeping fluid. There were several doctors in the barracks and they'd done what they could, but Michael wasn't improving and was so weak Abel had to support him while walking. Hiding that from the guards wasn't easy. Abel lived in fear that Michael would be noticed or collapse during roll call and he'd be sent to the infirmary. Abel would sooner have him shot in the head.

"God forgive me, but I miss Jakob," said Michael.

Abel smiled. "We all do. Hope left with him."

"Don't say that. God is with us." He patted the badge on his chest. "He gave us the best chance."

"Yes," said Abel.

"You must believe," insisted Michael.

A door banged open and the Kapo came in yelling and hitting their bunks with his truncheon. The Poles jolted awake and one fell off the bunk with a yelp, only to be given a swift kick and a torrent of screaming about being clumsy.

Abel climbed off the bunk and looked over at Dr. Fleck, who

quickly moved between Abel and the Kapo. He and several other men shielded Abel as he hauled Michael off the bunk.

One of the Poles sneered and moved away. "What is wrong with him? Send him to the infirmary."

Ludwik, a usually quiet biologist, made a fist and said, "If Michael goes, so will you."

The Pole's eyes narrowed, but he shut his mouth before he headed out into the icy morning air.

"Thank you, my friend," whispered Michael. "You'll see. It won't be long now."

Abel held him under the arm as casually as possible and helped him to the door. "You can do it."

"I will because I know that Jakob will find my family. Help is coming. I feel it."

"Yes. Now quiet. Save your strength."

"You must believe."

"I believe," said Abel automatically as he helped Michael out of the door and down the block alley to the square. It was more crowded than ever since Germany invaded Poland. Abel had heard a guard complaining about the smell. He'd said that the camp should only have six thousand prisoners and it now had nineteen thousand. Abel could well believe it. Many of the men who had been arrested after Grynszpan killed the Nazi in Paris had been released, but the Germans always found more men to imprison. Czechs from the Sudetenland and then Czechoslovakia itself. Now Poland.

"Who's next?" Abel wondered aloud without much interest. He was where he was. A year in hell had taught him that nothing would change it.

A guard came charging by, yelling, "Go on there, you stinking Jew!" He raised his baton and cracked a man on the shoulder with it. "What did you say? What did you say?"

More guards came, passing Michael and Abel, and concentrating on the barracks that held the Jewish prisoners. Grief and guilt washed over Abel, making his heart feel like it was twisting in his chest and wringing out his soul.

Michael squeezed his arm. "It is a gift from God."

Two Jewish prisoners went down and were savagely kicked as Michael and Abel shuffled by.

"It's unfair," Abel whispered.

"It is God's will that we live." Michael sounded strong. His eyes sparkled with fervent belief or perhaps it was the fever Abel could easily feel through the thin fabric of his ragged shirt. "It is."

Abel nodded, but he knew it was Jakob's will that he and Michael lined up with the communists and not the Jews. How the old man had done it wasn't clear, but Abel was sure that it was him.

When the first wave of Czechs came into the camp, Jakob had been designated for release, but while he was waiting, the guards decided to make him useful and assigned him to help process the influx of prisoners. Thousands were flooding in and the system they'd so carefully designed was overwhelmed.

Abel hardly saw his dear friend for the next few days, except for a glimpse of him bent over a desk, carefully filling out paperwork and another when he was being escorted out of his barracks with his meagre possessions. The Kapo, who wasn't as harsh as the others, allowed him to shake Abel's hand.

"I will see you again, my Leopold," said Jakob, referring to his son who had died at Dachau and in whose name Jakob had saved Abel.

"I hope so," said Abel.

Jakob's eyes sparkled under his shaggy brows. "I know so."

The Kapo forced him away before he could say more, but Abel had the strongest feeling that the old man was up to something and a few hours later he was proved right when his Kapo came to get him, yelling about mistakes and idiocy. He and Michael were hit and kicked all the way to the Shunt Room, where prisoners were processed when they arrived. It was the first place where Abel had been beaten without knowing why, and it wasn't the last.

After they'd gone inside and been shoved through a door to the long room where prisoners were stripped and cataloged, an SS screamed in their faces and waved paperwork around. Michael and Abel looked at each other in confusion, but all was revealed when the officer ran out of steam. He told them that they were not specific when they were brought in with the filthy Jews and had been cataloged incorrectly. He seemed to think this was a kind of crime, but exactly why wasn't clear.

The officer slashed at them with a razor and demanded that they remove their striped pants. They did, shaking so hard that the knocking of their bony knees was audible. Abel fully expected to be cut, possibly slashed to the bone, but, like a miracle, it didn't happen. The officer flung the razor at him and ordered him to remove his badge from his pant leg.

Utterly confused, he and Michael removed the red triangle stitched over the yellow triangle. When they tentatively placed them on the desk, the officer threw up his hands and yelled, "*Dummkopf!*"

He pointed at a couple of punchcards on the table, screaming about "the machine" and then waving the handwritten paperwork in their faces.

"Do you want to be a dirty Jew? Do you want to be with the scum?"

Abel and Michael just stared at him, mute. There was no right answer, experience had taught them that, and there they were standing in front of a mad man with their genitals barely covered by their shirts.

Another guard came over and Abel recognized him as Weiß, some sort of assistant to the camp commander. The tiniest sigh of relief escaped from Abel's lips. Weiß could not be considered kind or just by any stretch of the imagination, but he wasn't irrational or unpredictable as many of the guards were.

"What is this?" Weiß glanced with disdain at their shaking thighs and the yellow triangles on their pant legs, denoting them as Jews.

"These stupid fools can't understand a simple order," snapped the guard and then quickly stiffened when he saw Weiß's irritation at his tone. "They were classified wrong and told no one."

"Impossible," declared Weiß and he turned away.

"But the cards," said the guard. "My orders…"

Weiß turned back and eyed the punch cards on the table. "What about the cards."

"They say they are Jews, but the papers say no." The guard handed the paperwork over to Weiß, who glanced through it swiftly.

"Who punched the cards?" he asked.

The guard named several SS and hastily said, "It was a simple mistake, but these dogs did not tell us. These asshole communists let us put them with the Jews." He sneered. "Maybe they like the smell."

Abel knew this was the time to speak, but he found he had no voice. Fear had taken it. But Michael, a man of both extraordinary courage and faith, said in a clear voice with no hesitation or tremor, "We are not Jews." He sneered identical to the guard and said, "The smell is worse than you know."

"It says here you were arrested in Vienna on the tenth of November last year and brought in with Jews," said Weiß.

"Yes," said Michael. "We were arrested while watching a synagogue burn. At first they thought we were Jews, but we had our identification."

"Why were you arrested?"

Michael shrugged.

"Why did you allow the yellow triangle to be sewn on your pant leg?"

"No one was interested in what we said." He pointed at the punch cards. "They said the card was law."

Weiß nodded and tossed the paperwork on the table. "Remove the yellow and sew on the red, tip up." To the guard, he said, "Double check all the other cards punched from their group and put them in the correct barrack."

Weiß walked away and the guard began yelling about how slow they were. His face went red and spittle hit their hands as they cut the threads that held their Jewishness fast to their fate, amazed that neither Nazi thought to take a look under the hem of their shirts.

After they sewed on their red triangles, tip up, they put on their pants, careful to conceal themselves, and walked out into a spring day that was suddenly fresh and hopeful. They got their thin blankets and tin cups and took themselves to the new barrack on a different block away from the Jews, asocials, and criminals to the section where political prisoners were housed.

No one questioned their inclusion. The badge was everything.

Later that afternoon when they'd been assigned a new work detail out of the dreaded gravel pit to a painting crew, Abel found his voice. "How can we…"

"Live?" asked Michael. "By the grace of God. It is *his* will."

"But to deny our faith," said Abel.

Michael gestured to a man lying next to the electrified fence. The body with its yellow triangle had been there for three days, shot a dozen times for wandering too close to the fence line. "Do you want to end up like him?"

"We can still end up like him. We all can," said Abel, thinking of his mother. She was a faithful woman, kind and proud of who she was. She'd taught her son to be the same. What would she say to her son with his red triangle? Would she be joyful at this small chance or ashamed? Abel honestly didn't know.

"It is a gift from God," said Michael, his eyes lit with hope. "We will take his gift and find a way to get out of here. When the time comes we will make them pay for what they do and they will suffer as we have, as our people have."

"If you say so," said Abel.

"I don't. *He* does. God has given us this chance. He changed our paperwork. He showed it to the guards. How else could this be? Once you are categorized, it is over. But not for us. God gave us this. How else could we go from being Jews and political prisoners to only political? Now we will get more food. We won't be worked to death in the pit or beaten as much. They don't shoot the red triangles as fast." Michael grabbed Abel's arm with tears in his eyes. "We're going to live."

Read the Rest in
One Child in Berlin (Stella Bled Book Three)

# ALSO BY A.W. HARTOIN

Nowhere Fast

Dry Spell

A Sin and a Shame

**Stella Bled Historical Thrillers**

The Paris Package (Stella Bled Book One)

Strangers in Venice (Stella Bled Book Two)

One Child in Berlin (Stella Bled Book Three)

Dark Victory (Stella Bled Book Four)

A Quiet Little Place on Rue de Lille (Stella Bled Book Five)

Her London Season (Stella Bled Book Six)

Double Duet (Stella Bled Book Seven)

**Paranormal**

It Started with a Whisper (Son of a Witch Book One)

Angels and Insects (Son of a Witch Book Two)

**Young Adult fantasy**

Flare-up (Away From Whipplethorn Short)

A Fairy's Guide To Disaster (Away From Whipplethorn Book One)

Fierce Creatures (Away From Whipplethorn Book Two)

A Monster's Paradise (Away From Whipplethorn Book Three)

A Wicked Chill (Away From Whipplethorn Book Four)

To the Eternal (Away From Whipplethorn Book Five)

# A.W. HARTOIN'S NEWSLETTER

To be the first to hear all about the A.W. Hartoin news and new releases click the link or scan the QR code to join the mailing list. Only sales, news, and new releases. No spam. Spam is evil.

Newsletter sign-up

# ABOUT THE AUTHOR

USA Today bestselling author A.W. Hartoin grew up in rural Missouri, but her grandmother lived in the Central West End area of St. Louis. The CWE fascinated her with its enormous houses, every one unique. She was sure there was a story behind each ornate door. Going to Grandma's house was a treat and an adventure. As the only grandchild around for many years, A.W. spent her visits exploring the many rooms with their many secrets. That's how Mercy Watts and the fairies of Whipplethorn came to be.

As an adult, A.W. Hartoin decided she needed a whole lot more life experience if she was going to write good characters so she joined the Air Force. It was the best education she could've hoped for. She met her husband and traveled the world, living in Alaska, Italy, and Germany before settling in Colorado for nearly eleven years. Now A.W. has returned to Germany and lives in picturesque Waldenbuch with her family and two spoiled cats, who absolutely believe they should be allowed to escape and roam the village freely.